Praise for earlier C
Chronicle m

A fun read with humour throughout…
Crime Thriller Hound

An excellent novel, full of twists and turns, plenty of action scenes, crackling dialogue - and a great sense of fun.
Fully Booked 2016

A highly enjoyable and well-crafted read, with a host of engaging characters.
Mrs Peabody Investigates

An amiable romp through the shady back streets of 1960s Brighton.
Simon Brett

A highly entertaining, involving mystery, narrated in a charming voice, with winning characters. Highly recommended.
In Search of the Classic Mystery Novel

A romp of a read! Very funny and very British.
The Book Trail

Superbly crafted and breezy as a stroll along the pier, this Brighton-based murder mystery is a delight.
Peter Lovesey

It read like a breath of fresh air and I can't wait for the next one.
Little Bookness Lane

By the end of page one, I knew I liked Colin Crampton and author

Peter Bartram's breezy writing style.
Over My Dead Body

A little reminiscent of [Raymond] Chandler.
Bookwitch

A rather fun and well-written cozy mystery set in 1960s Brighton
Northern Crime

The story is a real whodunit in the classic mould.
M J Trow

A fast-paced mystery, superbly plotted, and kept me guessing right until the end.
Don't Tell Me the Moon Is Shining

Very highly recommended.
Midwest Book Review

One night I stayed up until nearly 2.00am thinking 'I'll just read one more chapter'. This is a huge recommendation from me.
Life of a Nerdish Mum

The Morning, Noon and Night Trilogy

Book 1

Murder in the Morning Edition

Book 2

Murder in the Afternoon Extra

Book 3

Murder in the Night Final

Three Crampton of the Chronicle mysteries

Peter Bartram

First published by The Bartram Partnership, 2017

ISBN: 9781549600982

For contact details see website:
www.colincrampton.com
www.peterbartram.co.uk

All characters and events in this book, other than those clearly in the public domain, are entirely fictitious and any resemblance to any persons living or dead is purely coincidental.

Book layout and cover design: Barney Skinner

Also by Peter Bartram in the
Crampton of the Chronicle mystery series:

Headline Murder
Stop Press Murder
Front Page Murder
Murder from the Newsdesk
Murder in Capital Letters

CONTENTS

Murder in the Morning Edition

A Crampton of the Chronicle mystery novella

Peter Bartram

The Morning, Noon and Night Trilogy
Book 1

Chapter 1

My Australian girlfriend Shirley took a luscious lick of her ice-cream and said: "Why is that man wearing gloves on the hottest day of the year?"

Shirley flicked her gaze towards the man sitting three tables away. We were on the terrace of the Black Rock café, looking out over Brighton beach. The sun was shining from a sky as blue as Max Miller's jokes. It was August 1963 and a long hot summer was drawing to a close.

I resisted the temptation to swivel my head and stare. In my line of work, it's not wise to show too much interest in the wrong sort of people. I'm Colin Crampton, crime correspondent on the *Evening Chronicle*. The kind of characters I peek at on the sly would give you a punch on the snout if they caught you gawping.

And that's just the cops.

So without moving my head, I swivelled my eyeballs left until they felt they were about to fall out of their sockets. I squinted at the bloke through a grey mist.

I said: "One thing's for sure. He's not come for a fun day by the seaside."

I shifted my chair a little so that I could eyeball the mystery man more discreetly. He was a thin wiry bloke who looked like he hadn't spent his forty-odd years on earth wisely. He had a swarthy complexion, a small scar above his upper lip, and a penumbra of five-o'clock shadow around his jaw. Central casting wouldn't have thought twice about handing him a role as one of the black hats in a spaghetti western.

He was wearing a grey three-piece suit which would have been perfect for Sunday morning church or a meeting with his bank manager. On Brighton beach he looked out of place - like a smile on a traffic warden's face.

A small fawn attaché case lay on the table in front of him. Beside the case was a thick white envelope. His gloved fingers drummed impatiently on the case. His flinty eyes glowered at the envelope and then surveyed the bustling activity around him.

The café throbbed with life as more people arrived. They'd come from a train that had just pulled into Black Rock station on the Volk's Railway, a few yards from the café.

The fresh crowd irritated Glove Man. He glanced anxiously around.

At the table behind him, a spotty boy, watched by a stern-faced nanny, dug his spoon deep into a giant knickerbocker glory. To his right, a pensioner couple smeared strawberry jam on their buttered scones. To his left, a pair of young lovers took turns to snap pictures of one another with a fancy camera.

A perky waitress in black skirt and white pinafore swung her hips as she weaved between the tables.

Glove Man glared at her as she wiggled by.

Shirley slurped her ice-cream cone. "I bet those gloves set him back a few saucepan lids," she said.

"Saucepan lids?"

"Quid."

I grinned. "Could be as much as a Lady Godiva."

"What?"

"A fiver."

I focused in on the gloves while Shirley sucked her chocolate flake. It stuck out of the ice-cream like a telegraph pole in a swamp.

The mystery man's gloves were as different from the mitts I wore when I drove my MGB on a cold day as a beach pebble from the Kohinoor diamond. They'd been tailored from some fancy brown leather. Probably by some ancient craftsman with white hair and hunched shoulders who agonised over every stitch. They fitted Glove Man's hands like a second skin. He could have sat at the upright Joanna in my mum's old parlour and tinkled Rachmaninov's second piano concerto note perfect without taking them off.

And then knocked out *My Old Man's a Dustman* as an encore.

I switched my attention back to Shirley. A summer tan had gently bronzed her perfect skin. The fringes of her blonde hair ruffled in a gentle breeze. She was wearing a stylish pair of Gucci shades which made her look like a film star. Perhaps dodging the paparazzi at the Cannes film festival. Or sneaking into Cinecittà in Rome to act in a new Visconti movie. She was wearing a lemon yellow dress that seemed to have given up any hope of covering her legs shortly after it had left her bum.

Not that I'm complaining.

I'd been dating Shirley since last summer when she'd pitched up in Brighton. She was working her way around the world and had found a job in a seafront café to earn the money for the next leg of her trip. She was still putting money by, but I hoped it would be a long time before she bought her next ticket.

Shirley crunched on the last of the ice-cream cone and said: "Perhaps old Glove Man is on his way to a business meeting."

"That explains the suit and attaché case but not the gloves," I said.

"Perhaps the guy's got sensitive hands."

"So why's he drumming his fingers on the case like he wants to beat a hole in it?"

"He's impatient. He's waiting for someone."

"I don't think so. The person he came to meet has already left."

"How do you know that, clever clogs?"

"Because whoever it was left him the envelope. They would have been and gone before we arrived. If he were waiting to meet someone and give them the envelope he'd keep it in the case."

"Why the impatience?"

"He wants to put the envelope in the case. But he doesn't want to open the case with everyone around - some nosey-parker might see what's inside."

"So what's inside?"

"It must be something a casual passer-by would immediately recognise as important at a glance. Perhaps something suspicious."

Shirley's eyes widened in disbelief. "You can't know that."

"True. I don't know it for certain. But he keeps looking at the case and the people moving around him. He's choosing his moment when he can sneak the envelope in the case with no risk of anyone peeking inside."

"We'll never know," Shirley said.

She leaned forward and kissed me. Her lips tasted of ice-cream. Vanilla. Personally, I prefer chocolate. But when ice-cream comes served on Shirl's lips I'm prepared to compromise. Her lips felt cold and hot at the same time. I tried to figure out which I liked best. Decided it depended on what I was going to do next. And as we were sitting in the middle of a crowded café the options were limited.

I wrenched my mind back to Glove Man and said: "When he leaves, why don't we follow him?"

Shirley's eyebrows arched over the top of her sunglasses like the loops of the Loch Ness monster breaking the surface. "Nuts," she said. "We can't follow an innocent man."

"We don't know that he's innocent."

"Listen up, whacker. I believe a man is innocent until he's proven guilty."

"We're not pointing the finger of guilt at the bloke. We just want to find out why his fingers are in those fancy gloves while the temperature is over eighty."

"What for?"

"There could be a story in it."

"Man in glove sensation! Give me a break."

"I've known big stories begin from more trivial beginnings. Besides, you're the one who wanted to know why he's wearing gloves on the hottest day of the year."

"And I guess we'll never know."

I grinned. "Perhaps not."

Perhaps Glove Man was as innocent as a baby sleeping in a crib. But I've got a reporter's mind. Suspicious.

And I could think of at least one guilty reason for wearing gloves on a sweltering day.

Chapter 2

Two hours before Shirley and I spotted Glove Man, I'd stomped into my news editor's office and said: "I need a holiday."

Frank Figgis put down the Woodbine he was about to light and said: "I understand that. You've worked long hours and turned in some great stories. Take the afternoon off."

Figgis was a small man with a wizened face and hard little eyes which constantly darted about. He had black hair which he parted straight down the middle. His sixty-a-day habit meant he leaked smoke like a Puffing Billy.

I pulled up the guest chair and slumped down. "I'm talking about a proper holiday, not playing hooky for a couple of hours."

"You could always make it the whole weekend."

"You weren't by any chance related to Thomas Gradgrind?"

"Not that bloke who used to dodge paying for his round in the Coach and Horses?"

Figgis had read his Charles Dickens as well as I had. He knew Gradgrind was the cold fish in *Hard Times* who was obsessed by work. Figgis was as crafty as a card-sharp. He was trying to turn the conversation away from holidays. He never took one himself and didn't see why anybody else wanted them. But he was always open to a logical argument.

So I said: "No better time for a reporter to take a holiday than in the middle of the silly season. There hasn't been a decent crime story for weeks."

"Silly season is the worst time, if you ask me. When good stories are hard to find, that's when you need your best reporters."

Figgis's yellow-stained fingers curled around his fag and he lit up. The tip glowed red as he took a long drag.

"I'll take that as a compliment. But I'd prefer to take a holiday," I said.

"If we had just one decent running story that would keep us in front-page headlines for a few days, I wouldn't be so worried about letting you off the leash."

Figgis leant back in his chair and surveyed his classic front pages from the past. They were mounted in frames on his office wall. He had a wistful look in his eye.

"There was a time when we could rely on good crime stories even in the silly season," he said.

I pointed at one of the front pages. "Like the Trunk Murders in 1934?" I said.

"First story when I joined the paper as a tyro," Figgis said. "Bits of a woman's body were found in a cabin trunk up at Brighton station."

"And she didn't even have a platform ticket."

"What a great story!"

"Not for the woman," I said.

Figgis ignored me. He was heading down Memory Lane. And, when he was in this mood, it was a one-way street.

"Then there were the thugs up at the racecourse," he said. "Graham Greene even wrote about them in *Brighton Rock*. But you never hear about them these days. Whatever happened to the razor gangs?"

"Perhaps they're having a shave," I said.

Figgis harrumphed. He came back to the present with an unpleasant bump. Sat up straighter in his chair. Frowned at me. Rummaged among the papers on his desk.

"Couldn't you leave your holiday until November?" he said.

"As the poet said, 'No fruits, no flowers, no leaves, no birds, November!'."

"But what do you say?"

"No chance. I want a holiday while the sun still shines hot."

Figgis scratched his chin. "I'll strike a deal with you. Bring me a running story we can splash on the front page and you can take your two weeks holiday as soon as the paper hits the streets."

I shrugged. It was all I was going to get out of him while he was in this mood.

I leant across the desk and extended my hand. "Shall we shake on it?"

A damp leathery hand grasped mine and squeezed reluctantly.

I stood up and moved towards the door. Turned back with my hand on the knob ready for a quick exit.

"So we have a deal," I said. "And, in the meantime, I'll accept your kind offer and take the afternoon off."

Behind me, it sounded as though Figgis had just exploded.

"I didn't mean... You sneaky, crafty, tricky..."

I hurried out and slammed the door. What Figgis was going to call me almost certainly involved a four-letter word.

It might even be true.

In the Black Rock café, I leant across the table and tapped Shirley's arm.

I said: "We're not the only ones watching Glove Man."

I jerked my thumb towards Marine Parade, the road which ran along the clifftop behind the beach. "See that guy leaning on the railings up there. He's been watching Glove Man for the past five minutes."

Shirley peered discreetly over the top of her sunglasses. "Do you mean the guy in the jeans and leather jacket? The one with the James Dean comb-back hairstyle and the searching eyes?"

"That's him. He wasn't there when we arrived."

"He looks like a Rocker Boy who wants to be like Dean. He's even wearing one of those blousons with a turned-up collar. He's a bit of a hunk. But how do you know he's watching Glove Man and not just taking the sea air?"

"Because as the café filled up, he's changed his position at least three times as new arrivals obscured his view."

The café had become busier so that every table was taken. The spotty boy had gorged his knickerbocker glory and the nanny was wiping his face with a napkin. The Darby and Joan pair were digging the last of the strawberry jam out of a tiny pot. The young lovers snapped pictures of one another against different backgrounds.

I said: "I think Glove Man knows who Rocker Boy is."

"Why?"

"Rocker Boy wants to keep Glove Man in eyeball contact but can't afford to move too close in case he's recognised. If Glove Man didn't know him, Rocker Boy could be sitting at a nearby table, just like us."

"Do you think Glove Man suspects he's being watched?"

"No. But he's certainly on edge. He's still anxious to put that envelope in the attaché case without anyone seeing what's inside. And there are two more questions. Who is Rocker Boy? And why is he so interested in Glove Man?"

Shirley shrugged. "Beats me."

But my reporter's nose was twitching at the sniff of a story.

I wondered whether we'd stumbled into a police surveillance operation. Could Rocker Boy be an undercover cop? Was Glove Man a crook who'd been meeting an associate? And were we about to witness an arrest? If so, my hopes of getting the kind of front-page story that would put a smile of Figgis's face - and send me on holiday - had just soared.

I was turning this thought over in my mind when a shadow loomed over our table. I turned sharply and looked up. It was the young lovers with their camera. He was dressed in a floral shirt and a beach shorts cut just below the knee. She sported a pink blouse and red Capri pants. They had a couple of sloppy embarrassed smiles on their faces. The kind people have when they're about to ask strangers for a favour.

"We were just wondering..." began the man.

"... whether you could take a picture of both of us..." said the woman.

"...together," added the man.

"Nat's taken plenty of shots of me..." said the woman.

"And Nettie's got an album-full of me..." said Nat.

"But we haven't got any of us together..." said Nettie.

"Which is a shame..." said Nat.

"Because we're always together," said Nettie.

She slipped her hand into Nat's and squeezed it gently.

I grinned. "Where do you want to stand?" I asked.

"Could you snap us in Madeira Drive?" said Nat.

"With the pier in the background?" said Nettie.

"I'll just be a couple of minutes," I told Shirley.

"I'll wait here and watch our friends," Shirley said. She winked.

Nat and Nettie bustled off to take up position for the shot. It wasn't easy because there were crowds everywhere.

But I eventually got them positioned and Nat handed me the camera.

I raised it and the shutter clicked.

Snap.

"Sorry," I said to them. "That one was an accident."

I moved a couple of yards back and the shutter clicked again.

Snap.

"It's a very sensitive mechanism," Nat shouted to me.

This was getting embarrassing. But the pair were trying to shift position so there would be no-one in the background. They'd never do it - there were just too many people about. Eventually, they posed with plastic smiles and I pressed the shutter.

Snap.

"Another one for the album," I said.

I handed the camera to Nat. "Perhaps not up to Lord Snowdon's standard - but you're both in the picture."

They thanked me and made for the Volk's Railway. I headed back to our table.

I pushed through the crowds. Saw Shirley, and immediately

knew something was wrong.

She was on her feet. She twizzled her head from right to left like it was being driven by clockwork.

I ran towards her.

"What's wrong?" I asked

She turned and stared at me with saucer eyes.

"It's Glove Man," she said. "He's just vanished."

I swivelled to look at his table. A fat bloke with a knotted handkerchief tied over his bald head had taken up residence. He had his nose stuck in the menu.

I looked towards the road. Ran my gaze along the railings.

"Something big is going to happen," I said.

"How do you know?" Shirley asked.

I thumbed towards the railings. "Rocker Boy has also disappeared."

"Perhaps they're supernatural," Shirley said.

Chapter 3

"I don't think Glove Man or Rocker Boy is supernatural," I said. "I think they're super-sneaky."

Shirley and I had left our table in the Black Rock café and were scanning the faces in the crowds of holidaymakers.

"I had my eyes off Glove Man for no more than twenty seconds," Shirley said. "There was some noise from the road - cars honking and drivers shouting - and I looked up there. Rocker Boy seemed to be taking an interest in it. Quite a few people turned to see what it was. So I stood up to get a better look. Then when I switched back to Glove Man, he was hidden behind a large family who were arguing about where to sit. When they moved out of the way, he was gone."

"The commotion gave him a chance to move."

"Do you think he knew we were watching him?"

"No. I just think he was super-cautious."

"As well as super-sneaky," Shirley said.

"And super-slippery," I added. "He's slid out of sight as sinuously as an eel in seaweed."

"So that's that." Shirley said. She punched her fists on her hips in frustration.

"Perhaps it is. But maybe not. I'd hoped this might turn into a story. Perhaps a big one. Possibly even a front page splash. Then Figgis would have to give me the holiday he'd promised."

I continued to scan the crowds while I talked, but there was no sign of Glove Man. Or Rocker Boy.

"Let's put ourselves in Glove Man's place," I said. "Suppose we'd met somebody for a criminal purpose in a café. Perhaps to receive the envelope. What would we do next?"

"Get away as quickly as possible, I guess."

"Exactly. So how's he doing that?"

"Car would be dinkum. As long as he parked it somewhere

near."

"Agreed. But did he come by car? I don't think so. If it was parked nearby, surely he'd have returned to it as quickly as possible as soon as he'd received the envelope. I think his problem is he has to move either on foot or by public transport. Which was why he was so anxious to put the envelope in the case before he left the café. And he couldn't do that because the place was so crowded other people could have seen what was in the case when he opened it."

"Perhaps the diversion with the honking cars gave him his opportunity?" Shirley said.

"You're right. And then he moved. Fast."

"But where?"

"If he's leaving by public transport, the Volk's Railway would be a natural choice as the station is just a few yards from the café."

We strode off towards the station. A train that had pulled in while I was taking a photo of Nat and Nettie was still standing at the platform. We hurried up to it. A couple of dozen passengers had already clambered on board.

We craned our necks and looked at the crowd. There were a few faces we'd seen at the café. Nat and Nettie were at seats facing us half way along the train. They waved and we waved back.

"No sign of Glove Man," Shirley said.

"Are you sure?" I said. "Who's that sitting with his back to us in the carriage right at the front of the train?"

I pointed at a figure wearing a white shirt with sleeves rolled up to the elbows.

"Some people never forget a face. I never forget the back of a head," I said. "It's helped me spot people who didn't want to be found more than once."

Glove Man had been clever. He'd taken off his jacket and waistcoat. By rolling up his shirt sleeves he'd done his best to fit in with the casual dress of the holiday crowd around him.

But I was willing to bet he hadn't taken off his gloves.

"That's super-scheming," Shirley said.

"Not to mention super-sly," I added.

We'd taken seats on the train a couple of rows back from Glove Man.

When they'd seen we were climbing aboard Nat and Nettie had looked miffed when we hadn't joined them. But Shirley and I made out like a couple of romantics who wanted to be alone. A role we played without trying too hard.

And it looked as though we would have our compartment to ourselves. Except that seconds before the whistle blew a fat bloke with a ten-pint belly climbed on board. He had a torso like a beer barrel. He strode to the far side of the compartment, looked across the beach and farted.

"Just smell that fresh sea air," he said to anyone within earshot.

"I'd prefer to," I said.

He sat opposite and scowled at me.

A whistle blew and the revs from the train's motor stepped up a gear. Couplings clattered as the train pulled out of the station.

"Call this a train," Shirley said. "It looks more like one of those trams you see in Sydney."

She was right. Forget the Flying Scotsman. Forget the Orient Express. Forget the Twentieth Century Limited. Volk's Railway's trains consisted of one or two open-sided cars with half-a-dozen pairs of facing benches.

I said: "This is the oldest electric rail service in the world. It started in 1883. But don't expect a long ride. There are only three stations and we'll be at Paston Place, the first of them, in less than five minutes.

The train chugged along at a stately twenty miles an hour with the beach to the left and Brighton's Madeira Drive to the right. Traffic on Madeira Drive was heavy. Open-topped tourers cruised by. Men wore yachting caps. Women had scarves tied over their heads. A few strollers waved happily at the train as we rattled along.

In a way, I envied them. They were on holiday and I wasn't. I'd taken an afternoon off to spend with Shirl. And now even that had turned into a hunt for a story.

Damn Figgis!

But, perhaps, I would land a scoop.

The train slowed as it approached Paston Place. I nudged Shirley and pointed forward.

Glove Man was putting on his waistcoat and jacket. Perhaps he planned to leave the train. Or perhaps he simply thought he'd played at being a tourist long enough to throw off any tail.

As the train pulled into the station, the brakes hissed. The wheels squealed. The couplings rattled. Some passengers shuffled into position to get off. A few on the platform shifted about ready to climb aboard.

On Madeira Drive, the roar of an approaching motorcycle engine rose to a crescendo. I twisted in my seat to get a better view.

The cycle's rear-end fishtailed as the rider skidded to a halt. He was dressed in motorcycle leathers and had a red spotted bandana tied over the lower half of his face. I didn't think he was wearing it to keep the flies out of his mouth. But if he'd intended it to be a disguise, it had failed as far as Shirley and I were concerned. I recognised the James Dean quiff of hair and the searching eyes.

He vaulted off the bike and sprinted into the station. He raced the length of the platform like he was going for an Olympic gold.

On the train, passengers turned to watch as the figure flashed by. I jumped to my feet, but Beer Belly had moved first. And fallen over.

He floundered in the middle of the compartment like a beached whale and blocked my exit. Meanwhile, Rocker Boy had reached the front of the train. I watched as he leapt into the compartment with Glove Man. Rocker Boy aimed a vicious haymaker of a punch at the side of Glove Man's head. He caught him on the jaw, just under the ear. Glove Man staggered sideways three or four steps but retained his balance. He pushed Rocker Boy back with both hands, but then leant down to reach for the attaché case.

Big mistake.

Win the fight first. Claim the prize afterwards.

Rocker Boy moved forward. He aimed another haymaker at Glove Man's head while he bent forward for the case. Glove Man's neck flopped to one side. For a moment, I thought it might be broken. But then his head started to rotate in that lazy circular way before someone faints. He was trying to stay on his feet. But I guessed the savage blow to the side of his head had damaged his inner ear. Now his sense of balance would be shot to pieces.

Glove Man staggered across the carriage a couple more steps. Then he fell backwards, like a stately tree collapsing under a woodman's axe. He toppled out of the compartment and fell on to the stony beach. I heard a crack as his head hit the pebbles.

And then Rocker Boy moved again. He leapt out of the train - but this time he had something with him.

Glove Man's attaché case.

By now the train, was in uproar. Women screamed. Some cried. Children shrieked.

Men shouted orders at one another.

Stop him!

Grab the case!

Trip him up!

But after the beating Glove Man had taken, nobody stepped forward. It was the old story: when there's a tough decision, be brave - send someone else.

A lone figure towards the back of the train yelled: "Keep calm. If it's the Russians the ticket inspector will stop him." But nobody was listening to his views.

Everyone's eyes were focused on the sinister figure in motorcycle leathers and bandana. They cowered in their compartments yelling at one another to stay out of harm's way as the figure rushed by.

Ten-Pint Belly scrambled to his feet and I pushed past him to the platform. Shirley hustled out behind me. I yelled over my shoulder: "See what's happened to Glove Man. I'm following Rocker Boy."

She shouted: "Leave Glove Man to me, cobber."

I raced after the fast retreating figure determined to discover who Rocker Boy really was.

I wanted to know what was in that case.

And I had a smile on my face. I had a scoop that would bring me that holiday I wanted.

I could almost feel the sand between my toes.

Chapter 4

I pounded down the platform after Rocker Boy.

My relaxing afternoon wasn't turning out to be quite as restful as I'd imagined.

To my right a procession of shocked faces - gawping mouths, saucer eyes - stared from the train.

Ahead, Rocker Boy shoved the ticket collector aside as he raced into the street. The attaché case swung from his right hand as he ran.

I forced myself to run faster. Found an extra spurt of speed. Wondered what to do when I caught up with Rocker Boy.

Perhaps I could bring him down with a rugby tackle from behind. But I wouldn't fancy my own chances of surviving that - not with hard concrete underfoot. Especially as I'd hit the ground first.

The ticket collector gave me a dazed look as I rushed by.

In the street, fifty yards ahead, Rocker Boy had reached his motorcycle. He glanced back. I caught a flash of indecision in his eyes.

He'd won the fight with Glove Man. But he hadn't thought through his getaway.

He'd assumed he'd have time to mount his bike, rev the engine, and roar off into the traffic while stunned onlookers pointed fingers and tried to absorb the shock.

Now he realised he'd made a mistake. He'd put the cycle key in his right pocket. He had to do something with the attaché case before he could retrieve the key.

He stooped forward to put the case on the ground. Changed his mind. Switched it to his left hand. Stuck his right hand in the pocket of his motorcycle leathers and fumbled for the key. But the leathers were tight and his hand would be sweaty. He couldn't grasp the key easily.

He glanced back. I was twenty yards away and closing fast. I scowled at him to show I meant business.

He looked at the bike. His arm jerked convulsively as he tried to pull the key from his pocket. But it had snagged on something.

And now my menacing scowl was just ten yards away.

He glanced at his bike and me. Took a decision. Yanked his right hand out of his motorcycle leathers. Transferred the case back to it from his left

And ran.

His head swivelled left and right watching for traffic as he cut across Madeira Drive. But he was lucky. There was a gap between a taxi and an ice-cream van. He scooted between the two.

And I skidded to a halt while the van slowed in front of me.

By the time it had moved, Rocker Boy was across the road and leaping the first steps which lead up the cliff to Marine Parade, the main coast road.

I was panting like a fell runner. My legs felt they'd turned to blancmange. And my shirt felt like it had been glued to my back.

But dressed in motorcycle leathers Rocker Boy would feel worse. He'd feel like a chicken roasting on a spit.

So I pushed the pain from my mind and thought of white sand rippling through my toes as I strolled along a palm-fringed beach.

But I had to catch Rocker Boy first. I took the first steps three at a time. Cut back to two after a couple of leaps. Then decided doing one at a time would be quicker in the long run. And by the time I was half way up wondered whether I'd do the second half quicker if I had a little sit down. My heart was pounding like a steam-hammer.

I looked up. Rocker Boy was struggling. He was moving like a man whose clockwork had run down.

I pushed myself onward hoping my heart wouldn't burst through my chest and leave a nasty stain on my new shirt.

I reached the top of the steps feeling a bit like Atlas must have done when he was told he had to carry the world on his shoulders for the rest of his life. Except Atlas wasn't facing a punch-up with a leather-clad rocker.

Marine Parade was thick with vehicles. Two lanes in a constant stream in both directions. Cars, vans, buses, lorries rolled by in a kind of moving traffic jam.

Twenty yards to my left, Rocker Boy glanced over his shoulder. He was moving like a man swimming through molasses. When he'd looked at me down on Madeira Drive, there'd been contempt in his eyes.

Catch me if you can!

Now there was fear. I was moving like a rhino with a wooden leg, but I was moving faster than he was. In ten seconds, perhaps five, I'd be on him. He knew it.

His head swivelled left and right as he hunted for a way to escape. I followed his line of sight.

A blue bubble car was approaching from the right in the inner lane. There was a small gap before the Brighton Corporation bus which followed it. Nothing in the outer lane in front of the bus.

I read Rocker Boy's mind. If he could sneak through the gap between the bubble car and the bus, I'd be blocked by the bus and the stream of traffic behind. He'd dodge between vehicles to the other side and get away up a side street.

I was five yards from him as he flexed his knees and leapt for the gap. He took off like a man who sees salvation within his reach. He dashed in front of the bus.

He glanced right and his body went rigid. Half a second later, a Ford Zephyr, overtaking the bus in the outside lane, hit him. His arms flailed and the attaché case flew from his right hand. His leg bent where it shouldn't as his body was lifted onto the

Zephyr's bonnet.

The car skidded to the right, swerved back and Rocker Boy slipped from the bonnet like butter sliding off a hot potato. But traffic was moving fast in the on-coming direction. Rocker Boy tumbled onto the road just as a furniture van accelerated to avoid the Zephyr's swerve.

Even above the traffic noise, there was a thump and then a soft bump - almost sensual in a foul kind of way - as the wheels of the heavy van rode over him.

Then the air was rent by the squeal of brakes and the roar of decelerating engines. People shouted. Some screamed. Further back, drivers - unaware of why the traffic had stopped - honked horns.

A dark pool of blood oozed obscenely from under the furniture van. I felt like an elephant was dancing in my stomach. Something sticky rose in my throat and I belched. My tongue felt like a doss-house doormat. A cacophony of horns and engines and loud voices filled my ears. I couldn't tear my eyes away from the horror of the crumpled limbs and swelling pool of body fluids that stained the road.

My breath was coming in short pants and my vision was hazy. I dragged my eyes away and looked down.

And jumped with shock.

The attaché case was lying close to my feet in the gutter. As it had flown from Rocker Boy's hand, it must have skittered across the road.

I leant down and picked it up. Glanced around, but nobody was watching me. Everyone's attention was focused on the accident. On the horror that was festering under the furniture van.

I walked slowly back to the steps which led down to Madeira Drive. Sat on the top step and opened the case.

I was still breathing heavily, but I couldn't contain a gasp.

The picture of a distinguished man with a domed forehead,

long wavy hair and penetrating gaze looked up at me. Benjamin Franklin. Author, politician, philosopher, scientist. And one of the Founding Fathers of the United States.

And there were lots of him. On the front of hundred dollar bills. All neatly banded into bundles. I picked up one of them. Counted the bills. The paper rustled importantly between my fingers as I flicked through the bundle. Twenty bills. So two thousand dollars. There were six bundles. Twelve thousand dollars.

It was a handsome sum. Correction, an enormous sum. One a thief would pay a high price to steal. But, perhaps, not as much as Rocker Boy.

So that was why Glove Man hadn't been anxious to open his case when there were prying eyes about. But it didn't explain who Glove Man was.

The envelope he'd had on the table beside him in the Black Rock café had ended up at the bottom of the case. Perhaps its contents would tell me more.

I glanced around to make sure nobody was watching, but all attention was focused on the horror behind me.

I reached into the case and took out the envelope.

Chapter 5

The envelope was addressed: Mr Arthur Crouch, Brighton Beach.

I put my hand inside and pulled out a British passport.

A thing of beauty to the traveller. The deep blue cover with Her Majesty's coat of arms emblazoned in gold shimmered in the sunshine. I ignored the lions - *passant* and *rampant gardant* - and other heraldic fripperies and focused on the motto: *Honi soit qui mal y pense.*

Shame upon him who thinks evil of it.

Intended originally as a warning to uppity medieval peasants tempted to stick a pitchfork up the Order of the Garter - and the knights and barons who wore it.

But that was a motto coined in the days when knights were bold and ladies fair.

Which ruled out Glove Man.

I flipped open the passport cover and turned a couple of pages.

And there was Glove Man pictured in monochrome scowling into the camera. There was no doubt. The swarthy complexion, the scar above the upper lip, the five-o'clock shadow were all present and correct. If anything, brought into sharper contrast by the black and white photograph.

The passport had been issued in the name of Arthur Beddoes Crouch. His place of birth was Leamington Spa, Warwickshire.

He'd been born on the thirteenth of April 1921 - which made him forty-two. His occupation was described as funeral director. The passport had been issued just two weeks earlier.

I slipped the passport back into the envelope and pulled out the document. A first-class airline ticket for a British Overseas Airways Corporation flight from London Heathrow to New York Idlewild airport. Leaving at eight-thirty this evening.

I glanced at my watch. Three-twenty. Crouch would have had to hustle to make his flight. He'd looked like a man who didn't leave much to chance. But he hadn't factored in the brutal attack on the train.

I slid the airline ticket and passport back in the envelope, roughly resealed it and shoved it back in the attaché case.

Why had a funeral director who was in a hurry to leave for the United States with a stash of cash been attacked? It left plenty to think about. But not now.

After the accident, the chaos was building around me.

I looked back towards the road. It was gridlocked around the furniture van. Traffic was at a standstill. Drivers had climbed out of their cars to share the experience in that peculiar way the British do after a disaster. No doubt a well-meaning local would soon appear with a tray of tea.

But some braver souls crept closer to the tragedy and peered under the van. They wished they hadn't. They were now throwing up on the pavement.

In the distance, a cop car's bell rose above the sound of the blaring horns and revving engines. Perhaps two cop cars. The ringing was insistent.

I looked at the attaché case in my hand and wondered what to do. It belonged to Crouch. But the last I saw he was lying unconscious beside the railway track. Perhaps he was dead. One thing was for sure: it didn't look like he'd be lounging back in his first-class airline seat sipping champagne this evening.

The attaché case was evidence in a criminal investigation. My duty as a good citizen was to hand it to the cops when they arrived. But my duty as a journalist was to get a great story for my paper. Crouch may have been the victim. But I suspected he was also a crook. He had some serious questions to answer. And I wanted to be the first to ask them.

The police bells were closer now. I decided I'd serve my duty as a journalist first - and be a good citizen later.

I hurried down the steps to Madeira Drive. Sprinted across the road and into the station.

The train hadn't moved. It wouldn't be going anywhere for some time. It was now a crime scene.

Passengers from the train milled about on the platform. They had querulous faces. They asked questions of their neighbours who shook their heads. Nobody had any answers yet. They'd witnessed the fracas at the front of the train. Now they were trying to make sense of it.

I scanned the platform for Shirley. She was towards the front of the train talking to Nat and Nettie.

I hurried up, put my arm around her and gently squeezed.

"Jeez, Colin, what's happening?" she said.

"Rocker Boy is dead. Crushed by a furniture van on the main road. But I've recovered the case."

I held up the trophy.

Shirl's eyes widened in shock.

"How did you get that?"

"I'll tell the full story later. First, I need to find Glove Man - incidentally, his name is Arthur Beddoes Crouch."

Shirley pointed to the front of the train.

"The driver went down onto the track to look at him. I came back here because I was coming to find you - you crazy bastard."

During the struggle with Rocker Boy, Crouch had fallen out of the front compartment of the train on the beach side - away from the platform.

Shirley and I hustled down the platform and climbed through the front compartment.

But the man lying on the track beside the train wasn't Crouch.

It was the driver.

He had a purple bruise on his forehead which leaked blood. He was rubbing his head and moaning.

We jumped down and hurried to his side.

Shirley pulled out a handkerchief and gently mopped the

blood from around the bruise. We helped him to sit up. He stared at us through glazed eyes.

"He hit me," he said. "He hit me with a rock from the beach."

"Take it easy," Shirley said.

During the next few minutes, the story emerged. The driver's name was Ernest. After the struggle, Ernest had climbed down from the driver's cab to see what had happened to Crouch. Ernest thought Crouch had knocked himself out. But if he had, it was for no more than a few seconds. When Ernest leant over him, Crouch had seized a rock from the beach and smashed the poor bloke.

Ernest pointed with a wavering hand. "He ran off - towards Palace Pier."

I stood up and scanned the beach, but there was no sign of a fleeing figure in a grey suit. And if there had been, he'd have surely stood out among the bronzed bodies in swimming cozzies.

If Crouch was a funeral director, I was a saggar maker's bottom knocker. (Even though one had been on the BBC's *What's My Line*, I wasn't sure exactly what he did.)

The robbery was going to be a big story. The accidental death of Rocker Boy - whoever he turned out to be - could be bigger. But Crouch's attack on the driver and hasty exit from the scene leaving a passport, air ticket and twelve thousand dollars behind, had to be bigger.

The cops would be focused on the chaos up on Marine Parade. Some of them may already have been puking up their sausage and chip lunch after viewing the grisly scene under the furniture van. But before long, they'd appear at Paston Place station. And I'd be forced to hand over the attaché case. Which meant I had just minutes to get what information I could from it.

I said to Shirley: "Do your Florence Nightingale act with Ernest. I need to speak urgently to Nat and Nettie."

Shirl gave me a queer look but didn't argue.

I clambered back into the train. Climbed through the compartment. Jumped down onto the platform.

Nat and Nettie were standing by the side of the train. They had those vacant eyes which people get when they're in shock.

I hustled up and said: "If we were back at Black Rock café, I'd give you both a cup of hot sweet tea. As it is, I can only offer sympathy for the ordeal."

They nodded and managed a couple of thin grins.

I said: "I've got a favour to ask. I've got a document in this attaché case I need to photograph. Could I borrow your camera?"

Nat looked at Nettie, then back at me. "I don't know… I've only three exposures left on the film."

"I'd only need a couple of them - and I'd be happy to pay. I'll even get the film developed for you for free."

"We normally take it to…" said Nat

"…the chemists," added Nettie.

"I'm a newspaper reporter with the *Evening Chronicle*. We have a photographic department which could have the film developed. Even provide enlargements for you."

This time, Nettie looked at Nat.

"I suppose, if we could get the pictures…" she said.

"…before the end of our holiday…" Nat said.

"…it would be all right." Nettie added.

Nat handed me the camera. I climbed into one of the empty compartments on the train. Opened the attaché case. Found the envelope and took out the passport. I opened it at the page with Crouch's photograph and personal details. I'm no photographer - as the accidental snaps earlier had proved. So I used all three exposures to take close-up shots of the passport. Then I wound on the film and took it out of the camera. Shoved it in my pocket.

I stepped out of the compartment and handed the camera back to Nat.

"I've kept the film," I said. "If you let me know where you're staying, I'll make sure you get enlargements of the shots before your holiday ends."

"Thank you. I guess this is a holiday..." Nat said.

"...we won't forget." Nettie added.

They gave me the address of a guest house in New Steine and said they'd be there until the end of the week.

I nodded my thanks and moved back to the front of the train.

Before I could, a couple of uniformed plods rushed onto the platform. And after them, moving at a more sedate pace, Ted Wilson. His face was red and shining. His beard looked shaggier than usual. And he'd got his serious eyes on.

But Ted's appearance was good news. He was one of the honest cops in the town - and my only reliable contact in the force.

He came up to me and said: "If there's trouble, I might have known you'd be mixed up in it."

"Great to see you, too, Ted," I said.

"So what have we got here?"

"It's a long story." I held up the attaché case. "But this seems to be at the centre of it."

I handed Ted the case and winked. "Don't spend it all at once," I said.

Chapter 6

Jeff Purkiss's jaw dropped like a puppet's whose strings had just been slashed.

"You handed twelve thousand dollars to the police?" he said. His eyes goggled in disbelief.

"In an attaché case. With a passport. And a first-class air ticket to New York," I said.

"I'd have spent ten thou' of that on good whisky, bad women and the flutter of a lifetime on the gee-gees up at the racecourse."

"What would you have done with the other two thousand?" I asked.

"Oh, I'd have wasted that."

Jeff was the landlord of Prinny's Pleasure, a downbeat drinking den in the North Laine part of town. The pub got its name from a legend that the Prince Regent had used the place for secret assignations with his top squeeze, Mrs Fitzherbert. The signboard hanging outside the pub commemorated the unlikely event. The board featured a portrait of Mrs Fitzherbert with her hand raised in a regal wave. Except that the ancient signboard had warped so badly it now looked as though the good lady was giving a rude V-sign to passers-by.

Inside, Prinny's Pleasure had green flock wallpaper that long ago had turned grey. There was a sticky carpet which made little squelchy sounds when you walked over it. Not surprisingly, the place didn't attract many customers. But that suited me just fine. When you're a crime correspondent, your contacts among the cops and the criminal classes don't want an audience when they're hobnobbing with the press.

I said: "I didn't have much choice about handing over the attaché case as the bloke who owned it had scarpered after braining the driver of a Volk's train - and the cops were flooding the area."

"Even so, you could have stuffed a wad of those big ones into your pocket before the fuzz showed up."

"I've written a story for tomorrow's *Chronicle* about the robbery of the case and its recovery. I believe Figgis is thinking of heading the story the Great Train Robbery. Anyway, with my byline on the piece, I could hardly swan around town spending hundred dollar bills. Now you can get me a large gin and tonic with one ice-cube and two slices of lemon."

Jeff grabbed a glass and pressed it against an optic. While he was looking for a lemon that hadn't grown mould, I thought back to the afternoon.

After Ted Wilson had turned up, I'd spent an hour at Paston Place station going over the events with him. Each fresh development in the tale had Ted's eyebrows rising higher so I thought they were going to disappear into his hairline.

"I don't like the sound of all this," he'd said. "On the face of it, there are two crimes. First, assault and robbery on Crouch. And second Crouch's assault on the train driver. I can understand the motive for the first. I could name fifty crooks in this town who'd whack their grandmothers to grab twelve thousand dollars. What I can't understand is why Crouch was so keen to clobber the driver and scarper to avoid getting the loot back."

"That's bothering me, too," I'd said.

I'd handed Ted the attaché case and he'd carried it off with about as much enthusiasm as if it contained a nuclear weapon. We'd agreed to keep in touch.

Jeff put my G and T on the counter. "If you'd kept the moolah, you could have been drinking champagne."

I was about to reply, but the pub door slammed open and Ted Wilson stood framed in the doorway. He glanced left and right and hurried inside.

I said: "Better add a large whisky to the order."

Ted walked up to the bar, pulled up a stool and slumped on it. His back was hunched and his eyelids drooped at the corners from tiredness.

"This case is turning into a monster," he said.

"Want to tell me about it?"

"Perhaps you can explain what's going on. Because I can't make head nor tail of it."

Jeff poured the scotch. We took our drinks to the corner table at the back of the bar.

Ted said: "When I left you this afternoon I thought at least we knew who the main protagonists were in this farrago. Now I don't even know that."

I took a long pull on my G and T. "Tell me more."

"Well, for a start, the fellow with the attaché case is not Arthur Beddoes Crouch. His passport is a forgery. A good one, certainly good enough to get him through airport checks, but perhaps not top of the range."

"You're not telling me anything I don't already know."

"How come?"

"When he didn't hang around after the original robbery, there had to be a reason. Especially as he'd lost a stack of money many people wouldn't see after three years' work. He'd know he'd be questioned by police as the victim of a serious crime - and he couldn't risk that. That's why he scarpered."

"The air ticket was genuine," Ted said. "It looks as though it was issued through a travel agent and we're running that down at present. But I think it will prove to be a dead end."

"I agree. He'll have paid for the ticket in cash so there was no payment paper trail for the cops to follow if anything went wrong."

"What about fingerprints on the attaché case?" I asked.

"None. It'd been wiped clean. Of course, you kindly added your own before handing it in."

"So that was why Crouch had been wearing gloves," I said.

"He was wearing gloves on the hottest day of the year?"

"A fancy pair. He could have threaded a needle wearing

them."

Ted took a swig at his whisky. Gave a long sigh. Relaxed a little.

He said: "The problem is that we've got too much mystery at both ends of the investigation."

"In what way?"

"I thought we'd be able to establish who the character you call Rocker Boy was when we'd recovered his body." Ted took a strong pull at his scotch. "Or what was left of his body. Never a pleasant task when part of it involves using a dustpan and brush."

"I saw enough to know that wasn't going to be a pretty business. Not that retrieving dead bodies ever is."

"We went through all his clothing but he had nothing which would identify him."

"Not even a motorcyclist's licence?"

"His pockets were empty."

"What about a photographic appeal? You know - contact the police if you know this man."

"A photograph of what?"

"His face. We'd run it in the *Chronicle*."

"Not much left of it. Not enough for the refined readers of your rag."

I took a gulp of the gin. Felt like another. But decided against.

"And that's not all," Ted said. "When we ran down the registration on his motorcycle, that proved false."

"Could you track him through the vehicle identification number?"

"We'll do what we can on that. But a bloke who seems to have done everything to ensure he couldn't be traced if anything went wrong, will have covered himself on that front as well. He probably bought the bike under a false name."

"So nothing?"

Ted hesitated. Picked up his glass and had a swig of scotch.

There was something. But he was undecided whether to tell me about it.

I said: "Off the record?"

"You're reading my mind again."

"If I could read minds, I'd be doing a variety act at the Hippodrome."

Ted's lips twitched into a grim little grin. "This really is off the record."

I gave him a three-fingered salute. "Scout's honour."

"You weren't even in the scouts. But this doesn't go any further at the moment. Agreed?"

"Agreed," I said without crossing my fingers.

"The character we scraped off the road this afternoon did have something on him."

"On paper?"

"On his skin."

"A tattoo," I said.

"Strange one, too. A quotation on each arm. 'Dream as if you'll live for ever' on the right. 'Live as if you'll die today' on the left.'"

"Mean anything to you?"

"Nothing. And I can't see it giving us a definite lead."

"Any theories?"

"Not many. And none that I'd want to see printed in the *Chronicle,*" Ted said.

"So what are you going to do next?"

"I think it will come down to basic police work. We'll see if we can identify the main actors in this drama. But what I'd like to know is: what are you going to do next?"

I swallowed the last of my G and T. Gave Ted my wide-eyed innocent look.

"After the adventure we've had today, I'm going to take Shirley out for a slap-up dinner," I said.

Chapter 7

Shirley pointed at my plate and said: "I don't know how you can eat that after seeing a man's brains splattered all over the road."

I said: "The oysters are delicious. And his brains weren't splattered over the road. Even if they had been, they wouldn't have been sprinkled with Worcestershire sauce, then lightly grilled with little lardons of bacon."

"You're heartless."

"And you're beautiful when you're angry."

Shirl grinned and dug into her prawn cocktail.

We were seated on a plush red banquette at a corner table in English's, a period piece of a seafood restaurant in Brighton's Lanes. The room had starched napery, crystal glasses, and the kind of heavy cutlery which makes a statement that eating good food is a serious business. As it should be. The place looked like a stage set for Edwardian roués. You half expected to see Edward the Seventh in a discreet alcove fondling Alice Keppel's thighs under the table.

It was nine o'clock and the light outside was fading.

And so was I.

It had been quite a day. After I'd left Ted Wilson, I'd hurried back to the *Chronicle* where I'd spent half an hour batting out a story about the latest developments in the Volk's train robbery. It would be the lead in the morning edition of tomorrow's paper. And, I reckoned, enough to make sure Figgis honoured our deal about my holiday.

Shirley raised her wine glass, took a sip of the Sauvignon, then said: "What do you think the blue heelers will do with all that cash?"

"They'll lock it in the safe in the cop shop's evidence store," I said. "In the lead to my story I wrote there was twelve thousand dollars in the case. So that should deter any light-fingered PC helping himself to a little pocket money."

"You think they'd do that?" Shirley popped the last prawns into her mouth.

"Not Ted Wilson who took the case. But Detective Chief Superintendent Tomkins, who'll run the investigation, is as bent as a fiddler's elbow. I wouldn't trust him. In any event, even the cops would have trouble spending hundred dollar bills in Brighton."

"Twelve thousand dollars sure is a pile of boodle."

"Yes. About nine thousand six hundred pounds. Enough to buy about three medium-sized houses in Brighton. A fortune to most people when you consider average pay is not much more than seven hundred pounds a year."

A waiter clad in a long white-starched apron appeared and cleared away our plates.

"Surely a funeral director would have to bury a whole graveyard of stiffs to make that kind of money," Shirley said

"I don't think Arthur Beddoes Crouch was a funeral director. In fact, Ted told me his passport is a fake so he's not even Arthur Beddoes Crouch. He's a crook - and by the size of his pay-off a good one. The trouble is that now the story's out there every journo in the land will be chasing leads."

"But you were at the scene of the crime."

"True. But that's an advantage that will fade pretty quickly as new facts emerge."

The waiter reappeared with our main courses - sole *Veronique* for Shirley and lobster thermidor for me. We hoisted our heavy cutlery and started to eat.

Shirley let the waiter shuffle off to another table before she asked: "So what will you do?"

I said: "In a story like this, the way to stay ahead is to answer the big questions before the competition. I think the key is to unravel the relationship between Crouch and Rocker Boy.

There are three possibilities. The first is that Crouch and Rocker Boy didn't know one another. Rocker Boy just happened to be passing, saw a guy dressed in a three-piece suit and carrying an attaché case and reckoned there must be something worth nicking in it."

Shirley speared a grape in her *Veronique* with her fork. "But you said in the café that Rocker Boy was watching Crouch from a distance because Crouch knew Rocker Boy."

"I still think that's most likely. But there's an outside chance that Rocker Boy was hanging back simply to make sure Crouch didn't realise he was being watched. But the second possibility is that Crouch and Rocker Boy were members of rival gangs who both knew about whatever criminal enterprise landed the loot. Crouch had it and Rocker Boy was determined to grab it off him."

I tucked into my lobster. The combination of the mustard sauce and Parmesan cheese was delicious.

"No honour among thieves, you mean?" Shirley said.

"Something like that. But I think the most likely explanation is that Crouch and Rocker Boy are involved in the same crime - and have fallen out over who pockets the proceeds. It would explain why Rocker Boy didn't want Crouch to see him before the attack. And how Rocker Boy came to know where Crouch was. Whatever the crime, it must've been big."

"And now neither of them have the loot," Shirley said. "So both have lost out."

"I guess so." I forked up some more lobster. "But train robberies are so rare at least I've got a front-page splash - and a holiday - out of it. When I turn up at the police briefing tomorrow morning there's not a reporter in the land who'll be able to take that away from me."

As it turned out, I was wrong on all counts.

The following day started badly.

I arrived late at the police press briefing because my alarm clock failed to go off - and I overslept.

The reason the ancient time-piece refused to ring was because my landlady, Mrs Gribble - known to her tenants as the Widow, but never in her hearing - had cleaned it. She'd used some kind of wax material which had leaked into the innards and gummed up the little hammer which rattles between the bells on top.

So when seven-thirty came, the bell did not toll for me.

I should mention that Mrs Gribble is to cleaning what Genghis Khan is to landscape gardening. She owns an ancient Electrolux vacuum cleaner which does more damage than a Sherman tank. She wields the cleaner brush and hose like she's repelling a zombie invasion. She leaves behind her a wasteland of chipped furniture, ripped rugs and busted objets d'art - not that I own many objets d'art.

I once asked her not to clean my room. She fixed me with a gimlet eye and said: "It's no trouble."

I'm ashamed to say I resisted the temptation to say: "It is to me." There are times with the Widow when cowardice is the best policy.

Anyway, the upshot of the latest cleaning catastrophe was that I didn't wake until twenty-five to nine.

I'd hoped to saunter into the nine o'clock press briefing ten minutes early. That would give my fellow hacks plenty of time to feed their simmering resentment that I'd scooped them. Instead, I ended up barging through the door, like the runner up in an obstacle race, at two minutes to nine.

I was panting like a prisoner on the run and promised myself I'd get into training. Sometime.

But if I was late, the cops were even later. There was no sign of the big-wigs at the top table.

So I slumped down in a chair at the back. It was a good vantage point to view the room and see which reporters had been sent from Fleet Street to cover what I was proprietorially thinking of as "my story". I noted a healthy turn-out from most of the nationals - The *Mirror, Express, Mail* and even the *Telegraph* had sent their finest. Nobody from the *Sketch,* but then the paper looked like it was put together by the office cleaners. And a fracas on Brighton seafront was much too trivial to bother the snooty *Times.*

I was reflecting on all this when a horny hand tapped me on my shoulder. I turned my head. The hand led to an arm encased in a moth-eaten grey jacket. It smelt faintly of the yellow mildew you see growing on gravestones.

I looked up. Jim Houghton was grinning at me.

Jim was my opposite number on the *Evening Argus,* the other daily paper in town. He'd been at the game much longer than me - and showed it. He had a lined face with a bulbous nose and a hank of greasy hair which flopped over his forehead when he became angry.

Jim grinned exposing a row of teeth as craggy as Macgillycuddy's Reeks.

He said: "I'm surprised the police are going ahead with this briefing."

My eyes widened at that. "What do you mean? The robbery on Volk's Railway is the biggest crime story we've had during this silly season." I gestured at the crowd on the seats in front of me. "Not often we get so many from Fleet Street here."

Jim flicked a lazy gaze over them. "They'd have had their marching orders from the news editors when it looked like there was nothing better to cover. No doubt most of them were on yesterday's Brighton Belle out of London slavering at the prospect of an all-expenses paid night out in Brighton. They won't be so happy now the big story is breaking elsewhere."

I cursed the Widow under my breath. Because I'd overslept, I'd dressed and rushed to the cop shop without even glancing at the morning's papers.

But I put on my confident face and said: "So, Jim, what story trumps a great train robbery of twelve thousand dollars?"

Jim grinned. "A greater train robbery of two million pounds."

Chapter 8

I teased the story out of a couple of friendly hacks in the next few minutes.

In the early hours of the morning, the Travelling Post Office train from Glasgow to London - better known as the Night Mail - had been attacked by a gang of robbers. They tampered with the signals near Bridego railway bridge in Buckinghamshire. Then they'd stormed the train and coshed the driver. They'd overpowered the workers in the high-value packages coach. Early reports suggested they'd made off with more than 100 sacks of mail. Nobody yet knew how much cash had been stolen. But, I was told, the cops were briefing it could well be more than two million pounds. If that were true, it would be the largest robbery ever in Britain.

As it turned out, the story broke too late to appear in the edition of the morning papers sent to the south coast. But it was in the London finals - and on the radio. But the Widow's antics with my alarm clock meant I'd stumbled into the briefing room like an innocent abroad.

I was thinking hard about how this might play in the press conference about the Volk's robbery, when the door at the back opened and the cops trooped in.

Detective Chief Superintendent Alec Tomkins led the way followed by Ted Wilson. A uniformed cop I didn't recognise brought up the rear. He had a bundle of papers stuffed under his arm. He'd be playing the bag carrier role and wouldn't be saying much. Whenever journalists were in the room Tomkins was the gobby one.

I'd crossed swords with him more than once in the past. He'd dearly have loved to handcuff me, sling me in a cell - preferably one with a few rats scuttling around in the corner - and forget I was there. But the chief constable's passion for public relations meant he had to pretend to be co-operative. He was a tall man with a full head of hair combed straight back from the forehead. He had a beaky nose and bushy eyebrows. It gave him all the charm of a nightclub bouncer.

Right now, he had an expression on his face like he was chewing on a wasp.

And behind him, Ted Wilson looked like he'd just spat the wasp out.

It wasn't difficult to deduce what had happened. They'd been having a barney backstage before they came on. As the investigating officer, Ted would have wanted to lead the press conference. But as a fully paid-up credit-hogger with a vain streak as wide as his kipper tie, Tomkins would want to bask in the glory of a robbery where the cops had already recovered the boodle. Actually, I'd recovered the money, but I'd no illusions that fact was going to be part of the narrative this morning. Still, it figured prominently in the story which should appear on the front page of the *Chronicle*'s morning edition.

The pair glared at each other as they seated themselves at the top table. The uniformed plod hovered in the wings fidgeting like a bloke who wasn't looking forward to breaking up the fight.

Tomkins surveyed the room with a truculent eye. Gave a tight grin which showed he was satisfied with the turnout. He picked up a paper and said: "I'm going to read a short statement. Kindly keep your questions until the end."

The bloke from the *Express* stuck his arm up and said: "Will there be plenty of time for questions?"

Tomkins glared at him and said: "I've asked you to keep your questions until the end."

"But this is a question about the questions," the bloke said.

"I don't care what kind of question it is," Tomkins snapped. "It can wait until I've read my statement. I'm not going to be dictated to about how I run my press conference by a jumped-up journalist."

The *Express* bloke looked like he was going to leap out of his seat and clock Tomkins on the snoot, but his neighbour restrained him. A murmur of resentment rumbled through the press pack.

Ted Wilson leaned forward and played the peace-maker. "I'm sure that there will be plenty of time for questions after the chief super has had his say," he said.

Tomkins glared at him. Turned back to the paper in his hand and started reading it.

As expected, it was a paean of praise for the brave police, prominent among them one Detective Chief Superintendent Alec Tomkins, who had foiled an audacious robbery on Brighton's historic Volk's Railway. Tomkins finished speaking and put down his paper.

I'd been watching my fellow hacks. Nobody had been taking notes. Tomkins' attitude to the *Express* reporter had narked everyone.

Tomkins surveyed the room with a benevolent sneer. "Now I will take questions," he said.

The *Express* bloke stuck his hand up. "After the big heist in Buckinghamshire, this just looks like tiny trouble on a toy-town train."

The journos laughed. Tomkins eyes popped and his face coloured.

The guy from the *Mirror* said: "I can see the headlines now: Beach Bandit Botches Burglary."

More laughter. The press pack was paying Tomkins back for putting down one of their own.

"Passenger Pirate Pinches Plunder," chipped in the hack from the *Mail*.

"Seaside Snatcher's Swipe Spoiled," said the bloke from the *Telegraph*.

The room was in uproar. Journos were swapping jokes, calling to their mates, laughing themselves silly.

Tomkins eyes flashed angrily. He shot to his feet. He'd lost it. He was shaking with anger. His face was red. Sweat beads rolled down his forehead. He shook his fists.

"Shut up!" he yelled. "You disgrace to the press. I should lock you all up," he screamed.

The room went silent, like the air had just stopped transmitting sound waves. Then the bloke from the *Express* stood up. Approached the top table. Held out his wrists. Said: "It's a fair cop, guv. Put the bracelets on me now."

That was it. We all erupted with laughter. The press pack hadn't had a briefing like this before. It was better entertainment than *Sunday Night at the London Palladium*.

Even the bag carrier was chortling quietly. Tomkins glared at him and his face changed like he'd just swallowed a warthog. Tomkins yelled: "You're all a disgrace," and stormed from the room.

It took five minutes for us all to calm down. I watched as Ted Wilson sat at the top table waiting for the merriment to subside. He had the look of a man who knows he has just won a small victory.

The room finally fell quiet. Ted leaned forward, and in a voice as unctuous as a palace flunky, said: "Are there any more questions?"

I left the press briefing not knowing whether to laugh or cry.

It had been fun watching Fleet Street's finest baiting Tomkins. But it was a tough reminder that my Volk's train robbery wasn't as big a story as the events further north. Still, as I pushed through the newsroom doors at the *Chronicle*, I was confident it was strong enough to lead the day's paper. And ensure Figgis signed off on my long-delayed holiday.

The newsroom was buzzing with excitement as I hurried over to my desk. The whole place seemed to be working on a story.

The crescendo from thirty typewriters pounded at the same time sounded like a machine gun attack.

Cedric, the copy boy, flashed his toothy grin as he hurried by. "Heard about the great train robbery?" he said.

"I was on the Volk's railway when it happened, Cedric."

"No, Mr Crampton, I mean the real one."

Cedric bustled off. I frowned. No doubt the lad would learn tact in time.

When I reached my desk, I found a note rolled into my typewriter carriage. It read: "I'd like a word with you. FF."

I hurried round to Figgis's office, knocked and barged in before he could shout: "Enter."

He was sitting behind his desk squirting petrol into his cigarette lighter. The sharp reek of the fluid over-powered the smoky smell of the furnishings.

I said: "I see from your note you'd like a word with me. I hope the word is 'holiday'."

Figgis looked up from his lighter and said: "At the moment, the word is 'trouble'."

I pulled up the guest chair and sat down.

I said: "I think you better explain that."

Figgis tossed the empty petrol cylinder into his waste basket. He reached for his Woodbines, shoved one between his lips and clicked the lighter. The thing sent up a flame like a solar flare which scorched his nose. He dropped the fag and the lighter and let rip with a string of words most of which never made it into the Oxford Dictionary.

He rubbed his nose and said: "So much for new technology. In future I'm sticking to matches."

I said: "Was it the lighter that's been giving you the trouble?"

"No," he said. "His Holiness upstairs."

Gerald Pope - the nickname was never used in his hearing - was the *Evening Chronicle*'s editor. He was a twerp who'd got the job because his posh voice and flawless table manners had impressed the paper's proprietor. Pope usually steered clear of the grubby business of news reporting. Instead, he spent his time badgering the feature writers with ideas that would seem tired in a parish magazine.

A little worry-worm started wriggling in my mind. "What's His Holiness been up to now?"

"Interfering in the business of news editing. He doesn't understand it."

"What's he done?"

"He's ordered me to run with the train robbery on the front page."

"You mean *my* train robbery?"

"No, the other one." Figgis sucked so hard on his fag the end lit up like a red light.

"You can't mean he's bounced the best Brighton crime story we've had in the silly season for ages off the front page."

Figgis nodded.

"That's ridiculous," I said.

"I've used every argument I can think of with him, but he's adamant. I even showed him a proof of a front page I'd had made up. Didn't change his mind. He says that as everybody is talking about the so-called Great Train Robbery at Bridego bridge in Buckinghamshire people will expect to see it on the front page. He doesn't realise that people buy local papers for local news."

"But the fact you intended to use my story means you'll stick to our agreement about my holiday?"

Figgis stubbed out his ciggie and reached for another.

"'Fraid not. With so much happening I need you here more than ever. Give it a couple of months and take time off then."

"I want a holiday while it's still summer, not when the mists of autumn are gathering."

Figgis leant back in his chair: "I'm afraid my decision is final."

I stood up and strode towards the door.

"You said you wanted a word with me," I said. "I've got one for you. Oath-breaker."

"That's two words," Figgis said.

"Not if you use a hyphen."

I stomped out and slammed the door.

Chapter 9

There was more bad news when I reached my desk in the newsroom.

A message from Ted Wilson said that he would be releasing the picture of "Arthur Crouch", the fugitive victim of the Volk's robbery, later in the day.

The picture of the photo - or should that be the photo of the picture? - in Crouch's passport that I'd taken with Nat's camera would be in all editions of the *Chronicle*. But no longer as an exclusive. Now it would compete with the official cop version, which would probably be of better quality. We'd end up using it ourselves.

So a useful edge I'd had on the story had slipped away.

Damn.

Of course, Ted would want Crouch's picture in as many papers as possible. He wanted to know who Crouch really was as much as I did. But when he circulated the picture, every paper in the land would get involved in the hunt. They'd hope to be the paper a reader would contact to say: "I know that man." With the nationals running the picture as well, the chances of the *Chronicle* getting lucky were slim.

I sat back in my old captain's chair and surveyed the newsroom with a detached eye. The pre-deadline frenzy was building. Journos made frantic phone calls, flipped through notebooks, rummaged in press cuttings files as they realised they didn't have enough info to meet their word count.

I'd had more than enough words for my story - and now His Holiness had banished it to an inside page. For all the impact it would make there, he might as well have had it printed in Cyrillic script under the jobs wanted adverts.

But bitterness is an unattractive trait. I decided I would not be prey to it.

Instead, I would work to get back in front on the story. The so-called Great Train Robbery may involve more money, but I felt mine had more mystery.

Everyone was chasing after Crouch because they didn't know where he was. We knew where Rocker Boy was - in the drawer of a freezer cabinet in the coroner's mortuary. But we still didn't know who he was. I had a hunch that if could I identify him, it could help lead me to Crouch. The more I thought about how Rocker Boy had watched Crouch from the shadows, the more I felt that Crouch knew who he was.

And that they weren't the best of buddies.

Shirley had said that Rocker Boy reminded her of James Dean - almost as though he had been modelling himself on the dead movie star. And Ted Wilson had revealed that Rocker Boy had a tattoo on each arm with a quotation.

Those two facts might be enough to let me trace who Rocker Boy really was. I stood up and headed for the morgue, the library where the paper filed thousands of press cuttings.

When I walked into the morgue I found Henrietta Houndstooth, who ran the place, sitting alone at her desk.

She was wearing a tweed suit that would've looked good on a grouse moor. She peered over the top of her glasses and said: "I thought you'd end up in here before the day was out."

Henrietta was one of those people who seemed to know what's happening before anyone else. She should have been a reporter but when I'd once mentioned the idea, she'd thrown up her well-manicured hands in horror.

"Poking around in other people's troubles - not my cup of Earl Grey," she said.

I scanned the room. "On your own today?"

Henrietta had a staff of three formidable middle-aged matrons who clipped cuttings from the paper and filed them. Mabel, Elsie and Freda were known around the paper as the Clipping

Cousins. But they were related more by a love of gossip and making trouble than by blood.

Henrietta said: "Freda's on holiday and Mabel is being fitted with a new surgical stocking."

I raised my eyebrows at that.

"I know," Henrietta said. "Apparently there's a new brand out. It 'grips your leg like a lover's caress' according to the makers. Mabel's wanted one ever since she heard a member of the Tiller Girls wears them."

It was news to me. I'd never noticed anyone in the chorus line wearing support hosiery - certainly not during their high-kicking dance routines.

I said: "I didn't realise Mabel had a problem."

"Varicose veins. Haven't you ever seen up her skirt?"

"Henrietta! Really!"

"Sorry. Silly question. But I can tell you it's like looking at the tributaries of the Amazon up there."

"And you haven't got Elsie to help you, either."

"She's had to rush out because she heard her Lennie's been injured."

"What happened?"

"He was competing in a 'Put 'em Down' contest."

"What?"

"You put live ferrets down your trousers and the last contestant to release them wins. Apparently, one of Lennie's ferrets bit him."

"Where?"

"In the two bullocks."

"That must have been painful."

"The Two Bullocks. It's a pub. Some dive out in the country off the London Road. It's where the ferret fanciers meet. Lennie was actually bitten in the leg."

Henrietta closed a file on her desk and said: "You didn't come in here to gossip about the Clipping Cousins."

"True. I believe you keep an archive of back copies of *Picturegoer* magazine somewhere in the filing stacks."

"We collected them when old Brian Trubshawe was film critic," Henrietta said. "I've never had the heart to throw them out."

"I'd like a quick shufti."

"Any reason?"

"I need some background about James Dean."

"The star of the film *Rebel Without a Cause*. Killed in a car crash. An icon for teenage angst."

"Got it."

Henrietta grinned. "I think you may be in luck. Brian kept a card index file of about two hundred film stars. It lists the main articles on them in the *Picturegoer* archive. I'll dig out the index for you."

Twenty minutes later, I was back at my desk with a small stack of back issues of *Picturegoer* - the numbers which Brian's index had told me contained articles about James Dean.

I shuffled the magazines into date order and started at the beginning. Dean, I learnt, had worked at a number of jobs, including farm hand and dental technician, before he got his break as an actor. He studied at acting academy and then picked up a steady stream of roles in television plays. His big break came when he was cast in the complex role of Cal Trask in a film adaptation of John Steinbeck's novel *East of Eden.* The role proved Dean was an actor with range and box office pulling power - and soon the offers started to flood in. But Dean had a love for fast cars - especially Porsche - and a tearaway life style. And this led him to his death in a car crash at a crossroads in California. Strangely, he was one of those rare people who are enhanced rather than diminished by death. He became an icon for youngsters seeking a better future - but not sure how or where to find it. One article mentioned how his death magnified his fame and spawned new fan clubs around the world.

I found what I was looking for in an article published in *Picturegoer* in early 1956. The piece was a retrospective on Dean's career but it included a sidebar with some of the more significant things he'd said during his short life.

And one of them was: "Dream as if you'll live forever. Live as if you'll die today."

The quotations tattooed on Rocker Boy's right and left arms.

Did this mean that Rocker Boy was a James Dean fan? The dare-devil tone of the quote would appeal to anyone attracted by a harum-scarum lifestyle. So it wasn't conclusive in itself. But, as Shirley had noticed, Rocker Boy seemed to have styled himself on James Dean. The quiff of hair backcombed in a pompadour style, the leather jacket with the raised collar, the cigarette casually hanging between his lips. And if Rocker Boy was a Dean fan did he belong to a club? Indeed, was there such a club anywhere in Sussex?

I had the answer from the clippings files in the morgue within ten minutes. A single cutting dated a year earlier mentioned a James Dean chapter of motorcycle rockers who met at the Ace of Spades café in Peacehaven, a small town six miles east of Brighton.

I closed the file, leant back in my chair and thought about my next move.

Then I called Shirley's number. She picked up after three rings.

I said: "I have a lead on Rocker Boy. So get your denims on, babe. Tonight we're gonna be the leaders of the pack."

Shirley said: "You're crazy - and if you're suggesting what I think you are, the answer is no.

"That's final. No, no, no."

Chapter 10

Shirley and I were riding a motorcycle along the coast road east of Brighton.

Ahead of us, the road climbed steeply towards the Seven Sisters cliffs. It was early evening and the sun was setting behind us. To the right, the sea sparkled with diamond points of light.

Shirley tugged on my right earlobe and shouted: "Can't you go any faster?"

I opened the cycle's throttle and the megaphone exhaust roared like a bear with toothache. The speedo climbed past eighty.

Shirley yelled: "*Yeeeeow!*"

I knew Shirley would fall in with my scheme once she'd seen the cycle. It was a classic machine - a custom-made Triton constructed from a Norton Featherbed frame and a twin-cylinder Triumph Bonneville engine. It had clip-on low handlebars and swept-back exhaust pipes. It was elegance and arrogance combined - and all on two wheels. It belonged to Freddie Barkworth, the *Chronicle*'s chief photographer, and he loved it like a sister.

It hadn't been easy to persuade Freddie to lend it to me for the evening. In the end, I'd promised to take full responsibility for any damage and to give him first crack at any picture opportunities which came out of the story. He'd given me a ten-minute crash course on how to ride the machine.

Shirley hugged her arms more tightly around my waist as I pushed the speed towards ninety.

She shouted in my ear: "If we want to win the rockers' confidence the bike is a great convincer. I'm not so sure about our own rig-outs, though."

Shirl was right. With only a couple of hours to spare, it hadn't been easy to turn ourselves into a pair of rockers looking for their next ton-up thrill. Shirley had made the best fist of it. She was wearing a denim jacket she'd bought a year or so back over a pair of Wrangler jeans. She sprayed a mist of lacquer into her hair. She'd backcombed it into a kind of beehive which she'd covered with a red scarf. She'd pass for a rocker's moll.

I wasn't so confident about my own get-up. I'd hurried out and bought a pair of Levis but they looked new and still had that shop-packaged smell that new clothes take a few days to lose. I'd borrowed a leather jacket from Freddie, but he was six inches shorter than me so the sleeves ended way above my wrists. Besides, Freddie was no rocker. So the jacket lacked the metal studs and pin badges rockers usually wore. A suspicious rocker would soon suss me for a ringer.

Ahead, the first houses on the outskirts of Peacehaven came into view. As we approached, the sun disappeared behind the hills and the town plunged into shadow.

I hoped it wasn't an omen for our visit.

The Ace of Spades café was a long single-storey shack which looked like it had been made out of two old railway carriages laid end-to-end.

It had a row of misty windows at the front and a pair of double doors in the middle - where the two carriages joined.

Five motorcycles were standing to the right of the doors. I'm no bike expert, but they looked like recent models and gleamed with their owners' pride. There was a single cycle on the left side of the doors. It looked older than the rest. The paintwork was chipped in places and there was a cut in the leather of the pillion.

Shirley pointed at it: "It's the ugly duckling of the fleet."

"And not one that will turn into a swan, like in the fable," I said.

We climbed off the Triton and left it parked next to the ugly duckling where it would attract plenty of attention. We headed towards the door.

Shirley said: "What's the plan?"

I said: "We don't have one. But if Rocker Boy was known around here, perhaps someone has heard something. If we could get a name, it would give us something to go on. Best tactic in a situation like this is to sit back and take no notice of other people. As the new guys in town we'll be the centre of attention."

I opened the door and we stepped inside. My eyes smarted from the heavy fug of bacon and cigarette fumes hanging in the air. On the juke box, Eddie Cochran was belting out *Summertime Blues*.

To the left, a small counter was smothered in bread crumbs and tea slops. A glass cabinet on the counter held two sausage rolls and a currant bun. On the bun one of the currants moved. A woodlouse, alarmed by our shadows, scurried for cover.

There was a small kitchen behind the counter. On the stove, a saucepan of brown stuff bubbled like a mud pool. A blubbery bloke, who could have doubled as Michelin Man, was picking his nose. He had a bristly chin and piggy eyes. He was stripped for action in a sleeveless string vest and boxer shorts. His eyes fixed on me like I'd just announced I was going to burn the place down. The eyes moved to Shirley and softened a bit. Like from diamond to tungsten.

He said: "What's your pleasure?" in a voice that suggested nothing would give him more delight than to strangle us.

I said: "Two coffees."

He banged a couple of grubby mugs on the counter, spooned in some instant coffee from a tin and topped up with water from a kettle which had been boiling on the stove next to the brown stuff.

He said: "A shilling."

I handed him a coin and we made our way into the other part of the shack where a collection of ill-assorted tables and chairs had been roughly arranged in two rows.

I glanced quickly around the room. There were nine people in the place - six men and three women - all but one grouped around a long table.

They turned as we walked in. Hostile eyes followed us as we made our way to the table closest to the door.

"We got company, Boss," said a youth with a widow's peak hair-do and a leather jacket with the words "Hell's Fire" on the front.

Boss flexed his shoulders to show he'd heard or perhaps just to prove he could do it. He had a pompadour haircut, rather like Rocker Boy's. He wore a leather jacket with studs on the shoulders and "Death before Dishonour" in gothic lettering on his back.

He said: "Yeah, I see with my own eyes, Chunky." He grinned and everyone around the table grinned too.

Boss said in a voice intended to carry. "I need coffee."

The others around the table exchanged worried glances.

Boss did that shoulder flexing thing again. He said: "Herbie, you awake?"

One of the gang had been sitting alone on a table at the back of the café. He stood up, like the headmaster had just walked into the classroom. He was wearing a denim jacket rather than leathers. He had moist eyes, a freckled face and thinning hair that no amount of Brylcreem would fashion into a pompadour.

He grinned uneasily: "I'll get you coffee, Boss." His tongue ran nervously over a row of gapped teeth.

He scurried towards the counter.

"Make sure the coffee is just how I like it, Herbie."

The others giggled and nudged each other to prove they loved seeing Herbie humiliated.

Eddie Cochran chose the moment to finish *Summertime Blues*. A heavy silence settled over the place. There was a clunk, a click and then another clunk. And on the juke box Gene Vincent started in on *Be-Bop-A-Lula*. A couple of the girls started to sway to the music. One of the boys said something, another nudged his mate and the atmosphere relaxed a little.

Shirley and I sat at the table and studied the steam rising off our coffee.

I whispered: "Don't look round now, but at the far end of the place there's what looks like a little shrine to James Dean."

"Rocker Boy who ended as raspberry jam on the road?"

"The real one."

A small ledge next to the window carried a couple of pictures of Dean in cheap frames. There was the stub of a candle in a holder. On the wall behind there were half a dozen action pictures of Dean - mostly, I guessed, stills from his films.

We sipped our coffees.

I said: "I hope one of these guys makes a move in our direction soon. I'd hate to have to order more of this sludge."

But it looked as though we'd suffer that fate. We sat through Chuck Berry's *Johnny B Goode,* Bo Diddly's *You Can't Judge a Book by Looking at the Cover,* and Gene Vincent's *Pistol Packin' Mama,* before a shadow loomed over our table.

I glanced up. Boss was glaring down at us. He didn't look like he was about to offer us more coffee.

He said: "That Triton outside yours?"

I nodded.

"How long you had it?"

"Long enough to know it's a great bike."

"What did you pay for it?"

"What it's worth."

"Where did you buy it?"

"Private sale."

"Don't say much, do you?"

"Is there any reason I should?"

He nodded at Shirley.

"Who's the bint?"

Shirley's eyes flashed like warning lights. "Watch your mouth, whacker."

The guy's lips twitched into an indulgent smile.

"Not from round here, are you?"

"Got a problem with that, cobber?" Shirley said.

"I might have."

A couple more rockers sensed something was going down. They got up from their table and fell in behind Boss. The atmosphere had become tense. Shirley and I stood up. A look passed between us. We both knew what it meant. We couldn't take on a posse of rockers. If the situation turned ugly, we'd run.

Meanwhile, I tried to cool the tension.

I said: "We're just passing through."

Boss sneered. "When people pass through here, they pay a toll."

"Who says?"

"I do. I say what goes on round here."

"Not that fat old basket behind the counter?"

"He knows which side his bread's buttered."

"Seems to be his sole knowledge of food."

"I don't answer to him. Not to anyone. Except the memory of the great J D."

I pointed towards the James Dean stuff in the corner. "You think that tawdry little collection about a great actor gives you the right to throw your weight around?"

"He's the guvnor. The tops. Don't you dare belittle him. I'll make you repeat his name a hundred times as I grind your face into the floor."

"Violence is your creed, then?"

"Violence is strength." He pointed to the slogan on his leather jacket: Death before dishonour. "See those words - that's how we live."

"Trouble is if you choose death you never get a chance to decide you would have preferred dishonour."

"The power of the fist is what counts."

"James Dean didn't think so."

"What do you know about J D?"

"More than you, it seems. I know that he said, 'Only the gentle are ever really strong'." I offered up a silent prayer to *Picturegoer* where I'd read the quote earlier that afternoon.

"I'll show you how gentle I can be."

Boss moved towards me. I stepped back. Grabbed my mug from the table. Threw it in a looping arc across the room. It landed with a crash on the James Dean table. The candle toppled over. One of the picture frames smashed.

Boss's eyes glazed with confusion. He turned round. Chairs tipped over as everyone rushed to their feet.

But we only heard that sound as Shirley and I raced for the door. We hustled through and slammed it behind us.

The Triton's wheels skidded on the gravel in the parking lot as I fired the throttle. As we reached the road, the rockers piled out of the café and ran for their bikes.

Chapter 11

"That went well," Shirley yelled in my ear as we accelerated away from the café.

Freddie Barkworth had boasted to me that his Triton could top a ton on the open road.

Now we were about to find out.

I opened the throttle and the roar of the exhaust echoed off the houses as we raced out of Peacehaven.

I felt Shirley press into my back as she leant forward to hold on tight.

She shouted in my ear: "Jeez, Colin. Next time you pick a fight, try to limit the numbers."

I yelled over my shoulder: "Boss was picking the fight. But that talk of 'death before dishonour' was a give-away. They knew Rocker Boy, I'm sure of that."

As I roared down the hill into Newhaven, Shirley glanced behind her.

"There's five of them - and they're about a quarter of a mile back," she shouted.

"We'll head into the country and I'll lose them in the back lanes."

Car horns blared as I shot through a road junction in the centre of Newhaven. There was a tight corner ahead, but I kept up the speed and the bike yawed at a forty-five degree angle as we turned into a road that led north.

"Yikes," Shirley shouted. "Now I know what it's like on the wall of death."

As we left the town and hit the winding country lanes, I opened the throttle again and the speedo passed ninety. But it wasn't enough to shake the posse behind.

The speedo nudged one hundred but I realised I wasn't going to lose them with speed alone. Every few hundred yards farm tracks led off the road. Some of them were short and led to barns. Others wound their way into woods and disappeared. If we could turn into one of the longer tracks without the pack seeing us, we could hide while they roared by.

Ahead the road curved to the left. I pushed the speed higher and the bike leaned inwards as we roared round it. About fifty yards further on, a track led off the road to the right and disappeared behind a cowshed.

I squeezed hard on the brake. The cycle fishtailed as we lost speed. As I approached the turning, I glanced in the rear view mirror. The road was empty.

I swerved across the road, bumped through a puddle and skidded on some mud as the bike bounced onto the track. I turned behind the cowshed into a farmyard and switched off.

I swivelled round to Shirley and put my finger to my lips.

Ssssh!

We sat rigid while we waited. In the distance the roar of the posse's cycles approached. I listened for any change in the tone - that would mean they were slowing down. When the volume reached its crescendo, it rattled the boards in the cowshed as the cycles raced by. Then the roar died as they curved around the next bend.

I let out a long sigh. "I think we've thrown them off."

"What happens when they can't see us up front?" Shirley said. "They'll turn around and come looking."

"There are more twists in this road than a con-man's corkscrew. They'll have to ride a fair few miles before they can be sure we're not still ahead of them. By then, they won't know where we've turned off. We'll get our breath back and then return the way we came."

"And hope there's no tail-end Charlie limping along behind."

"I kept an eye on the rear-view mirror and I only saw five bikes."

"There were six outside when we arrived."

"Perhaps the sixth stayed at the café for another cup of their delicious coffee."

Shirley looked at me and raised her eyebrows.

And then we heard a lone motorcycle in the distance. The growl of its engine rolled across the silence of the countryside.

"Someone else entirely," I said. "We'll wait here until he passes."

The engine roar ratcheted up the decibels as the cycle rounded the last corner before our turn-off. Then there was a sharp squeal as tyres skidded on the road. The thrum of the engine fell like a dying heartbeat. There was a splosh as the machine splashed through water.

And then the motorcycle appeared around the corner of the cowshed.

The rider put his feet to the ground, turned off the engine, and raised his goggles to his forehead. The lower half of his face had been tied with a green bandana. He pulled it down so it flapped like a flag at half-mast around his neck.

Herbie fixed his watery eyes on us.

I said: "OK, so you've got your scout's tracker badge. How did you find us?"

Herbie's lips split into his tooth-gapped grin.

"I notice things, see," he said.

"Me, too. But I didn't see anything."

"That's because what I noticed was behind you."

"Like a pantomime villain."

Herbie looked confused. So I said: "Just tell what it was behind us that you noticed."

"When you rode in here, you splashed through a puddle. It left the road wet, see. Day like today, that would dry off in about ten minutes."

"Could have been a tractor."

"I noticed something else. Fresh motorcycle track in the mud beyond the puddle."

Shirley said: "Trouble is, tracker boy, you're too late. Your cobbers are five miles down the road now chasing thin air. There's two of us and we're leaving."

Herbie swung his right leg over the bike and dismounted. He propped up the bike and walked towards us.

He said: "Don't you want to know what else I noticed, see?"

I looked closely at him. You can usually tell when someone is planning to thump you. They'll develop a nervous twitch. Or start balling their fists. Or have murder in their eyes. Herbie didn't have any of them. He was just a sad guy in worn clothes who was the butt of his mates' ill-natured jokes - and who noticed things. See?

I said: "You noticed something else, didn't you?"

"And I bet you want to know what it is."

"Spit it out and I'll make a donation to the fund for your new front teeth."

"They'll be gold teeth when you hear what I noticed, see."

"Our interest in James Dean?"

"I saw you peeking at our shrine. Then you bust a picture frame. Boss don't like that."

"Boss will get over it. But tell me more about James Dean. You had a member of the pack who looked like him."

"Could have been him, see. He came six, perhaps seven, months ago. Boss didn't want him at first. But then Marlene, Boss's chick, got round him - like she always does. But he had to do the initiation."

"What was that?"

"He had to put one of those town boys - the kind that hang around outside Sherry's - in hospital. Not just casualty, see. Proper hospital."

"And he did that?"

"He said he did."

"But you didn't believe him?"

"If he put town boys in the hospital why weren't there

something about it in the paper?"

"But he got into the gang?"

"It's a chapter, see."

"Did he undertake any other gallant acts of derring-do?"

"What?"

"Did he put anybody else in hospital?"

"No, he was quiet. Like me. I think he liked me, not like the rest of them who're always mocking my cycle just because it's old and making me pay for their coffee, see. They call me a dickhead behind my back. He talked to me about what we did and where we went. Interested he was. That's why I didn't say anything about the town boys he was supposed to hit."

"But you've not seen him today?"

"No."

"What was his name?"

"I could tell you that, see."

"But you're not going to."

"I might. You talked about a donation. If I could get my teeth fixed I think the others would like me more."

I nodded. "How much to get your teeth fixed?"

"Fifty pounds. In cash."

I thought about that. It was tidy sum for a tip-off - even on a national newspaper. Could I persuade Figgis to stump up the sum out of the news budget?

I said: "OK. What's the name?"

Herbie grinned again. "I'm not stupid, see. Money first, name after."

We dickered for a bit, but Herbie wasn't going to come across with the name until he had folding stuff in his hand. I arranged to meet him with the cash at Prinny's Pleasure the following morning at eleven.

Herbie headed back to his bike.

Shirley stepped forward.

"Herbie."

"Yes."

"I don't think you're a dickhead."

Herbie's face lit up like Piccadilly Circus's neon. "You don't?"

"No. Now ride north because we're heading south."

Herbie mounted his motorcycle, kicked the starter pedal and roared out of the farmyard.

We listened as the engine faded into the distance.

"That was the easy bit," I said. "Now comes the hard stuff. Sweet-talking fifty pounds out of Figgis."

Frank Figgis picked up the piece of paper I'd just placed on his desk and said: "What's this?"

I said: "It's a chit for you to sign so I can draw fifty pounds from the cash office to pay a contact for a tip-off."

It was the following morning. I'd been awake half the night wondering whether Herbie really did know the name of Rocker Boy. It would be easy for Herbie to pluck a name out of the telephone directory.

But before I handed over the pay-off, I'd make clear how the rules of the newspaper tip-off game worked. He'd get gold-plated anonymity if what he told me was accurate and given in good faith. That included me not revealing my sources and being carted off to chokey by the cops if they put the squeeze on me. But if he ripped me off, he should expect to see his name in a headline in the paper. Just like the people he'd betrayed.

In the end, I'd decided on the gamble, which was why I was now facing Figgis.

"For that kind of money I'd expect a complete list of the team that organised that Night Mail train heist at Bridego bridge." Figgis reached for his Woodbines and lit up.

"The so-called Great Train Robbery," I said.

"If you could find a Sussex angle on that story, I could persuade Pope to pay any amount of money for tip-offs."

"Where would I start?" I said. "Even the cops don't yet know who organised the scam. And our own Volk's train robbery has more than enough mystery. If we could find Rocker Boy's name before the cops crack the case we'd have a national scoop."

Figgis scratched his chin. "How reliable is your contact?"

"As reliable as any chancer who wants to make easy money from a newspaper. You know how this game works."

Figgis nodded. "Played it enough times myself. But these are high stakes."

"High stakes bring big returns," I said.

"Only when they win."

I frowned. "So you're turning it down?"

He reached for his pen and scribbled a petty cash chit. "I always was a bit of gambler."

"This one's a racing cert," I said.

Chapter 12

Three hours later I wasn't sure that Herbie was the racing cert I'd made him out to be.

I'd been nursing a gin and tonic in Prinny's Pleasure for nearly an hour and watching the door. There was no sign of Herbie. No sign of anyone. Prinny's Pleasure was that kind of pub. Landlord Jeff liked it that way.

Fifty quid was big money to a man like Herbie with a motorcycle to run. He wouldn't turn up the chance of stuffing a wad like that in his back pocket. But I sensed that Herbie was a man living on his own finely balanced edge. It seemed clear the rest of the Ace of Spades bikers despised him. Herbie lived with it because he was desperate to belong to something. Anything. Even a bunch of bikers who ridiculed him. So he'd developed survival tactics - the kind that allowed him to make out as the runt of the pack.

And then along came Rocker Boy. A new member. But accepted quickly in a way Herbie never would be. Even by Marlene, Boss's chick. And yet it seemed that Herbie had formed some kind of bond with Rocker Boy. Enough to want to share information about him. But he was worried about that. Perhaps because he knew other members of the pack wouldn't approve. Or perhaps because Rocker Boy wouldn't want it. Well, Rocker Boy was in no position to object and I wondered whether Herbie knew that. If he did, I sensed, he was going to be devastated.

I drained the last of my G and T and thought about ordering a refill. But I was kidding myself. Herbie had bailed out. He wasn't coming. And my one lead into the identity of Rocker Boy was gone.

Jeff had been down in the cellar hauling up crates of bottles. I stood up and walked over to the bar. Peered over. A hatch in the floor behind the bar led directly down to the cellar.

Jeff's head appeared in the hatch. His face was blackened by sweat-stained dust smuts. The remnants of a cobweb hung from his left ear. He was wearing a grubby string vest and pair of grey trousers with a hole in one knee.

I said: "I've never seen you without a shirt on before. What are those grey smudges on your arm?"

Jeff climbed out of the hatch into the bar and shook himself a bit like a dog that's just emerged from water. For a few seconds a little dust mist enveloped him.

He said: "I'd rather not talk about them."

I pointed at one of the grey areas and said: "That's a tattoo of a girl's name but the last letters have been smudged."

"I wish you hadn't seen that. It caused me a lot of trouble."

I looked closer. "Caroline isn't it? But the 'ine' is in different letters than the 'Carol'. What's the story behind that?"

Jeff shrugged his shoulders and perched on a stool. "It was while I was doing my National Service up at Catterick Camp. I met a girl called Carol. She worked in the NAAFI."

"You swept her off her feet?"

"You could say that. I knocked her down with my bicycle. Came round a corner too fast. But she weren't hurt and we seemed to hit it off. I got the Carol tat done after our second date."

I pointed at it. "Isn't that impulsive?"

"No, it's Times Roman."

"I know that. I meant weren't you getting ahead of yourself."

"You could have a point there. On our third date she dumped me. Said she could read me like a book. I told her that if she named the book, I'd have it tattooed down my back. I reckoned I could have got most of *Murder on the Orient Express* in small letters. Said it would give her something to read in bed after we were married. But she said she wouldn't fancy reading my bum to find out whodunit."

"So you were left with a memory of a love affair that- never-was on your arm for ever?"

Jeff reached for a glass, turned to the optics, and poured himself a large measure of scotch. "Big problem," he said. "How could I go on other dates with the name of my first love on my arm?"

"You could have had the word 'Christmas' tattooed above 'Carol'."

"Thought of that. But I'd have had to tattoo *Silent Night* or something underneath and there wasn't room. For two years, I steered clear of women. And then I had a stroke of luck. I met a girl called Caroline. I asked her out and she accepted. I raced off to the tattoo parlour and got them to add the 'ine' but there was a mix up and they did it in the wrong typeface. I thought of sticking a plaster over it and pretending I'd been bitten by a dog, but it didn't matter anyway. She never turned up. So I've got this on me for ever."

A thought had crossed my mind as Jeff was talking. When Ted Wilson had been telling me about collecting the remains of Rocker Boy, he'd said that he'd had nothing on him. But, of course, he did have something on him. He had a distinctive tattoo.

"Dream as if you'll live for ever" on the right arm.

"Live as if you'll die today" on the left.

It would be a long shot. But if I could trace the tattooist, perhaps I could identify Rocker Boy after all.

It was past six o'clock by the time I reached the last tattoo parlour on my list.

Beelzebub's Ink occupied a grubby lock-up shop in a side street not far from an entrance to Shoreham Port.

I was feeling as scratchy as a blunt gramophone needle. I'd spent the afternoon getting the bum's rush from a succession of tattoo artists whose only interest was to decorate my body with the artwork of their choice.

I ask you! Who wants a pack of hounds chasing a fox down their back? Even if all you can see of the fox is its brush emerging from the only hidey-hole available.

I climbed out of the MGB and took a look in the window. The centrepiece was a picture of the torso of a fat bloke who'd had a three-masted schooner tattooed on his stomach. A notice underneath read: "Amaze your friends. Ripple your tummy muscles and make it look like the ship's going to sink."

I walked over to the door. A sign read: "Welcome to our overseas customers. Bugger off if you don't speak English."

A twee little bell, out of character with the place, tinkled as I pushed open the door. Inside, the walls were painted black. Pictures of tattoos festooned the walls. At a glance, I saw a python coiled around an arm, a pair of knuckles reading "Love" and "Hate", and a red admiral (butterfly, not Russian naval officer) on a woman's breast.

At the far end of the room was a black seat which looked like a cross between a barber's chair and a beach lounger. A thin bloke, naked from the waist up, was lying in the chair. He had closed eyes and was biting his lower lip. An obese man in black T-shirt and ill-fitting jeans displayed a generous builders' cleavage as he bent over the thin bloke. Fatty was wielding an implement that buzzed like a September mozzie.

He turned when he heard the door slam shut behind me and switched off the implement.

The thin bloke opened his eyes and said: "*Tyi zakonchen?*"

Fatty said: "Shut your mouth, you commie bastard. I've still got to do the heart."

The thin bloke smiled and nodded.

I walked towards the chair and said: "Wonderful thing, customer service, Beelzebub."

"The name's Thor. And, anyway, what do you want? You don't look like the kind of geezer who wants 'Meat and two veg' tattooed next to his wedding tackle to give his new bride a surprise on her honeymoon."

I said: "Perhaps another time. I was wondering whether you've tattooed these quotations on anyone."

I handed Thor the paper I'd written them on.

He looked at it. Handed it back to me.

"No."

But he'd looked at it a little too long. He'd recognised them. It would have been a custom job. Not like the pythons and the butterflies.

I said: "It would be really helpful if you could think about it."

"Already thought about. And I've got work to do."

I nodded at the thin bloke in the chair and said: "Good afternoon."

Thor said: "No use speaking to him. Russian sailor off one of the cargo boats in the harbour. Wants me to tattoo a heart with the words 'Boris, my best friend' on his chest. Done the words. Just got to do the heart. So bugger off and let me get on with it."

"Boatswain's mate, is he?"

"He will be when he goes back with this."

"Speaks English does he?"

"Not a word. Just brought what he wanted on a paper."

I smiled: "He's a thin bloke. But wiry. Could give a lot of trouble I'd have thought. Especially with the boatswain and a ship's company with him."

"He'll give no trouble."

"He will if I hold a mirror over his chest with his original paper by the side."

Thor stared at the bloke. He looked back with worried eyes. But Thor's were more concerned.

"Bugger Beelzebub!" Thor said.

"Yes, you've tattooed 'Boris, my best fiend'. I guess the boatswain won't be too happy about that."

"The ship sails on the midnight tide. He won't see it before then."

I raised an eyebrow. "Won't he?"

Thor pulled up a wooden chair and sat down. "OK, it was about two months ago. Bloke came in one afternoon. Wanted those quotations on his arms. Never heard them before. But pleased to do it - especially as he seemed like a cut above my usual customers."

"Cut above?"

"Something about him. Had an inner confidence. Not like the losers we usually get in."

"Get a name?"

"Not really. I think he said most people called him Chaz. But nothing that would identify him."

"What happened to the paper he'd written the quotations on?"

"Took it with him. One thing though. He did mention he had a girlfriend called Michelle. From something he said I thought she worked at the Metropole Casino. As a croupier."

"He said that."

"Not directly, but there was idle snippets of chatter while he was in the chair."

I'd got everything I would from Thor.

I said: "You better see if you can work an 'r' between the 'f' and the 'i'."

He looked at the Russian. I headed for the door.

"What should I do if I can't?" he said.

I turned at the door. "Retire," I said.

Chapter 13

I found a telephone box in Shoreham close to the tattoo parlour and put a call through to the newsroom.

My plan was to track down the croupier Michelle and discover what more she could tell me about Chaz. But I'd been out of touch with the office all afternoon. I needed to check in to discover whether there'd been any developments I ought to know about.

I was put through to Figgis. He picked up after one ring and barked: "What is it this time?"

I said: "Not the same as last time."

"It's you. Where the hell have you been all afternoon?"

"Giving tattoo artists the needle."

"I won't even ask about that. Besides, you're needed elsewhere."

"Where?"

"Devil's Dyke."

"What's happening up there? At this time of year it's usually crowded with rubberneckers admiring the views."

"Not when there's a dead body in the scene."

I yanked out my notebook and flipped it open. "When did you hear about this?"

"Fifteen minutes ago. From your old mate at the cop shop."

"Ted Wilson?"

"He's expecting you."

Figgis started to say something else. But I'd already slammed down the receiver and was running for my car.

The sun was sinking in the west by the time I pulled the MGB into the car park at Devil's Dyke.

Dark shadows were forming in the valleys of the Downs. A hundred yards to the south of the car park the cops had taped off an area around a clump of trees. A couple more cops were carrying a tent down the slope towards the trees. They'd erect it over the body while the forensic boys went about their work.

I hurried down the slope after the tent carriers.

I was stopped at the blue tape by Kathy Kelly, one of Brighton police's all-too-few women cops.

She grinned as I approached. "The guv said it wouldn't be long before you showed up."

"That's my one fault. I'm too predictable."

Further down the slope, Ted Wilson emerged from the clump of trees. He spotted me and signalled to Kathy to let me past the tape. She lifted it up and I ducked under.

Ted lumbered up the hill towards me sweating more than I thought the temperature merited. His suit was more crumpled than usual. The turn-ups on his trousers had picked up a drift of dead leaves. His beard stuck to his face like a pantomime villain's. The point on the pencil sticking out of his breast pocket had broken.

He panted up to me and said: "It's another of your rocker chums. I'd like you to take a look to see if you recognise him - but you're not going to like what you see."

I felt my heart do a double back flip and plunge off a diving board. When it landed, it felt like the water had been drained from the pool. A blue haze swirled around my eyes.

I now knew why Herbie hadn't shown up at Prinny's Pleasure.

I said: "Before I look, what did they do to him?"

Ted took out a handkerchief and wiped the sweat off his forehead. "They went to work with a knife. Nothing's missing - as far as I can see from a quick look - but they knew how to hurt him in all the tender places."

"He was tortured?"

"No rack or thumbscrews, but torture by any other name."

We reached the body. It was sprawled behind the cover of a thorn bush. The cops had covered it with a tarpaulin.

Ted said: "Pull back the covering - head only."

A uniformed plod lifted the tarp. I looked down at a nightmare face set in a scream. The eyes were still open and seemed to bulge in terror from their sockets.

Ted said: "We haven't done anything about the body until the medical examiner gets here. Do you know the victim?"

"His name is Herbie. I don't know his second name, but I was due to meet him this morning in Prinny's Pleasure. He never showed."

Ted said: "We need to talk - but not here."

It wasn't difficult to find a table in the nearby pub.

Normally, on a summer's evening the place would be crowded with romantic couples gazing into one another's eyes while the sun set over the most glorious scenery in Sussex. But the presence of a dozen cops and a dead body had dulled their ardour.

I played it straight with Ted and told him about how Shirley and I had come to visit the Ace of Spades. I told him about the rumpus inside the café and the daredevil chase through the countryside. I told Ted how Herbie had found us and how he wanted money to tell us more. Ted's eyebrows had twitched upwards a few times while I spoke but he said nothing.

I finished, hoisted my glass and took a much needed gulp of the double gin and tonic.

Ted said: "So now we have two dead men - Chaz and Herbie - but no idea who they really are."

"Did Herbie have any identification on him?"

"We haven't examined the body in detail yet, but I'm guessing not. People who stoop to that kind of torture don't leave a body with a name and address label tied round the big toe."

"I suppose you'll be interviewing the rocker gang at the Ace of Spades."

"Obviously, but I don't want you publishing that until we've had the chance to round them up. Perhaps they'll give us more of a lead on Chaz."

I took another pull at the gin. I didn't want Ted catching a glimpse of a guilty secret on my face. I hadn't told him about the lead I had on Michelle, Chaz's girlfriend. I'd played straight with Ted but I wasn't planning to hand him a hot lead on a plate.

I said: "Any theories on what's behind this killing?"

"I could ask you that."

"It has to be connected with yesterday. Herbie wanted to tell us something about Chaz. He was scared but greedy - and the greed overcame the fright. But I think the rest of the gang found out."

"How so?"

"Herbie wasn't riding with the rest of the gang when he found us. He'd explained that partly because his own motorcycle was older and not as fast as the rest - one of the reasons they mocked him, I expect. But there'd have been questions afterwards about why he never caught up with them."

"He could have lied."

"I imagine he did. But under the bluster, Herbie was the nervous type. The truth would have shown on his face even as the lies formed in his mouth. They'd only have needed to catch him in one lie, to drag the rest out of him."

"Looks like it took some heavy-duty persuading to do it."

I nodded. Herbie had paid a painful price for his greed. Had he told Shirley and me what he knew in that farmyard, we could have made sure he was safe.

I said: "I suppose there'll be a press conference tomorrow with Tomkins smirking over the proceedings."

Ted grinned. The first time that evening. "Actually, it will be me. After his outburst the other day, Tomkins is on leave. Orders of the chief."

"So you'll be the one grabbing the headlines?"

"Don't know whether I'll have anything big to report."

"Don't worry," I said. "I know how to find my own stories."

Shirley looked at the thing on her plate and said: "How do they make a fried egg come out in a perfect circle? Whenever I do it, they run all over the pan."

I said: "They fry them in a mould."

It was an hour and a half after my meeting with Ted Wilson. Shirley and I were in The Golden Egg restaurant having a quick supper. Eggs and chips. With brown sauce. An English delicacy.

Shirl put down her knife and fork. "I like food that looks like it's been cooked by a chef with passion - not a maths wonk trying out his geometry."

I said: "If you'd seen what I've seen this evening, you wouldn't have much of an appetite for anything. At least I've got a murder for the morning edition that even Pope won't be able to bounce off the front page. But that's not all."

Shirley dipped a chip in her egg yolk and said: "Tell me."

I described how I'd visited Beelzebub's Ink and found out about Chaz - and that he had a girlfriend, Michelle, who worked at the Metropole Casino.

I said: "When we leave here, I'm going to the Metropole to see if I can find Michelle. I'd like you to come because we don't know how close Chaz and Michelle were. We don't even know whether Michelle realises that Chaz is dead."

"Guess I'm going to play the sob sister for this outing," Shirley said.

"We may be the first to tell her."

"Don't worry. I've got a big shoulder to cry on."

"You may need it," I said.

Chapter 14

Michelle's face was streaked with tears and her nose was red.

She wailed: "Chaz can't be dead. He told me he'd only be away for a couple of days."

Shirley gave Michelle a clean handkerchief and she snivelled into it. We were in the manager's office at the Metropole Casino. I'd told him we were bringing Michelle sad news of bereavement. He was only too keen to offer some privacy. When a croupier weeps over a roulette table, it doesn't encourage the punters to place bets.

Michelle Jarrett was a petite woman in her early twenties with auburn hair and a cute baby doll face. She had a pert button nose and large green eyes which looked permanently surprised. It wasn't difficult to see why Chaz had fallen for her.

It hadn't been easy breaking the news. I'd told Michelle that Chaz had been killed in a traffic accident. To soften the blow, I'd kept back the news that he'd just snatched a case with twelve thousand dollars in it. But I'd have to raise that matter eventually. I couldn't rule out that Michelle knew about Chaz's plans.

But when you're a reporter faced with a difficult interview, you start with the easy questions.

So I asked: "How long had you known Chaz?"

Michelle blew her nose and wiped her eyes. "We met four weeks ago yesterday. In Sherry's. I was with some girlfriends and he came up and asked me to dance. I thought I'll just have the one dance with him but…"

"You knew you wanted more," Shirley said.

Michelle nodded. "I could have danced all night." She managed a tight little smile. "That's a song, isn't it?"

"And then you started dating Chaz regularly?" I said.

"Most nights. We were getting to know each other well. I liked him. You see these rocker types strutting around in their leather and think they're tough. But Chaz wasn't like that. He seemed very gentle on the surface, but underneath you could tell he was strong."

"Did he tell you his full name?"

"It was Rickman. He was Charles Rickman. But he said everyone called him Chaz."

"Including his rocker friends?"

"I knew about them but he never introduced me. I said I wouldn't mind meeting them. Chaz had told me they met up at a café in Peacehaven, but I don't think he wanted me to see them."

"Or perhaps he didn't want them to see that he'd bagged himself a honey," Shirley said.

Michelle's gaze flicked to Shirley to acknowledge the compliment. "I don't know about that," she said. "I am sure Chaz had a passion for his motorcycle. He took me for some rides on it. But he didn't fit my image of a rocker - certainly not what I've heard about them from my mates. He just wasn't rough like that."

"Where did Chaz live?" I asked.

"He told me he had a flat out in Coldean. But I never went there. He said he was ashamed of the place because he never had time to tidy up."

"I said I'd help him. We'd make a fun evening of smartening up his flat, but he wasn't keen. He said the neighbours downstairs had a dog that was always barking and it got on his nerves."

I wondered whether the flat existed - or whether Chaz didn't want to reveal to Michelle where he really lived.

"Did Chaz have a job?" I asked.

"Yeah. He told me on our second date. He worked at a place called Nobby's Novelties. They sell all that rubbish you see in the souvenir shops on the seafront. Seashell houses and Royal Pavilion keyrings - that sort of thing. They're like a company that supplies the stuff to the shops..."

"A wholesaler."

Michelle nodded.

"What did Chaz do there?" I asked.

"He told me he was a warehouseman. He made up the orders when they came in and sometimes went out to deliver them."

"On his motorcycle?"

"Sometimes, if he could get the package in the panier on the side of the bike. Otherwise, he took the company's van."

I leaned forward: "You said Chaz told you he was a warehouseman - as though you weren't sure whether that was true."

Michelle glanced anxiously at Shirley.

Shirley said: "Relax, kid. All this goes no further than these four walls."

I said: "You couldn't quite make him out, could you?"

Michelle twisted her handkerchief round her fingers. Looked at Shirley again, then back at me.

"I really liked him," she said.

"But..."

"But I couldn't get to the bottom of him. Do you know what it's like with some people? It's like they only show you part of themselves."

I gave Michelle my encouraging smile. "I know about hundred people like that."

"And I know one," Shirley said with a pointed stare at me.

Michelle gave the handkerchief a couple of extra twizzles around her finger. "I think he wanted to be an ordinary bloke, like the others you meet down Sherry's. Only interested in two things - football and fanny."

She blushed. "Shouldn't have said that."

Shirley laughed. "You speak out, kiddo. It's only the truth."

Michelle produced another thin smile. "Chaz wasn't like the blokes I'd been to school with at the secondary mod. They'd come up to you all teeth and pimples hardly able to string two words together. Chaz spoke nice, like. Although I think he tried to hide it. But he couldn't help himself. I remember once I asked him whether something I'd read in the paper was true. *'In con vert it brate abl'*, he said. Or something like that. I can't even remember the word now."

"Incontrovertible," I said.

"Yeah, that was it. And another time, he took me to a posh fish restaurant in the Lanes. He knew which knife to use to butter his roll with. Other blokes I'd knocked about with thought it was the height of refinement to put the salt on their chips after the vinegar."

I sensed that Michelle had recovered a little from the initial shock. I didn't want to hit the poor girl with another bombshell, but I needed to know whether she'd known about Chaz's robbery plan.

I glanced at Shirley. She knew what my look meant. It was time to tell Michelle the full truth about Chaz's death. Shirley frowned at me but shrugged.

I said: "There's something you need to know about how Chaz died."

Michelle's eyes widened with alarm. "You said he was run down in the road."

"He was, but it was why he was in the road that's important."

During the next few minutes, I told Michelle the full story. There were tears, but not as many as I'd expected. After the initial shock there were not many left. And Shirley did her best to soften the blow.

I finished and sat back looking at the poor woman.

"I can't believe it," she said. "I'd been dating a criminal. I don't believe it."

"No-one knows why Chaz snatched the case," Shirley said. "Perhaps it was an impulse. Foolish, but we're allowed one foolish mistake in our lives. I've used up my one hundreds of times."

I looked at Michelle. She'd been shaken by the news and I was convinced that she hadn't known what Chaz planned to do. In fact, the more Michelle had opened up, the more it became clear that she didn't really know him.

That made two of us.

I said: "I'll have a word with the manager. Tell him you've had a shock. I'm sure he'll give you the rest of the night off."

Michelle nodded her thanks.

I said: "The police are investigating Chaz's death but at the moment I'm not going to tell them about you. And I won't be mentioning you in anything I write for the *Chronicle*."

Eventually, Ted Wilson would have to be told. But a worry was nagging at the back of my mind.

Herbie had wanted to tell me about Chaz - and he'd been tortured and killed. I didn't want Michelle to suffer the same fate.

Chapter 15

I arrived in the newsroom at the *Chronicle* the following morning with a lot on my mind.

After we'd left Michelle the previous evening, I'd told Shirley about my concerns. She urged me to tell the police everything I knew about Chaz and Michelle. But I'd warned her that Brighton cop shop had more leaks than the *Titanic*. If I told Ted Wilson he'd be discreet, but he'd inevitably share it with colleagues who'd blabber the news all over town.

In fact, I'd had a brief word with Ted before I'd reached the newsroom at the morning's police press briefing. He'd told me a hit team of officers had raided the Ace of Spades café late the previous evening. They'd picked up most of the rocker gang and were questioning them about Herbie's murder and other crimes.

But Boss, the leader of the pack, had eluded them. That didn't surprise me. Boss had struck me as the kind who'd be well clear of the scene of the crime when the cops came calling. He'd be happy for others to take the rap.

I thought Boss could have killed Herbie, but that didn't answer the main question - what was Chaz's role in all of this?

The more I'd thought about what Michelle had told us, the more I realised that Chaz was a man of mystery. She'd known him probably better than any of his rocker friends, including Herbie. Yet she'd admitted she couldn't get to the bottom of him. But perhaps his employer at Nobby's Novelties would know more.

I'd pulled a thin file on the firm from the morgue and it lay open on my desk. There was one clipping in it dated eighteen months earlier. It was a company profile piece written by Susan Wheatcroft, the paper's business correspondent. The story told how former chief petty officer Jerry Clark had recently started the business. He'd retired from the submarine service in Portland, Dorset. He'd rented a warehouse in Portslade, a small town four miles west of Brighton, and started hustling his novelties - the kind of tat you see in souvenir shops - along the south coast. The article related how Clark had circled the globe as a submariner. Now he was putting his worldly experience to use sourcing products from countries where manufacturing costs were low. Susan described how he'd bought model sailing boats from Bulgaria, ashtrays shaped like scallop shells from Russia, and rubber crabs that floated in the bath from Poland.

"It's a question of buying cheap overseas and selling for a good profit in Britain," Clark had told Susan. "That's the way to make a profit and build a successful business."

I finished the piece, closed the file and sat back in my captain's chair. The buzz of activity in the newsroom was building to the first deadline of the day. Cedric bustled by.

"Read the latest news, Mr Crampton?"

"I write it, Cedric."

"They reckon those great train robbers have nicked more than two and a half million quid. The amount seems to go up every day. Great story for someone, eh, Mr Crampton?"

"Yes, a great story, Cedric. But I've got my own."

I picked up my notebook and headed for the door wondering whether the rubber crab entrepreneur would be able to tell me any more about Chaz than Michelle.

Nobby's Novelties operated from a two-storey brick-built warehouse in a street not far from the harbour.

The building was a squat structure with a flat roof. It looked as though it had been there since Victorian times and had all the charm of a workhouse. The bricks were blackened by soot and the windows were mounted high in the walls so that passers-by couldn't see in. When the place was built the windows would have been positioned so the staff couldn't see out. The thrifty frock-coated businessmen who'd first owned it wouldn't have liked workers distracted for one second from their daily toil.

A notice on the front door read: "Entrance: Trade Only". Well, I was hoping to trade in information, so I opened the door and stepped inside. I found myself in a narrow corridor which led to the back of the building. To my left, a set of double doors opened into a large room with lines of floor to ceiling shelves arranged in aisles.

I pushed my way inside and stood at the head of one of the aisles.

Somewhere on the other side of the room a machine was running. It made a rhythmical sound like wheels bouncing over a hump in the road.

Bobble-de-bobble-dah. Bobble-de-bobble-dah.

The air was cut with a sharp aroma -like someone was burning rubber and squeezing the zest out of a hundred lemons at the same time.

I made my way through the aisles towards the sound.

Bobble-de-bobble-dah. Bobble-de-bobble-dah.

I stepped out from between the aisles. A young lad wearing a brown overall and frayed plimsolls was standing by the machine. The thing looked like an oven with a conveyor belt running through it.

The lad was feeding books loosely wrapped in cellophane on one end of the conveyor. They trundled slowly through the oven. When they came out, the heat had shrunk the cellophane so that it gripped the book like an outer cover.

The lad turned as I approached. He looked a bit worried and said: "You're not a factory inspector are you?"

I said: "Not today."

He looked relieved, so I nodded at the machine and said: "Hot work, I expect?"

He wiped some sweat from his face.

"The chief wants all these books shrink-wrapped by the end

of the day."

"The chief being Jerry Clark?" I said.

"Who else?"

"Where can I find him?"

"I expect he's upstairs. He usually is."

I left the lad piling more books on the conveyor and headed back to the stairs in the corridor.

The top of the stairs opened into a long room with larger windows. The walls had been painted cream and the floor laid with green carpet tiles. There were three desks facing the windows. The first two each had a stack of empty wire baskets, a blotter pad and a telephone - but no busy bees shuffling papers or taking orders.

The third desk at the far end of the room had a man sitting behind it. He had a telephone receiver in his hand and was dialling a number when I came in. He put down the receiver, stood up and walked towards me in a rolling gait which I guessed he'd picked up from years at sea. He was a short stocky man with broad shoulders and a barrel chest. He had a fleshy face with a broad nose that was criss-crossed with veins. His hair was close cropped in what I reckoned must have been his regular submariner cut. He was wearing a cheap grey suit with a dolphin badge in his left lapel.

He greeted me with a smile like I was the man from Littlewoods come to tell him he'd scooped the pools.

He said: "It's Mr Carpenter from the Beach Boutique isn't it? Good morning to you, skipper."

I said: "No, it's Colin Crampton from the *Evening Chronicle*, Mr Clark."

The smile drained from his face. "A newspaper? You've come about advertising perhaps. We don't have any spare cash at the moment."

"Me, neither. Catching isn't it?"

Clark frowned.

I said: "I'm one of Susan Wheatcroft's colleagues. You must remember Susan. She wrote a really flattering profile of Nobby's Novelties in the *Chronicle* about eighteen months ago."

Clark tapped his forehead. "I do remember. Very, er, personable young lady. Said she was interested in nautical affairs."

"Susan doesn't mind whether her affairs are on land or sea as long as there are plenty of them."

Clark grinned. It was the grin of a wolf. Or, as he'd been a submariner, perhaps a shark.

"So what can I do for the *Chronicle*, skipper? Another profile is it?"

"Not exactly, but Susan said you were very helpful."

"Always pleased to help the press, especially when there's something in it for me."

I ignored that and said: "Do you have an employee called Charles Rickman? You may know him as Chaz."

Clark had been standing easy, but now his body stiffened.

"I can't discuss individual employees. It wouldn't be right."

I decided to tell him what I already knew. "I've been told Chaz is a warehouseman here."

"That's right, but he's not here. In fact, I haven't seen him for a couple of days."

"He's on holiday?"

"No. In fact, I don't know why he hasn't come to work."

"Didn't you get in touch with him to find out why?"

"Chaz isn't an easy person to contact. He moves around. He gave me an address when we took him on, but I think he's moved since then."

"I have some bad news for you, Mr Clark. We believe Chaz was killed in a motor accident on Marine Parade three days ago."

Clark didn't throw up his hands in horror. Or start weeping and wailing and gnashing his teeth. He just looked at me blankly. At first, I thought he couldn't take in the news. Then I realised his eyes were moving in that shifty side-to-side way they do when people are thinking fast. Clark was deciding whether he should look surprised. Or whether to admit he'd already heard the sad news. Finally, his jaw dropped.

"That's terrible," he said. "Riding that motorbike, I suppose."

"No, he was on foot."

"I don't understand."

"Chaz was making a run for it after grabbing an attaché case containing twelve thousand dollars from a man travelling on the Volk's Railway."

"I read about that but there was no description of the thief in the papers."

"That was because the body was too badly mangled in the accident."

Clark rubbed a hand over his forehead. "Horrible," he said.

"We can't work out how Chaz knew the victim was carrying so much money on him. Do you have any idea?"

Clark shook his head. "It's beyond me. Why should any man want to carry around that amount of money - especially on that tiny train? Do you know who the victim was?"

"That's another mystery. After the robbery he vanished and has made no attempt to get his case back."

"With the money?"

"With the money."

Clark seemed more concerned that a stack of unclaimed cash was lying around than that his former employee had been splattered over the road.

He said: "Will there have to be a positive identification?"

"The police will be in touch. The identification may have to be by his clothing rather than his body. He had a girlfriend. She might be better placed to do that."

Clark seemed relieved. "Unpleasant job for the poor girl."

I turned and headed for the door. "Pity your visit couldn't be a happier one," he said.

"That's true."

"Wait a moment, skipper." He turned and hurried back to his desk. Opened a cardboard box lying beside it and took out something. He came back across the office and handed it to me.

"One of our new lines, just in. Take one."

"What is it?"

"It's a Russian nesting doll. They call them matryoshka dolls in Russia. If you pull it open in the middle, you'll find a smaller doll inside - and even smaller ones inside that."

I took the thing. It was made out of wood and brightly painted in reds and yellows. She had black hair and pink cheeks. At first, I thought the face was cute. But then I looked closer.

I could have sworn the eyes were mocking me.

Chapter 16

Frank Figgis took a bite of his bacon sandwich and followed it with a long drag on his fag.

I said: "The bacon was already smoked."

He said: "No harm in making sure." Crumbs sprayed out of his mouth and spattered over his desk.

It was lunchtime and we were in his office at the *Chronicle*.

I said: "Smoking and eating at the same time isn't good for you."

He put down the sandwich. "In that case, I'll finish that later. Besides, if I eat any more I'll get indigestion. Especially after the news you've given me."

I'd just told him about my meeting with Jerry Clark, the novelty king.

"So that's a dead end," Figgis said.

"Not entirely." I tried to put a positive spin on the meeting. "What Clark told me confirms that the guy who died on Marine Parade was Charles Rickman, also known as Chaz. But we still don't know where he was living - and Clark was vague on the matter. In fact, he didn't seem to care."

"So you can't take that line of enquiry any further?"

"It doesn't look like it. The rockers at the Ace of Spades are hostile, the girlfriend Michelle is distressed, and Clark can't be bothered that his employee just resigned the hard way."

"So we're stumped." Figgis picked up his sandwich and tossed it in the bin. "Who needs food? I get all the calories I need from fags."

I ignored that and said: "I think there may be another way of cracking this story."

"Follow the money. The cash in the attaché case."

"We don't need to follow it. It's locked up at the cop shop," I said. "But if we could discover who Arthur Crouch is, I think we might get a good idea why he was carrying the cash. In fact, if we could find him, we could ask where he got it."

"But he's disappeared, too. He could be anywhere."

"I think the best way to discover where he is now is to find where he's been. If we knew more about where he's stayed, we could pick up clues about where he's hiding. Remember, alongside the cash, he's also lost the fake passport and airline ticket. It's going to take time to replace those - especially as the passport will need to be in a new name. Every day that Crouch is in hiding gives me a chance to find him."

"You don't even know where to start," Figgis said.

I fanned away smoke from his Woodbine. "My theory is that Crouch took delivery of the case and the envelope at the Black Rock café because he was staying in that area - somewhere in Kemp Town. There are dozens of hotels and guest houses in the area - and hundreds of landladies who take in lodgers. I think someone will know him."

Figgis stubbed out his fag and reached for another. "Seems a long shot to me. Crouch's picture has been in the papers for the last couple of days. If your theory is correct, one of these landladies would have seen it and come forward."

"Not if Crouch had paid them well to keep quiet."

Figgis nodded while he considered the point. "OK. Spend the afternoon on it. If you turn up a lead, I'll authorise more time. Otherwise, that's the end. Curtains. Fair enough?"

"Fair enough," I said.

I was sure Figgis couldn't see my crossed fingers under his desk.

Shirley adjusted the straps on her backpack and said: "What's the point of calling at a guest house which has its 'No Vacancies' sign up?"

I said: "It gives us a good reason to ask about other places which might not be full."

I was carrying a small suitcase stuffed with crumpled-up newspaper.

It was a couple of hours after my talk with Figgis. I had a hunch that Crouch must have stayed somewhere in Kemp Town. That's why we'd seen him at the Black Rock café nearby.

I'd recruited Shirley to help in the search. We were calling on hotels and guest houses disguised as a couple looking for lodgings.

We'd just drawn a blank at the second guest house on our list.

I said: "If I appear on a landlady's doorstep as a reporter asking questions she'll just clam up. She won't want a nosey journalist poking into her guests' affairs. Not good for business. But if we pretend to be American tourists looking for somewhere to stay, we might provoke some comments about other Americans who've been staying locally. There can't be many who lodge in this part of town."

"Just one little detail you've overlooked, cobber." Shirley said. "I talk like a proud Aussie and you're accent is spiffily English."

"You make me be sound like Alvar Lidell reading the news on the BBC. My voice is nothing like that. Besides, I can put on an American accent. And as for your Aussie vowels, I don't suppose many Kemp Town hoteliers will be able to tell the difference from a Yankee talking. If we're asked, we'll say you come from a remote part of Alabama."

We reached the third guest house on our travels, a place grandly called The Bolingbroke. We'd drawn blanks at the first two.

"This looks more promising," I said. "It's larger than the previous two. Perhaps it gets more visitors."

The Bolingbroke occupied a large four-storey terraced house in a road off the seafront. The façade was stuccoed and scored to look like fancy Portland stone. The front door and window frames had been freshly painted royal blue. Iron railings screened off steps that led down to a basement.

We tramped up to the front door like a pair of weary travellers looking for a place to rest our heads. A notice next to the doorbell said: Proprietor: Mrs Phyllis Spannier.

I rang the bell and we waited.

The door was opened by a thin middle-aged woman with a pinched face, tight lips and suspicious eyes. She had dark brown hair most of it gathered under a scarf which was fastened with a front knot. She was wearing a housecoat decorated with an ivy motif.

She pointed at the "No Vacancy" sign in the window and said: "Can't you read?"

I put on my best cowboy accent and said: "Sure can, ma'am, but the place looked so hospitable-like, we just had to stop by and say 'howdy'."

Close your eyes and you could have thought it was John Wayne talking.

The tight lips loosened a little. "You're Americans?"

"From the great U S of A, ma'am. Just flown in on the red eye this morning and lookin' for a place where a pair of lonesome travellers could find a warm welcome and a soft bed."

Phyllis brightened a little more. "Well, you won't find either of those here. At least, you would if we weren't fully booked. But we are. Fully booked, that is."

"Can your ladyship point us in the direction where a couple of hungry Yanks can fuel up on pancakes and maple syrup?"

"We don't get many Americans in this part of town. Sorry."

Phyllis reached for the door handle. She'd had enough Yankee charm.

I said: "Guess we'll just have to hitch up the wagon train and move on."

I glanced at Shirley and she shrugged. We turned for the street.

"Now I come to think of it, you could try Mrs Harrison at The Hawthorns. She mentioned a week or so ago, she had an

American gentleman staying. Don't know whether he's still there."

The Hawthorns, Phyliis said, was in a street a little back from the seafront so it didn't fill up so quickly. I made a mental note of the address.

When we were back in the street - and out of view of The Bolingbroke - I said to Shirley: "We can't visit The Hawthorns as American tourists in case Harrison's guest is a genuine Yank and still on the premises. He'd see through us straight away. But if there's a possibility the guest was Crouch, I'll have to show Mrs Harrison the photo I took of his passport picture to get a positive ID.

"So I'll need to make this call alone - as a reporter. But let's meet up this evening."

"Where?" Shirley asked.

"How about the *Chronicle* at half past six? Hopefully, I'll be there with some good news we can celebrate."

The Hawthorns proved to be an Edwardian semi-detached house which had been extended with some rooms in the roof.

It occupied a corner site in a side road off Eastern Avenue. The notice in the window said: "Vacancies". There were cracked tiles in the garden path, peeling paintwork round the window frames, and brickwork which badly needed repointing. It didn't look like the kind of accommodation a guy with a case full of dollar bills would choose. But perhaps that was the reason he did.

I knocked the door - the bell was out of order - and waited.

The door was answered by a bustling plump number with a moon face, short fair hair, and a broad smile that flashed like a neon sign. She was wearing a grey cardigan over a light green blouse and brown slacks.

She said: "It's seventeen and sixpence a night including a full English breakfast. If you want a continental breakfast, the ferry for Dieppe leaves Newhaven at half-past eight every morning."

I grinned: "Personally, I'm a bacon sandwich man, Mrs, er..."

"Colman. As in the mustard rather than the fellow who brings the nutty slack. And the bacon sarnie's fine providing you have white bread and brown sauce, ducks."

"Is there any other way?"

She peered round the side of me as though looking for someone else and said: "Where's your luggage?"

I said: "I'm travelling light." I pulled out my reporter's notebook. "This is all I need."

"What for?"

"I'm Colin Crampton. I'm a reporter on the *Evening Chronicle.*"

"You won't find much news around here, ducks."

I decided shock tactics might work best with Mrs Colman. I pulled out the picture of Arthur Crouch from my inside pocket and showed it to her.

"I believe this man stayed with you a few days ago," I said.

Mrs Colman's eyebrows twitched upwards with recognition. Then she eyed me suspiciously. "What's it to you if he did?" she said.

"Background enquiries on a story," I said. "Do you know what off-the-record means?"

"It means you keep my name out of it, ducks. Right?"

"Right. But it also means you have to tell me everything you know. It's a two-way deal. You understand?"

"Suppose I've got no choice. Anyway, I didn't take to him. Said his name was John Taylor."

"Not Arthur Crouch."

"No. And I don't think Taylor was his real name. I asked him whether he spelt it Tailor or Taylor and he hesitated before he answered. I mean, who has to think how they spell their name?"

"How long was he here?"

"Let me think. He came last Thursday - that would the first of August. Left on Wednesday, the seventh."

"What did he do while he was here?"

"Went out most days. I don't know where, although he went to London one day, because I found the stub of his train ticket in the bin in his room."

"When was that?"

"On Tuesday. The sixth. Didn't get back until past midnight, either."

"Did he tell you anything about himself?"

"We exchanged a few pleasantries. Good morning. Lovely day. That sort of thing. But I could tell he wanted to keep himself to himself."

"Did you ever see him with a fawn attaché case?"

"No. He didn't have much luggage at all. Just a small holdall with a change of clothes in it."

"How did he pay?"

"In cash. Just how I like it."

"I don't suppose he left a forwarding address."

"He didn't leave anything - except a nasty smell in his room. He used this cologne - but not a brand I've ever heard of. Smelt like burnt bones, it did. Still haven't been able to clear the stink."

I closed my notebook. "Thank you, Mrs Colman. When it comes to observation, you're as keen as mustard."

She nodded. "Yeah, I've only heard that one a thousand times before. Now, if you'll excuse me, I've got a nasty smell in a guest's bedroom to get rid of." She shut the door.

I turned and headed back to the street. I'd discovered where Arthur Crouch, aka John Taylor, had stayed. But my hope that it would provide clues about where he was now hadn't worked out.

I'd hit another dead end.

Chapter 17

I arrived back in the *Chronicle* newsroom feeling like I'd finally hit a brick wall.

Head first.

I'd tried to find out who Chaz Rickman really was and where he came from. And failed.

And now I'd failed to uncover whatever strange story lurked behind the persona of Arthur Crouch, aka John Taylor, the man not eager to collect his twelve thousand dollars.

As far as I could tell, the police investigation was faring no better. I'd had no word from Ted Wilson.

I slumped back in my captain's chair. My eyes fell on the Russian nesting doll which I'd left on my desk. The one that had come from Jerry Clark at Nobby's Novelties. I thought I'd give it to Shirley.

I picked the thing up and opened it. As Clark had said there was a smaller version of the doll inside - and a tinier one inside that. I thought about what Winston Churchill had once said about Russia: "a riddle wrapped in a mystery inside an enigma".

It could be applied to this story. Chaz's robbery of the case was the riddle. Crouch's failure to reclaim his money the mystery. And the reason for killing poor Herbie the enigma.

I was musing on this when Freddie Barkworth bustled into the room. He came up to my desk and put down a thick envelope.

"Sorry I haven't done these before. With a couple of the other photographers on holiday, I've been rushed off my feet."

Of course, the other pictures from the film in Nat and Nettie's camera. I'd used it to take a picture of Crouch's passport. Freddie had developed the film and printed the passport picture, but said he'd enlarge the other shots later.

I said: "Thanks, Freddie. I almost forgot about these. I guess they're the other pictures the pair had been taking of one another. I'll drop them off at their guest house."

"Seemed to have a passion for shooting each other," he said. "Waste of good film if you ask me." He grinned in his lopsided way and headed off to his darkroom.

I picked up the envelope and shook out the photos. There were twenty. I flipped through. They all seemed to have been taken at the Black Rock café the afternoon Shirley and I had spotted Crouch.

Freddie was right. There were alternate pictures - first of Nat taken by Nettie, then Nettie taken by Nat. A moving cast of passers-by acted like film extras in the background of the shots.

I looked through them, shuffled them together and put them back in the envelope.

There are times, I've found, when the eye registers something but the brain takes time to note its significance. I sat at my desk staring into space with that feeling right now. I'd been looking at a bunch of boring holiday snaps, but I'd not been seeing them. The old brainbox hadn't taken it all in. But there'd been something that had passed before my eyes which I should have registered.

That was important. That changed everything.

I shook the photos out of the envelope again. I began to look at each one carefully. I'd been too focused on Nat and Nettie in the foreground. Not enough on the background.

A lot of the photos seemed to have been taken before Shirley and I had arrived at the café. There were different people sitting at some of the tables. Other people moving around the area - walking by or looking out to sea.

I guessed that Freddie had given me the prints in the order in which they'd appeared on the film. That gave me a clear timeline through them. And on the first print, the table Crouch had occupied was visible in the background but vacant. But by the fifth print Crouch was sitting there. But neither the attaché case nor the envelope was on the table where they'd been when

Shirley and I saw him.

On the eleventh print I discovered why.

A stocky figure with broad shoulders and a barrel chest was approaching Crouch's table.

And he was carrying an attaché case in his left hand and an envelope in his right.

Jerry Clark.

I jumped up from my desk and hurried to Figgis's office.

Figgis studied the picture of Clark with the attaché case and the envelope for almost a minute without speaking.

Then he said: "So what does this mean?"

I said: "It shows that Clark delivered the money to Crouch which his employee Chaz then stole."

"That makes no sense."

"It does if the pair had cooked up a conspiracy. Suppose Clark owed the money to Crouch - perhaps for some crooked business deal - but decided he wanted a way to get the money back? What better way to pay it and then steal it back? It would be a plot full of dangers - and Chaz had paid them in full. But it might be something a desperate man would attempt."

Figgis scratched his chin. "I agree it doesn't look like Clark was paying Crouch as part of a legitimate business deal."

"That's right. Clark has obviously built a successful firm, but I don't think it's one that's able to draw twelve thousand dollars in cash. In any event, if the deal was above board, why hadn't Crouch reclaimed his money from the police?"

"Too many questions," Figgis said.

"And there is one man who can answer them. Jerry Clark. I'm going to see him now."

I opened the front door of Nobby's Novelties' warehouse and stepped inside.

I hadn't expected the door to be unlocked. After all, it was half-past six. Well past office hours. But perhaps Clark was working late. Perhaps he was expecting a visitor. If so, I'd pop up like an unwelcome surprise.

I closed the door behind me. I moved into the corridor and gently pushed open the door to the left which led into the warehouse

I listened.

Bobble-de-bobble-dah.

The shrink-wrap machine was running. That rubber-lemon odour cut the air.

There was another sound. The tinny clump of boxes being loaded onto metal shelves came from the rear of the place.

I moved silently further inside and looked around. The large room was arranged in six main aisles with metal shelves from floor to ceiling. Down the first aisle I could see a couple of gaps, one every ten yards or so. I guessed they formed part of cross aisles so the whole place was laid out like a matrix - a kind of symmetrical maze.

I crept down the first aisle. The shelves were loaded with boxes, each with a red label listing the contents. I moved past boxes labelled egg cups (Bognor Regis), tea cosies (Seaford), drinks coasters (Eastbourne). I reached the first cross aisle (toilet roll holders, Bexhill-on-Sea). I listened again. At the back of the warehouse, another box thumped onto a metal shelf.

Clunk!

I made my way towards the sound. Clark was in shirt-sleeve order a few feet from the *bobble-de-bobble-dah* machine. A book with a red and yellow cover was lying nearby. The book had a cartoon of a laughing man on the cover.

Clark was bending over a cardboard box (tea towels, Ditchling Beacon). He was holding a large Stanley knife and slitting the tape which sealed the box. He was so absorbed in his work he only noticed me when I rapped lightly on the metal shelving.

He looked up and I saw shock and then anger in his eyes.

I said: "I didn't think a bloke who walked around with an attaché case stuffed with dollars would have to do the heavy work."

He stopped opening the box, stood up and scowled at me. "What the blazes are you talking about?"

But he knew all right. His hand tightened around the Stanley knife.

I said: "You can save the 'who me?' act for the jury. I have a photograph of you delivering a case with twelve thousand dollars to Arthur Crouch. If that's his real name."

"I've never heard of Arthur Crouch. Or twelve thousand dollars."

"You don't make that kind of boodle flogging novelty toilet roll holders. Where did it come from before you passed it on to Crouch?"

"That's my business."

"What I can't figure out is why your employee Chaz Rickman should then steal the cash. Was it a scam? Was the plan that the money should end up back here? Or did he double-cross you?"

"I thought I could trust Chaz. But he made mistakes. They paid the price."

I felt like a thousand volt charge of electricity had just shot through my brain.

"You said 'They paid the price'. Who are 'they'? Who paid the price apart from Chaz?"

"Just a turn of phrase."

"You killed Herbie. He paid the price along with Chaz."

"I don't know a Herbie."

"How did it happen? Did Chaz discover the secret of your scam? Did he tell Herbie about it?"

Clark hefted the Stanley knife in his hand. Glowered at me with death-ray eyes.

I said: "That knife hasn't only been used for opening boxes."

He said: "Submarines are confined spaces. Weeks at sea, not

surprising trouble breaks out sometimes. It's the chief petty officer who deals with it. Quietly. No fuss. Don't want fuss in a sub."

He looked again at the knife and back at me. As though he were a butcher eyeing up a side of beef and deciding where to make his first cut. He'd used it to slice up Herbie - and now he planned to use it on me.

He wanted to rush me. But there was a pile of boxes (William the Conqueror baby's bib, Hastings) between us. He moved sideways, away from the boxes. I stepped back. He tensed his right leg to rush me, but his left leg caught on the side of a box and he crumpled to the floor.

I turned and took off down the nearest aisle. There was no way I would tangle with a killer with a knife. I dashed past boxes labelled kiss-me-quick hats (seconds), books - *Saucy Seaside Jokes,* Duke of Norfolk commemorative saucers (cracked). I swerved right into the first cross aisle, moved across a couple of junctions and turned into the fourth aisle along.

At the back of the warehouse, I heard Clark cursing. Not quietly with no fuss. But, then, we weren't in a submarine. I crouched down behind a box (napkin rings, Queen Mother's portrait) to figure out my next move. This wasn't going to be an interview where I asked questions and wrote down the answers in neat Pitman's in my notebook.

A few aisles away I heard footsteps. Clark was sneaking up on me with cat-like tread. Like a cat wearing clogs. I moved further down the aisle to the next cross-over point (Prince Regent wig, "Hair-raising fun"). I peeked around the corner of the shelves. Nothing.

Two aisles over I heard Clark clump along. I moved silently in the opposite direction.

This was crazy. It could go on for hours. I had to find a way out.

I peered back down the aisle towards the door. Wondered

whether I could make a dash for it and get away. But that could let Clark off the hook. I'd call the cops, but by the time they arrived he'd have scarpered. I crept silently into the next aisle (coloured sands, Isle of Wight). The flap of the box was open. I peered in. The box was half full with glass tubes containing the multi-coloured sands arranged in cute designs. I reached in and pocketed a couple of tubes.

At the far end of the aisle, I spotted a telephone on the wall.

I shouted: "This farce has gone on long enough, Clark. I'm calling the cops."

Before he had time to answer I dashed for the phone.

I could hear him galumphing after me in an adjacent aisle.

I reached the phone and seized the receiver.

Clark burst out of an aisle. His face was contorted red with rage. He rushed towards me. Like a steam engine accelerating downhill.

I dropped the receiver. Reached into my pocket for one of the sand tubes.

Cracked it hard against the wall. Then slung it at Clark's face. It broke open before it hit him. Sand sprayed over him, like a whirlwind had just blown in from the Sahara. The sand lodged in his eyebrows, caught around his nose, stuck to his lips.

He closed his eyes involuntarily. Stumbled and dropped the Stanley knife.

I darted forward and grabbed it.

Clark opened his eyes. Saw I had the knife. Turned and rushed down the corridor to the stairs.

I headed after him. But not so fast I might run into him if he suddenly decided to change direction.

Clark pounded up the stairs at a surprising speed. Perhaps all those years of training on how to get out of a sinking sub had come into use.

I took the steps two at a time after him.

Clark cannoned into his office. The office where I'd interviewed him earlier in the day. Where he'd handed me the Russian doll.

He crossed the room and pushed through a fire-escape door.

I followed him. He was climbing an outside metal staircase which led up onto the flat roof. He looked back from the top of the stairs and grinned.

Not the grin of a man who expected to be caught. Who expected to hear a judge sentence him to hang by the neck until dead.

I took the stairs one at a time. I reached the top panting.

Clark was on the far side of the roof. He teetered on the edge.

He was looking directly at me. Not with hatred now.

I tried to fathom the emotion on his face. It wasn't what I expected. Then I got it.

Pity.

Clark felt pity for me.

He edged back so his heels were just over the edge of the roof. He was taking the weight on the balls of his feet.

He shouted: "You just don't understand what this is all about. Like so many others. Hundreds will come after me. Thousands. No, millions. You can't defeat us. My death is a small price for the victory that's coming."

I hurried forward. "We can talk more about this."

"The time for talking is over. Now it's time for action. For sacrifice. The cause is bigger than one man. Others will come for you. You won't escape."

He smiled. Then he leant back. His body twisted through a perfect arc, at first slowly, then faster. And he fell.

I rushed forward in time to see Clark's body hit the concrete yard below. It bounced once, then lay still. His scalp had split open and blood oozed into a pool around it. His left leg stuck at an impossible angle from the side of his body. I couldn't tear my eyes away from the horror. My body started shaking convulsively.

I stepped back from the edge of the roof. Took a deep breath to steady myself. Told myself the vision would fade. I closed my eyes and continued to suck in deep draughts of air. My body stopped shaking and relaxed.

Relief that the danger had passed flooded through me.

I turned round.

Boss was standing on the far side of the roof. He held a long crowbar.

He grinned: "One down, one to go. And the next one won't be me."

Chapter 18

"When Clark said others would come for me, I wasn't expecting such speedy service," I said.

Boss moved one step closer. "Two bodies on the concrete. The rozzers will think they fought on the roof and fell together to their death."

"Just like Holmes and Moriarty at the Reichenbach Falls."

"You won't feel so clever on the way down."

"But Holmes came back."

"Today, you're playing Moriarty."

Boss swished the crowbar in a forehand drive and then a backhand pass. A bit like Lew Hoad practising his shots before a Wimbledon final.

I said: "You may think you're the king of the road on your motorbike but you're an ordinary Joe up on the roof."

I wasn't so sure. Boss was taller than me and heavier. If it came to a tussle he'd have the weight advantage.

I said: "Before you toss me off the edge, will you answer a question?"

"The condemned man's last request?"

"If you like."

Boss thought about it. I could see the cogs moving in his brain. He said: "Why not?"

I said: "Why did Herbie have to die?"

"He was going to grass on us."

"How did you know?"

"He didn't ride with us. Claimed he couldn't catch us and turned back. But there was mud on his bike that couldn't come from the roads. They were dry. We wanted to know where he'd been. Weren't convinced with his first answers."

"So you and Clark tortured him. What did you hope to learn?"

"What he knew."

"What's your connection with Clark?"

"I don't even share that with dead men."

"I'm not dead yet."

"You soon will be."

I moved a step closer.

"There must be a motive that turns a mixed-up rocker into a cold-blooded murderer," I said.

"Don't you call me a murderer - or a mixed-up..."

But Boss didn't finish because I rushed him.

He'd become complacent. The crowbar had dropped to his side.

He couldn't believe I'd attack him. So he was slow to raise his arm with the crowbar. But by then it was too late. I cannoned into him like I was trying to run through the whole England back pack at Twickenham. Boss stumbled and fell backwards. I tumbled on top of him.

The crowbar weapon had been an advantage while he was standing at a distance. Now it was an encumbrance. Before he had time to let go, I lifted my elbow and smashed it into his face. Blood spurted from his nose and I knew I faced an argument with Figgis over an expense claim for a new shirt.

Boss dropped the crowbar and brought his arms around me in a bear hug. He was trying to squeeze the air out of me - and he was strong enough to do it. But I took a deep breath and got in a short jab with my fist to his jaw. I heard teeth crunch together and he shook his head in pain.

But I was running out of air. Boss rolled himself sideways and grabbed at my throat. It was like a giant claw had gripped me. I tried to shout but all that came out was a mouse-like squeak. I grabbed Boss's hands and tried to rip them from my throat but he was squeezing too hard and I was running out of air. Somehow, Boss levered himself up on to a knee and I found myself under the weight of his torso on the ground. I expected him to punch me, but he let go of my throat and I breathed in deeply and choked.

I tried to scramble up, but Boss pushed me to the ground. He twisted himself round and grabbed my feet. He stood up and hoisted my legs into the air so the bottom half of my body was upside down. He began to drag me across the roof on my back. I flailed with my arms but there was nothing I could do. I couldn't stand up and I couldn't reach Boss.

I felt the sharp gravel of the roof's asphalt covering dig into my back, but that was the least of my problems. Boss was dragging me towards the edge. He was going to throw me over. I summoned the last of my strength and sat up. I lashed out with my arms at Boss's legs and landed a blow but it bounced off his motorcycle leathers.

He swivelled me round. He was going to push me off the roof head first. He shoved me forward. But it wasn't as easy to push as to pull. I dug my hands into the ground and pushed back. Boss leaned forward to kick my arms away. I leaned back to avoid a boot aimed at my shoulder and my head flopped over the edge.

"Another two feet and you fall," he said.

I said: "Better be quick then, before those cops behind grab you."

"Old tricks won't save you. I turn round. You scramble up and belt me one. Try again, sucker."

And then three uniformed plods who'd crept silently up the stairs grabbed Boss's arms and pulled him back.

Behind him came Ted Wilson - and then Shirley.

She rushed towards me as I scrambled back onto the roof.

"Nice of you to drop in before I dropped off," I said.

Shirley and I clinked glasses and I took a long pull at my gin a tonic.

We were in Prinny's Pleasure a couple of hours after my adventure on the roof at Nobby's Novelties. They were two hours in which I'd been examined by a doctor, been interviewed by the cops, and written a piece for the *Chronicle*. Some time, I'll explain those hours more. For now, I didn't want to think about them.

I said: "I still don't understand how you got the cops to act so fast - or knew where to send them."

Shirley said: "It was when I came round to meet you at the *Chronicle* offices at six-thirty, like we arranged. When I found you weren't there, I thought you'd blown me out. Then I ran into Frank Figgis in reception and he told me how you'd seen a photograph of Clark delivering that attaché case to Crouch. I just knew a crazy bastard like you would want to confront him for an exclusive. So I called your mate Ted Wilson and told him what I knew."

"And good old Ted came running," I said.

"Just as well for you," Shirley said.

"Ted will be pleased that he collared a big arrest," I said. "Boss as good as admitted to me that he and Clark killed Herbie. I don't think the cops will have too much trouble finding the forensic evidence to get a conviction."

"So case closed." Shirley sipped at her white wine.

"I'm not so sure," I said. "I still don't know why Clark killed himself - or what his connection was to Boss and the rockers. The evidence of the money seems to suggest that Clark was using Nobby's Novelties as a cover for illegal activities. But what?"

"Could be drugs."

"Or money laundering. I've been wondering why Clark was handing over the money in dollars not pounds. Then there are the strange things he said before he killed himself. About millions coming after him. And that stuff about the cause being bigger than one man. What cause?"

"Perhaps he'd just flipped his lid."

"Could be. He was a tough man. But he'd know there was no way he'd avoid the noose for the murder. Perhaps he thought it would be quicker to end it now."

"Saves a lot of trouble all round," Shirley said.

"Perhaps. But it also stops him being asked any questions. Maybe that's why he killed himself. So there was no way the cops could prise out of him what his scam was."

"Dead men tell no tales."

"True, but frustrating for me. I'd have liked to discover what his real relationship with Chaz was - and why Chaz was stealing money Clark had just given to Crouch.

"And it's doubly frustrating because Crouch is the only one of the three still alive - and we don't know where he is."

Shirley drained her glass in a couple of gulps. "Still, Herbie's murder is solved. Isn't that a just end?"

"I'm not so sure. To me, it feels as though this whole case has just begun. But, hey, nearly getting thrown off a roof makes you hungry. Why don't we eat? I know a great Chinese restaurant."

Murder in the Afternoon Extra

A Crampton of the Chronicle mystery novella

Peter Bartram

The Morning, Noon and Night Trilogy
Book 2

Chapter 1

I was alone in interview room three at Brighton police station when the door opened and a man walked in.

He was nearly six feet tall, had stooped shoulders, thinning hair and a frown like the wrinkles in a widow's stockings. He was wearing a crumpled grey suit with a brown waistcoat. There was an egg stain on the waistcoat pocket. He carried a black medical bag and had a stethoscope slung round his neck.

He said: "I'm a doctor."

I said: "I'd never have guessed."

He put his bag on a table. "Some people mistake me for an undertaker."

"It must be your cheery smile."

The wrinkles in the frown deepened.

He asked: "Are you Colin Crampton?"

"Yes. Crime correspondent of the Brighton *Evening Chronicle* at your service."

He said: "I've been told to examine you."

"Like a laboratory specimen?"

"No, like a patient."

"I've not reported sick."

"I understand that you've been thrown off a roof."

"No, just dragged to the edge on my back. I didn't make the journey down."

"Anything damaged as a result of the dragging?"

"Some of the roof asphalt was torn."

"I mean in you."

"No bones broken. All organs working as expected."

"Everything alright downstairs?"

"As far as I know. You could always pop down and ask the sergeant who mans the reception desk."

"I mean your downstairs."

I knew what he meant. Why he couldn't use the correct medical term "wedding tackle" I don't know. As I was feeling a bit skittish after my near-death experience, I decided to have some fun at his expense.

"Mrs Gribble, my landlady, lives in my lodgings' downstairs. I live upstairs."

The doc ran a hand over his forehead like a man who knew he wasn't going to complete the job he was sent to do.

"Was it by any chance a doctor who tried to chuck you off the roof?" he asked.

"No, a murderer. A nasty streak of malevolence in motorcycle leathers called Boss. He pushed me to the roof's edge but the cops grabbed him before he could finish the job. He'll be in the cells now."

"I know. I've just examined him. He complained of feeling faint."

"Attempted murder does that to some people."

"So do heights. Apparently, he can't stand them. He never explained why you were both on the roof."

"I was up there because I'd pursued his partner in crime - one Jerry Clark, the proprietor of Nobby's Novelties, and the owner of a warehouse full of cheap tourist tat. He wasn't anxious to explain why he'd paid twelve thousand dollars in hot money to a mystery man called Arthur Crouch. I was just asking questions but the cops would've been hard on my heels. Clark chose the quick way down rather than capture."

"He jumped?"

I nodded. "I don't think he thought he could fly. Anyway, he won't be needing the services of a doctor. Now, if you were an undertaker..."

The doc sighed wistfully. "I've often thought it would be an easier life. So I can put you down as in rude health?" he said.

"Never ruder," I said.

The doc picked up his medical bag. "I wish I could say the

same."

He opened the door and went out.

Twenty minutes later I was at my desk in the newsroom at the *Chronicle.*

After the doc had left, I'd decided I'd wasted enough time at the police station. I'd answered the cops' questions about the events on the roof - but I had to write a piece for the paper about it. So I'd slipped down the back stairs and left through the door they normally use to hustle villains into the cells. The cops - especially my old mate Detective Inspector Ted Wilson - would be angry I hadn't yet provided a written statement. But if they wanted to read about it, they could buy a copy of the next *Chronicle.*

So I pulled my trusty typewriter towards me and rolled copy paper into the carriage. I sat back in my captain's chair and looked idly around the room. The place was deserted. Not surprising as it was Saturday evening. My fellow hacks would be downing pints in pubs or eyeing up the talent in Sherry's dance hall.

Me? I was hungry. There's nothing like nearly being murdered for working up an appetite. I planned to take my girlfriend Shirley to dinner. But first I had to write the story - which meant assembling the elements of a complicated tale in my mind.

I began to type...

Dateline: Brighton, Saturday 10 August 1963.

Trevor Kerby, 28, an unemployed gasfitter from Newhaven, has been charged by Brighton police with the murder of the motorcycle rocker found dead at Devil's Dyke on Friday.

Kerby, who uses the nickname Boss, is alleged to have killed Herbert Grover, 26. Both men were members of a motorcycle "chapter" which met regularly at the Ace of Spades café in Peacehaven.

A police source told the Chronicle *that Mr Grover had sustained serious injuries before he was killed.*

Police allege that Kerby conspired with Jeremy Clark, 42, owner of Nobby's Novelties, a fancy goods wholesaler, to kill Grover.

Clark, a former Royal Naval chief petty officer on submarines, killed himself by jumping from the roof of his company's warehouse in Portslade. Clark's apparent suicide happened after the Chronicle *confronted him with his alleged part in the killing.*

The Chronicle *has discovered that Clark supplied the attaché case containing $12,000 which was stolen from a mystery man known as Arthur Crouch.*

The money was grabbed from Crouch during a daring raid on a Volk's Railway train on Tuesday afternoon. It has emerged that the money was snatched by Charles Rickman, a warehouseman at Nobby's Novelties.

Rickman was killed in a road accident while trying to escape with the money. Mr Crouch has not come forward to reclaim his $12,000, which is being held at Brighton police station.

Police are investigating whether the robbery and the killing of Mr Grover are related. Other members of the Peacehaven motorcycle chapter have been questioned by police, but released without charge.

Detective Inspector Ted Wilson, who is heading the case in the absence of Detective Chief Superintendent Alec Tomkins, who is on sick leave, said: "We would like to hear from anybody who was in the area of Devil's Dyke on Friday, when we believe the killing took place. We will treat all information in confidence.

"We would also like to hear from anybody who knows Mr Arthur Crouch or who may have any idea where he can be found."

Kerby will appear before Brighton magistrates and is expected to be remanded in custody pending further enquiries.

I rolled the last folio out of the typewriter and put it in the pile with the others.

The story told what I knew - but there were more loose ends than a bowl of spaghetti.

I opened my notebook and listed the questions I needed to answer.

What was the connection between Clark and Kerby, aka Boss, the thuggish rocker? Was Boss Clark's hired muscle or did the relationship go deeper?

Where did Clark get the twelve thousand dollars, forged passport, and airline ticket to New York he handed to the man known as Arthur Crouch at a café on Brighton beach? And what is Crouch's true identity?

Why did Clark's employee Charles Rickman, aka Chaz, steal the cash, the passport and the ticket from Crouch? And where is Crouch hiding now that he's lost the passport and ticket that would have allowed him to flee the country?

I leaned back in my chair and thought about the questions. I couldn't think of a way to answer any of them. Of the four players in this drama, two - Chaz and Clark - were dead. Boss was in the cells at the cop shop. He had the slogan "Death before Dishonour" emblazoned on his leather jacket - and looked like the kind of bloke who meant it.

Crouch might be persuaded to speak - but nobody knew where he was. He hadn't come forward to pick up his boodle - a giveaway sign that it was hot money.

I stood up and headed for the door. It was late and I was hungry. I wasn't going to find answers to any of these questions tonight.

Or perhaps ever.

But two hours later, I realised I could be wrong.

There was one way I might uncover the true identity of Arthur Crouch. If I could do that I might have the clue that would let me unravel the rest of the mystery.

This epiphany happened while Shirley and I tucked into a late supper.

We were at a corner table in the Forbidden City Chinese

restaurant in Preston Street. The place had yellow table cloths with a red dragon motif. Chinese lanterns hung from the ceiling. They cast a pale pink light. The chopsticks came in a long paper envelope - as though they'd arrived in the post. The menu was stained with someone else's dinner. Spare ribs in barbecue sauce, I think. The air smelt like it had been fried in oil.

We'd scoffed prawn balls in sweet and sour sauce and chicken chow mein.

Then Shirley leaned forward, licked her luscious lips, flashed her big blue eyes and said: "Let's order some Peking duck."

I reached for the menu, found the duck - and knew what Archimedes felt like when he jumped into his bath.

Or when the apple fell on Isaac Newton's head.

Or Benjamin Franklin flew his kite.

It was like a thunder flash had gone off in my brain. I just stared at the menu.

Shirley said: "You look like you've just forgotten your own name."

"It's the menu," I said. "It's made me realise what I've overlooked about the mysterious Arthur Crouch."

"Show me."

I leant across the table and pointed at the menu.

"See this item. It says 'Peking Duck'."

"So?"

"Well, strictly speaking, it should be written 'Peking duck' with a lower case d. You only use capital letters for proper nouns - like names and places. A duck is a common noun."

"I don't give a wallaby's whoopsie whether it's proper or common as long as it's crispy."

A waiter materialised alongside the table and I gave the order.

I said: "It's always the unexpected detail which trips up crooks. In this case, it's a capital letter. That envelope Crouch received from Clark was addressed to him at Brighton Beach. Capital Bs on both words. I'd assumed it was written that way as Crouch was getting the envelope while he was sitting at a café by the beach. But when we write Brighton beach in the *Chronicle*, the beach always has a lower case b."

"So what?"

"So I think Clark had written Brighton Beach on the envelope with capitals because he knew Crouch had come from the town with that name. It's part of the Borough of Brooklyn in New York."

"Seems a pretty thin theory to me."

"There's supporting evidence. Crouch had an airline ticket to New York and he'd been paid in dollars."

"But the passport was British."

"I think that's because it would have been too difficult to forge an American one in this country. If Crouch is a crook, he won't care which passport gets him into the States. I'd bet my portion of Peking duck he plans to disappear when he's passed immigration."

The waiter appeared with duck, hoisin sauce, pancakes and garnish.

I said to Shirley: "If Arthur Crouch does hail from Brighton Beach, I think I could trace him on his home turf."

Shirley helped herself to a pancake, spread it with hoisin sauce, added shredded cucumber and spring onion, loaded some duck and rolled it up.

She said: "You've overlooked one key point, mastermind."

"That Crouch isn't in Brighton Beach at the moment."

"Right, Einstein. Remember that his passport was stolen. Without it, he can't leave Britain."

"So he'll be in hiding while he orders up a new one from his forger. But that will take time. It can't be in the same name because the cops now have the original. There'll be an all-ports alert on Arthur Crouch. And he'll have to change his appearance because the authorities have the photo from his first passport. And his photo has been in all the papers. I wouldn't mind betting that the photo from the stolen passport is similar to his real appearance. He had no reason to disguise himself all the while nobody knew what he was up to. So if I show the photo around Brighton Beach, I think there's a good chance someone may recognise him."

"Sounds like a long-shot to me. New York is a big city."

"Sure. But if he's been mixed up in a crime in this country, chances are he's on police or FBI records in the States. Perhaps they'll recognise him."

Shirley took another bite of her pancake. "Perhaps, if you can get the Yankee cops to play ball."

"I'll take my chance on that," I said.

"And what if you're wrong, Big Brain?" Shirley said. "You're staking a lot on being right about Crouch coming from Brighton Beach, New York. Suppose that envelope really was intended for Crouch on our Brighton beach."

"Then I've made a capital error."

"And a bad pun. I shouldn't be encouraging you to go."

"If Frank Figgis, my news editor, lets me go, I'll bring you back a present."

Shirley leaned across the table and kissed me. "Make sure you do."

A waiter came and cleared our plates. He left two fortune cookies on the table.

I said: "Why don't we find out what the future holds for us?"

Shirley reached out a hand for one, then withdrew it. "I don't know. I find these things creepy."

"It's just a bit of fun. Nobody believes what's written inside them."

"You go first, then."

I shook my head. "No, it's ladies first."

Shirley reached for a cookie and broke it open. Her eyes widened as she read it: "'You will have a surprise.'"

"Right there. Here comes the waiter with the bill."

Shirley shrugged. "Read yours then."

I broke it open and read the message silently. "You're right, this is stupid." I screwed it up and tossed it into the ashtray.

Shirley's hand darted out and grabbed it before I could stop her.

She unscrewed the paper and read the message. She looked at me with saucer eyes. "You know what it says, don't you?"

I quoted: "Danger lies over water."

Chapter 2

I arrived at the newsroom the following morning after a restless night.

I'd done my best to make light of my fortune cookie message, but Shirley took it seriously.

I'd argued that she could have easily picked the cookie with the water warning. In which case, I'd be lecturing her about her visits to Saltdean Lido. But she said that it was fate that determined which cookie we chose. I thought of saying it wasn't fate, it was the damned waiter who'd chosen them from a box of dozens and dumped them on our table. But it was clear that Shirley had made up her mind on the matter.

In the end, I'd had to agree to think again about taking a trip to Brighton Beach. In any event, I didn't think I'd be able to persuade Figgis to let me make the trip at the *Chronicle*'s expense.

So I arrived at my desk in a scratchy mood.

That wasn't improved when my telephone rang. I lifted the receiver and a voice that sounded like a wire brush scratched across a washboard, said: "Come into my office with alacrity."

I could tell by the tone that Figgis had something on his mind. I stepped briskly round to his office. I knocked and went in before he could growl: "Enter."

I said: "I've come to your office alone. I'm afraid Al Acrity is off work today."

Figgis's hard-boiled eyes moved from the fag he was lighting to me. "I'm in no mood for your cracks this morning."

"Despite having a cracker of a front-page story delivered at great personal danger to myself last night?"

He took a long drag of his Woodbine and his face muscles sagged that bit lower, like Christmas decorations on Boxing Day.

He said: "I'll grant that. We're splashing with it on the front page. But that's not what's giving me grief this morning."

Smoke leaked out of his mouth, nose and ears. Briefly, I wondered whether it leaked anywhere else. But that was too macabre to think about.

So I said: "What's the trouble?"

"It seems that His Holiness was having dinner with the Chief Constable last night."

Gerald Pope - His Holiness throughout the newsroom, but never on the rare occasions he made a visit - was the paper's editor. He was a posh type with little aptitude for the hard-knocks world of newspapers. But at least he'd have known which knife and fork to use when the fish course came round.

I said: "Pope's always hobnobbing with some dignitary."

"Yes, and like a cushion he always bears the imprint of the last bum to sit on it. In this case, Chief Constable Harding has filled his head with a load of nonsense about the so-called Great Train Robbery and the lack of coverage about it in the *Chronicle*."

The robbery had taken place two nights earlier at a remote spot called Bridego bridge in Buckinghamshire - well clear of the *Chronicle*'s patch. A gang of desperados had lifted more than two million quid from a Night Mail train - then vanished into the countryside. Scotland Yard's finest were baffled, but the papers were having a great time. A robbery this size coming in the middle of the silly season was like having Christmas, birthday and a wedding anniversary happening on the same day.

Except that Pope wasn't happy the *Chronicle* hadn't splashed it all over our front page.

"We've had our own home-grown train robbery to entertain readers," I said.

"I know that, but Pope thinks it's small beer compared with the big one - and now he's giving me earache about our Volk's robbery coverage."

Figgis seemed more edgy than normal when Pope made one of his ill-judged editorial decisions. I couldn't understand why. Perhaps he was just getting old. Or perhaps he'd had a nasty warning in a fortune cookie.

I didn't bother too much about the reason. Because with Figgis on the back foot, I had an opportunity. There's never a better time to ask someone for a favour than when they need your help first.

I said: "I could write a couple of backgrounder pieces on the robbery - perhaps get some quotes direct from Harding. Maybe he's just after getting his own name in the paper to show he's taking an interest in the investigation. After all, with Scotland Yard handling the case, he must feel a bit like the country bumpkin on the side-lines - especially as Sussex is well away from the scene of the crime."

Figgis sat up straighter in his chair. "You could do that?"

"Be my pleasure. I could manage the first piece for the night final today."

"That should get Pope off my back."

"There is one other point," I said. "As soon as I get the visa, I want to go the United States to follow up the Volk's train robbery story."

Figgis's jaw dropped so fast, the fag stuck to his bottom lip fell into his lap. There was a bit of a panic while he wrestled with his trousers.

I said: "I don't suppose there are any fire hazards down there these days."

Figgis frowned but chose to ignore that.

Instead he said: "A trip to the States would use up the editorial travel budget for an entire year. Besides, I need you here."

"And I need a holiday - and you promised I could take one if I landed a front-page splash. I've more than delivered on my side of the bargain - so now it's payback time."

Figgis was a tough operator, but he was also a shrewd newsman. Over the next ten minutes I put all the arguments together about how I would trace Crouch and use that to crack open the story.

I said: "It would give us a string of exclusives. His Holiness could boast to whomever he's breaking bread with that the paper was out front rather than piggy-backing on somebody else's story. Besides, if this is as good as I think it will be, the paper could make syndication fees out of the copy I write."

We dickered and argued for half an hour - or four fags in Figgis time.

He said: "I can't stop you taking holiday time owed, but you do this in your own time and at your own expense. And if you're not back here in two weeks' time, I wouldn't bank on a future at this paper. Pope will have you out of the door faster than you can say Big Apple."

I stood up and headed towards the newsroom. "And we wouldn't want a big apple giving His Holiness the pip," I said.

Chapter 3

The man in seat 14B on the flight from London to New York turned to me and said: "If we're going to crash it'll be in the next thirty seconds.

"It's the time when the engines need to deliver full power to get this old crate into the air."

I dragged my gaze away from the receding suburb of Hounslow as the aircraft gained altitude and its wheels retracted. I looked at him from the corner of my eyes.

He'd hustled onto the plane at the last minute and taken his seat next to me. He was the wrong side of fifty but carrying his age well. He had an aquiline nose jutting above a well-trimmed moustache. He had dark hair that was turning grey and a pimple at the edge of his jaw, just below his left ear. You could mistake it for an earring in the half light. He was wearing a brown suit that would have the boys at the *Tailor & Cutter* cooing with delight. His green and red stripy tie - could have been old school or old regiment - was fastened in a Windsor knot. And he wore a pair of cufflinks with his initials inscribed on them in flowery script - R, C, F, D.

I would have bet ten bob the first three stood for something like Rupert Clarence Fotheringay.

The plane's engine note rose, then fell.

I said: "If the engines fail, the plane belly-flops with all the elegance of a hippo falling off a diving board. My fortune cookie the other evening warned me there'd be danger over the water, so I'm not getting worried until we reach the Atlantic."

"Actually, old boy, we've just passed over the River Thames."

"Well, that just proves you shouldn't believe everything you read in fortune cookies."

The bloke grinned and stuck out his hand. "Reginald Derwent."

"I had you down as a Rupert," I said.

A frown wrinkled on his forehead. I nodded at the cufflinks.

He laughed, but it was forced. "Very observant. Reginald Christopher Fulbert Derwent. Friends call me Reggie."

"Am I a friend?" I asked.

"Let's say an honorary friend for the next eight hours. No sense in sitting next to one another like a pair of Trappist monks."

I stuck out my hand and we shook. "In that case, Colin Crampton. Friends call me Colin."

My new friend Reggie settled himself back in his seat and said: "Please forgive my opening conversational gambit, Colin. I didn't intend to be alarmist. One finds it so difficult to know how to begin a conversation with one's neighbour on a long plane journey. Not like a train. You can't say, 'Where are you getting off?' or 'Do you mind if I open the window?'"

"Do you often visit America?" I asked.

"Now and then."

"Where will you be staying?"

"Here and there."

"Planning to do anything interesting?"

"This and that."

"Very informative," I said.

"How about your trip? Business or pleasure?"

"Pleasure," I said. "A brief holiday."

"Interesting," he said. "Do you often take your portable typewriter on holiday with you?"

My wits sharpened at that remark. He must have seen me holding it in the departure lounge. I'd already stashed it in the overhead locker before he'd boarded the plane. And what was it to him if I was travelling with my trusty Olivetti?

I said: "Never travel anywhere without it. It's like some people take a Saint Christopher disc."

"Or a lucky rabbit's foot," he said.

"Except the foot didn't prove very lucky for the rabbit."

Reggie rubbed the bridge of his beaky nose with his forefinger. "I'd assumed you had the typewriter because you were going to write something. Novelist, are you?"

"Journalist."

"Ah, a member of the Fourth Estate. Fleet Street is it?"

"Brighton. *Evening Chronicle*."

"Interesting," he said. "We have a lot to thank our provincial press for. Had any good stories lately?"

"Nothing much," I lied.

"Really? I think I saw a paragraph or two in *The Times* about a robbery on the seafront. The quaint little Volk's Railway, wasn't it?"

"Yes, it was the Volk's Railway. And I hadn't realised it had been picked up by *The Times*. I thought the nationals couldn't look further than that so-called Great Train Robbery - the one at Bridego bridge in Buckinghamshire."

Reggie stroked his chin while he thought about that. "Bad business," he said. "Can't have fellows stopping trains in the dead of night and grabbing anything that takes their fancy. That sort of thing ought to be confined to America."

I said: "Is your own visit to America business or pleasure?"

"Definitely," he said.

"Bit of both is it?"

"I expect I'll find out when I get there."

"What line of business are you in?" I asked.

"Civil servant. Bureaucrat. Paper shuffler. Nothing of note, but one delivers one's nothing with a certain pride."

"What do you do?"

"Routine work. Papers come into my in-tray and I move them across to my out-tray."

"But not when you fly to America for a bit of business and pleasure."

He gave me a sharp look, then smiled. But it was a smile that didn't reach his eyes. "No, not then. But this is a rare trip out of the office. Hardly ever move from the chair behind my desk. Seat of my trousers gets so shiny, you could see your face in it."

"Always assuming you could get your head far enough between your legs," I said.

There was movement in the aisle further down the plane.

"Well, here's some good news," Reggie said. "The steward with the drinks trolley approaches. We'll have a noggin or two. And if I'm not mistaken there'll be some pukka victuals to feast upon later. Then I'll tell you a bit more about myself."

That's rich, I thought. So far you've gone out of your way to tell me nothing at all. Still, what more do you need to know about a bloke who says "pukka victuals" when he means "tasty nosh"?

"Damn and blast."

We were two hours into the flight and Reggie was not happy.

"This is like trying to load cartridges into a double-barrelled shotgun while wearing a blindfold and mittens."

Reggie's fingers were clawing at a small tightly wrapped packet which contained two sugar cubes.

"Allow me," I said.

He handed me the packet. I inserted a fingernail under the fold in the paper and nicked an opening. "You should be able to get the sugar out now."

"Thank you so much, Colin. I really don't know why airline food always has to be wrapped up in something. It's a constant source of annoyance."

Strange, I thought, that a civil servant who admits to making only rare trips abroad should find the food a "constant" source of annoyance. But perhaps it was just a turn of phrase.

I said: "The point about airline food isn't that it has any nutritional value. It's a form of occupational therapy. If it takes you five minutes to unwrap a sugar cube, that's five minutes you don't worry about the plane crashing."

"Never thought about it that way."

He dropped the sugar cubes into his coffee. He picked up a mint wrapped in gold foil, looked at it, but decided not to bother. He tossed it back on his tray.

He said: "I guess you face more testing problems in your job than sugar cube wrappers."

"Most of them come shrouded in smoke. Frank Figgis, my news editor, is a sixty-a-day man."

"Runs a tight ship, this Figgis?"

"No, he runs a tight newsroom. We never put the paper together at sea."

Reggie cleared his throat in what may have been a mirthless laugh.

"But it's true that journalists face dilemmas, isn't it?"

"Certainly. Sometimes we can't find the facts we need to make a story stand up. Sometimes we worry we leave ourselves open to libel even though we know what we've written is true. But, in the end, if a story needs to be told, it should be."

Reggie took a sip of his coffee. Made a contented little sigh. "Even if it causes damage to others?"

"That depends on who the others are - and what damage they will suffer."

"Suppose, old boy, you had a story that would damage the country if it were told. Would you publish that?"

"People who claim a story would damage the country often mean the story would damage their own interests."

"But if a person in authority came to you and appealed to your sense of patriotism. You know, 'my country right or wrong'."

"G K Chesterton said nobody would think of saying that except in desperate circumstances. It was like saying 'my mother drunk or sober'. In any event, I don't have a story that would damage my country's interests."

Reggie drained the rest of his coffee. "Just an abstract discussion," he said. "It's interesting to learn that patriotism is in short supply in the journalist profession."

I didn't remind him that Samuel Johnson, who'd done a bit of journalism himself, had said that "Patriotism is the last refuge of the scoundrel."

And I was beginning to wonder whether Reggie was a patriot - or a scoundrel.

After finishing his coffee, Reggie decided he needed a "spot of shut-eye, old boy," before we arrived in New York.

I settled back in my own seat and thought back over our conversation. I couldn't make much of it. Perhaps it was just idle chit-chat among neighbours to while away the time. But I couldn't help feeling there was more to it. But what? I had no idea.

When we reached Idlewild Airport, Reggie was ahead of me in the queue for immigration control. He turned and waved to me as he went through the gate.

Then he bustled off and was lost among the crowds.

And I was left wondering what the hell I was going to do now I was in America.

Chapter 4

"Hi, honey, you got a face looks like the Empire State building just toppled over and fell on your foot."

The waitress in Big Buck's diner was called Mabelle. I knew that because she had a plastic badge pinned to the right breast of her scarlet apron which said: "Mabelle".

Mabelle had a cute oval face with high cheekbones framed with a frizz of curly blonde hair. She had the kind of surprised eyes that could have got her into show business or into trouble. Under the apron she wore a fawn T-shirt and blue jeans. On her feet she had a pair of plimsolls which I later discovered she called sneakers. Whenever she sneaked across the diner's tiled floor their soles made a low sibilant hiss, like a pair of nuns whispering their prayers.

But she wasn't sneaking right now.

She held one hand on her right hip and tapped a sneaker against the floor impatiently.

I said: "It's not my foot that's hurting. I'm tired and I don't know what to eat. The clock on the wall says it's three in the afternoon, but my stomach says it's dinner time."

Mabelle said: "The clock don't need no food. You listen to your stomach, honey."

I shrugged. "What do you recommend?"

"Buck grills a mean cheeseburger. Folks come from as far away as Twelfth Street to eat it. Everything else he touches turns out as crap."

"Suppose it'll have to be the mean cheeseburger, then."

"With fries?"

"You mean chips?"

"Chips is what you lose in the casinos in Atlantic City, honey. Fries is what you have on the side of your burger. I'll bring you coffee."

The nuns whispered as Mabelle headed for the kitchen to place my order with Buck.

I felt the hard deal chair press into my back as I leant back and surveyed the place. I'd arrived in Brighton Beach on the New York metro fifteen minutes earlier. The metro line ran up the centre of the town's main street like it owned the place. It was hoisted above the road on giant metal legs. Trains rumbled overhead so the street sounded like it had a regular thunderstorm.

I'd hauled my suitcase down the steps from the metro station into the street. I'd turned left for no particular reason other than it seemed the best thing to do. I knew nothing about this town. I could be anywhere.

But I'd found Big Buck's diner a hundred yards along the street. It sat in the shadow of the overhead metro like a toad cowering under a rock. One thing was for sure. Arthur Crouch would've never eaten here.

I'd opened the door and walked in knowing I was going to regret the decision. The place was empty and felt like it had got used to the condition. The floor was criss-crossed with black lines where dust had settled into the grouting between the tiles. The walls were painted green. The tables had plastic tops and metal legs. The chairs were upright, wooden and not built for comfort. The place smelt like someone had roasted an ox a week ago and not opened the windows since.

While I waited for Mabelle to bring my coffee, I thought some more about Reggie Derwent. I was still wondering whether my meeting with Reggie was the chance encounter he'd made it out to be. For somebody who'd rushed onto the plane just before the doors closed, he seemed cocksure certain about which seat he had to occupy. And then there was the way he'd turned the conversation to the Volk's Railway robbery - as though nothing else in the world was more interesting to chat about. I couldn't shake off the feeling that he'd been grilling me for a reason. But what reason I couldn't imagine. Besides, when we'd landed at Idlewild, he'd disappeared into the crowds. I'd never see him again.

I had to be positive. I'd persuaded Figgis that I could track down Crouch - and that we'd land a scoop that would make the nationals drool with envy. Now I had to do it. But having finally reached Brighton Beach, I was baffled about where to start.

I was puzzling over this conundrum when Mabelle reappeared at the side of my table. She set a mug of coffee and a plate in front of me. The plate held the cheeseburger. Something yellow, like pus from an open wound, oozed from the centre.

I pointed: "What's that?" I asked.

"Monterey Jack cheese - melted just as the chef likes it." Mabelle said.

I picked up one of the fries and took a bite. At least it was hot and, hmmm, actually crisp and tasty.

Mabelle watched me eat the chip while she decided whether to ask me something.

"You're not from around here?"

"How do you know?"

"Anybody around here would recognise the cheese in a burger. Besides, you talk funny. You from Vermont or somewhere up in the hills?"

I took another chip. "Brighton, England."

"Hey, they really got a Brighton in England? Bet it ain't got a beach like ours."

"It has, all pebbles."

"I guess they named your town after ours."

"Other way round. The place was named after my Brighton by a bloke called Henry C Murphy. The C stood for Cruse. He was a newspaperman, like me - edited a paper called the *Brooklyn Daily Eagle* way back in the late nineteenth century. It's all in *Encyclopaedia Britannica*."

Mabelle's eyes had narrowed when I'd mentioned I was a

newspaperman. Now she glanced around the diner, checked there were no other customers, and took the seat opposite me.

"Hey, if you're a reporter, you could write about me. Help me get my big break."

"What break would that be?"

Mabelle leaned closer. Helped herself to one of my fries and took a bite.

"I ain't just a waitress working a diner, you know. I'm a dancer."

"Ballet or ballroom?"

"Exotic. Had an act with a snake. A python. Cute little critter called Percy. Did my act at the Hoochie-Coochie Club down near the boardwalk. You must know it."

I shook my head.

"No? OK. Must admit I never saw you there. Anyway, did this act. Tasteful. Classy, like. You could have taken your grandmother. Dance of the Seven Veils. Well, Percy filled in for the veils as they came off."

"There's no business like show business. Even for a snake," I said.

"Yeah, when Percy'd had his treat he'd perform like a star. Liked a mouse before a show, though."

"To eat?"

"Well, not to play Parcheesi with. Anyway, this night I didn't have no mice, 'coz the store had sold the last one to some snotty kid who wanted a pet. So Percy had to go without his treat. Before I went on stage, I put him down for just ten seconds while I made sure my veils were covering the hills and valleys - and you know what the darned critter did?"

"He made his getaway."

"You got it, buster. And then Leone De Luca, the grease-ball who runs the joint, said I was to blame for his constipation."

"How come?"

"Well, you know what a python does when it lams outta

somewhere?"

"Makes for water?" I said.

"Yeah. De Luca said he couldn't sit on the can without thinking a slimy head was gonna slither round the bend in the pipes and bite him in the ass. Jesus H Christ. He didn't have to fire me. He could have got a laxative."

The pus had stopped oozing from my cheeseburger. The thing had congealed and turned cold.

I said: "How did you come to work here?"

"Two days after I'd been kicked out of the Hoochie-Coochie and landed on my butt, I met this guy who said he was looking for a girl who wanted to work for big bucks. I thought, 'That's great, I wanna make big bucks.' So I accepted on the spot."

"And when you got here you found you were working for Big Buck's."

Mabelle's shoulders slumped. "Yeah. Guess I made a big mistake."

"You should've got Buck to write it down."

"How do you mean?"

"Write big bucks with small letters and it means lots of money. With capitals at the start of each word, it's this place."

"Sure, wise guy. Next time I'm offered a job I'll get a lawyer to check the punctuation. But I got plans. I'm gonna get outta here soon. But, hey, I'm telling you my life story and you ain't writing no notes for your article."

I grinned. "Perhaps another time," I said. "When I've finished the piece I'm working on at the moment."

"You staying local long, then?"

"I'm not sure yet. And I'm not even sure I'm staying local, unless I can find a cheap hotel to fit my budget. The paper doesn't pay generous expenses."

"Yeah, I've worked for cheapskates, too. But I could put a good thing your way. My aunt Ernestina takes in lodgers - her rates are real low, too. I could take you round there after I finish my shift."

Mabelle told me her aunt lived just a few blocks away near the junction of Sixth Street and Neptune Avenue. I arranged to meet her back at the diner in a couple of hours.

"What did you say your name was?" Mabelle asked.

"Colin," I said. "Colin Crampton."

Mabelle rolled the name round her mouth meditatively - like she was sucking a boiled sweet.

"Colin Crampton," she said. "Sounds real classy. And from England. I bet you know the Queen and everything."

Chapter 5

An old bloke wearing faded jeans and a shabby jacket shuffled into the diner.

He carried a ripped canvas bag. Old clothes burst out of splits in the canvas like the socks wanted freedom from the underpants. He hobbled across the room and took a seat at the back.

Mabelle took a look at him, released an annoyed hiss. "Guess I'll have to hustle - you want more coffee before I serve the hobo?"

I shook my head. "I'll meet you back here in two hours," I said.

"Yeah, you can tell me whether the Queen likes cheeseburgers," she said.

She looked pointedly at my uneaten meal. "You done?" she said.

A fly landed in the yellow ooze.

"I am now."

Mabelle took the plate and stomped back to the kitchen.

I picked up my suitcase and portable typewriter and lugged them outside. I had two hours to kill in a town I didn't know.

I walked back towards the metro station. The sidewalk was crowded with people hurrying home. Two trains overhead set up a thunderstorm as they rattled into Brighton Beach station. A minute later, a crowd of people swarmed down the steps into the street.

Next to the metro station a newsstand was open for business. I took a professional look at the papers. The *New York Times, Herald Tribune* and *Time* magazine were all on display. So was a paper called the *Brighton Beach Banner* (incorporating the *Coney Island Chatterer*). The paper was thinner than the rest, but I paid twenty cents for a copy and tucked it under my arm.

I strolled along and looked in the shopfronts. There were cut-price grocery stores offering three tins of beans for a dollar. There were bargain basement hardware shops with ten per cent off everything until the end of the week. (They didn't say which week.) There were second-hand clothes joints promising "mad discounts" on winter socks. So not exactly Third Avenue - or wherever New York housed its fashionable shops.

I passed a doughnut store. The door was open. The scent of sugar and batter made my stomach rumble. I'd only eaten a couple of chips at Big Buck's. I went into the store and bought a bag of three doughnuts. I came out carrying them, my suitcase and portable typewriter.

I had to find somewhere I could sit down. My arms ached and I felt like I could sleep for a century.

At the junction of Brighton Beach Avenue and Seventh Street I turned right towards the ocean. Seventh Street was quieter. The sidewalk wasn't crowded and there was little through traffic. The houses were modest and neat - some brick but also some timber-frame buildings. The street felt like one of those places where people minded their own business. A street where people lived quietly with nothing to worry them. Unless they knew a performing python was loose in the city's sewers.

It took me ten minutes to reach the ocean. The gently sloping sandy beach seemed to stretch for miles. The sun was low in the sky and the slanting rays made the ocean beyond sparkle with little points of light.

Down by the water, a woman walked a pair of cocker spaniels. A small group of children were building a sandcastle. A couple of young guys played catch with a baseball.

I found a bench, sat down and ate my doughnuts. I unfurled the *Brighton Beach Banner* and read it while I chomped away. The paper may have been a thin weekly but it took a brave editorial stance. The front page splash exposed a "numbers racket" which it claimed was run by a local hoodlum called Leone De Luca.

That had my attention. De Luca was the constipated guy who sacked Mabelle because he feared a python down the pan. It looked as though Mabelle moved in rough company. But I guessed if you were a stripper you didn't get to meet too many pillars of the community.

I finished the doughnuts and folded the paper.

A gentle breeze wafted in from the ocean, but the air was warm.

I closed my eyes, turned my face towards the sun and let its evening rays warm me.

I winced with pain.

Something hard prodded into my ribs.

I opened my eyes. A cop was standing by me holding a nightstick. He moved to prod me again, but I brushed it away.

He snarled: "Hey, buster, you step out of turn with me and I'll run you down to the station house."

I said: "If it's on the way to Big Buck's diner, that'll save me a walk with this heavy case."

The cop was wearing a blue blouson. It was held in at his waist by a black belt with a gun holster. His peaked hat was pulled low over his forehead. He had a broad nose, thin lips and a scowl he must have worked on for years.

He said: "City ordnance number one three seven nine: no sleeping on the beach."

"I wasn't sleeping. I was contemplating the meaning of the universe."

"You had your eyes closed."

"Only in philosophical meditation."

"Don't get smart with me, buster. Anyway, you ain't from round here. Where you come from?"

"England."

"A limey, eh? We had trouble with limeys before."

"Back in 1776, I believe. But surely old friends can put that little bit of unpleasantness behind them?"

"Jesus! I wish I hadn't woken you up now." He tossed his head in a despairing gesture and ambled off.

I glanced at my watch. In fact, I had fallen asleep and now I had less than ten minutes to meet Mabelle.

I grabbed my case and typewriter and headed for Big Buck's.

It had just turned eight when Mabelle and I arrived at Ernestina Koch's house.

Just after eight - but my body was screaming to me that it was one o'clock in the morning. My limbs ached for sleep.

Mabelle had chattered all the way on the walk from Big Buck's. She told me how working at the diner would be easier if Big Buck wasn't such a crap cook. She told me how she had to sweet talk the punters who didn't like their food. She told me how she got a mouthful of swear words from Buck when she passed on complaints. She told me how she wanted to return to the stage as an exotic dancer if she could persuade grease-ball De Luca to take her back. She told me she worried about what had happened to Percy the python.

Ernestina Koch's lodging house turned out to be a two-storey building with a flat-roofed single storey extension tacked onto the side. The place had been given a slap of fresh paint in the last couple of years. Probably by the decorator who'd submitted the lowest estimate. Paint flaked from walls where damp plasterwork hadn't been repaired.

"You'll love it here," Mabelle said as we stepped up to the front door. "Aunt Tina is such a welcoming hostess. She's a real people person."

An old-fashioned bell chain hung by the front-door. Mabelle gave it a tug and a noise like a tin can rattling on a chain sounded somewhere in the house.

The door was opened by a thin woman with a thin face. She had a narrow mouth, suspicious eyes and a nose that was too big to fit in with the rest of her features. Her grey hair was parted in the centre and tied back in a bun.

She looked at Mabelle like she was the rent collector and said: "What brings you round here? I told you once, if I've told you a hundred times, I ain't lending you no money to buy no snake."

Mabelle flashed me a coy smile. "Auntie Tina, please. You're embarrassing me in front of my friend. I'm not here about Percy."

The people person turned a critical eye on me. "And who might you be?"

"Colin Crampton," I said. "One of Her Majesty's journalists, just landed from England, and eager to find a place to rest my weary head."

I stuck out my hand and Ernestina reluctantly shook it. "I suppose you better come in."

We trooped in and walked down a narrow hallway into a room with not many windows and too much furniture. Ernestina gestured me to an over-stuffed sofa and I sat down.

"How long you want to stay?" she asked.

"It depends how long my research takes but possibly two or three days."

"I gotta room at the side looking out over the extension. It's got a single bed and bathroom down the corridor. It's eight dollars a night without breakfast."

"I'll take it," I said.

"Hey, ain't that swell," Mabelle piped up. She'd sat down next to me.

"I guess you'd like some coffee," Ernestina said.

"That would be swell," I said. In America for only hours and already I was picking up the lingo.

Ernestina bustled off to the back of the house and we heard crockery rattling as she prepared the coffee.

Mabelle nudged closer to me on the sofa and said: "I guess you didn't come to Brighton Beach to write about little ol' me."

"'Fraid not."

"You chasing a big story, then?"

"I hope so. Otherwise my news editor isn't going to sign off on the expenses for the trip."

"Must be difficult being a reporter. Pitching up in a place you never been to before and all that."

"Sure. Especially the 'all that'."

Mabelle giggled softly.

"Maybe I could show you around."

"I haven't decided where I'm going yet."

"But you must know what you gotta do."

"I've got to identify a man who's in England now, but probably came from Brighton Beach."

"I know a lotta people in this ol' town."

I looked at Mabelle. Her eyes were burning with curiosity.

"I've read there are thirty thousand people here. You can't know all of them."

"I've seen plenty at the diner," she said. "And at the Hoochie-Coochie - before I got the sack."

"I'm not sure the person I'm trying to identify would've visited either."

"I've seen people in other places, too."

"Like where?"

"Like in the street."

Mabelle had a point. In a small town, people see the same faces again and again as they go about a daily routine. Doesn't mean they know who the people are. But even if Mabelle recognised the face, it might help.

I said: "If I show you a photo of the man I want to identify, will you promise to keep it confidential if you recognise him?"

Mabelle nodded and leaned closer towards me.

I reached inside my jacket pocket and took out the photo.

I said: "This is a recent shot."

I watched her face closely as I passed the photo to Mabelle. She held it up to the light for a couple of seconds.

Her eyes widened in surprise.

She handed the photo back to me. Her arm was tense. She was breathing faster.

She looked at a spot on the wall and said: "Never seen the guy in my life."

"You don't recognise him at all?"

"I said so didn't I? You gonna make a federal case out of it?"

I smiled: "I never doubted you for a minute."

Mabelle stood up and moved to a chair on the other side of the room.

Ernestina bustled into the room with three mugs of coffee on a tray.

She looked at me, then at Mabelle.

"You been pestering this nice young man about your snake?"

Mabelle pouted. "No. I just needed more room."

I took my coffee and had a sip. I wasn't feeling so tired now I knew Mabelle had lied. I felt I'd won a small victory. As she'd recognised the photo, I was now sure Arthur Crouch came from Brighton Beach.

Chapter 6

I went to bed as soon as I'd finished my coffee.

Mabelle had gulped hers like she hadn't drunk for a week and then scarpered. She couldn't get out of the place fast enough.

I'd had no chance to challenge her about her lie before she'd made her hasty exit. I couldn't do it in front of Ernestina in case it blew up into a row. And, anyway, I sensed there was a bit of frost between Aunt Ernestina and her errant niece.

Now I was lying on a lumpy mattress staring at a brown stain on the ceiling and wondering what the hell I was doing. My eyelids felt like iron shutters but I couldn't sleep. Too many questions were chasing around my mind.

And the one that was running faster than all the others was: why didn't Mabelle admit she knew who Arthur Crouch was? Perhaps it was because she knew he was a crook. But that wouldn't necessarily seal her lips. If she knew him but didn't want to say so, there had to be a reason. Could it be because she'd also been involved in his criminal activity, whatever that was? Or could it be that she was scared about the consequences if she shopped his true identity to a journalist - because then the news would very soon reach the cops? Or perhaps it was because she knew him through her own career as a stripper. Mabelle was an attractive woman who would certainly cut a striking figure when she'd shed her seven veils. Percy the python wouldn't be enough to frighten off the most ardent suitors. And, anyway, Percy had disappeared.

Mabelle's reaction had made me wonder who I could ask with confidence in what seemed to be a tight-knit community. If Crouch had been - perhaps still was - a captain of the criminal world in these parts, he might have powerful friends. Perhaps dangerous friends. They wouldn't take kindly to a Brit turning up and asking awkward questions. I realised that I would have to think carefully about whom I shared my knowledge of Crouch with in this town.

But I wasn't going to solve these problems tonight. I was too tired and I was alone in an unfamiliar city. I closed my eyes, manoeuvred into a less lumpy portion of the mattress and tried to sleep.

I felt a sharp prick in my leg. It seemed I wasn't alone after all.

I was awoken by the revs of a loud engine and the clang of metal.

I heaved myself out of bed, went to the window and pulled the curtain to one side. My room looked out over the flat roof of the extension. Its roof was just a couple of feet below the window ledge. In the street, a Brooklyn garbage truck was crawling down the street. A team of garbage collectors hustled around it. They hauled bins from yards in front of the houses and tossed the contents in the back of the truck.

I looked at my watch. Half past eight. I'd slept deeply - despite the attention of the bed bugs. There were five bite marks on my legs and a couple on my stomach. I decided that if Ernestina couldn't find me a bug-free room, I'd pack my case, twitch my mantle blue, and head to fresh woods and pastures new.

I found Ernestina in her kitchen, a small room with a damp musty smell somewhere between a laundry and a funeral parlour. She was sitting at a table leafing through the pages of a clothing catalogue. She had it open at the corsets.

She looked up as I walked in and said: "You look perkier than you did yesterday. There ain't nothing like a good night's sleep."

I said: "I'll let you know when I get one. It turned out I was the midnight buffet for the bed bugs. I need a bug-free room."

"You saying my bed got little critters living in it?"

"I can show you the evidence."

"You've got no evidence that I want to see."

"Then perhaps I should show the city council's sanitation department the evidence. The garbage men are in the street at the moment."

Ernestina closed the catalogue and angrily folded her arms. "Well, I don't want no trouble so you can take the back room. I've got another lodger coming this evening - Hank Shultz, one of my regulars - and Hank ain't a complainer like some people I could mention. He'll sleep like a baby in the side room."

"In that case, I'll move my things into the back room."

I left Ernestina muttering under her breath about "trouble-making limeys" and went upstairs.

I gave the bed in the back room a close inspection before I unpacked my suitcase. I lay on the bed to think about my next move. My experience with Mabelle had convinced me it would be dangerous to walk around town flashing the photo of Crouch in front of random people.

I considered showing the picture to the local police. But my experience on the beach with the uniformed cop made me feel they wouldn't welcome an outsider barging in and asking awkward questions. They wouldn't divulge confidential information to an out-of-town reporter who turned up on their doorstep. Besides, I couldn't rule out that there'd be bent cops in the local force who passed along tips about possible trouble in return for pay-offs.

The more I thought about it, the more I realised I'd ruled out pretty much all the population of Brighton Beach from helping with my enquiries.

But there was one man I hadn't ruled out. I hauled myself off the bed, shrugged into my jacket and clattered down the stairs.

Ben Stoker took a long drag from a thin cheroot and studied the card I'd flipped across his desk.

He put the card down and exhaled a long stream of smoke. "So you're a crime reporter on the *Evening Chronicle* in Brighton, England."

It hadn't been difficult to find the offices of the *Brighton Beach*

Banner (incorporating the *Coney Island Chatterer*). It occupied a building on Neptune Avenue not far from Fifth Street. I had no trouble getting in to see the editor either. When I'd walked into the paper's front-office, the only obstacle was a pile of returns of last week's paper stacked next to the door.

Stoker picked up a heap of galley proofs he'd been correcting and tossed them into an out-tray. He was the wrong side of sixty. The lines on his forehead and around his mouth had sharpened the edges of his face as though a sculptor had carved them. He could have still cut a handsome figure but dark bags under his eyes smudged his cheeks. They made him look like a man who'd just gone ten bruising rounds with Rocky Marciano. Stoker had thick black hair which he combed back from his forehead and held in place with hair cream. He was wearing a grey-striped shirt rolled up to the elbows and a blue tie held in place by a gold tie-pin.

When he spoke it was like only the front part of his brain concentrated on what he was saying. The rest was thinking about something else. He was a man with a lot on his mind - and not just what he was going to put on the front page next week.

He said: "We had a crime reporter once. Now all we've got is the crime."

I said: "I read your splash in last week's paper about the numbers game scam. I got the main drift of the piece but missed out on the background detail."

"Sure. We should've run a sidebar to explain it, but I've got no-one here to write it."

"From what I understand, the numbers game is an illegal betting racket."

"You got it. Mobsters run around town selling tickets. Mugs buy a ticket with three random numbers. They win if their numbers match the last three digits of what's called 'the handle'. That's a random number which no-one can foretell. In most cases, it's the last three digits of the total value of money staked by gamblers in a day at a well-known racetrack, such as Belmont Park. The figures for the previous day are published in most New York daily papers like the *Times* and the *Trib.*"

"So with three random numbers, the chance of winning is nine hundred and ninety-nine to one?"

"Simple math, but the punters don't get it. That's where the racketeers make their money. They pay out no more than six hundred to one on winning tickets."

"So that forty cents on the dollar goes into their own pockets," I said. "Don't the cops do anything about it?"

Stoker took a final drag on his cheroot and stubbed it out in an ashtray. He threw back his head and laughed. "Sure, they put on a show once in a while. But that forty cents in the dollar margin isn't there for nothing. Some of it ends up in a slush fund for pay-offs. Are you gonna tell me there's no cop in Brighton, merry old England, that hasn't once in a while taken a bent penny?"

"No."

"Same here."

I said: "I saw the splash in last week's paper. Can't have made you popular with the numbers guys."

"If you don't make enemies on a campaigning newspaper you're not doing your job right."

"But they have to be the right kind of enemies," I said.

Stoker grunted.

"And you need the resources to take them on," I added.

He grunted again. "The *New York Times* we ain't. But there was a time when we had the team to take on any scam artist on our patch."

"But not now?"

"Time was when I thought we had a gang of scribblers could expose a big scandal and win a Pulitzer Prize for our work."

"American's top award for great journalism?"

"Sure. Dreamed of it myself. Walking up to collect the award.

Ben Stoker, Pulitzer Prize winner. Look at me now? Struggling just to keep the paper alive."

"You could still run investigative pieces," I said.

Stoker shrugged. "You're a newspaperman. You know what it takes to run big stories. You need time - and that means money. When I bought this paper back in the days when Harry Truman was still in the White House, we'd carry seventy pages of advertising every week. You saw the last paper."

"I counted eight pages of ads."

"You're sharp. But, yes, and half of those sold on discount. My last reporter left a month ago to join the *Herald Tribune*. I ain't got the budget to hire more. So now it's just me and a handful of voluntary stringers who phone in stories to keep the paper going. Don't know how much longer I can carry on."

"You're thinking of selling?"

Stoker threw back his head and laughed. It was a deep rumbling laugh that started in the chest, magnified itself in his throat, and burst out of the mouth like a factory klaxon blasting off at closing time.

"Sure, I'm thinking of selling. On your way in, you probably noticed the queue of buyers snaking round the block."

"No buyers?" I asked.

"There's a buyer. Snap up the paper tomorrow, if I let him. But the man is an animal - he's behind everything that stinks in Brighton Beach. Leone De Luca. He's ruthless and he's vicious. He's the kind who'd sell his old mother's bones to boil for glue if he thought he could make a tax-free dollar from it. You've not been in town long enough to know him."

"I've heard the name a couple of times. And I know the type from my own town."

"I'd rather close the paper and sink the presses in the Hudson River than sell to him. But it looks as though he may get the paper anyway. And when that happens he'll turn the *Banner* into a cheerleader for every racket in town. Trouble is, there's nothing I can do to stop him."

I thought about that for a moment. Mabelle knew Crouch and had worked for De Luca. So did Crouch know De Luca? If Crouch were a captain of crime, I figured he did. That gave me an idea. I leaned forward and looked Stoker in the eye.

"Perhaps there's a way we can help each other," I said.

Chapter 7

Ben Stoker arched his eyebrows in disbelief.

Stoker was a decent bloke wondering whether he still had anything to be decent about. Disbelief was allowable.

"Sure, you can help me save the paper," he said. "Just hand over three thousand seven hundred and forty-three dollars in cash."

"You'll have to explain that," I said.

"It's the money I owe the loan company. Eighteen months ago the presses needed a major overhaul just to keep them running. I didn't have the cash to stump up for the work so I took out a loan, repayable over five years. Looked right at the time, but since then things have got worse. It's been a question of making the monthly loan payment or paying the newsprint bill. No contest. Without newsprint the paper doesn't come out."

"How many payments are overdue?"

"Three. Under the terms of the agreement when that happens I have to repay the full loan. When I missed the third regular payment last week, that clause kicked in. Any day now, I expect to get a notice to pay up in full. So unless someone dumps a heap of greenbacks on this desk, I'm out of here."

I took a deep breath. I felt my stomach tighten, my heart beat faster. Stoker was the kind of bloke who held his emotion inside. Even so, I could tell he was stuck somewhere between anger and helplessness. He was going to lose his paper and there was nothing he could do about it.

I said: "I guess you asked for a further extension and the loan company turned you down."

"Nope."

"Why not?"

"Because the loan company sold the loan to Leone De Luca."

My jaw dropped south at that. Stoker read the shock on my

face.

"Can they do that? Is it legal?" I asked.

"Sure, it's legal. I checked it out with the paper's attorney. But it stinks. I took out a loan with a reputable loan company - then I find I owe the money to a shark."

"Why did the loan company sell the loan on?"

"Why does anyone do anything when De Luca asks them? Because they know what will happen if they don't. And I guess De Luca spread a few of his dirty bucks around to encourage the loan company's vice-president to sign the deal."

"And De Luca wants to buy the *Banner* because it's a thorn in his flesh?"

"And a pain in his ass."

"Yes, I've heard he's especially sensitive in that department. But you've kept the pressure on De Luca in the paper?"

"If you've gotta go, might as well be in a blaze of glory. When I publish that last issue there won't be a fanfare of trumpets or a procession along the boardwalk, but there'll be a hell of a story on the front page."

"I'd like to see that." I meant it.

"Sure. When I got into this game I dreamed of one day winning that Pulitzer. Put me up there with journalism's greats. It won't happen now."

"Dreams should never die," I said.

Stoker nodded thoughtfully, but his mind was on his current problems.

He said: "So you see, friend, unless you've got a stash of cash in your billfold, there ain't much you can do to help me."

Stoker's eyes bored into me as I reached into my inside pocket and brought out my wallet.

I said: "You're right about the cash. But I've got something else I'd like to show you."

I took out the picture of Arthur Crouch and laid it on the desk in front of Stoker.

"What's this?" He reached for a pair of wire-framed glasses, looped them around his ears and leaned forward to look more closely at the picture.

I spent five minutes telling Stoker how Shirley had spotted Crouch wearing gloves on a hot day, how Chaz tried to rob him on the Volk's Railway, and how I recovered the attaché case Crouch was carrying.

"There was twelve thousand dollars in the case, a false passport, and an air ticket to New York," I said. "The envelope with the passport and ticket was addressed to Arthur Crouch, Brighton Beach. Put all that together and you have a big league crook."

"Seems logical," Stoker said. "I don't recognise the name. But that's because it'll be false."

I nodded. "What about the picture?"

Stoker picked it up and held it six inches from his nose. He let out a long sigh.

"You know, I've seen this face before. Couple of years ago there was a lot of trouble in nightclubs around New York - around the whole States. There are some legit spots, but there are plenty of places that are dives - clip joints which aim to separate mugs from their money. De Luca has one here in Brighton Beach - the Hoochie-Coochie Club. Well, gang bosses used to stick to their own territory but some got greedy. They set up joints on rivals' home turf. It got pretty rough. Doormen got beat up and there were a couple of arson attacks. Miracle no-one was killed. Cops were getting involved and none of the racketeers wanted that. They made a point of sorting out their own shit. Anyway, I got a tip there was gonna be a meeting of the bosses - a mobsters' peace conference, if you like - at the Hoochie-Coochie. So I hired a freelance photographer to snap the comings and goings. In those days, I still had a few dollars to pay a lensman. In fact, the event turned out to be a damp squib, but my man hid up in the hardware store opposite the club and got some shots - and I gotta feeling your Crouch is in one of them."

"But having a picture won't give us a name."

Stoker levered himself out of his seat and moved towards a bank of filing cabinets. "It could do," he said. "In those days, I had a contact in the Hoochie-Coochie. Used to meet her in a milk bar up in Bay Ridge. I remember she put names to some of the faces we'd shot. Not all of them."

"Do you still have your contact at the club?"

Stoker reached the filing cabinets, looked back at me over his shoulder. "She's still at the club, but she ain't a contact anymore. Tips came at twenty dollars a pop - and I can't pop the loot these days."

He yanked out one of the filing cabinet drawers and rummaged inside. Pulled out a fat buff folder.

"These are the shots," he said.

He crossed back to his desk and put the folder in front of me. "Be my guest - you can use one of the reporters' desks over by the door. Don't mind if I get on with these proofs, do you?"

I said: "If my Crouch turns out to be a known Brighton Beach crook, I'll write the story for you. No charge."

Stoker grinned, for the first time since we'd met. "That's what I figured."

I carried the folder over to the reporters' desk and sat down. Opened the folder. There must have been around forty or fifty photos in the file - most eight by tens, the size a paper would use for reproduction. They showed shady types in sharp two hundred dollar suits, mohair coats and slouch hats. The kind of characters you'd cross the street to avoid. Most of them kept their heads down so their faces didn't show. Those that didn't should've. That mobsters' convention had attracted some ugly types. It didn't take me long to run through the prints - with no luck.

But the greatest interest was in a couple of dozen sheets of contacts - pages of thumbnail shots printed size-for-size from rolls of negatives. Each sheet held around thirty shots. I held the sheets up to the light one by one and studied each contact carefully. Someone - presumably Stoker - had put a little tick against each contact which had a name. But on the first sheet, only three hoodlums had been identified.

Fifteen sheets into the pile my eyes felt like they'd been rinsed in turpentine. Many of the shots showed the same crooks. I despaired of spotting Crouch. There was no reason why he'd had to be at the Hoochie-Coochie. I picked up the next sheet with no enthusiasm - but then my eyes widened and focused. The pictures showed two men coming out of a well-lit doorway. The shots had been taken in quick succession, probably by a camera with a motorised shutter. The man on the left of the shots was old, thin and walked with a slight stoop. Or perhaps he'd knocked back too much bourbon in the club. Or perhaps he'd partaken of the club's other pleasures - and at his age, too. He was another blank face as far as I was concerned.

But I knew the face of the man on the right. No question. His hair was styled differently to when he rode the Volk's Railway. He was wearing a sports jacket with a show handkerchief neatly folded in the breast pocket. He had his hand on the other man's shoulder and a shit-eating grin on his face - as though he was delivering the punch-line of a dirty joke.

There was no doubt in my mind. He was the man I knew as Arthur Crouch.

A neat tick by the photo told me that at least one of the figures in the picture had a name. I turned over the contact sheet praying that it was Crouch.

A note on the back read: "17. R/h Elliott Bellwether."

I sat back and grinned. A wide satisfying one.

So Arthur Crouch's real name was Elliott Bellwether.

But who was Bellwether?

I glanced across the office. Stoker had his head down over his desk correcting proofs. I pulled the folder towards me and was about to close it, when a scrap of paper slipped out from between two of the photographs. A name and phone number was written on it. The same handwriting as that on the back of the contact sheets. Presumably Stoker's.

The paper read: Tulip Fragrance and added a New York city phone number.

I pulled out my notebook and scribbled the name and number in it.

Then I closed the file, keeping the sheet with Bellwether's pictures separate.

Stoker looked up at me with tired eyes as I approached his desk.

"Any luck?" he asked.

I showed him the picture and said: "Elliott Bellwether. Ring any bells with you?"

Stoker squinted at the picture. Stroked his chin, perhaps to make sure it was still there.

"Yeah, I remember at the time we wondered what he was doing at the meeting. The guy's an attorney but doesn't seem to practice much. He doesn't run to an office or appear in court. Lives in a swish pad down near the ocean." He mentioned an address. Looked at the picture again with questioning eyes.

"Perhaps he's one of those *eminences grise,*" he said.

"A power behind the throne. Behind Leone De Luca's throne?"

"Could be, but I've not heard him take any of De Luca's business - civil or criminal. And there's plenty to take."

"Perhaps he was working for the other bloke in the picture. Any idea who he is?" I asked.

Stoker gave his chin another speculative rub. "No joy on that one. Although, wait - I recall my contact said she'd heard he was from out of town, perhaps Oklahoma."

"I feel a song coming on."

Stoker frowned. "I feel a funeral dirge coming on."

I said: "Mind if I borrow this contact sheet for a day or two."

Stoker shrugged: "Keep it. It's one thing De Luca won't get his hands on when he takes over here."

I stuffed it in my pocket. I said: "I'll call you if I get a lead on anything."

"Sure."

I left Ben's office wondering whether Tulip Fragrance was at home.

Chapter 8

I rang Tulip Fragrance from a pay phone in a drug store a hundred yards down the street from Stoker's office.

I figured that if Tulip was a girl who worked at a nightclub into the small hours, she'd be a girl who slept in during the morning. I just hoped she'd be sleeping in alone.

The phone was answered after nine rings.

A sleepy voice said: "If you're looking for a girl, Tulip's petals ain't open yet."

I said: "Ben Stoker sends his regards."

She said: "Who did you say?"

"Ben Stoker. Editor of the *Brighton Beach Banner*." Silence. "Incorporating the *Coney Island Chatterer*," I added.

"You're tugging my titties. You're not Ben."

"That's the correct answer for ten dollars. You win another ten when you answer a question I have."

"You've got a funny voice. Like that English actor. What's his name?"

"David Niven?"

"No. Sydney Greenstreet. *Casablanca* is just my all-time favourite movie."

I said: "My real name's Colin Crampton. I have a proposition for you."

"I don't turn tricks before lunch. It ain't nice."

"Turning tricks or lunch? Never mind. It's important that I see you. I believe Ben used to pay twenty dollars for tip-offs."

"I ain't doing nothing that's getting me into trouble."

"Nothing I've got to ask will prevent you from leading your spotless life."

Tulip giggled. "You're funny - like Sydney Greenstreet. Are you also as fat?"

"No. And if you let me come and see you I'll prove it."

"Ten minutes, then." She reeled off an address in Sixth Street, north of Neptune Avenue. "Ring the bell twice. And no funny business."

The line went dead.

It took me eight minutes to reach Tulip's apartment.

It was on the second floor of a six-storey block that was probably put up during the nineteen-thirties. Perhaps with money from Roosevelt's New Deal. Thirty years on the place was showing its age. It was built out of large brownstone bricks. In some places they bulged and ties had been put in to prevent walls cracking. The metal window frames were grey with old rust. Most of the tiles on the steps leading to the front door had cracked.

There was a row of six bells with a name card in a brass holder beside five of them. The card in Tulip's holder was missing. I rang the bell anyway. And waited.

A minute later the door opened. Tulip was a tall girl with a statuesque figure that was all breasts and buttocks. She could have modelled for an egg-timer. One of those where the sand runs through once for soft-boiled and you turn it over again for hard boiled. But I wasn't thinking of eggs right now. Tulip had skin like brushed velvet, a mouth with lips that came together in a gentle pout, and large brown eyes with long lashes. Her arms were slender and her hands delicate. Her fingernails were as sharp as an eagle's talons and painted scarlet.

She was wearing a flame red dress which hugged in all the right places. It had a couple of straps which looped over each shoulder. The hem ended just above her knees.

Tulip's eyes danced with amusement as she looked me up and down like I was a racehorse and she was just about to stake a bundle.

She said: "You're sure nothing like ol' Sydney. And with that jacket and tie, you look like some real square cat."

I said: "But I'm thoroughly house trained and won't make a mess on the carpet."

She said: "I ain't got no carpet. But if I did, I'd make sure it was a magic one - so I could fly away from this dump."

"Before you do, perhaps I could come in."

"Guess I better show you some real American hospitality."

I stepped into the hall and we climbed the stairs together.

"You ain't from round here?" Tulip said.

"England."

"Gee, you gotta butler?"

"I had to fire him on account of he didn't tug his forelock correctly."

Tulip giggled in a soft husky way, like steam escaping from a pipe.

She opened the door of her apartment and led the way inside.

She was right. The place didn't have a carpet. The floorboards had been stained and polished but were now scratched and dark with age. The wallpaper featured isosceles triangles in a geometrical pattern that would have old Pythagoras thinking up a new theorem.

Tulip wiggled her hypotenuse across the room and sat down in a fat old easy chair, one of a pair. I took the other without waiting to be invited.

I said: "I'm looking for a man."

Tulip said: "This ain't that kind of place, honey child. But you can swing any way you want in this town."

"I'm not looking for any man."

"Anything that keeps the world turning is fine by me."

"The man I'm looking for is almost certainly in England at the moment."

"Then you're looking in the wrong place."

"But I think he came from Brighton Beach."

Tulip held up her hand. "Just a minute, honey child. You're moving too quick for me. We gotta agree the terms of trade here."

"Ben told me he paid you twenty dollars."

"Sure, Ben was a regular gentleman. I could trust Ben to keep his mouth buttoned. He knows the information I got is dangerous."

"Dangerous - to whom?"

"To me, honey. If certain people knew I was sharing it about. And, gee, I just love that English way you say 'to whom?'."

"I understand the need for discretion. Ben told me."

"Why ain't Ben come himself?"

"He's a bit short."

"Ben ain't short. He's six foot three. In his socks."

"He's a bit short of twenty dollar bills. I, on the other hand, have a small wad of bills with your name on. If you can help me with one teensy-weensy bit of information."

Tulip giggled again. "Teensy-weensy. You crack me up."

"Let's hope nothing falls off until we've finished. I'd like to show you a photograph and ask you whether you recognise anyone in it."

Tulip grinned. "Not so fast, honey. Let's see the greenbacks first."

I reached inside my jacket for my wallet. Opened it and counted out twenty dollars. Stood up, crossed the room and handed the money to Tulip.

Then I took the photo out of my pocket.

I said: "This is a contact printed from a negative, so it's small but the two figures in it are clearly shown facing the camera."

I handed the photo to Tulip. She took it and held it in front of her face. Her eyebrows slanted inwards as she concentrated.

She said: "When was this picture taken?"

"Ben tells me about two years ago. When there was a lot of trouble in the nightclub world - with beatings and burnings."

Tulip nodded. "I remember that was a bad time. Even the Big L was worried."

"The Big L?"

"De Luca. The guy who owns the Hoochie-Coochie. Leone De Luca."

"Ben told me there was a meeting there. Of nightclub owners. To try and resolve their differences."

Tulip gave a little snort. "Sure - instead of beating the crap out of each other."

"But do you know these blokes?"

"Sure. The guy on the right is called Elliott Bellwether. Weird name. He's friendly with Big L - you sometimes see them huddled over a bottle of Jim Beam in the booth at the back of the downstairs bar. Pally as a pair of pickpockets they are."

"I've heard Bellwether is a lawyer, but he doesn't practice."

"No? Not down at the courthouse, maybe. But what do you think all that talk is in the back booth. Not scuttlebutt about the latest ball game."

Tulip could be right. A lawyer doesn't need to dress in black jacket and striped trousers or sit behind a mahogany desk to dispense legal advice. If you're telling a racketeer how to skirt round the law, the back booth in a dive like the Hoochie-Coochie will do just fine.

I asked: "Ever seen the second bloke in the picture?"

"Sure. And just two weeks ago."

That sharpened my interest. "As recently as that?"

"Sure," Tulip said.

"He was with Bellwether?"

"Yes. I was with a client, but I saw the pair of them sitting at the bar. Then they ordered some food and had it served in a private dining room upstairs. Up there for three hours they were. And well soused when they came down - the pair of them. Pleased with themselves. Patting each other on the back. A real pals-for-life act."

"Who is the second bloke?"

"I don't know for sure. But I know his name."

Tulip looked at me with teasing eyes as though she couldn't decide whether to tell her secret.

I put on a posh English accent and said: "One would be awfully interested to hear it."

Tulip giggled. "It was Newton. I was talking with Millie the hat-check girl when the pair came out and Bellwether said something like, 'Mr Newton's hat, please'."

"And that's all?"

"Not quite." Tulip did that teasing eye thing again.

I obliged with: "Come on old fruit, spill the beans."

She giggled, more loudly this time. "His first is Willis. As he was leaving, Bellwether said, 'Thanks for all your advice, Willis. There'll be some bonus bucks for you if the big job comes off.'"

"The big job," I said. "You definitely heard those words."

Tulip nodded.

"But they didn't say what the big job was?"

"In front of a hostess and hat-check girl? Wise up, buster."

"Did De Luca sit in on the meeting two weeks ago?"

"Sure. Not much happens in the Hoochie-Coochie unless Big L gets a slice of the action."

"How well do you know him?"

"As well as a girl can know any man. Well enough to know that Big L is not big everywhere."

"What's he really like?"

"He's mean and he's vicious. But when he's with his top-drawer friends, he acts big and talks big - and thinks he's as good as them. But that's because deep down he knows he's not."

"And he entertains these top-drawer friends at the Hoochie-Coochie?"

"Only the ones he wants to compromise. He prefers to mix with the nobs in that snooty gentleman's club down near the beach."

"What's it called?"

"I think it's the Founding Fathers. But De Luca ain't no

founding father. He's got big ambitions to be like one of them - but if your daddy were the wrong man, there's no way you gonna be a founding father."

"And De Luca's daddy was the wrong man?"

"I don't think Big L even knows who his daddy is."

"But De Luca did know Bellwether and Newton?"

"Sure he knew them. And I reckon he's up to his scrawny neck in whatever scam they were planning."

I said: "One last question. Between the time the photo was taken and two weeks ago, did you ever see Bellwether and Newton together?"

"Nope. But that doesn't mean they weren't together some other place. They seemed mighty pally when they met. As though they were renewing an old friendship. Know what I mean?"

I stood up.

Tulip looked disappointed. "You gotta go? I thought we could get acquainted more closely."

I smiled. "Some other time, perhaps. Maybe I could catch you at the Hoochie-Coochie."

"Sure," said Tulip. "And give my regards to Ben. Tell the old bastard if he needs a loan, I can stump up five dollars."

"I'll pass on the message," I said.

Tulip stood up. "Guess I better get some beauty sleep before the club tonight."

I walked over to the door and opened it. Paused on the threshold. "Beauty sleep? Leave some for the rest of us."

I heard Tulip giggling as I went out and closed the door behind me.

Chapter 9

One thing you learn fast when you become a crime reporter is that there are no limits to dishonesty.

I was thinking about this as I walked down Sixth Street towards Neptune Avenue. Arthur Crouch had turned out to be called Elliott Bellwether. But wait a moment... There is no rule which says a crook has to limit himself to one alias. Suppose Elliott Bellwether's real name was something else. Or suppose he had a whole address book of other names.

So far I had only two contacts who knew Arthur Crouch as Elliott Bellwether. Ben Stoker and Tulip Fragrance. But if Bellwether was known around town as a lawyer - albeit not practising - perhaps that was his real name.

I reached the corner of Sixth and Neptune. My plan had been to head back to the *Banner's* office and tell Stoker what I'd learnt from Tulip. But I had a better idea. At least, I knew where Bellwether lived - when he wasn't hiding in England waiting for new false papers. Stoker had described Bellwether's apartment as a swish pad near the ocean. I headed south towards the boardwalk.

As I walked, I thought about the other name I now had in the frame - Willis Newton. Tulip thought he was from out of town, perhaps Oklahoma, a thousand miles away in the prairies. I didn't think Stoker would recognise the name because he hadn't recognised his picture. And when Tulip had originally looked at the pictures - after the meeting at the Hoochie-Coochie club two years ago – she hadn't known Newton's name either. It was only two weeks ago when she'd heard it used for the first time. If Newton came from Oklahoma, it was going to be more difficult to discover who he was. As a reporter, I'd start with the telephone directory. But what if Willis Newton was also a *nom de guerre*? But I didn't think so. From the way Tulip had described it, Bellwether had referred to his name quite naturally.

But I didn't have time to pursue that line of thought, because I'd reached the apartment block where Elliott Bellwether apparently lived in a swish pad. It didn't look too swish from the outside. In fact, it looked like a child's drawing of a block of flats. Tall, square, flat roof and with oblong windows equally spaced along the front on each floor. No doubt the architect wanted to get home early that day.

There was a canopy over the entrance and a glass door which opened into a foyer with a faux marble floor.

I pushed on the glass door but it was firmly locked. A panel with thirty-two buttons was recessed into the wall next to the door. Each of the buttons was labelled with the name of the occupant. Bellwether occupied the penthouse apartment at the top of the building. So, perhaps, despite outside appearances, the bloke did live in comfort. At least he'd have a sea view. Three thousand miles of ocean all the way to Europe.

A man who spent too much time gazing at that could build a whole castle of dreams. Perhaps one of those dreams was the "big job" Tulip heard Bellwether mention to Newton. I wondered what that could be. Bellwether had been carrying twelve thousand dollars when he'd been attacked on the Volk's Railway. That was a tidy sum. Perhaps it was his share of the pay-off for the "big job".

I was musing on this when the glass door opened and an old man stepped out. He had a bald head with a fringe of white hair. He had a pencil moustache and wore glasses with thick black frames. He was wearing a blue corduroy jacket and grey flannel trousers.

I thought of stepping around him into the foyer while the door was still open. But the old boy had suspicious grey eyes behind those thick-rimmed glasses.

So I stood to one side to let him through and said: "Morning."

He nodded at me and said: "Morning."

I said: "Do you happen to know whether Elliott is in?"

When you use a first name, people assume you already know the person you've mentioned. They're much more likely to answer your questions.

The old boy said: "Elliott. Don't know any Elliott."

I said: "Elliott Bellwether. Penthouse flat."

"Oh, him. Don't often see him. He keeps himself to himself."

"So you don't know whether he's in?"

"You think I'm his social secretary?"

"No, it's just that I'm over from England and hoped to catch up with him. We met briefly while he was in the old country a couple of weeks ago and I was hoping to renew our acquaintance."

I didn't mention how we met - and I didn't say that I was certain Bellwether was still in the UK.

"Well, I guess you'll have to catch up with him some other time."

I looked up admiringly at the building. "Nice place," I said. "Elliott didn't tell me how long he'd been living here."

"Longer than me. And I've been here eight years."

"I guess with a penthouse apartment, Elliott gets a lot of visitors."

"Some we could do without."

My eyebrows lifted half an inch at that. "What do you mean?"

"I mean we could do without foreign types. Two months ago I was coming down the stairs, I heard two people talking in some language I didn't know while they waited for the elevator. One of them was Bellwether. I recognised his voice from a couple of times we'd exchanged pleasantries when we'd passed in the foyer."

"Elliott never told me he spoke foreign languages."

"I had him down as the kind of guy who doesn't tell people a lot of things."

"Do you know which language it was? I'd like to surprise

Elliott that I know next time I meet him."

"Do I look like a professor of linguistics? All I know is that it sure wasn't a language I've heard spoken. And we got folks who come from other countries down at the Old Timers' Lunch Club. And that's where I'm due now. So if you'll excuse me..."

He hurried down the street and turned the corner.

I thought about hanging around outside to intercept more residents, but from what the old boy had said, it didn't seem like any others would be able to add anything useful. And his mention of lunch made me realise I hadn't had anything to eat since breakfast.

I decided to grab a sandwich and then see what I could discover about the second mystery man.

Willis Newton.

I found Brighton Beach public library easily after I'd eaten a salt beef sandwich in a diner close to the boardwalk.

The library was one block from the boardwalk on First Road at Brighton Beach Avenue. The place was housed in a brick building which was in a sort of art deco style, but not enough to get Clarice Cliff excited.

Inside a young woman with shoulder-length brunette hair tied back in a bun was standing at the issues desk. She had peachy cheeks, a wide mouth, and a pert button of a nose. She was flipping through a pile of filing cards. Her name badge read Joy Novak.

I walked up to the desk and said: "If you shuffle and cut those, we could improvise a game of poker."

Joy looked up and said: "Only if you want to lose your shirt. My father taught me to play poker when I was four."

I said: "And you haven't looked back."

She gave me a sharp look and said: "I manage. Anyway, are you looking for a book or trying to pick me up?"

"I'll start with the book. Do you keep the index of The *New*

York Times in this library?"

"Normally not. But the library at Borough Park is being renovated and the indexes and microfilm for the *Grey Lady* have been moved down here until the work is finished."

"Could I look at the indexes?"

She put down the filing cards and said: "Follow me."

The indexes - a separate volume for each year - had been stored in a side room off the main library. The most recent volume covered 1961 and other volumes ran back as far as 1908. While I'd been eating my sandwich in the diner, I'd thought that if any newspaper had ever carried a story about Willis Newton, it would be in the *New York Times*. It was the nearest thing the United States had to a national newspaper. It carried stories from right across the country.

But now I was sitting in a poky room facing a shelf full of *Times* index books, it didn't seem such a great idea. It would take me hours to work through them. But perhaps I could find a way to shorten the task. I had the picture of Newton and Bellwether in my pocket. I took it out and had another look.

Newton was no youngster. From the way his face had lined, his hair receded and he'd grown a beer gut, I reckoned he must be at least seventy. My best guess would be between seventy and seventy-five. So, as this was 1963, it was reasonable to assume he could have been born around 1890. But it was unlikely his criminal career had bloomed in any serious way before he was twenty. Which put 1910 as my marker date. That meant I needed to look through all the indexes between that date and 1961, the last volume available.

I sat there pondering whether to work backwards or forwards. Backwards would give me details of Newton's most recent criminal enterprise. But forwards would build a picture of how his criminal career developed.

And, I reminded myself, only if the *New York Times* had carried a story about him. Which could be a long shot.

I reached for the 1910 volume and leafed the pages to the letter N. I ran my finger down the column hunting for any references to Newton. I was surprised how many of them there were. The most famous of them all - Sir Isaac - merited six mentions during the year in various scientific articles. But there was no Willis Newton.

I closed the book and glanced at my watch. I'd spent fewer than five minutes on the volume, so perhaps this wouldn't take as long as I'd imagined.

I reached for 1911 feeling like a man about to crack a story.

But as I closed the volume for 1923, my optimism had taken a severe knock.

Willis Newton seemed to have led a blameless life. Or certainly not one worthy of mention in the *New York Times*.

I reached for the 1924 volume, turned to the Ns. Ran my finger down the column. And there it was: Newton, Willis.

And not just one article either. Willis Newton had hit the headlines in the *Grey Lady* - and, I suspected, newspapers across the country - for the summer of 1924.

I felt like a set of illuminations had lit up in my brain. As bright and brash as the ones that flashed along Brighton prom. It was going to give me a string of headlines - and make my name as a reporter.

For I now knew why Elliott Bellwether was mates with Willis Newton.

And why Bellwether was in Britain with twelve thousand dollars in his attaché case.

Chapter 10

Over the next two hours, I pieced the story together.

I made a list of all the references to Newton in the *New York Times'* indexes, then looked up the relevant articles on the microfilms of back issues.

The story began on 12 June 1924 when a postal train carrying boxes of bank notes from the United States' Federal Reserve Bank left Union Station in Chicago. The train was due to travel hundreds of miles north and west, stopping at small towns along the way to offload the notes to local banks.

But the train never made it further than a remote point where a road crossed the rail tracks at Rondout, Illinois. Willis Newton had crept aboard the train secretly before it left Chicago. As the train headed north towards Wisconsin, he moved through the coaches and climbed aboard the engine. He intended to force the driver to stop the train at the Rondout crossing point. The plan was that other members of the gang hiding at Rondout would storm the train and steal the money.

It didn't work out quite like that. Faced with a violent threat from Newton, the driver was so nervous he overshot the crossing point. Newton forced him at gunpoint to back up. In the confusion, one gang member shot and injured one of the others. And, in the panic, someone shouted Newton's name which was overheard by one of the train's crew. Yet despite the fracas at the scene, the gang made off with three million dollars in cash, the biggest train robbery of all time.

And my research didn't end there. I moved from index to microfilm reader and back again until the table was littered with books and boxes of film.

I discovered that even before Newton had masterminded the Rondout heist, he and his brother Wylie had robbed five other trains. Their takings from the previous thefts hadn't put them in the big league and they'd served their time in prison, but one thing was for sure. After the Rondout snatch, Willis Newton was the number one man when it came to train robberies.

He was a team player, too. I read the *Times'* reports of the Rondout trial. Newton had joined up with a pair of Chicago gangsters and a crooked postal inspector to rob the train. He knew the value of working together - and the rewards it could reap. And he knew the value of planning - and how it could all fall apart when things went wrong.

But what was the connection with an audacious heist thirty-nine years ago and the Volk's Railway robbery? I tried to put the events in order in my mind.

It started two years ago when the nightclub peace summit took place at the Hoochie-Coochie Club. Newton had been there because he owned nightclubs - financed by proceeds from his robberies. Bellwether was there, no doubt as De Luca's legal advisor. Newton and Bellwether may not have known one another before the meeting - but they were certainly firm friends after it. I had Ben's photograph which showed the pair of them hugging one another like a pair of drunken freshmen at a fraternity initiation.

Move forward two years and somehow Bellwether became involved with the gang planning the Bridego robbery. It was an ambitious undertaking and nobody had ever done anything as big in Britain before. But they had in America. And it just so happened that Bellwether knew the very man who had pulled it off. He arranged to meet Newton again and ask for his advice. And from the way the robbery was carried out, it looked as though Newton had provided it. For the train was stopped at a crossing point - Bridego bridge - where the gang could storm it, a repeat of the tactics used in the Rondout caper.

But how did the advice get from Newton to the British gang? Newton could hardly come to Britain himself. With a long prison record, he'd show up on passport checks at air terminals and sea ports. The answer was clear. Bellwether was the go-between who passed information from Newton to the British gang.

When I'd interviewed Mrs Colman, Bellwether's landlady in Brighton, she'd told me he'd arrived a week before the robbery took place. (Of course, she knew him as Arthur Crouch.) And he'd visited London a couple of days before. He was like the consultant who comes in with all the answers. But, as a foreign national, he couldn't be involved in the raid. So, I reasoned, it was arranged that after he'd delivered his advice, he intended to leave the country the evening before the raid took place. That way he couldn't be questioned if something went wrong. When the heist went down, he'd be flying westward across the Atlantic. Except that it didn't work out like that - and now Bellwether was hiding out in Britain.

I slumped back in my chair. I was exhausted. My mind was whirling - wouldn't stop - like a fly-wheel in a machine, rotating even though the electricity had been turned off. I couldn't take in the implications of it all.

I got up, shrugged into my jacket and walked back to the library's issues desk.

Joy was still shuffling filing cards.

She looked up as I approached the desk and smiled. "Did you find what you were looking for?"

"Most of it," I said absent-mindedly.

"Glad to be of service."

I turned to leave.

"I'll give you that game of poker some time," she said.

"Look forward to it."

She winked. "If you're a gambling man, we could make it strip poker. Although, I should warn you I never lose."

I managed a half-hearted grin. "I'll come wearing an extra pair of long johns and sock suspenders."

"You'll still lose."

"Not today. I'm feeling lucky."

Joy's mocking laughter followed me as I pushed through the door.

I reeled into the street stunned by the conclusions I'd reached in the library.

My body pulsated with excitement - and not just at the prospect of beating Joy at strip poker.

If the links I'd made were correct, there'd been a conspiracy which reached across the Atlantic from America to Britain to rob the Night Mail. It was the biggest story I'd ever landed. It would make headlines around the world.

But I couldn't write any of it because I didn't have a shred of proof. Figgis would have tossed my copy straight in his bin - and then lectured me on the expensive perils of libel.

Besides, even if my theory was correct, there were still holes in the story. Still things I couldn't explain. Like why Chaz had robbed Bellwether. And why Jerry Clark had thrown himself to his death.

It seemed I'd discovered all that I could in America. If I could find answers to the other questions, they'd be in England.

Long shadows from the buildings across the road reminded me it was late in the afternoon. I wouldn't be in time to catch a plane back to Britain tonight, but in the morning I'd head for Idlewild and Blighty.

I decided to use my last night by paying another visit to Big Buck's diner. The food was no attraction but I wanted to discover why Mabelle had lied about not knowing Bellwether when I'd shown her his photo. Although she'd left her aunt Ernestina's in a hurry, there was no reason why we shouldn't still be on good terms.

Big Buck's was busy when I arrived. A group of hard-hats who'd just knocked off from a nearby building site downed beers. An office type in a grey suit had loosened his tie and undone the top button of his shirt - all the better to tackle one of Buck's giant burgers. A young man and woman sat at a table at the back. They shot furtive glances around the room before gazing adoringly into one another's eyes. They'd be an illicit office romance preparing for the dreadful moment when they had to part and return to their lawful spouses.

The room was alive with cheerful chatter. It was the end of the day. There was beer to drink. And Trini Lopez was belting out *If I Had a Hammer* on the jukebox.

Most of the tables were taken but there was a free one over by the window. I walked over and sat down. Looked out of the window. Rush hour traffic clogged Brighton Beach Avenue in both directions. The driver of a yellow cab blasted his hooter at a newspaper delivery truck that blocked a lane of the road. The truck driver yelled something at the cabbie. The cabbie gave him the finger. City life.

Mabelle hurried out of the kitchen like the chef had just put a bomb on to boil. She was carrying a fresh tray of beer for the hard-hats. She slammed the beer down on the table.

She looked across the room and spotted me. I smiled and waved. She frowned, looked away briefly, and then back at me. She smiled, but it was a smile as warm as a penguin's tail. She glanced back at the kitchen, took out her order pad and made her way across the diner. She slouched up to my table like there was nothing she wanted to do less in the world.

She said: "Didn't expect to see you in here tonight."

I said: "Couldn't resist Big Buck's delicious cooking. Besides, I wanted to see my favourite waitress. On this side of the Atlantic."

"Sure. If Raquel Welch walked in all eyes would be on me."

I said: "Is there a draught in here or has the temperature dropped since yesterday?"

"If you want the weather forecast, buy the *Herald Tribune*."

"I just wanted to thank you for helping me find a place to stay. Do you feel like a drink after work?"

"Sure. In my own company. You gonna order. I can't stand around shooting the breeze all night."

I glanced at the menu. "Bring me the omelette with French fries and a beer," I said. "Hope you get over whatever's bothering you."

Mabelle stomped off with my order.

I sat there wondering what had brought on the frost. It had to be the photo. She'd been keen to get to know me until she'd seen it. Now I felt like I'd just walked in ringing a leper's bell.

A couple of young blokes walked in. They wore leather jackets and had Elvis haircuts. They took a table close to the door and studied a racing paper.

Mabelle bustled back from the kitchen with a couple of plates of burgers. She thumped them on the table in front of the illicit lovers. She scarpered back to the kitchen. Made a point of not looking at me.

I just stared out of the window. Rush-hour traffic still clogged the street. A bus stopped immediately outside the window. I couldn't see across the road.

Further up the street, the traffic lights changed to green. The bus's engine rumbled. A cloud of fumes poured out of its exhaust as it pulled away.

For a moment, the traffic cleared. The fume cloud lifted and I could see the other side of the street. A man was staring into a shop window. He turned as he realised the traffic had cleared.

Even at seventy yards I recognised the aquiline nose, the well-trimmed moustache and the pimple on his jaw.

Reggie Derwent, my travelling companion from the plane, had been watching me.

I leapt up, threw a couple of dollars on the table, and shot out of the diner.

Across the street, I saw Reggie's mouth drop in surprise. Then he moved like a whippet with its tail on fire. The lights had turned red and the traffic had halted. I think he thought I hadn't spotted him. He hustled down the street and turned into an alley.

I stepped into the road. A horn blared and a Ford convertible swerved to avoid me. I jumped back onto the sidewalk. The lights turned green and a fresh stream of vehicles flowed by. I hopped from one foot to another in frustration. It was a minute before I could dash between a gap in the cars to the other side of the street.

By the time I reached the alley, Reggie had vanished. I ran between two towering brick walls, wondering which way he'd gone. I asked myself: what would I do if I wanted to throw off my mark who was now in hot pursuit? I'd use the back doubles to try and circle round behind my pursuer so he was heading away rather than towards me.

I hustled down the alley, past piles of garbage. The place reeked of rotting fish. I dodged slimy puddles on the flagstones. An overflow pipe high up in a wall leaked brown water. The passage came out into a narrow street running at right-angles to it. I had three choices. I could carry on down the alley which continued on the other side of the road. Or I could turn right or left.

What would Reggie have done? A fugitive always turns away from his pursuer. I'd come from the right towards the alley so Reggie's natural instinct was to turn left. But Reggie was no novice at this game. He wanted to get behind me. He'd turn right.

I ran up the road. It turned left in a dog-leg into a dead-end. I was panting like a marathon runner as I reached the end - the backs of three buildings which presumably faced on to a street in front. I stopped, bent double, let my breathing return to normal and listened.

Silence.

Or not quite silence. I could still hear the distant hum of traffic.

But no running feet. No slamming doors. No revving car engines.

Reggie had vanished as rapidly as he'd appeared.

I felt tired and defeated. I tramped back up the road. It turned into the alley. It was dark and deserted. The only sound the steady drip of water from the overflow. A dustbin rattled and a dark shadow dashed across the alley. Could have been a cat. But I wasn't sure.

I decided to keep to the busier streets.

I'd come to America to hunt for a man.

A cold shiver ran down my spine. Someone was hunting me.

Chapter 11

I kept a close watch over my shoulder as I made my way through Brighton Beach's unfamiliar streets.

I was looking for a quiet bar where I could have a drink to steady my nerves. And try to figure out what the hell was going on.

Rico's was a small bar in a side street close to Corbin Place. It had a narrow frontage with brown bricks and a small window which was too high to see in from the street. Ideal for a shaken journalist who needed to down a large gin and tonic unobserved.

Inside the bar was a long narrow space, a bit like a railway carriage with no compartments. I ordered a G and T and something called a club sandwich. It turned out to be a mini-mountain of bread inter-leaved with chicken, bacon and lettuce.

I made my way to the back, past tables with three lone drinkers. All looked like regulars who'd come in for a heavy session.

I took a good pull at the G and T, then bit into the sandwich. It was surprisingly tasty. Whoever made it had used mayonnaise like cement between the layers of bread to stop the whole thing toppling over.

I relaxed a little and began to think about Reggie Derwent. I'd had my suspicions about him when he'd hustled onto the plane at the last minute and taken a seat next to me. Now I knew why. He was following me. And I suspected he was a master of the craft. Most followers lurk in the shadows. It takes a bold man to conduct his pursuit in plain sight.

But what kind of bold man was Reggie?

He didn't strike me as a cop. For a start, the Savile Row suit he was wearing would have cost a cop three months' salary. Besides, I knew all the 'tecs in Brighton's small force.

And I didn't think he came from Scotland Yard either. He

simply wasn't the type. Besides, Scotland Yard weren't involved in the Volk's Railway case. No reason they should be. The cops still thought it was a local matter.

Unless they'd made the connections I'd just made between Bellwether and Newton - and knew there was a link with the Bridego robbery. I didn't see how they could have unless they'd identified Arthur Crouch as Elliott Bellwether. I doubted they'd done that before I - and Reggie - had flown out of Heathrow.

But if Reggie had been tagging along unseen in my wake, he could've made the connection by now. And, if so, who did he report it to?

I chomped my way through the rest of the sandwich while I thought about that.

Could Reggie be a private detective hired by a party that had an interest in the robbery? The Royal Mail would be anxious to recover the money and avoid a huge compensation pay-out to customers.

Reggie looked like a bit of a toff - not like your average private dick. But not all private eyes slept in their clothes and chewed gum. If Reggie was tailing me for a client, it would've had to be someone who knew that Crouch, aka Bellwether, was a link between the Volk's Railway and Mail heists. And I didn't think anyone knew that apart from me.

Which raised a darker thought in my mind. One person who seemed to know what was going on was Jerry Clark. He'd delivered the twelve thousand dollars to Bellwether. And he'd been so keen not to be caught that he'd killed himself. But he'd also issued a chilling warning before he'd died: "As for you, others will come after me. You won't escape."

Was Reggie one of those coming after me? Perhaps he was part of the criminal conspiracy behind the robberies. If he were an assassin, he was a gentleman with it. But he was also anxious not to confront me an hour or so ago. Perhaps the plan was to discover what I'd learnt before he closed in.

If that were the case, he could do that easily by following my track to the library. Perhaps he was there now charming the information out of Joy Novak. Perhaps already down to his Savile Row socks in a game of strip poker. In which case, he would know as much as I did. And his mission would be complete, apart from eliminating me.

I drank the last of my gin and tonic and made a firm decision.

Tomorrow I would return to Britain on the first available plane.

Unless Reggie got to me first.

When I arrived back at my lodgings, I found a fat man sitting in the best chair in Mrs Koch's parlour.

He had a moon face with puffy cheeks, a bulbous nose and hanging jowls. His brown hair was parted down the centre and combed out so that it hung over his ears. He had a barrel chest and a three-hamburger stomach which bulged over his belt. He was wearing grey flannel trousers and a blue shirt which strained at the buttons.

He looked up as I walked in and said: "Hi, you must be the limey the old crow told me about. No offence intended."

I grinned. "None taken. At least, not by me. I can't speak for the old crow obviously. And where is Mrs Koch?"

"Visiting her sister in Newark. Won't be back until morning. I'm Hank. Hank Shultz." He extended an arm like a tree branch and I shook his hand. It felt like grasping a bunch of bananas.

"Colin Crampton."

Hank pointed to a bottle of bourbon on a side table and said: "Care to join me?"

I took the only other easy chair in the room and said: "Try and stop me."

Hank reached for a spare glass and poured me a medicinal measure. He handed me the glass and we toasted each other.

"Here's to crime," he said.

"I'll drink to that. Without it, I'd be out of work."

Hank shot me a worried look. "Not a cop, are you?"

"No."

"FBI?"

"No."

"Christ! You're friggin' CIA. No offence intended."

"None taken. I'm a journalist. Crime reporter on a newspaper in Britain."

Hank blew out his cheek in that puffy gesture people make when they're relieved about something. "So you won't be writing about me."

"Why, are you a criminal?"

Hank laughed, baring a set of teeth so uneven they looked as though they'd been implanted by a blind dentist wearing welding gloves.

"No. Not me. But I cut a tough deal. Honest Hank, they call me. On account of it's a kind of joke. Like one of them words which is kinda supposed to mean the opposite of what you say. Ivory? No, that's elephants."

"Irony."

Hank grinned. "Sure, irony. Hey, you're a real clever guy. We're gonna get along swell."

I sipped at the bourbon and felt the warmth as it made its way down my throat.

"So what's your line of business, Hank?"

He took a good pull on his drink and inspected the glass. Decided the tide had gone down enough to merit a top up. Poured himself another generous measure.

"I'm in the fun business, Colin."

"You sell fun?"

"I can see you're not quite with me. Brainbox a little slow tonight? No offence intended."

"None taken."

"Great. Yeah, I sell fun. Specifically, and to be precise and not beat about the bush, because I'm a guy who comes right to the point - no prevarication from me - I sell the thing that gives people more fun than anything else in the world."

"Contraceptives?"

Hank laughed. "I see your point, Colin. But let's say I sell the thing which gives people the second most amount of fun in the world."

"Which is?"

"Fruit machines. Yep, who'd have a thought a little ol' boy from Cranky Corner, Louisiana would make it big in the great gaming machine industry? You know, people say to me: you ain't only big in fruit machines, Hank, you're just big. But I don't mind. You know why?"

"Because no offence was intended?" I said.

Hank nodded, took another gulp of his bourbon.

"Yep, I've made it big in Greasy, Oklahoma, in Sweet Lips Tennessee, and in Loafers Glory, North Carolina, but there's one place I want to make it big. You know where?"

"The Big Apple," I said.

"You got it. If you're gonna be big, you need to be somewhere that is big. This is my fifth trip here - and this time I'm gonna land the big one."

"A contract?"

"Yep. Over at Coney Island - and there ain't no jumped-up mafia punk gonna stop me."

Hank reached for the bottle and splashed more bourbon into his glass. Took a serious gulp. Looked at the glass and decided it needed another refill.

I said: "Who's the jumped-up mafia punk who's trying to stop you?"

"Grease-ball called Leone De Luca. You know the guy?"

"I've heard the name," I said. "What's his beef with you?"

"The guy thinks he owns Coney Island - at least the right to supply all the gaming machines to the fun parks there. Last time

I was here he came round with a couple of his goons. Tells me to eff off to Lick Skillet, Tennessee or wherever I do my business. I told him Sweet Lips - and it's a classy town so he ought to try it. He says if I show myself in this town again, I could have an accident. He doesn't scare me."

I said: "I hear he scares a lot of people."

"That's because no-one stands up to him. And he greases the cops."

"With Vaseline?"

"With payola. Dollars."

Hank reached for his glass. Saw it was empty. Picked up the bottle. Looked glum when he saw he'd finished the bourbon. Slumped in the chair and burped.

He said: "Say, why don't we go out and get a couple of drinks? We could take in a cathouse. Get ourselves some pieces of sassy ass. No offence intended."

"None taken. You make it sound irresistible," I said. "But I need an early night. I'm heading back to England tomorrow. And nothing is going to stop me."

Chapter 12

I slept fitfully.

I don't know whether it was the bourbon or the club sandwich. Or a combination of both. But I tossed and turned on Mrs Koch's lumpy mattress.

At least I didn't have the itchy company of the bed bugs in the side room. They'd be feasting on Hank Schultz. No offence intended, of course.

At around two, I drifted into a light slumber. It was one of those restless sleeps where your dreams seem so vivid you feel they have to be real. I was sitting on a stool in a bar next to Hank. The lights were so bright I couldn't see anything beyond them. Hank kept passing me glasses of bourbon. I drank them, but I didn't become drunk.

And then the lights in the room dimmed and I realised that Hank had taken me to a cathouse. I was in a brothel. Girls were lounging on *chaises longue* around the room. But the girls had no faces. It was like the place where their face should be was a coloured light. Then one of the girls stood up and sashayed across the room. And her face appeared.

It was Shirley. My girlfriend Shirley.

I called out to her: "I'm over here, Shirley." But she ignored me. She only had eyes for Hank. She walked up to him and stroked his face. He smiled, a sloppy lascivious smear of a grin with his tongue hanging out of the side of his mouth. He looked like an old bulldog having his tummy tickled. Then Shirley led Hank across the room and they went through a door. Shirley looked at me and shook her head. It was a message that I wasn't to follow. Then she shut the door.

I stared at the door and the lights started to become brighter. The door began to disappear as the lights shone more fiercely into my face. And all I could hear behind the door was Hank moaning - crying out with pleasure.

In the dream, I tried to block my ears against the moans.

And then I came awake. Suddenly. Like my brain had been plugged into a nuclear power plant.

And I heard Hank moan again.

Not in pleasure.

In pain.

He cried out - a long stifled cry which could have been "help". There was a crash as some furniture fell over and a glass smashed.

I sat up in bed in a cold sweat.

I threw back the bed clothes and leapt out. I hauled open my bedroom door and hurtled down the corridor towards Hank's room.

I heaved open Hank's door and rushed into the room. Hank had fallen off his bed and was lying half propped against the wall. His face shone as white as an arctic glacier. His eyes stared as though he'd just seen the gates of Hell open in front of him. His mouth had dropped open in a silent scream.

And a knife was sticking from his chest.

As I crossed the room, blood frothed in his mouth and he vomited.

I felt my heart thump like a steam-hammer. The club sandwich danced a roundelay in my stomach. I belched and tasted bourbon. I took a deep breath to steady myself.

Hank slipped sideways down the wall while scarlet arterial blood pulsed from his mouth. The pupils of his eyes had shrunk so they looked like tiny holes.

I couldn't bear to look anymore. I dragged my eyes away from Hank's body. And realised the window was open.

Hands were gripping the windowsill from outside. Thin bony fingers held on like claws. I rushed across the room, but the hands released and I heard a body drop onto the flat roof of the extension.

I thrust my head out of the window and looked down. A man had landed on his back on the roof. He was about twenty-five, slim and wiry. He was splayed with arms and legs outstretched. He was dressed in a black sweatshirt and trousers. He wore those running shoes which Mabelle called sneakers.

The fall had winded him and it was a few seconds before he could scramble to his feet. There was enough light from a streetlamp to see he had a narrow face with pronounced cheeks and a prominent chin. His eyes were close together under eyebrows that hardly registered. He had thin lips which were compressed tightly together - perhaps as a result of the pain from the fall.

He pushed himself into a sitting position, looked up and saw me. His eyes widened in surprise. He sat for a moment like someone who's had a shock. I could almost see his brain pulsing with thought. He didn't know what to do.

He scrambled to his feet. I was a witness - and therefore a danger to him. He wanted to kill me. He moved towards the window. But to climb back he'd need to grip the windowsill and I could break his hands while he tried to pull himself up.

He spat in disgust on the roof, turned and vanished over the side. I heard a drainpipe rattle as he shinnied down it and a thump as he hit the ground. Then he emerged from the shadow of the house and ran down the street.

I couldn't follow him, even if I'd been able to jump out of the window. My bare feet would have been cut to pieces.

I turned from the window and looked again at Hank. He'd fallen flat on the floor. The blood had stopped pumping from his mouth. It formed a sticky pool to the side of his body. I knelt and felt for a pulse in Hank's neck. The flesh was warm but lifeless.

Hank had intended no offence for the very last time.

I hurried out of the room and down the stairs. Mrs Koch kept her telephone in the kitchen. I lifted the receiver and called the cops.

A cop car screamed to a halt outside the house four minutes later.

Its siren blared and its blue light flashed.

Impressive. In Brighton, after four minutes the cops would still be finishing their tea and biscuits in the canteen before they decided whether to ride their bikes or walk.

There were two cops in the car. They killed the lights and sound, scrambled out and hammered on the door.

I opened it. The first cop in was six foot tall, and had a face with a bent nose and a crooked jaw, like he'd walked into a wall.

He barked: "Where's the body?"

I said: "First floor, side bedroom."

He pounded up the stairs.

The second cop was shorter by six inches, had folds of fat under his eyes and a double chin.

He grabbed my shoulder, turned me round and handcuffed me.

I said: "Is this any way to treat an informant? Not to mention a visitor to your shores."

Shorty said: "All we know is we got a radio call to get here fast and make an arrest. Don't matter whether you've come from over the rainbow to us."

"It does matter that the true killer scrambled out the window and is now legging it out of the area while you waste your time with me."

"First thing I saw, you got blood on your pants."

I looked down. "My trousers. I knelt down to find out whether Hank was dead."

"Sure, you did. Or perhaps you helped make him dead. We don't know."

The first cop came down the stairs.

He said: "Stabbed. A messy business. The perp will have

blood on his clothes."

He looked at my trousers and then at me. "Anyone else in the house?"

"No."

"Ever hear of anyone getting stabbed through a brick wall?"

"No."

"Then looks bad for you," he said. "The lieutenant ain't gonna like this."

I wasn't much enjoying it myself.

Lieutenant Jess Sheldon leaned back in her chair and said: "You got everything you want?"

I crossed my legs, looped an arm over the back of my chair and said: "I can't think of anything. Except possibly my freedom."

We were in an interview room at a police station somewhere in Brooklyn. The place was a square box painted a dirty cream with a dado rail round the wall picked out in mucky green. It reminded me of a British Rail waiting room on a little-used branch line.

Sheldon said: "You're entitled to a lawyer at public expense."

I glanced at the clock on the wall. Two forty-five in the morning.

I said: "Why disturb him? At this time of the night, the poor bloke will be snoring in his jim-jams."

Sheldon clenched her cheeks to stop herself smiling. She was in her early forties. She had a pleasant open face that would have been great on a probation officer but must have been a drawback for a cop dealing with hard types. But there was something about the set of the jaw and the determination in the hazel eyes that would warn even the toughest cons they weren't going to get any favours.

She turned to the small cop sitting next to her. He had a bald head and the crumpled body posture of someone who knows his lot in life is to be a second stringer.

"Sergeant Middleton, who were the arresting officers?"

"Kaplinsky and Rogers, Lieutenant."

"Jesus. They might as well have sent Abbott and Costello."

She turned back to me and said: "We'll start at the beginning. Tell me everything."

So I did. Well, perhaps not everything. But I told how I'd shared Hank's bourbon. How we'd gone to bed. How I'd been roused by cries from his room. How I'd found him. And how I'd seen the killer escape across the flat roof of the extension.

"Then I called the cops as a civic duty and got arrested for my pains," I concluded.

Sheldon nodded. "For now, let's consider you a witness. Did Hank Shultz give you the impression that he felt his life was in danger?"

"Not specifically. He was the kind of guy who blunders through life not taking much notice of the dangers around him. He did mention that he'd had a run-in with someone called Leone De Luca over gaming machines business in Coney Island."

"We know Mr De Luca," Sheldon said. "He is a person of interest to us. Great interest. Did Shultz mention any specific threat De Luca had made?"

"He said a couple of De Luca's goons had warned him off last time he was in Coney Island. He didn't seem to take the warning seriously. But by this time, he'd worked his way to the bottom of a bottle of bourbon. Perhaps the drink made him feel brave."

Sheldon thought about that for a moment and then said: "Let's turn to the man you saw escaping over the flat roof. Did you get a good look at him?"

"I saw him about five feet away. But only by the light from a streetlamp."

"After this interview, I'd like you to go with Sergeant Middleton and see if you can create an Identikit likeness of the man."

She turned to Middleton. "Get that set up now, Stew."

Middleton uncurled himself from his chair and went out.

I said: "Now the hired help is out of the room, you can ask the serious questions. Is that the plan?"

"You're perceptive, Mr Crampton. Let's cut to the chase. What are you doing in America?"

I thought about that for a moment. Decided to break the habit of a lifetime and tell the truth.

"I came here to identify a man who'd been robbed in Britain."

"Why couldn't you identify him in Britain?"

I told Jess the story. About the mystery of Arthur Crouch, the man who wore gloves on the hottest day of the year. About the robbery on the Volk's Railway. About how Crouch didn't hang around to reclaim his twelve thousand dollars. About how Chaz and Jerry Clark died - and about how Boss tried to kill me.

Jess leaned forward. "And have you identified Crouch?"

"Yes. I believe he is a man called Elliott Bellwether. And I think he's acted as a link-man - and kind of consultant, if you like - between Willis Newton and a gang of unnamed train robbers in England."

Jess nodded. "Newton - you're sure it was Willis Newton."

"Yes, I have a picture of him with Bellwether coming out of De Luca's nightclub."

"Last I heard, Newton was living a quiet life, but not a blameless one, somewhere in Oklahoma. If he's been seen on my turf, I'd like to know more."

I grinned. "Perhaps we could do a deal. Hands across the sea, and all that."

Jess frowned, a two-wrinkle job on her forehead, but I could tell it was more for show.

"The New York Police Department does not do deals with journalists."

"And the Pope doesn't have a naughty thought if a nun shows a flash of ankle."

"If we could tie De Luca into this, I could take one nasty guy off the streets for years," Jess said.

I said: "The punk who stabbed Hank would have been acting on De Luca's orders. I guess De Luca was more concerned about the threat to his gaming machines business than Hank thought."

Jess nodded. "I'll buy that. But I won't be able to prove it. Even if we catch him - and we will - the punk won't confess. But if we could nail De Luca on an international conspiracy... well, that would be a federal case."

I said: "I need to know more about Bellwether. I've discovered his name, but I know nothing about his background."

Jess handed me a writing pad and pen. "I want everything you know about the links between Bellwether, Newton and De Luca written down. Now. Then I want you to work with Middleton to produce an Identikit picture of Shultz's killer. Give me both of those, and I'll see what I can find about Bellwether. But no promises."

She stood up, stepped across to the door and went out.

I picked up the pen and began to write.

Chapter 13

A pale light had appeared in the east by the time I stepped out of the cop shop.

I'd written a two-thousand word account of what I knew about Bellwether, Newton and De Luca - and constructed the face of a killer. Middleton, at least, seemed happy with my Identikit work. He had the decency to run me back to Old Mother Koch's house of horrors to collect my things. Obviously I couldn't stay there while the place was a crime scene.

So unless I could find new lodgings, I'd be tramping the streets of New York like a hobo. Buddy, can you spare a dime?

Middleton left me standing outside Koch's house with my suitcase in one hand, my Olivetti portable in the other and not much else but my wits. I decided my best bet was to make for Ben Stoker's office. After all, I was a journalist with a story to tell.

It was seven when I arrived at the *Brighton Beach Banner*. The sun was up - but Ben Stoker wasn't. At least, he hadn't yet reached the place. There was a diner across the other side of the street - and it was open. I made my way over there, took a window seat so I could see the *Banner* offices and ordered eggs, bacon and coffee.

I was feeling tired but mellow by the time I saw Stoker walk down the street and unlock his office door. I paid my check, as the waitress called it, and headed across the road.

Stoker was in his office, sitting at his desk reading teleprinter messages that had come in overnight. He looked up as I knocked lightly on his door jamb and walked in.

I said: "Give me a desk and a stack of copy paper and I'll give you a murder story to splash in this week's edition."

Stoker said without any enthusiasm: "Yeah, the radio was reporting a stabbing this morning, but no details about the victim or motive. Haven't had time to follow it up."

He was slumped in his chair like a guy looking forward to a heart attack. All the fight had gone out of him.

"Your trouble's got worse?" I asked.

He nodded. "Can't get any worse now. Remember I was sweating on that loan. It's been called in. I have seven days to repay it or I lose the paper. The next edition will be the last. At least, the last I edit. I hate to think what De Luca will turn it into when he gets his greasy hands on it."

I moved across the room. Took the guest chair on the other side of Stoker's desk.

I said: "You've got to fight it."

Stoker shrugged: "What with? The last bill for newsprint cleaned me out."

"Fight with the richest commodity a newspaper has - the truth"

"Not much of that commodity left in this town."

"Then let's make some."

"Easy to say when you work for a paper with a full newsroom."

I wagged a finger at Stoker. "You want to stop the *Banner* falling into De Luca's hands? Then use the last edition to show why De Luca would be an unworthy owner - expose him as the vicious gangster he is."

"I can't do that. It's all I can manage to get any kind of paper out."

"I can."

He gave me a look like I'd just volunteered to play target practice for a firing squad.

He said: "You cross De Luca and you end up in the Hudson River. And not on the Staten Island ferry."

I said: "I've faced up to hard cases in my home town."

"It ain't so easy when you don't know the score."

"Gangsters are the same the world over - malice fuelled by hubris."

"You don't look like Nemesis to me."

"I hope not. She was a woman."

"I can't pay you."

"Make it in kind. I need a place to lay my head for a couple of nights while I wrap up my business in America."

Stoker shrugged. "I ain't gonna talk you out of this, am I?"

"No."

"I'm not even sure I want to. You can bunk down at my place. It ain't far from here."

"Then we have a deal."

Stoker smiled for the first time that morning. "We have a deal."

I crossed the office to a spare desk and took my Olivetti portable out of its case.

Stoker busied himself with his paperwork while I batted out six hundred words about the murder at Old Mother Koch's place. There's nothing like writing up a good murder, I've found, for kicking the old brainbox into action. By the time I'd rolled the last folio out of the typewriter's carriage I'd decided on my next move.

To bring down De Luca, I had to find evidence that would link him to a crime. He'd have planned Hank Shultz's killing so that the cops had nothing to connect him to it. But in even the best planned crime there's a loose thread hanging somewhere. Find that thread, tug on it, and the whole scam unravels.

Hank had crossed De Luca over his plans to sell gaming machines to the Coney Island pleasure parks. No doubt De Luca had imagined he had exclusive rights to that turf. He'd had a monopoly with the park operators - and would have made sure they paid high prices for their machines. If a guy like Hank came along with an offer that saved them money, some of them would jump at it. Which is when De Luca would have a choice - lose a customer or make sure they paid the penalty for shopping elsewhere. A gangster like De Luca would have thugs who'd make sure that customers didn't step out of line when a seller with a better offer came to call.

But that didn't mean those customers would like it.

And one of them could be willing to talk.

Across the office, Stoker was tut-tutting over a page proof. I called across to him that I'd be gone for a couple of hours.

I'd heard Coney Island was where New Yorkers go to look for fun.

But I wasn't expecting to find any.

I rode the metro to Coney Island's Stillwell Avenue stop.

The metro was crowded with folks heading into the city for the day's toil. I crushed myself up against a couple of city types with their noses stuck in the *Wall Street Journal*. No doubt they were planning their next take-over or stock deal.

I kept a close watch at the metro station in case Reggie Derwent was on my tail, but I didn't see him. I guessed my pursuit the previous evening might have forced him to fade into the background. But I'd have to remember that he could be somewhere. For the time being, I had Coney Island on my mind.

I had to push through the crush to get out at Stillwell Avenue. I shuffled along toward the exit with about a dozen other people and clattered down into the street. The road was thick with traffic, most of it heading north into the city. The driver of a Chevrolet pick-up leaned on his horn when a Ford pulled in front. A guy dressed in jeans and tee-shirt revved the engine of his Harley-Davidson as he weaved between the lines of cars. The brakes on a pink Cadillac squealed when it stopped suddenly after a nun dashed out from behind a bus. The driver gave herself the sign of the cross.

The air tasted like cotton wool soaked in lighter fuel.

I hurried south towards the amusement parks, the boardwalk - and the sea. There were few pedestrians on the sidewalk. A hundred yards ahead a mother pushed a pram. A sprightly old boy in sports coat and checked trousers bustled along with a brown bag of groceries in one arm.

I glanced back. A couple of hundred yards behind me two young blokes swaggered along. One had the muscly build of a tough guy who works out with weights. He was dressed in jeans and tee-shirt. The tee-shirt had a slogan on the front which I couldn't read at the distance. The other was thinner and wiry. He had grey trousers and a pullover with a hood. It was pulled up over his head, like a monk's cowl, so I couldn't see his face.

I pressed on, thinking hard about how I could get any of the traders in the amusement parks to talk. They weren't going to point the finger against De Luca, even if I promised them cast-iron anonymity. After all, I was a new boy in town - and one with an English accent - so why should they believe anything I told them? From what Hank had told me, De Luca kept his customers in line as ruthlessly as he kept competition out.

I suspected that if I announced myself as a reporter from the *Brighton Beach Banner* I'd be about as welcome as a Jehovah's Witness selling *The Watchtower*. Which left me with that age-old journalist's ploy - subterfuge. I could pretend to be Hank Shultz's business partner making a follow-up call. That would be risky, especially if any of the traders had already heard about Shultz's killing. But from the papers on the newsstands, the story didn't seem to have made the morning editions.

Ahead of me, a giant Ferris wheel marked the position of the amusement parks. I walked on and within a few minutes I was in the middle of it all. It reminded me of Brighton's Palace Pier. There was a carousel with liberty horses, bumper cars, a waltzer, a helter-skelter - and a ghost train. There was an arcade which housed dozens of slot machines and one-armed bandits.

I walked into the arcade and had a good look round. There were half-a-dozen hardened losers feeding dimes into slots. They'd pull the handle, tense up the neck muscles while the rotors spun, then clap their hand to their forehead when they lost. This would have been where Shultz had hustled for business.

The problem was I didn't know whom he'd hustled. At the far end of the arcade, an old bloke in a bottle-green janitor's outfit was sweeping up cigarette butts. In the change booth, a young woman stacked up piles of dimes. Neither would be the boss who took decisions on which machines to buy.

I stepped out of the arcade to rethink my plan.

And stopped dead in my tracks.

Over by the entrance gates, the two blokes I'd seen follow me out of the metro at Stillwell Avenue had just walked into the park. Now I could read the words on the muscleman's tee-shirt. They said: "Get smoochie-smoochie at the Hoochie-Coochie."

The two were standing beside an information board with a map of the park. They twizzled their heads back and forth like people looking for someone. The bloke with the monk's hood on his head took it down.

And I knew I was in trouble.

He was Shultz's killer. The guy whose murderous eyes I'd looked into less than ten hours ago.

I moved back into the shadow of the arcade and watched.

As I did so, the young woman who'd been in the change booth walked over and looked across the way. She turned and beckoned to the janitor. He shrugged and ambled over.

The woman pointed at the pair: "I've seen those before. Do you recognise them?" she asked the janitor.

He pulled her back into the shadow of the arcade. "Steer clear of them. They're De Luca's muscle. The guy on the right with the hood is a vicious piece of work called Dino. The body builder freak is a thug called Kurt."

"Why are they here?" asked the woman.

"To make trouble," the janitor said.

Trouble for me, I could've added.

I was the only witness who could ID Dino for Shultz's killing. It was no secret at Old Mother Koch's that I was a reporter. He must have picked up my trail at the *Brighton Beach Banner*. I hadn't seen him follow me onto the train - but I was too busy keeping an eye out for Reggie. And the train was too crowded to see everybody on it. When he'd reported back to De Luca, he'd have been ordered to find me and take me out of the picture. No loose ends.

I watched from inside the arcade. They'd seen me come into the park, but they'd lost me. They were arguing about what to do next. Dino wanted to go right. Kurt pointed left. They argued some more. Agreed on something. Split up and headed in opposite directions.

That was good for me. If I ran into either of them I'd only need to take on one. But by splitting up, they'd doubled their chances of finding me. I wondered whether the park had a security officer who I could ask for help. But he could also be De Luca's man. As the thought ran through my mind, a guy dressed in a shabby uniform ambled over and took up sentry position by the gate. He wasn't looking at people coming in. He was there to stop one person going out.

Me.

Dino disappeared stage right behind the helter-skelter, Kurt moved around the carousel. I was thinking fast. But not fast enough. I had to find somewhere to hide while I worked out what to do next.

I sprinted out of the arcade and kept close to the wall as I slipped behind the building. I found myself in a sort of fairway with a string of stalls - hoop-la, coconut shy, lucky dip, shooting range - down one side and the ghost train on the other. The train was a sizeable operation which ran on two levels. The punters sat in open cars which ran on rails. I call them cars but they looked like buckets with the front cut out and a seat inserted. You climbed in the front, sat down and the car trundled forward.

As I watched, the entrance doors opened and one of the cars holding two young kids rattled inside.

I felt exposed. Dino or Kurt could appear at any minute.

It would be dark inside the ghost train and there could be somewhere to hide. I hurried up, paid my dollar, took a seat in the next car.

I sat back as a gear crunched and the car moved forward. The doors had Dante's welcome to hell - Abandon all hope ye who enter here - painted on them.

They crashed open and I disappeared into the darkness.

Chapter 14

The first thing I saw in the ghost train was myself covered in blood.

I jolted back in shock. Well, you would, wouldn't you?

Not a pretty sight. A bit like seeing yourself in the shaving mirror after a heavy night.

Then I laughed.

I was looking at a mirror with streaks of blood painted down it.

The car clattered around a bend into darkness. Ahead, the kids in the earlier car screamed at one of the horrors.

I flinched as something soft and sticky brushed my face. A piece of gauze made to feel like a spider's web.

Ahead a woman let out a maniacal laugh. The kind you only hear in a mad house or the ladies' bar of the Fur and Feathers at closing time.

Twenty seconds into the ride and the ghost train had already assaulted my senses of sight, sound and touch.

But I hoped it would protect my sense of life.

A bright light flashed. I blinked. Ahead a skeleton rattled from a hook, its bones picked out in luminescent paint.

The train had been designed to run round a series of loops. As you turned each loop, a fresh horror appeared.

The car rolled on and a ghostly pirate brandished a sword dripping with blood.

I rattled up a gentle incline towards the upper level. In a Victorian Christmas tableau, Old Marley rattled his chains.

A headless corpse dressed in Tudor clothes carried his severed head under his arm. The head mouthed a word I couldn't hear. It may have been "ouch!"

A plague victim twisted in his coffin and moaned like a guy with a bellyache.

An old girl with white hair and ravaged face - a cross between a waxwork and a skeleton - wore a tattered wedding gown. She reminded me of Miss Havisham from *Great Expectations*. She produced the maniacal cackle of laughter I'd heard earlier as I clattered by.

I dragged my mind away from the exhibits to think hard about what I should do. I needed to climb out of the car - perhaps as it slowed to turn a loop - and hide. Perhaps I could find a back way out of the ghost train. Then, maybe, I could slip out of the park through a staff entrance.

My car rolled down an incline towards the ground level. The ride would end within a minute or two. Ahead, I heard the kids' car crash out of the exit doors. I decided I would jump out of my car when it slowed to turn through the next curve.

And then the car stopped.

Just jolted to a sudden halt.

My senses sharpened and I listened. No other cars were moving. The electric current driving the cars had been switched off.

But not the lights illuminating the tableaux. So no power failure.

Five feet ahead of me a ghostly highwayman brandished a blunderbuss. He rode a black horse. A wooden horse. But not like the one left outside Troy. So I wouldn't be able to hide inside it.

I climbed out of the car to see if I could hide behind the horse. But if the highwayman was Dick Turpin, Black Bess seemed to have caught a bad case of dry rot.

I had my ears focused for any sound.

The plague victim moaned.

Old Marley rattled his chains.

Miss Havisham cackled.

The headless corpse said "ouch!"

Then hinges creaked.

To my right daylight briefly filtered into the gloom as the entrance door opened. But not to let in another car. Footsteps stepped quietly - but not quietly enough - over the boards which formed the floor. Just one set of footsteps. They stopped.

I strained my ears so hard I could've swapped them with a bat and the bat would've got the better deal.

Silence.

And then a door slammed. To the left. The exit door. A man cursed softly.

He said: "Sorry, boss." Kurt.

A voice twenty yards to my right hissed: "Be quiet." Dino.

De Luca's goons had picked up my trail faster than I'd imagined.

But, then, no doubt they'd be known in the park. They'd only have had to ask stallholders whether they'd seen anyone fitting my description. And when the ghost train owner had been told to switch off the electrics, he wouldn't have argued.

Dino and Kurt had come to kill me. And, like an idiot, I'd set myself up in the perfect place for them to do it - in the dark, out of sight - and with plenty of opportunities to dispose of my body.

A kind of icy coldness crept through me as I crouched behind Black Bess and I shivered. Gooseflesh rose on my arms and back. Yet I also seemed to be sweating. I felt sweat pricking from the pores on my forehead. My body had slipped into panic mode.

Scrambled thoughts raced through my mind. What would happen to the old typewriter on my desk at the *Chronicle*? Who would drink with Ted Wilson in Prinny's Pleasure when I was gone? Would Shirley wear black underwear when she attended my funeral?

The plague victim moaned.

Old Marley rattled his chains.

Miss Havisham cackled.

The headless corpse said "ouch!"

I forced my mind to focus. It wasn't easy. I had to think of a way out of this mess.

Kurt's clumping footsteps approached from the left.

Dino's cat-like tread crept in from the right.

Kurt had looked like a hulk attached to a pair of fists. I could out-think him.

But last night Dino had had a knife. And knew how to use it. Perhaps he also had a gun. Perhaps he knew how to use that, too.

The thought chilled me again.

But it also forced me to realise I had to act.

I needed a weapon to defend myself. The pirate in the first tableau I'd seen had a sword. Was it real or like Black Bess made of wood? Even a wooden sword would be better than nothing.

But I couldn't reach it with Dino closing in from the right and Kurt from the left. Quietly, I moved to the back of the highwayman tableau. There was a dark backing cloth with a few silver stars and a crescent moon pinned to it. A half-hearted attempt to make it look like a night sky.

Silently, I lifted the cloth and peered under it. There was a narrow passage running behind the exhibits, perhaps a way to reach them unobserved if something went wrong while punters trundled by in the cars. I rolled myself under the backcloth and stood up.

It was like standing in a coalmine without a Davy lamp. I daren't move for fear of knocking into something. I stood like a statue and listened for footsteps.

The plague victim moaned.

Old Marley rattled his chains.

Miss Havisham cackled.

The headless corpse didn't say "ouch!" Perhaps it didn't hurt anymore.

Dino and Kurt were closing in.

If I stayed where I was I'd end up as the meat in the sandwich.

Dead meat.

I had to move. The simple thought made me realise my mind was working. I could scheme my way out of this.

Couldn't I?

Both sets of footsteps arrived in front of the highwayman tableau. I heard the low murmur of a whispered conversation.

With one eye, I looked around the edge of the backcloth. Kurt's Mr World-sized biceps were tense. He was fired up for a rumble.

But Dino had a gun. He held it confidently in his right hand, like it was an old friend.

The pair ended their *sotto voce* conference and moved off in opposite directions.

I had a plan. I had to get Dino and Kurt at one end of the ghost train so I could make my getaway at the other end. All the while they were spread out, they'd block my escape.

Behind the backcloth, I stretched out my right arm to make sure there was no obstruction. The way seemed clear. One careful step at a time I edged along the narrow passage.

The thump of heavy feet clumping on boards echoed from the upper storey. Kurt was on the prowl. But where was Dino?

For an instant, I wondered whether he'd discovered the service passage behind the exhibits. If he had I'd be in for an unwelcome surprise.

The plague victim moaned.

Old Marley rattled his chains.

Miss Havisham cackled.

From the upper storey, Kurt said: "Jeez, that old broad is scrambling my brain. Can't we shut her up?"

From behind old Marley, Dino said: "Shut your own mouth. This is a silent search."

I reached the far end of the service passage, shifted the backcloth half an inch to the side, and cautiously peered around it with one eye.

I was behind the pirate tableau. Dino had been around the first bend in the track. And he'd been heading away from me. I crept out and ran my finger down the pirate's sword. As I suspected, it was made of wood. It would be little use as a weapon against a man with a gun. Even Kurt would snap the flimsy item with a flick of one of his bulging biceps.

I was about to creep behind the backcloth when I noticed that the pirate also had a knife stuck in his belt. I grabbed the handle and yanked the knife out. There was a six-inch blade - and it was real. Cautiously, I ran a finger down the business edge. Sharp enough to cut through butter, but not to carve the Sunday joint. But it was better than no weapon. I stuck it under my own belt and slipped behind the backcloth again.

Dino and Kurt were becoming impatient. I could hear them hurrying along the track.

They couldn't find me. The longer it took, the higher the chances there'd be trouble. The ghost train's owner would have known to keep his mouth shut, but sooner or later some disgruntled customer denied a ride was going to start shouting the odds.

I crept further along the service passage. I'd had an idea but it would be risky.

What was I thinking? Just being here was a terminal risk.

I reached the point in the service passage behind the shaking skeleton tableau. I lifted up the backcloth a little to let light in. A black box was bolted to the floor. A wire stretched upwards out of the box to a bracket fixed from the roof. Then the wire ran horizontally under the roof out to the tableau. It passed through another bracket and down to the skeleton. The wire ran down the skeleton's back. Every twenty seconds a mechanism in the black box made the wire move up and down to shake the skeleton.

I pulled the pirate's knife out of my belt and sawed away at the wire where it emerged from the black box. The wire had been made from thin strands of metal woven together like a rope. As I sawed away, one strand after another snapped. I stopped sawing when only two strands remained.

I stood back and surveyed my handiwork. The skeleton was made out of wood, but had some metal pieces attached which made it rattle more fearsomely. It was heavy. I reckoned it wouldn't survive more than a couple of shakes suspended only by two strands of the wire. At least, I hoped it wouldn't because my plan depended on it.

If I could divert Dino and Kurt with the collapsed skeleton near the entrance, I would have an opportunity to sneak out of the exit.

I crept along the service passage as close to the exit as I could get and waited for the skeleton's next shake.

The skeleton shook. But it didn't collapse.

I could hear Dino and Kurt running around the track. They were frustrated they hadn't found me.

The bones rattled.

Twang!

One of the remaining strands snapped but the skeleton held.

But the noise had spooked my pursuers.

"That's him!" Dino shouted. "On the lower level. Get down here."

Two sets of feet pounded along the track. Dino's on the lower level, Kurt's from the upper.

"He must be near that skeleton," shouted Dino. "Where the hell are you?"

I crouched in the service passage and held my breath. The feet stopped. They'd approach the skeleton cautiously in case I'd planned an ambush.

I peeked out from behind the backcloth. Twenty yards away I could just see the skeleton around the loop of the track.

It shook again but didn't fall.

Dino came into view creeping silently. He held his gun

outstretched with both hands like a cop expecting a shootout.

And then it all happened in a second.

Behind Dino, the plague victim moaned.

Dino swung round like a man expecting to be attacked from the rear.

The skeleton shook once - a rickety rattle of a shake.

Twang!

And collapsed.

It fell in a raucous clatter of falling femurs and ribs and vertebrae. The pelvis split in half. The finger bones bounced like hail stones. The skull hit the ground like a bowling ball and rolled away.

At that exact moment Kurt raced around the curve towards Dino.

Dino, wired with tension, swung back.

And fired.

One shot.

But it was enough. Kurt screamed and collapsed. He clutched his right thigh. Blood spurted through his fingers. His face contorted in agony.

"You crazy punk," he yelled. "That's the second time you've got the wrong guy."

Dino dropped his gun and slumped down beside the track.

I shot out of my hiding place and hurtled through the exit into bright sunlight.

I badly needed some air.

Kurt's words pounded in my brain.

"That's the second time you've got the wrong guy."

Kurt was the second guy.

Hank Shultz was the first guy. But he was the wrong guy.

Dino hadn't wanted to kill poor Hank.

He'd wanted to kill me.

Chapter 15

I drained the last drops of coffee and put my mug back on the table.

"That was good," I said. "I wouldn't mind another cup."

Jess Sheldon pulled a disapproving face. "We're not the local diner, you know." But she nodded to a uniformed cop who took my mug and refilled it from a metal pot.

We were in an interview room at the cop shop. I seemed to be spending a lot of time in there lately. It was three hours after I'd hurtled out of the ghost train at Coney Island.

Jess said: "You've explained what happened inside the ghost train, but what happened outside before the cops arrived?"

I said: "Folks outside the ghost train heard the gun shot. They started shouting and the park's security guys came running. They sealed the ghost train while someone rang the cops. When the cops arrived, they went inside and found Dino trying to bind up Kurt's leg wound with part of Miss Havisham's wedding gown."

The uniformed cop put a fresh mug of coffee in front of me.

The two wrinkles appeared in Jess's forehead as she frowned. She said: "What I can't figure is what you were doing in the ghost train."

"I was working on the theory that Shultz was killed because he posed a threat to De Luca's rackets in Coney Island. I thought it might be possible to pick up some local colour, as we journalists like to call it, by visiting the place and talking to the locals."

"But ended up getting yourself targeted by the very punk you'd tagged as Shultz's killer."

I nodded ruefully. "I wasn't expecting that."

"So Dino hoped to rub you out because you were the only witness who could positively ID him."

"There's more to it. I think - no, I'm sure - Shultz wasn't

Dino's target. It was me. When Kurt was shot he yelled at Dino something about him being the second wrong target hit. The first had to be Shultz."

"How do you figure you were the mark?" Jess asked.

"Because I was the only other person in the place. Old Mother Koch was visiting her sister in Newark and wasn't due back until the morning."

"So if you were the mark, why did Dino croak Shultz?"

"Because he'd been given the wrong information."

"You can't know that," Jess said.

"Not for certain, I agree. But I think I can infer it - and strongly. Consider how Dino worked the killing. He took the trouble to climb onto the flat roof extension at Old Mother Koch's rather than work a window on the ground floor. That's because he knew - or thought he knew - where his mark was sleeping soundly. In the side bedroom looking out over the extension roof."

"But you were in the back bedroom."

"Right. I spent the first night in the side bedroom, but didn't like the company."

"Company?"

"Bed bugs. I told Koch I wanted a different room. But Dino thought I was still in the side room. He'd been given the wrong brief."

I took a swig of coffee.

Jess thought about that for a minute. "Who knew you slept in the side room on the first night?" she asked.

"Only two people - Old Mother Koch herself and Mabelle Willow, her niece. She's a waitress at Big Buck's diner. But only Koch knew I'd moved to the back room. Mabelle would've thought I'd still be tucked up soundly in the side room."

Jess sat back in her chair. Toyed with a loose strand of hair at the side of her head. "I don't buy it. You're suggesting Mabelle briefed Dino on where he'd find you. What's her motive?"

"I don't think she briefed Dino direct. She may not even know him. I think she passed the information to De Luca. Mabelle wants a favour from De Luca. She's tired of her life waiting table at Big Buck's. She wants to get back to her life as an exotic dancer. She told me she'd been performing her act at De Luca's Hoochie-Coochie club but got fired when she lost her snake."

"So the girl was looking for her big break. She didn't have to conspire in murder. She just had to hustle her assets," Jess said.

"She'd hustled. And from what I'd seen, her assets were considerable. But they weren't enough. She needed something that a man like De Luca couldn't ignore and I unwittingly showed it to her. The photograph of Elliott Bellwether."

"The guy you asked me to find more about?"

I nodded. "We know that Bellwether had been meeting Willis Newton the train robber at the Hoochie-Coochie because Ben Stoker has photos of them outside the club. Mabelle has seen Bellwether at the place and suddenly an English guy pops up with his picture and starts asking questions about him. When I showed her Bellwether's picture she denied knowing him, but I could tell that she did - but didn't want to say. Now we know why. She saw an opportunity to tip off De Luca that an English journalist was in town asking awkward questions about one of his close confidantes."

"And you think she spilled the beans to De Luca?"

"I'm sure of it. It was a way to get her stripper's job back. When I called at Big Buck's diner last night, she could barely bring herself to speak to me. It was either guilt or she'd been warned off by De Luca. Possibly both."

"If you're right Mabelle could be looking at a conspiracy rap."

I picked up the mug and drank the last of the coffee.

"This all started because I showed Mabelle the Bellwether picture. Yet I still don't know anything about Bellwether. Have you been able to uncover anything?"

Jess shook her head.

"Nothing at all?" I asked.

"Nothing worth knowing," she said.

"He doesn't figure in police files?"

"None that I've seen - and I've looked."

"That includes files held by the New York Police Department?"

"Yeah."

"And the FBI?"

"At my level, I don't get automatic access to FBI material."

"But you'll have contacts and will have asked them," I said.

"Sure. The Feds hoard information like a miser minds his gold. They hate giving it away."

"So nobody knows anything about Bellwether?"

"Nothing that I can access." Jess looked down at her notes. Avoided my eyes.

I said: "There is something, isn't there?"

"There might be. But nothing I can see. Or you."

"But you tried?"

Jess put her hands on the table and leaned forward. "This goes no further. Agreed?"

"Cub's honour," I said.

"I'll take that as a 'yes'. I asked an old mate from the FBI down in Washington. He put a call into a colleague of his. Next thing he knows, he's standing on his boss's rug receiving the bollocking of his career. Apparently, Bellwether is off limits even at his level."

"So someone somewhere knows something interesting about Elliott Bellwether."

"Sure they do. But they ain't saying."

I thought about that for a moment. Then I said: "De Luca could tell us more about Bellwether if you put pressure on him. We know he's behind Shultz's murder, which must give you leverage over him."

"Sure. I know that. But Dino won't squeal on De Luca - it's an honour thing with mafia types."

"Even though he'll go to the electric chair."

"He goes without talking, he becomes a legend. And his aged mother gets some mafia bucks as his silence money. He goes after squealing, he's reviled as a schmuck and his aged mother suddenly finds they won't serve her at the local grocery."

"I'd rather be a live schmuck than a dead legend."

"Let's hope you never have to make the choice."

I grinned. "There's another way we could learn more about Bellwether."

"How?"

"From De Luca."

"He'll never talk."

"He might do if he faced a conspiracy charge for Shultz's murder."

"I'll never make that stick."

"You could if Mabelle testified that she told De Luca about me showing her Bellwether's picture. It might make him uneasy enough to trade information in return for a deal."

Jess considered the point. "There might be something in that. It would depend on how much Mabelle told me."

"Don't you mean us?" I said.

"You think I'd let a Brit reporter sit in on an official suspect interview? No way."

I quoted the first amendment of the American constitution about the freedom of the press, but it made no difference.

We argued. Tit for tat. It got heated.

Jess pointed out my presence could taint the quality of evidence given in the interview if a case ever came to court. But she agreed to brief me off-the-record after the interview. And she said if Mabelle came across, she'd personally arrest De Luca for questioning about Shultz's murder.

What Jess said was logical and fair, but I was angry. I suppose it should have satisfied me. But it didn't. I smouldered with resentment. Hank Shultz was dead. Perhaps he would have ended up dead anyway if he took on De Luca. But he wouldn't be dead yet.

I should've been the one lying on a mortuary slab. And when someone else has been killed in mistake for you, it's not enough still to be alive. You have to do something personal to avenge the killing. I knew De Luca was behind Hank's murder and I wanted to nail him for it.

Jess was a good cop and she played by the rules. But De Luca didn't. In this town, he made the rules. But I would break them.

I stood up and said to Jess: "Will you at least call me when you've interviewed Mabelle?"

Jess nodded. "Sure. Where will you be?"

"I'll be at the *Brighton Beach Banner* offices. Or, perhaps, somewhere else."

Jess shot me a warning look. "Which somewhere else?"

"That depends," I said.

Chapter 16

The Founding Fathers' Athletic & Gentlemen's Club reeked of old money like a farmyard reeks of manure.

The place occupied a corner site near the river in one of the smarter parts of Brooklyn. It was a solid brownstone building with large windows to let the light in and thick walls to keep the riff-raff out. A set of polished granite steps led between two towering pillars to a pair of carved oak doors.

Tulip Fragrance had told me De Luca often used the place. It was part of his plan to put on a respectable face. And it gave him the chance to hobnob with bankers, politicians and scions of the old Brahmin families.

I hoped he was using the place now. But there was only one way to find out.

I marched up the steps, opened the door and stepped into a wide hallway lit by a large chandelier. To my left a chesterfield and a couple of chairs had been grouped in front of an open fire. To my right, a man with broad shoulders and narrow hips was sitting in a red leather porter's chair. He was wearing a blue uniform with gold braid edging.

He stood up as I came through the door and moved towards me.

He said: "Can I help you, sir?" in a voice which made clear helping me was the very last thing in the world on his mind.

I said: "Leone De Luca is expecting me."

He said: "Mr De Luca is fencing."

"Stolen goods?"

"With State Senator Calvin Picklestitch III."

"Foils or epées this week?"

"Always épées, sir. I believe Mr De Luca prefers sport where the whole body is a target."

"I'd heard that as well. Remind me, where is the fencing

court?"

"I believe you'll find the gentlemen in the sports bar by now."

"Straight ahead through those doors and turn left?"

"No, sir. That is the bridge room. The sports bar is the last door on the corridor to the right."

I nodded my thanks and headed swiftly across the hall.

"What did you say your name was?" he called after me.

"I didn't," I said as I went through the doors and turned into the corridor.

There were only two men standing at the sports bar.

I recognised De Luca immediately from the pictures Stoker had published in the *Brighton Beach Banner*. He was a short man who held himself like a fighting cock. He had a lean face with pronounced cheeks and deep set eyes. His thick wavy hair, combed straight back from the forehead, showed the first silver streaks. He had a lithe body with enough muscle to suggest he worked the weights from time to time.

His companion, the third Picklestitch, looked like a man made from left-over bits of the first two. He had an outsize head with a pronounced forehead. Add a bolt through his neck and he'd have been a dead ringer for Boris Karloff as Frankenstein. He had arms that were too long, legs that were too short and a stomach that was too fat.

The pair of them were dressed in the white jackets and breeches with long socks they'd worn for fencing. They'd taken off their masks all the better to down the dry martinis - I'd spotted the olives on sticks - they were raising to their lips.

I walked over to them, stuck out my hand and said: "Good afternoon, Mr De Luca. I'm pleased to meet the man who's tried to kill me twice. I won't wish you better luck next time."

De Luca ignored my hand like it was infected with a deadly disease.

"This is some kind of gag by those guys at the poker game,

right?"

His tone suggested he wanted to laugh off the intrusion in front of his influential friend. But his eyes focused on me in a rocket-fuelled hate glare.

"No. The only joke is that your man, Dino, missed his mark both times. He's now at the cop shop helping Lieutenant Sheldon with her inquiries into the case. By the way, he doesn't send his regards."

De Luca thumped his glass on the bar spilling some of the martini.

I grinned. I was getting to him.

"Who are you?"

"Colin Crampton. Reporter currently attached to the *Brighton Beach Banner*."

I turned briskly to Picklestitch. Extended my hand and we shook. His hand felt as flabby as a walrus's flipper.

I said: "Don't feel you have to leave us, senator. I'll want to get some quotes from you for the piece I'm writing about the links between elected politicians and organised crime."

"What piece?" bleated Picklestitch.

"My piece for the *Brighton Beach Banner*. I'm sure your constituents will be interested to learn you're matey with such a pillar of the community as De Luca here."

Picklestitch's shoulders worked up and down like pistons. He was in a panic. "I... I... I have an urgent meeting with the Governor. I must be on my way."

He left his martini on the bar and hurried to the door. The too-long arms swung like an ape's. The too-short legs scurried like a dachshund's.

I turned back to De Luca. His body had tensed. His fists were clenched. His lips compressed in fury. He was fighting every fibre in his body to stop himself attacking me on the spot.

I said: "I wouldn't kill me here. The club's membership committee don't like dead bodies on the carpet. They smell in the hot weather and it lowers the tone."

De Luca shot a furious glance at the barman who was enjoying the exchange and hissed: "What is all this?"

"Let's call it background on the newspaper story I'm writing about your life of crime. And how it's about to end."

"Crime? Don't know what you're talking about. I'm an honest businessman. I mingle with respected politicians."

"Who can't get out of the room fast enough when a reporter threatens to link their name to yours."

De Luca stepped closer so the earwigging barman couldn't hear. I could smell the sour sweat on De Luca's body.

He said: "You've got nothing on me. I've dealt with nosy reporters before. They end up in the hospital - or the graveyard."

"You've missed your chance with me, De Luca. And don't think it'll be third time lucky. Because it's not just me on your case. Your men Dino and Kurt are being interviewed by the cops - and one of them will break and implicate you."

De Luca laughed. "If that's all you've got against me, you're dead. I own the cops in this borough."

"Not this cop."

"You could interrogate Dino and Kurt with lights and electrodes and they wouldn't break."

"They will this time."

"I'll take my chance on that."

"And will you take your chance when the cops interview Mabelle?"

"Who's Mabelle?"

"Mabelle Willow. The girl with the pet python. Don't say you've forgotten already. She's the girl who tipped you off that I'd shown her Elliott Bellwether's picture. She told you I was a journalist in town asking awkward questions. You decided I had to be stopped asking them. And Mabelle was only too eager to help - no doubt to get more work stripping at the Hoochie-Coochie Club - and tell you where I could be found. Even the bedroom I was sleeping in. Except that she didn't know I'd moved rooms. And Dino croaked a harmless slot machine salesman. It'll all be in my story, De Luca."

He reached for his martini. He downed it in a swallow. Looked no better for the effort.

He said: "Mabelle will keep quiet."

"Or what? Her snake gets it?"

"I'll take my chances. You're a busted flush, Crampton."

"I haven't played my best card yet. Bellwether."

"You know nothing about Bellwether."

"I know everything about Bellwether. I know how he met Willis Newton, the king of the train robbers, at your club. I know how you collaborated in a heist to rob a mail train in England. And I know how Bellwether was skimmed of his fee for advising on the scam by a motor-cycling thief called Chaz. I've made all the links De Luca, and you sit right in the middle of the story. And that story's going to appear on the front page of the *Brighton Beach Banner* this afternoon."

"The *Banner* doesn't come out until Saturday."

"With a story this hot we don't wait. We're running an Afternoon Extra edition," I lied.

To add a touch of truth to the porkie, I glanced at my watch. Nodded with approval.

"Story should be set in type by now and the press ready to roll in forty minutes time. Ben Stoker's got two hundred kids from the local William E Grady High School lined up to sell the paper around town. By this evening, they'll be all over Manhattan, too. Wouldn't be surprised if the *New York Times*, the *Herald Tribune* and the rest don't pick up a story this big in the morning."

De Luca pulled up a bar stool and sat down heavily. He glared at me like he wanted me dead, but he knew he had a problem to deal with. He'd greased enough palms to make sure that a hostile story in the *Banner* did him no damage. But the piece I'd just outlined would get picked up by the big New York papers.

Perhaps even the TV stations, like NBC. It would cause trouble. Get questions asked in unexpected quarters. Like the FBI and J Edgar Hoover. Perhaps even attorney-general Bobby Kennedy. They'd be powerful enemies he could well do without. Besides, the press coverage would scupper his attempt to portray himself as a respectable businessman. Even misfits like Picklestitch wouldn't want to fence with him.

I watched De Luca's face. He hated it, but he knew he had to cut a deal.

He said: "What do you want?"

I said: "It's my story. If I tell Ben I want it pulled, he has to pull it. It's my copyright."

"And what would make you pull it? Money? Drugs? Girls? All three?"

"A piece of paper."

De Luca rocked back on his stool. "A piece of paper?"

"You hold a loan over the *Brighton Beach Banner*. I want a notice of cancellation delivered to the *Banner*'s offices in the next thirty minutes."

"Jeez. I can't do it in that time."

"There's a phone behind the bar. Use it now to make the call and give the order."

De Luca glanced at the phone - then the barman. "What are you grinning at, ape? Hand me that phone."

I leant against the bar while De Luca made the call. He took the phone from his ear.

"It's being done," he said. "Now you call and pull the story."

I rang the *Banner*'s number hoping Stoker was still in the office - and would catch on fast.

He answered: "*Banner*."

I said: "Ben, that story I wrote before I left the office. I want you to pull it."

"Pull it? That's a great story. I've already subbed the piece."

I said: "Trust me. It will pay to pull it. Just do it." I replaced the receiver before he could answer.

He'd scratch his head and wonder what the hell was going on. But he didn't know where I was calling from, so he couldn't ring back.

De Luca asked: "The story is out of the paper?"

"It's out of the paper. And my work is done."

De Luca climbed off his stool. Moved towards me.

"Mine isn't," he said. "Say farewell to your best friends. Make your will. Book your plot in the cemetery. Order your funeral flowers. You're dead."

I said: "Not while you rely on a pair of bunglers like Dino and Kurt. They couldn't kill a cockroach - even if it sat up and grinned at them."

He said: "Next time, I won't send an errand boy. It'll be me. And I'll have my epée."

I reached into my pocket and pulled out a Biro. "And I'll have this," I said.

"Think that will save you?" he said.

"I'll risk it. After all, you've just discovered that the pen is mightier than the sword."

Chapter 17

"You take some risks," Ben Stoker said. "One of these days..."

I grinned. "I was lucky. I caught De Luca hobnobbing with one of his so-called influential friends. It was easy to embarrass him. Even better, I did it in a place where he couldn't kill me without raising complaints about blood on the carpet."

We were in Stoker's office at the *Brighton Beach Banner*. It was early evening, just a couple of hours after my confrontation at the Founding Fathers' Athletic and Gentlemen's Club.

"But I must admit, I wouldn't have done it if Jess Sheldon hadn't barred me from her interview with Mabelle Willow. That made me red with anger."

"But De Luca is a dangerous man to cross."

"Even dangerous men have their weaknesses. And with men who've made their fortunes from crime it's often the desire to become legit. They find that money doesn't buy respect - at least, not from the people they'd like to respect them. That's why De Luca joins posh clubs like the Founding Fathers. It's a place where he can meet people like that state senator, a collection of odd body parts called Winklesnitch or something."

"Picklestitch."

"Yes. It was fortunate De Luca was having a drink with him when I pitched up. I was able to embarrass De Luca in front of the senator, just the kind of person he wants to impress. Once he was on the back foot, it was just a question of manoeuvring him into a position where he believed he was in real danger of being exposed in the *Banner*."

"Sounds a thin beat to me."

"Maybe. Jess might not get much out of Dino and Kurt, but she could threaten Mabelle with a conspiracy charge. That may be enough to get her talking. If she does, De Luca could have some awkward questions to answer."

"De Luca is a master at answering awkward questions - especially when his lawyers are in the room. And you can be sure they will be if Sheldon comes calling."

"There may not be enough yet to link De Luca to the killing of Shultz and the attempt on me, but he couldn't be sure. And with Picklestitch alert to the fact that the newspapers were on to him, he had to close the trouble down. That's why I pitched him the idea you were about to bring out a special Afternoon Extra edition naming him as a master criminal."

"Sure, I don't know how you did it, but that loan cancellation has saved the paper. When that guy came through the door and threw the papers on my desk I thought it was some kind of hoax - especially after that weird phone call from you."

"I had to make it look convincing to De Luca who was standing right next to me."

"You certainly did that. Three thousand seven hundred and forty-three dollars of convincing."

"And there's a great murder splash to lead the front page tomorrow," I said.

Stoker reached across his desk for a page proof. "You haven't seen this yet."

He handed me the page. My story was the splash under the headline KILLER KNIFES VICTIM IN BED.

Further down the page, there was another headline in screamer type: MAN SHOT IN CONEY ISLAND GHOST TRAIN.

"There's nothing like a good murder to get people buying newspapers," I said.

Stoker's mouth grimaced in a moue of doubt. "Perhaps," he said.

I stood up. "I guess this is the point in the movie where I ride off into the sunset."

Stoker stood and extended his arm across his desk. I took his hand and we shook.

"If you're ever looking for a job…" he said.

"...I'll be sure not to apply to the *Banner*."

Stoker laughed.

"And don't give up on that Pulitzer Prize," I said.

Stoker gave a rueful smile. "I guess that might be a dream too far - even with your help."

I picked up my suitcase and portable Olivetti and went through the door.

As I closed it behind me, I heard Stoker's telephone ring.

Two hours later, I was sitting in the departure lounge at Idlewild Airport waiting for my flight back to London.

I was drinking a cup of lukewarm coffee and thinking about the latest twist in the story.

The phone call Ben Stoker received just as I was leaving his office had come from Jess Sheldon. She'd interviewed Mabelle. The girl had turned out to be as slippery as her snake. She'd said she'd told De Luca that I'd shown her a photograph of someone who visited the club regularly. But she'd claimed she'd mentioned it as casual talk. She'd admitted mentioning to De Luca that I was renting a room from her aunt Ernestina, but denied telling him which room I slept in. Sheldon said the evidence didn't provide enough to warrant interviewing De Luca as an accessory to Shultz's murder.

And that wasn't the end of it. A top lawyer had turned up at the cop shop to defend Dino. No need to guess who was funding the legal brains. Now Dino wanted to plea bargain. He hadn't intended to kill Shultz at all. It had all been a private beef over some business deal between the two. Dino only meant to frighten Shultz. In the dark, he had slipped and accidentally knifed the poor sap. Dino would take a manslaughter rap in return for no more than eight years down the river in the pen.

It was Sheldon's considered opinion that De Luca would walk away from the whole affair. But, at least, he'd keep his head down until the court had ruled on what to do with Dino - and

Kurt, who was still in hospital having his wound tended.

I took a final sip of coffee and put the cup back in the saucer. There was one element in the story that Sheldon hadn't covered - De Luca's link with Bellwether. It was the link that interested me most. And if there was an answer, I thought that I'd find it back in England.

I was looking forward to getting back to the *Chronicle*.

And to Shirley.

Which reminded me. I'd missed Shirley's birthday while I'd been in Brighton Beach. I'd promised to bring her back a present. There were a few shops on the far side of the departure lounge. I stood up and strolled over to them. I stuck my hand in my pocket and pulled out a couple of notes and a few small coins. I had precisely two dollars and thirty-five cents of my American money left.

It wasn't going to buy Shirley much of a gift.

I mooched among the shops looking in the display cases. One held a collection of watches. My eye was taken by a small watch with a gold bracelet made of tiny links. It was as delicate a timepiece as I'd ever seen. Shirley would love it, I thought, simply because of its beauty. The price tag read: $195.

I was so absorbed in this thought that I didn't notice a tall man standing alongside me.

He said: "There are guys who'd pawn their last pair of pants to give their girl a watch like that."

I glanced sideways at him. He had a pleasant lined face with even features and the kind of intelligent eyes that come from reading people rather than books. His brown hair was cut short in a conservative fashion. He was wearing a grey three-piece suit with a striped tie. He had a show handkerchief in his breast pocket. I put his age at about forty.

I said: "I've been looking for a birthday present for my girlfriend but these trousers wouldn't raise enough cash at the pawnbrokers."

He glanced down and nodded. "I wouldn't disagree with that."

"They've taken a beating over the last few days."

"So I gather."

I looked at him sharply. "What do you gather?"

"That you've had a busy time in America."

I frowned. "Who are you?"

He smiled. Reached into an inside pocket and brought out a small leather folder. Opened the folder and took out a card. Handed the card to me.

I took the card and read: Rudolph Strongbow.

I said: "This card doesn't tell me anything about you."

"That's the way we like it."

"We?"

"The organisation I work for. Instead, let's talk about you. You came to America to trace the identity of one Arthur Crouch. You discovered he was better known on these shores as Elliott Bellwether. You found he consorted with a gangster called Leone De Luca and a train robber named Willis Newton. You got mixed up in an accidental murder and ran into more than you bargained for in the Coney Island ghost train. Am I right so far?"

I squared up to Strongbow and said: "Spit out what you want, then scarper. I've got a plane to catch."

Strongbow grinned in the kind of infectious way that might even have had me smiling too under other circumstances.

He said: "We also have an interest in Elliott Bellwether. A considerable interest in him, as it happens. We know he's in England, but not where. Of course, we've asked official agencies for help in tracing him. They've got other fish to fry - isn't that what you English say? But you're a reporter - you know what happens when official enquiries start. We've followed your progress in tracking him. Impressive. We think you might be able to help us."

"To do what?"

"To find Bellwether."

"And if I find Bellwether, what do I do?"

"You contact me."

"How?"

"Through a telephone number."

"What number?"

Strongbow said: "Turn over the card."

I did. It had a London telephone number on the back.

"A secretary will take a message and pass it to me immediately," he said.

"I'm a journalist chasing a story. Why should I want to help you?"

"We can be very generous to people who help us. Naturally we expect to pay a fee."

He signalled to the woman behind the watch counter. Asked for the gold watch. Paid for it from a bundle of bills the size of a giant's fist. Handed the watch packaged in a neat box to me.

"Shall we call this a down payment? Give it to your girl. Shirley isn't it?"

He strode off, turned after three paces. He gave an encouraging nod.

"But what's this all about?" I asked.

"That's what we'd like to know."

He turned and strode off across the concourse. A confident walk, with head up and arms swinging.

I stared after him with my mind in a riot.

Murder in the Night Final

A Crampton of the Chronicle mystery novella

Peter Bartram

The Morning, Noon and Night Trilogy
Book 3

Chapter 1

The sign on the wall behind the immigration desk at Heathrow Airport said: "Welcome to Britain".

But the look on the face of the bloke standing behind the desk said: "Bugger off."

He had a face like a suet pudding. Flabby cheeks, jowly chin, pudgy bags under his eyes.

He wore those glasses with round wire-frames and spindly arms with hooked ends. He'd wedged the hooks behind his ears like grappling irons. I once saw a similar pair of specs in a photo. They were perched on the nose of Heinrich Himmler. Perhaps Pudding Face used the same optician.

I shuffled up to the desk at the end of a long queue of travellers. We'd just staggered off the red-eye from New York. The clock on the wall said it was eight o'clock in the morning.

But the beat in my soul said it was three o'clock in the night. Lullaby time. I should've been tucked up in bed with my teddy. Or my girlfriend Shirley. Or both.

My brain cried out for sleep, but my body told me to shuffle on.

I reached the head of the queue.

Pudding Face held out a flabby hand and said: "Passport."

I handed it over. He flipped it open at the page with my photo and potted personal details.

He asked: "Where have you come from?"

I said: "The Land of the Free."

His cheeks drooped a bit and he said: "You're the tenth person to say that in the last half hour."

"Does that mean I get a prize?"

"It means you answer some questions. Are you Colin Crampton?"

"That's what it says in the little blue book you're holding."

"Your occupation is listed as journalist."

"Crime reporter on the Brighton *Evening Chronicle*."

He sniffed. "Have you been consorting with criminals in the Land of the Free?"

"Not through choice. I don't always get to pick the people I have to interview. I expect you know the problem."

He wrinkled his nose. I couldn't tell whether he was annoyed or wanted to sneeze.

He pointed at the photo in the passport and said: "Is this you?"

"A few years ago when I was young and carefree."

"It doesn't look much like you."

"That's because the photographer told me not to smile."

Pudding Face turned a page in my passport. "What colour are your eyes?" he asked.

"Bloodshot," I said. "I've just spent a night without sleep in an airline seat designed for a midget with six-inch legs."

"Any distinguishing characteristics?"

"Yes. When I put the seat back in the sleep position I was looking up the nose of the bloke in the row behind."

"Your characteristics, not the airline seat's."

"Only my warm personality and the desire to seek the best in everyone I meet."

Pudding Face snapped the passport shut. He handed it back to me. Looked over my right shoulder and said: "Next."

I glanced over my shoulder. "There isn't anyone," I said.

"There will be," he said. "There always is."

I shoved the passport back in my pocket and shuffled toward the door marked "Exit".

Welcome to Britain.

Shirley opened the little black box I'd given her and stared open-eyed.

"Jeez, Colin, did you rob a jeweller's?" she said.

The box contained the lady's gold wristwatch Rudolph Strongbow had pressed into my hand at Idlewild Airport in New York. The one that cost a hundred and ninety-five dollars.

Strongbow was the mysterious all-American hunk who'd bearded me in the departure lounge. He'd seemed to know more about my business in America than I knew myself. He wanted to find the whereabouts of Elliott Bellwether, a crooked New York lawyer who was on the run in Britain after becoming the victim of a train robbery. I'd have liked to know where Bellwether was myself. We had unfinished business. But I wasn't going to tell Strongbow about that.

Shirley took the watch out of its box and held it against her wrist.

"It's gorgeous," she said.

"When I was looking for your gift, I thought there's no present like the time."

Shirley groaned. "But how did you afford it?"

I said: "You mean when I only had two dollars thirty-five cents of my American money left. Strongbow pitched up with a proposition and wouldn't take no for an answer. The watch is, apparently, a down-payment on my fee for unspecified services to be rendered at some undefined time in the future."

A tiny wrinkle appeared on Shirley's brow. "You've lost me already. Why don't you start at the beginning?"

We were sitting in the Regency restaurant on Brighton seafront. I'd phoned Shirley at her flat from a call box to suggest lunch as soon as I'd stepped off the train at Brighton station. After the flight from the States and the train journey from Heathrow airport, I felt like a run-down clock that needed winding. I wanted my bed. But I also wanted Shirley. Preferably both together. I couldn't wait to see her again.

And here we were at a window table looking out to sea. In the middle distance, crowds of holidaymakers strolled on the West Pier. It was one of those days when the blue of the sky merges in a hazy line with the green of the sea. The triangular sails of small yachts cut the line of the horizon.

I said: "I'll tell you the full story, but first I wanted to wish you a belated happy birthday."

I raised a glass of the chilled sauvignon the waiter had brought and toasted Shirley. She leant forward and kissed me.

"Now tell me about this Strongbow guy," she said.

So I did. Between mouthfuls, as we tucked into our lemon soles, Jersey Royal potatoes dripping with butter, and a green salad lightly dressed with olive oil.

Shirley pronged one of the tasty spuds on her fork and raised it half way to her mouth.

"And that's how I came by the watch," I concluded.

Shirley lowered the fork and put it on her plate.

"I don't get it. A guy walks up to you in an airport and asks you to trace another guy you're already looking for. He doesn't know where this guy is but he knows all about you. Who is this Strongbow?"

"My guess is CIA."

"Who?"

"Central Intelligence Agency. It's the United States' civilian foreign intelligence service. Spies or spooks to you and me."

"Like James Bond?"

"He's British - Secret Intelligence Service, also known as MI6. And fictional. But, yes, if Strongbow is who he hints he is, he operates in the same kind of shadows. Maybe he's licensed to kill."

"But you're not sure?" Shirley picked up her fork again and scoffed the spud. A little dribble of butter ran down her chin. I leant over and wiped it off with my napkin.

"There's another possibility - that he's a crook. We know that Elliott Bellwether is. But he's a crook who's failed in his mission. He was robbed of the money he'd made from whatever criminal enterprise he'd undertaken. If he had other partners, they wouldn't be pleased the money has gone missing. They might even wonder whether Bellwether planned to double-cross them. Perhaps he was in league with Chaz, the motorcycle rocker who robbed him. Perhaps the pair had planned the scam to make it look like Bellwether had been robbed - and then intended to share the money between them."

"But Chaz was flattened by a furniture truck."

"Yes, if a double-cross was their plan, it went about as wrong as any plan could. The money has gone, but that doesn't mean Bellwether's partners wouldn't stop looking for revenge. Honour among thieves? Don't bet on it."

Shirley picked up the watch and looked at it again. "So my present could've been paid for with hot money?"

"We don't know that for sure. Strongbow could be what he implied to me - CIA. But we can't be certain."

Shirley held the watch up to the light. The sun's rays through the window caught it. They created tiny pools of light on its surface. Shirley fixed the watch strap around her wrist and fastened the clasp. She held out her arm for me to admire.

"It looks good," I said.

"Too good," she said. "Suppose this was paid for with cash ripped off from some unsuspecting bozo... Every time I checked the time, I'd feel like a heel."

She unfastened the clasp, took off the watch and placed it carefully back in the box. She closed the box. Pushed it across the table to me.

"Keep it for now until we know more."

I shrugged. "If that's what you want. But it means I don't have a present for you now."

Shirley flashed me a saucy sideways look. "We could celebrate my birthday in another way."

"With champagne?"

"No."

"With cake?"

"No."

"With a party?"

"For two."

"Where?"

"At my flat."

"When?"

"No time like the present."

I glanced at my watch. Ten past two. "I think my news editor Frank Figgis was expecting me back in the office by three o'clock."

Shirley grinned. "Better call him and say you'll be late."

Chapter 2

I walked into the newsroom at the *Chronicle* with a smile on my face as wide as the Brooklyn Bridge.

I just love those birthday presents where the giver gets as much pleasure as the receiver.

So it wasn't surprising that the old clock on the newsroom wall had just ticked onto twenty to five when I pushed through the swing doors. There was a chorus of backchat as I crossed the newsroom to my desk.

"Did you give your regards to Broadway?" Phil Bailey yelled across the room to general laughter.

"Were the gang still on Forty-Second Street?" Sally Martin shouted.

"Neither as it happens," I said. "But I did say hello to old Coney Isle in a way I won't forget."

I sat down in my old captain's chair and surveyed my desk. A thin film of dust had settled over piles of old papers and my Remington typewriter. I created a little mist above the desk as I blew it off.

I flipped open my notebook at the notes I'd made in America about Elliott Bellwether. I reached for copy paper and rolled it into the typewriter. I sat with my hands poised over the keys. To the best of my knowledge, Bellwether was alive and hiding somewhere in Britain. It was obvious he was a crook, but the only hard evidence linking him to crime was a fake passport. So this was a difficult story to write. It held more traps than a poacher's knapsack. Traps like libel which costs big money. Or contempt of court where you end up in chokey.

But this was a big story and had to be told. My mind buzzed with words. I started to type.

Dateline Brighton, 18 August 1963.

The man who was robbed on Volk's Railway 11 days ago has been named as Elliott Bellwether, an American lawyer.

Mr Bellwether was attacked on a train at Paston Place station where his attaché case was snatched. The case was later found to contain a false passport in the name of Arthur Crouch together with $12,000 in American currency and a first-class air-ticket to New York.

The case was recovered after the robber, Charles Rickman, was killed in a motor accident on Marine Parade while trying to escape. Mr Bellwether has not reclaimed the case and contents which are being held at Brighton Police Station.

The Chronicle has established that Mr Bellwether is well known in Brighton Beach, part of the Borough of Brooklyn in New York City. He is believed to be an associate of Leone De Luca, a nightclub owner, who has been involved in several police investigations but never charged.

He is also known to have met Willis Newton, an American who has served several prison terms for robbing trains and banks but who is currently free.

Mr Bellwether, who local people say does not practice as a lawyer in New York courts, lives in a luxury seafront penthouse apartment not far from Coney Island, famous for its amusement parks.

Brighton police have not been able to establish the purpose of Mr Bellwether's visit to Britain. He arrived in the country on the first of August and lodged at the Hawthorns Guest House in Kemp Town for a week.

The air tickets show that Mr Bellwether was due to fly back to America on the evening of seventh of August, just hours before the Great Train Robbery at Bridego Bridge, Ledburn in Buckinghamshire took place. There is no suggestion that Mr Bellwether was connected to the robbery.

Like hell, there was! But I'd written the last sentence to keep the libel lawyer's blood pressure down.

As I rolled the last folio out of my typewriter, Frank Figgis appeared at the side of my desk.

He took a long drag on his Woodbine and said: "Did you give your regards to Broadway?"

I said: "We've already done that one. And before you ask I didn't see the gang on Forty-Second Street either."

Figgis was never a snappy dresser but he seemed to be shabbier than usual. His shirt was creased. There was a gravy stain on his tie. His trousers were crumpled. And he was wearing odd socks.

He saw me studying him closely. His hard marble eyes shifted down to take in the waistcoat fastened on the wrong buttonholes, and the scuffed shoes.

"His Holiness has been riding me like a Grand National winner the last few days on this Bridego robbery story," he said.

Gerald Pope, the paper's editor, was the dim scion of some minor aristocratic family. The type that usually ends up as the vicar of an ancient church with a leaking roof and a congregation of two deaf parishioners. Instead, he'd been pushed into newspapers because his father knew someone else's father who owed him a favour. Pope rarely took any interest in the newsroom which was just fine with everyone who worked in it. He spent his time complaining that the weather forecast we published was always wrong. Once, I suggested Figgis should tell him that the forecast was right but the weather was wrong. But Figgis bottled it.

It was odd that Pope had become obsessed with the Bridego robbery, especially as it had happened well outside the *Chronicle*'s circulation area. Besides, the nationals were running acres of coverage of it. The *Chronicle* had had nothing new to add.

Until now, that is.

I said: "Any reason why Pope should be taking a special interest in the Bridego story?"

Figgis glanced around the newsroom. Typewriters had fallen silent. Phone calls hastily ended. Reporters who'd been planning a quick exit discovered a reason to linger. Everywhere people pretended to study their notebooks. Or rummage bits of stray lint out of their desk drawers. Or change the ribbon in their typewriters. Ears wigged. Everyone wanted to know the answer to my question.

Figgis said: "Come into my office."

I stood up, picked up the folios of my story and followed him across the newsroom. Behind me the buzz of whispered conversations started up.

Figgis opened the door to his office. I took a deep breath before I stepped inside. His sixty-a-day habit meant the room smelt like a coke oven had just exploded. In the First World War soldiers used to get invalided home from the trenches for breathing air like this.

Figgis sat at his desk and I pulled up the guest chair. He lit another fag and took a drag.

He said: "Keep this to yourself."

I drew my fingers across my lips in the zipped sign. I've always found its useful when you're asked to keep a confidence - and it's not a legally binding commitment if you want to break it.

"I think Pope is using this story to get me out of the paper," Figgis said.

"Whatever for?"

"I don't know. Perhaps I've read the situation wrongly. He just seems jumpy about the whole robbery."

I thought about that for a moment and then said: "The cops had discovered the Bridego robbers' hideout - a place called Leatherslade Farm - the day before I left for America but they weren't saying much about it. Have there been any developments since?"

Figgis balanced his fag on the edge of an ashtray and ran his fingers through his thinning hair. "Not much. They don't want to give a lot away. But I hear from my old Fleet Street drinking chums that the cops have lifted some fingerprints from the place. Perhaps that will lead to arrests. And yesterday, there was an item on the tapes that a couple of strollers had found a briefcase, a holdall and a camel-skin bag in Dorking Woods in Surrey. There was more than a hundred thousand quid in the bags."

"'If you go down to the woods today, you're sure of a big surprise,'" I said.

"Some surprise," Figgis said.

"And the strollers handed the cash to the cops?"

"Touching that there are still a few upright citizens about, isn't it?"

"But no arrests yet?" I asked.

"Not that we know of. And I'm sure the cops will be crowing about it as soon as they feel their first collar."

I leant back in my chair and said: "I think I may be able to take some of the heat off you." I handed him the folios of my story.

Figgis took them, put on his glasses and read them more slowly than he'd normally do. He took his glasses off and rubbed the bridge of his nose.

I said: "There's only a tenuous link to the Bridego robbery in the story for obvious legal reasons, but there's more."

I told Figgis about my theory that Bellwether had been recruited as a kind of consultant for the team running the Bridego heist. How Bellwether had been the conduit used to relay Willis Newton's first-hand experience of pulling off a big train job. And how there were striking similarities between a three million dollar steal Newton's gang had pulled on a mail train at Rondout, Illinois years back. And I told him how I believed Bellwether was still hiding out in Britain - and how Rudolph Strongbow had tried to recruit me to find him.

Figgis stood up, walked over to his window. And opened it.

I said: "Be careful. That fresh air could do you no end of harm."

Figgis turned towards me. "So could Pope if we don't get this right."

I was about to say something but somebody knocked the door. It opened. Cedric, the copy boy, stepped inside holding the latest edition of the *Evening Argus*, the rival paper in town.

He waved it around nervously. "Thought you might want to see this, Mr Figgis. It's their Night Final."

He stepped forward and put the paper on Figgis's desk. I had no difficulty reading the headline from where I sat. It was in the *Argus*'s biggest display type.

The headline read: VOLK'S TRAIN ROBBER'S HIDEOUT FOUND.

I grabbed the paper before Figgis could get back to his desk.

I devoured the story in seconds. The piece amounted to little more than a couple of facts resting on a pile of padding. While I'd been in America, Jim Houghton, my opposite number on the *Argus*, had landed his "scoop". He'd found where Charles Rickman - the man who'd robbed Bellwether on the Volk's Railway - had been living. According to the story, Rickman had lodged with a widow called Eileen Dudgeon at a house in the Westdean part of town.

The story informed me that Eileen was well-off and had lived in Brighton for more than ten years. Rickman had lodged with Eileen since he'd come to Brighton to work at Nobby's Novelties. That, Houghton reminded readers, was the company owned by Jerry Clark, the man who threw himself from the roof of his warehouse to avoid arrest for conspiracy to murder.

But Houghton had added an interesting footnote. Rickman's funeral was taking place at Woodvale Crematorium tomorrow morning. I decided I would put on my black tie and join the mourners.

But before then I had a question to answer. Who was this Eileen Dudgeon who was happy to provide bed and board to a man who turned out to be a train robber?

Chapter 3

If Eileen Dudgeon had ever featured in the *Chronicle*'s pages, the clipping would be filed away in the morgue.

When I walked through the door Henrietta Houndstooth, who ran the place, was standing behind her desk. She was running her fingers through her auburn bob-cut. She had a look on her face like she'd won the pools but lost the coupon.

I stepped smartly over to her desk and said. "If you're about to explode, keep a lid on it until I've fetched a dustpan and brush to sweep up the bits."

Henrietta let out a long sigh. "It's the Cousins," she said. "These past couple of days they've been driving me crazy."

The Clipping Cousins - Mabel, Elsie and Freda - were sitting at the large table in the centre of the office. They were three middle-aged matrons who'd been with the paper for years. They clipped each issue of the paper into cuttings which they filed in a vast maze of cabinets in a dusty archive behind their office. Normally, the table would be a chaotic jumble of newspapers, toffee papers and cake crumbs.

A friendly hum of gossip would buzz round the table like a wasp trapped in a jam jar.

But today, they sat as far apart as they could, like they suspected the others had an infectious disease. They barely looked at one another. They frowned, pursed their lips, clipped angrily with their scissors.

I whispered to Henrietta: "What's up with the Cousins?"

"It's the Women's Institute."

"Someone stolen their recipe for roly-poly pudding?"

"It's worse than that. Mrs Hogg-Tomlinson has resigned as chairwoman of the local branch after fourteen years and all three are vying for the job."

"Nothing wrong with healthy democracy."

"Perhaps not. But they're accusing each other of dirty tricks in the election campaign."

I strolled over to the table and said: "Hello, ladies. Is it my imagination or has the next ice age started in here?"

Mabel eased a painful ruck in her surgical stocking, pointed at Elsie and said: "You better ask her. I don't go around promising the impossible."

Elsie swivelled so sharply in her neck brace I thought the damned thing was going to fall off. "I am going to get Frankie Vaughan as the speaker at one of our meetings when I'm chairwoman," Elsie spat back at Mabel.

Vaughan was a popular singer whose stage manner was as greasy as his Brylcreemed hair. He had this habit of kicking out his right leg at the high points of his numbers. It was a gesture which appealed to middle-aged women. I could never understand why. But, then, I'm not one. In any event, it seemed unlikely a star of the London Palladium would take time out to address a couple of dozen women in a draughty church hall in Brighton.

Mabel and Elsie glared at one another.

Meanwhile, Freda looked at me earnestly with her good eye. "Both of them don't stand a chance. I've got the jam makers' vote tied up."

Mabel and Elsie switched their hate glares onto Freda.

Henrietta came up alongside me. "I don't want to hear any more about this election today - or tomorrow. And I want yesterday's newspaper clipped and filed before any of you go home tonight."

The Cousins grumpily reached for scissors and pens.

I said: "May the best woman win."

"Thank you," they chorused together. Then shot daggers at one another.

Henrietta and I walked back across the room and she sat down behind her desk. I perched on the edge of it, like a bird on a window ledge.

"Goodness knows what will happen when they make their speeches at the hustings meeting," she said.

"The paper will have to send a reporter to that," I said. "Bill Clegg who writes the rugby coverage will be the man for the job. He knows all the dirty tricks in a scrum."

Henrietta grinned for the first time since I'd walked into the room. "Bet you didn't come in to talk about the Women's Institute."

"It wasn't the main item on my mind. I want to know whether the paper has ever written anything about one Eileen Dudgeon. And before you ask, I don't know whether she was a member of the Women's Institute - and I don't care."

Henrietta stood up and said: "Let's go into the filing stacks and see whether we have a folder on her."

The stacks - floor-to-ceiling cabinets, each filled with files of cuttings - were held in a maze of corridors lit by dim bulbs. The air was heavy with a musty odour as two million press cuttings quietly mouldered. The passageways between the cabinets were covered with cheap lino and creaked as you walked over them. I often wondered when the weight of cuttings in the drawers would be so great they'd crash through the floor into the advertising department below.

Henrietta stepped briskly along, no doubt without any of these troubling thoughts on her mind. We reached the Ds and edged sideways looking for the drawer that began DU. Finally, Henrietta stopped, reached down to a drawer second up from the floor and pulled it open. She stooped low and rummaged through the files in the drawer.

Her body tensed. She tut-tutted and shook her head.

I moved closer. "What's wrong?" I said.

"This shouldn't be here," she said. She pulled out a file and handed it to me.

The name on the file was Duane Eddy.

I opened the file and had a quick shufti. It appeared Eddy had played a concert in Brighton a few years earlier. There was a piece previewing the event, a backgrounder on the rock-and-roll star, and a review by one of the *Chronicle*'s reporters. ("Duane's Brighton rock.")

I handed the file back to Henrietta.

"This should be filed under Eddy, not Duane," she said.

"Easy mistake to make," I said. "The bloke has one of those reversible names. Whoever filed it probably thought Eddy was his given name. That's not going to be a problem for Eileen Dudgeon."

"No." Henrietta flipped through some more files. "No Eileen Dudgeon here," she said. "But we do have a Dudgeon, Sir Roderick." She pulled a buff folder out and handed it to me.

I opened it. There were three cuttings in the file. The first was dated five years earlier. It described how Brighton resident Roderick Dudgeon had been knighted by Queen Elizabeth for his services to the government. It didn't say what those services were. Perhaps lying low and keeping out of trouble.

The second cutting was dated three years earlier. It related how Sir Roderick had given a talk at a local Women's Institute meeting. His subject: potting chrysanthemums. And the third cutting, just eighteen months old, was a brief obituary. It described how Sir Roderick had been a senior civil servant "at the heart of government" and a "wise head in Whitehall". I read through the three paragraphs. The obituary's writer obviously hadn't had the faintest idea what Sir Roderick had done with his life. Apart from potting chrysanthemums.

Henrietta stood up and looked over my shoulder as I read the cuttings.

"Don't tell you much, do they?" she said.

"More than you think," I said.

I was wondering how a motorcycle rocker who hung out at a greasy spoon café and robbed a man on a train came to be lodging with the widow of a titled gent who'd spent his life "at the heart of government" and potting chrysanthemums.

But not, presumably, at the same time.

I was still thinking about it as I arrived back at my flat in Regency Square, an address which never quite lived up to its billing.

Charles Rickman - Chaz, as I'd come to think of him - was more Duane than Dudgeon. I could just see Chaz at a Duane Eddy concert playing air guitar at the front with the other hopefuls who dreamed of becoming something they'd never be. I also had a mental image of Sir Roderick Dudgeon. He'd be a stuffy type who thought the height of informality would be to sit down to luncheon wearing a tweed suit without a waistcoat. His wife - Lady Eileen, as I now needed to think of her - would be the product of a minor girls' public school. She'd employ a cleaner to come in twice a week, but do her own baking.

How was it that Chaz, who worked as a humble warehouseman for a company selling the kind of stuff that would have Lady Dudgeon calling in the bad taste police, came to lodge with her? No doubt she was a bit short of the readies now that Sir Roderick was no longer around to draw his civil service pension. But if she needed to rent a room, surely she'd have chosen a white-collar lodger? Like a bank clerk with a frayed collar and a fading picture still tucked in his wallet of the girlfriend who jilted him years ago. Or a lady librarian with a pince-nez balanced on her nose, her hair tied in a bun, and a secret stock of Mills & Boon romances under her bed.

None of it made much sense. The one bright spot was that it didn't seem Jim Houghton on the *Argus* knew about Eileen's background. If he had, he'd have surely mentioned it in his piece in today's paper.

I reached the front door and inserted my key silently into the lock. I opened the door, stepped quietly inside and crept towards the stairs.

It was no use. I might as well have turned up with a marching band playing something by Souza.

The Widow was out of her parlour before I could get my foot onto the first tread. Beatrice Gribble, my landlady, had hearing that would shame a bat. She was dressed in a long flannelette dressing gown and had her hair in pink curlers. She'd fixed a kind of net arrangement over the curlers so it looked like she'd just caught a load of prawns on her head.

She said: "Mr Crampton, I'd like to take a minute of your time."

"Of course. I'll save a minute for you - in about three years."

"It's urgent."

The Widow moved across the hall and blocked my route to the stairs.

When she was in one of these moods, it was usually quicker to hear her out.

So I yawned and asked: "What is it?"

"It's about the room on the first floor that's been empty since that nice Valerie Hanley moved to Hertfordshire. Something strange has happened."

"Valerie's ghost has put in an appearance?"

"It's stranger than that. A man presented himself on the doorstep this afternoon and asked to rent the room."

"What's strange about that?"

"I hadn't advertised it, so how did he know it was for rent? I normally put a card in Mr Patel's window, but I haven't done anything as some of Valerie's things are still in the room."

"Did the man say how he'd heard about it?"

"He winked at me. Well, really!"

From the look on her face, anyone would have thought the Widow had just been ravaged by a shipload of drunken sailors.

"No other explanation?" I asked.

"He said he'd heard about it 'on the grapevine'. Whatever that was supposed to mean."

"So you sent him packing?"

The Widow's cheeks coloured. As usual, there'd be more. Something she was embarrassed about.

"He asked me what the rent was. When I told him, he said he'd add an extra ten shillings a week because he wanted so much to live in Regency Square. I'm very tempted, but I don't know whether I can trust him because his eyebrows meet in the middle."

I ignored that and asked: "Did he say what he did?"

"A writer."

"That usually means unemployed."

"But he offered me a month's rent in advance. So he can't be hard up."

"And you've accepted it?"

"He moves in the day after tomorrow. Do you think I've done the right thing?"

"I'll let you know when I've taken a look at him." I pushed by the Widow and started up the stairs. "What does he call himself?" I asked over my shoulder.

"Mr Coniston. But what's in a name?"

As it turned out, more than I'd expected.

Chapter 4

Early morning mist drifted like wraiths through the woods as I drove along the narrow track towards Woodvale Crematorium.

I swung the car around the bend onto the forecourt of Woodvale's chapel. The gravel crunched under the MGB's tyres.

It was the morning after Mrs Gribble had bearded me with her worries about the new tenant. But I wasn't thinking about that as I climbed out of the MGB and looked around.

A light breeze ruffled the canopy of the trees surrounding the chapel. A couple of pigeons cooed at one another, then fluttered noisily into the woods. A Siamese cat appeared from behind a stone, looked at me in a disinterested sort of way, and slunk off into the undergrowth.

As I crossed the forecourt towards the chapel, a short man with stubby legs, a pudgy face and a bald head appeared around the corner. He was dressed in the full clerical get-up of cassock and surplice with a fancy embroidered stole looped round his neck. He glanced at his watch, tut-tutted to himself, and hurried towards me.

He looked at me with sad eyes and said: "I'm the Reverend Harrison Poulter. Are you with the deceased?"

I said: "No. He's in a coffin and there was only room for one."

Poulter's eyes swivelled upwards as though he were looking for help. "I meant are you with the funeral party?"

"At the moment, I'm on my own. But if someone wants a party, I'm game."

Poulter said: "I knew this was going to be a difficult ceremony. In a case like this, I'd normally get the organist to play *Sheep May Safely Graze* by Johann Sebastian Bach. I'd say a few words, and send the dear departed on his way. But the regular organist is off sick and I've had to fall back on Mr Younghusband who's not really up to it. He's got these new dentures which he grinds during the hard bits, but still plays most of the notes wrong."

"So his Bach is worse than his bite?"

Poulter sighed. "In fact, I've just heard that Bach is not wanted. We're having some modern music played on records. Not that I've heard of it. *Three Steps to Heaven* by one Eddie Cochran sounds as though it may be suitable but *Pistol Packin' Mama* by someone called Gene Vincent? Hardly ecumenical, is it?"

I said: "Who asked for the music? In fact, who made the funeral arrangements?"

"I believe the funeral is being paid for at public expense."

"A pauper's funeral?"

"We try and avoid that phrase in these more egalitarian times."

"But who's told you what music to use?"

"It came as a telephone message taken in the office. I don't think the caller left a name."

I was about to pursue that point when a taxi appeared out of the mist and drew to a halt. Michelle Jarrett, the casino croupier who'd been Chaz's girlfriend, climbed out of the back seat. She was wearing a black dress with a mauve chiffon scarf around her neck. She had a scrunched arrangement of feathers and bows on her head which was either a hat or a dead crow.

I walked over to her and said: "I'm sorry about Chaz."

She looked at me through teary eyes and said: "He lied to me. I read it in last night's *Evening Argus*. He said he lived in a flat in Coldean when all the time he was lodging with a lady in Westdean. Why did he do that?"

I said: "I don't know, but I'd like to find out."

"So would I. But it's too late now."

"It's never too late for the truth," I said. Then wished I hadn't. It was the kind of cod philosophy you saw printed on cheap gifts in the shops on the seafront. A solemn occasion and I was talking like a souvenir tea-towel.

Michelle looked at me in a kind of pitying way and tottered

off on three-inch heels across the gravel.

As she turned the corner to enter the chapel, a beaten-up old Wolseley emerged from the mist, made a circle turn on the forecourt and pulled up alongside my MGB.

The driver's door opened. Jim Houghton levered himself out of his seat and looked around. He spotted me and leered in the predatory way of a man who knows he's got a bundle of snide remarks to make and has just spotted a mug to use them on.

He limped towards me. He was wearing his trade-mark moth-eaten grey suit and a black tie. He had a small shaving nick on his chin. A hank of greasy hair flopped over his wrinkled forehead.

He said: "I'm surprised to see you here. After my exclusive in last night's paper you're running so far behind on this story you couldn't catch me, even if I took a fortnight's holiday."

I said: "Good to see you've lost none of your old charm while I was nailing the big story in New York."

There was a brief flash of worry in Jim's eyes. They flickered like there was a loose connection in the wiring.

"What big story?"

"You'll read it in the *Chronicle* today. I've uncovered the real name of Arthur Crouch, the man who was robbed by the late Charles Rickman on Volk's Railway."

"Real name? What is his real name?"

"It's not John Smith."

"You don't say." Jim turned. "I'm going in to get a seat at the front before it fills up."

He limped off and I stood there amidst the mist and the silence and felt the pleasure of a small victory warm me like a good brandy.

I had no intention of taking a seat at the front. If I took a seat at all, it would be at the back. That's where you see what really goes on. Besides, I was waiting for one mourner I thought would put in an appearance. Eileen Dudgeon. She'd provided Chaz with board and lodging for more than six months. So, surely, she would turn up to pay her last respects? If so, I planned to waylay her before she entered the chapel. I had some blunt questions I wanted to ask.

I was musing on this strategy when a distant rumble rolled through the woods.

At first it sounded like thunder. But it couldn't be. Instead of dying away, the rumble grew in volume. Besides, this wasn't thundery weather.

I stood and listened as the rumble grew to a roar that filled the air and echoed through the wood. And then they appeared out of the mist, moving slowly in a steady stream. There were motorcycles - dozens of them. I counted thirty-two before I gave up and simply watched.

The cycles fanned out across the forecourt and formed two lines, facing one another - like a guard of honour. I recognised one or two of the riders from the time Shirley and I had visited the Ace of Spades café in Peacehaven. Marlene, who'd been Boss's girlfriend, seemed to have shifted her affections. She rode pillion to a new guy, with a big chest and thick arms. He was dressed in black motorcycle leathers and had a red bandana tied around his neck.

The riders dismounted and stood beside their cycles, waiting. And then slowly the hearse appeared far back on the lane through the wood. For a moment, a puff of mist flurried out of the trees and obscured it. But then it emerged, smooth and stately, like a blackbird swooping from a cloud.

The hearse drove slowly onto the forecourt between the honour guard formed by the motorcyclists. As it approached, they reached for their throttles and revved their engines into a monstrous roar. Birds squawked and took to the skies. They wheeled in the air and screeched with anger.

The hearse turned and stopped in the middle of the forecourt. The riders turned off their engines and walked towards the chapel. I took out my notebook and jotted some quick notes to remind me of the scene.

Then I strode towards the hearse. The funeral director and pallbearers were already sliding out the coffin. It was a fine-looking item, fashioned out of oak, polished to a bright sheen, and fitted with handsome brass handles. It was a stately way for a train robber to travel on his last journey. The Reverend Poulter had said the funeral was being paid for at public expense. Either the public had suddenly become unaccountably generous - or someone had signed a big cheque.

The pallbearers hoisted the coffin and marched slowly towards the chapel door. From inside, a scratchy record of Eddie Cochran singing *Three Steps to Heaven* started up.

I followed the coffin into the chapel.

Eddie was finishing the last few bars as I took my seat at the back where I could keep an eye on the congregation - and the door, in case Eileen Dudgeon was a late show.

Poulter moved towards the coffin and started on the service: "'I am the resurrection and the life,' says the Lord. 'Those who believe in me, even though they die, will live, and everyone who lives and believes in me will never die…'"

The vicar droned on. At one point, Marlene stood up and read a poem. Something about "Speed is what I live for - give me life/ Faster, faster, faster, cutting like a knife." It went on for several verses in the same vein. Heads nodded, but I don't think anyone really knew what it meant.

We stood up and bopped around self-consciously while the record player belted out a tinny version of Gene Vincent singing *Pistol Packin' Mama*.

Then Poulter moved in for the final words: "We have entrusted our brother Charles to Christ's mercy…"

I knew the rest and headed quietly for the door. One question had nagged at my mind throughout the service. Why hadn't Eileen Dudgeon, the woman who'd put a roof over Chaz's head, come to pay her last respects?

Eileen Dudgeon lived in a substantial Victorian villa just up the hill from Withdean Stadium.

I had Jim Houghton's piece in last night's *Argus* to thank for the address. The place looked out over some woodland. The road was the kind of quiet backway where the residents of the posh houses would keep themselves to themselves.

Eileen's place stood about twenty yards back from the street behind an attractive garden planted with geraniums, foxgloves, nasturtiums and sweet peas. There was a small fishpond. A stone gnome with a red jacket, yellow breeches and a supercilious smile dangled a fishing line in the water. A stone-flagged path led up to the front door. My shoes click-clacked as I walked up it.

The front door had a lattice arrangement in the top half set with small windows. Beside the door was a bell pull - no common-or-garden buttons for the Dudgeons - and I gave it a hearty yank. It jangled away in the house with the kind of urgent tone which I imagined once had a butler hurrying.

But not today.

I tried again.

Nothing.

I peered through one of the small window panes in the front door. There was a wide hallway with a polished wooden floor and a Persian rug in the middle of it. There was a hat stand to one side of the hall and an occasional table on the other side. There were framed family pictures on one wall.

But I only took these details in later.

Because now I knew why Eileen Dudgeon had not been at Chaz's funeral.

She'd soon be attending her own.

Chapter 5

I marched across to the fishpond and seized the gnome by his scrawny neck.

I hurried back to the door, transferred my grip to the gnome's nether regions, and thrust his head through one of the small window panes. The one nearest the lock. That wiped the smile off the little beast's face.

I left the gnome in the porch looking sorry for himself, shoved my hand through the broken window and opened the door from the inside. I stepped in carefully avoiding the glass on the floor and moved to the woman's body.

She was lying part upside down with her legs on the bottom three steps of the stairs. Her head had twisted over onto her shoulder. She looked as though she'd tumbled down stairs head first. But had she tripped or was she pushed? It was difficult to say from the position of her body. And there was no obvious sign of a struggle in the hall or on the stairs.

It was clear from the angle of her head to her body that her neck was broken, but I checked for a pulse anyway.

Nothing.

I assumed this was Lady Eileen Dudgeon, but I've slipped up in the past with careless assumptions. So I knelt down and took a good look at her face. Then I went over to the family photos on the wall and examined them. The lady on the floor was the same as the woman who appeared in several of them.

I knew I had to call the police, but could I have a quick look round first? It would be a risk. Someone else might come to the front-door, see the broken window, and call the cops themselves. They might stumble in and find me. Worse, the cops might discover me rootling around with a dead body on the floor. Difficult to explain. Big trouble.

Yet the situation also presented an opportunity. If some of

Chaz's possessions were still in the house, they could provide clues as to who he really was. I assumed he had a room upstairs, so I stepped carefully over her ladyship and hurried up two steps at a time.

A couple of times previously, I've searched a house before calling the cops. I don't recommend it, but if you must, buy a pair of those thin rubber gloves that surgeons wear when they're cutting people up. You can buy them in Boots. (The gloves, not the surgeons.) The sales assistant gives you a bit of a queer look as though you're some kind of weird pervert, but the gloves stop you leaving your fingerprints all over the place. I always carry a pair in my jacket pocket. They scrunch up tight and take very little room.

I took them out when I reached the top of the stairs and put them on. A corridor had two doors off to the right and one at the far end.

The first room I pushed into had a large double bed, a couple of hefty wardrobes, and a dressing table loaded with bottles of scent and jars of unguents. Lady Dudgeon's room.

The second was a bathroom.

The door at the far end of the corridor opened into a light and airy room. There was a large window with a view of the house next door. There was a single bed that had been stripped of its bedding and was now covered with a heap of books, records and magazines. Shelves around the room had been emptied. Drawers pulled out and their contents dumped on the floor. The rug in the middle of the room had been rolled up. There were scratch lines along the wall at the back of the shelves. It looked as though someone had used a small-bladed knife to probe the wall for secret compartments.

The room had been searched in a hurry.

Which answered the question about whether Lady Dudgeon had fallen or been pushed.

It wasn't going to take Hercule Poirot to work out she'd been killed when she'd discovered the searcher. He or she had tried to make it look like an accident. Although that ploy would not have convinced anyone for long. As soon as the cops saw the bedroom, they'd realise the room had been turned over. Even Brighton's finest could draw the correct conclusions from that.

I put the question of who the killer was to the back of my mind for a moment. I focused on whether there were any clues about Chaz's true identity among the jumble of his possessions on the bed.

There were a dozen or so books about the actor James Dean and back issues of film journals featuring articles about him. There were motorcycle magazines, copies of *Melody Maker*, the pop music weekly, and an untidy heap of various newspapers - the *Chronicle*, the *Argus* and, surprisingly, some back issues of *The Times*. There were no clothes or any other personal items.

I looked at the stuff and couldn't decide what to make of it. I knew that the motorcycle chapter which Chaz had belonged to hero-worshipped James Dean. They'd even created a kind of shrine out of Dean memorabilia in the Ace of Spades café. So it wasn't surprising that Chaz had a room full of Dean material. But there was something strange about his. Most of it seemed relatively new and little read. The books had no creases on the spine and most of the magazines seemed to be in pristine condition. If Chaz had a lifetime obsession with Dean - like his motorcycle chums - why had he bought most of his Dean collection recently?

I didn't have time to answer that question now - because there was something else I wanted to look for before I called the cops.

I'd discovered the previous evening that the late Sir Roderick Dudgeon was a former civil servant. I wanted to see whether there were any clues in the house about what kind of civil servant he'd been.

I slipped back down the stairs, taking care not to tread on Lady Dudgeon on the last three steps. I hurried through the hall and poked my head around the first door on my left. A sitting room. I'd come back to that if there was time. The kind of clue I was looking for would be in the study. If Sir Roderick had one. And what retired civil servant doesn't? He needs the comfort of somewhere he can shuffle pointless pieces of paper about.

I found the study round a dog-leg in a corridor to the right. It was a dark room with browns and greys and lots of leather-bound books which I guessed Dudgeon collected for show rather than reading. There was a handsome desk with an inlaid green leather top. I opened the desk's drawers one by one. It looked as though Lady Dudgeon had done little to clear them since Sir Roderick had died. Perhaps she couldn't face up to the job.

But that suited me just fine. I found what I was looking for in the bottom drawer in the middle of a pile of old *Hansards*. It was an internal telephone directory for top civil servants. Perhaps Dudgeon hadn't realised it had slipped between the parliamentary reports. I opened the directory and flipped to Dudgeon, Sir Roderick.

I gasped. (Honestly! It was one of those times when I couldn't stop myself.) And with good reason. Until three years ago, Sir Roderick had been head of the Security Service.

Better known as MI5.

Carefully, I stuffed the directory back in the middle of the *Hansards*.

I went back into the hall, took off my gloves and grasped the telephone. Despite the shock, I was pleased I was still thinking straight. When you've taken care not to leave your dabs around, it's suspicious not to leave them where they should be. Then I called the cops.

It was three minutes before I heard the ringing bell of the cop car approaching from the far end of the road.

"One of these days the cops will slam the bracelets on you and march you off to the cells."

Frank Figgis's eyes twinkled in a way that suggested he was looking forward to the event.

I said: "As I told Detective Inspector Ted Wilson, any public-spirited person would break into a house to save an injured woman."

"Except that she was dead."

"I couldn't be sure of that from outside the house."

We were sitting in Figgis's office. I'd spent a busy two hours since finding Eileen. First, I was interviewed by Ted. Then I hurried back to the office to write up the murder story in time for the Night Final edition.

There was a knock on the door and Cedric came in. He handed a proof of the front page to Figgis, nodded at me and went out. Figgis looked at the proof and grunted with satisfaction. He showed the page to me. A screamer headline read:

SPY CHIEF'S WIFE FOUND DEAD

I'd taken a risk mentioning the fact that Sir Roderick had been the boss of MI5. If the cops asked me, I'd have to think of a credible reason for how I'd found out. I couldn't admit to rummaging in the old boy's desk. But that was a problem for the future. Right now, I had another thought on my mind.

I said: "I'm sure Lady Eileen was killed by whoever was searching Chaz's room."

"The big question is who was doing the searching - and the killing," Figgis said.

"I think it was Elliott Bellwether, the former Arthur Crouch - the mystery guy Chaz relieved of twelve thousand dollars and a false passport."

"Surely he'd keep a low profile while he plotted his escape from the country?"

"That's what I thought at first. But I've changed my mind. I'd assumed that he'd lie low while he fixed up a new false passport and plane ticket out. But now I wonder whether the people who'd employed him have cut him loose. My theory is that he provided advice on how to carry out the Bridego robbery. We know that the cops are closing in on the gang. If the gang arranged Bellwether's original fake passport, they might now be feeling the heat. Perhaps they can't deliver a second time. Perhaps they don't want to now the cops are on their tail."

Figgis reached for a Woodbine and rolled it speculatively between his fingers.

"But why kill Lady Dudgeon?"

"I think she was collateral damage. If it was Bellwether, I don't think he intended to kill her. Perhaps he thought the house was empty. I'm sure he's as puzzled as we are why he was robbed by Chaz. He knew Chaz was dead, but until Jim revealed where he'd been living in last night's *Argus*, Bellwether wouldn't have known anything else about him. Perhaps he thought he'd find something among Chaz's things that would get him out of his mess."

"But we still don't know where Bellwether is hiding."

I nodded. "That's true. And we're not the only people looking for him. I'm convinced Rudolph Strongbow, the CIA guy who gave me the gold watch for Shirley, is looking also. He handed me a contact number in London. I'm going to call it and see if I can get any further information out of him."

Figgis lit his fag and took a drag. "Be careful. Those guys really are scary."

Chapter 6

I lounged in the captain's chair at my desk in the newsroom and looked at the card Rudolph Strongbow had given me.

I turned it over and studied the phone number on the back: REG 7937.

I'd always thought there was a certain elegance to London telephone numbers. Three letters, four numbers. Easy to remember. Besides, the letters told you whereabouts in the sprawling city the telephone was located.

REG stood for Regent Street, a handsome boulevard of posh shops and offices that stretched from Oxford Circus to Piccadilly Circus. Some REG numbers would belong to premises in the street itself. But not all of them. To the east lay Soho, London's red-light district. I wondered exactly where Strongbow's office was among the good and the bad of the Regent Street telephone area.

And there was only one way to find out.

I leant forward, lifted the receiver, and dialled the number.

The phone was answered after three rings by a woman with a pinched voice: "Regent Street 7937. Thelma Hughes speaking."

In the background, I heard the growl of a car's engine start, rev a couple of times, and drive off. The woman was sitting close to an open window.

I said: "Am I through to Rudolph Strongbow's office?"

There was a slight pause and I heard some papers rustle.

Then Thelma said: "Would that be Mr Strongbow of the Acme Zip Fastener Company?"

I gulped in surprise - at Strongbow's audacity. So he'd created a false front for himself.

I said: "Is there any other Strongbow?"

"No."

"In that case, yes."

"How may I help you?"

In the background, I could hear a faint rhythmical thump. Like the drums of a small combo beating out a dance tune.

I said: "I have an urgent letter for Mr Strongbow. Could you please give me his office address?"

"Mr Strongbow has all his mail delivered to a post office box number," Thelma said. She quoted the number for me.

Ah!

I paused for a moment, while I thought about that.

A rough man's voice - presumably from outside the window - shouted something. It sounded like: "Free pund of yer pip ins a bob."

I said: "As the letter is urgent, I'd like to deliver it by hand."

Now a pause at the other end of the line.

The beat of the drum rose to a climax and ended. I thought I heard a flurry of faint handclaps.

Thelma said: "Mr Strongbow will not be in the office to receive your letter. Please use the post office box number."

"Perhaps I could take the office address for my files."

Thelma's voice took on a distinct frost. "The telephone number and post office box are all you will need to contact Mr Strongbow in the future."

The line went dead.

I sat back and thought about that. Thelma was very anxious that I shouldn't know where Strongbow was. If, as I suspected, he was a spook, that wouldn't be surprising. But there were too many unanswered questions about Strongbow. Before I traded information, I needed to know more about the man. And that meant finding where he hung out.

I could try and blag the address of Strongbow's office from directory enquiries. But that would be risky. If my scam went wrong, the Post Office would alert Strongbow to the threat. And he would know I was tracking him.

So did that mean finding his office was impossible?

I didn't think so. For a start, I knew it must be inside the Regent Street telephone area. That restricted it to an area bounded on the east by Charing Cross Road, on the north by Oxford Street, on the south by Shaftesbury Avenue, and on the west by Regent Street itself. It was still a large area with thousands of buildings and it would take days to search.

But I'd picked up some other clues during my call to Thelma.

I'd heard a car start up and drive off. Not unusual in London. But what was unusual for central London was that I hadn't heard any other cars. Most roads were clogged with traffic. In those, there was a background hum of idling engines. So the office could be close to a road where cars were restricted.

Then there was the sound of beat music and the faint ripple of applause. That was unusual for the middle of an afternoon. My area covered Soho and there were plenty of seedy drinking and striptease clubs in the area. So perhaps Strongbow's office could've been next door to one. Or even on another floor in the same building. That didn't sound like the kind of premises a CIA operative would hire, but perhaps that was the point. They operated in places people would least expect to find them.

And then there was the shout from outside the window by the man with the rough voice. I tried to recall his words: "*Free pund of yer pip ins a bob.*" Pure Cockney, the London slang. For my own benefit, I translated: "Three pounds of your pippins for a bob." The man was selling Cox's orange pippin apples for a shilling. He was a market trader. That would explain the absence of many cars. The street was filled with market stalls.

I knew from my time at university in London that there was only one street market in the area I'd defined. Berwick Street. And I'd bet a guinea to an orange pippin that Strongbow's office was within sight and sound of the market and close to a club. It could still be a challenge to find it and I would need some help.

I lifted the phone and dialled a Brighton number.

Shirley lifted a stained mug to her lips, took a sip, and said: "This tea tastes like wombats' piss."

"Drank much of it back in Oz, did you?" I asked.

"Tea?"

"No, wombats' pee."

Shirley clunked her mug back on the table and gave me a not-so-playful punch on the arm.

Ouch!

We were in a cramped greasy spoon caff in Peter Street, Soho. The place was run by a miserable bloke with a face like a squashed sausage. He was slouched behind the counter wearing a white apron stained with egg yolk and tomato sauce.

Shirley and I were sitting at a window table looking across the road at a broad-fronted four-storey building just around the corner from Berwick Street. The front wall of the building had been fly-posted with posters about a Billy Graham revival meeting. To the side of the posters, a brass plaque had turned dark with age. It read: Mercury Message Agency. First floor. REGent Street 7937.

"Is that it?" Shirley asked.

"I'm sure it must be," I said.

We'd spent nearly an hour inspecting every building within a hundred yards of Berwick Street market.

I said: "The clincher is that bloke over there." I pointed at a tubby barrel of a man in short-sleeved shirt and flat cap standing beside a fruit and veg stall. As we watched, he bellowed down the street: "Git yer luverly barn arse, sip en a bun."

I translated: "Get your lovely bananas, six pence a bunch. I'm sure that's the man I heard over the phone."

Shirley said: "But the place is above a strip club."

The building's ground floor had wide double doors which opened into a spacious foyer. Above the doors a red neon sign flashed: Naughty Knickers Club.

I said: "When I called the number, I thought I could hear

music in the background, but I wasn't expecting a set-up quite like this."

Inside, the foyer provided access to the club and the other floors. To the left, stairs led to the upper storeys. To the right, a desk was manned by a heavy-set ex-boxer type with a blunt nose and a cauliflower ear. He wore a dinner jacket so tight he moved with stiff limbs like a robot that needed oiling. Behind the desk, stairs led down to the basement where it seemed the girls danced wearing (or not) their naughty knickers.

Shirley said: "We can't hang around here much longer. I think old misery-guts behind the counter thinks we're going to steal the spoons."

"Now that I know Strongbow is using a message agency, I don't think we're likely to see him."

"So what's next?" Shirley asked.

"Let's give it five more minutes. We could keep misery-guts happy by ordering one of those doughnuts on the counter."

"Doughnuts? I thought that was a pile of elephant droppings," Shirley said.

I was about to urge Shirley to keep her voice low, when I noticed a bloke turn into the street from the far corner. He was dressed in a linen summer suit and a red bow tie. He wore a Panama hat with a scarlet band. He reminded me of Alec Guinness as Wormold in the film *Our Man in Havana*. He glanced behind to see whether he was being followed - in the manner of shifty types everywhere.

He slowed his pace as he approached the Naughty Knickers Club and looked round again. He glanced into the foyer as he walked by, took a few more steps, loitered as he looked all-round the street, then walked smartly back to the club. He stepped through the doors and went up the stairs like his trousers had just caught fire.

"Is that Strongbow?" Shirley asked.

"No, but I wonder whether he's one of his messengers. Let's

wait to see what happens. If he comes out again, we'll follow him."

The bloke I now thought of as Wormold came back down the stairs a couple of minutes later. He was carrying a large brown envelope which looked as though it held something thick. He set off in the direction he'd come.

We scrambled off our chairs and headed for the door.

Wormold had already turned the corner into Wardour Street and we followed. Our target was eighty yards ahead and heading north.

I said: "We'll need to watch our distance. He looks nervous - and he's keeping a keen watch for followers. I'll cross the road and follow on the other side. Targets always forget they can be followed by two people in different places."

I slipped between a taxi and a beer lorry, then jogged a bit to make up the distance I'd lost. Shirley was powering ahead on the other pavement. She weaved around a couple of guys carrying cans of film. It reminded me that Soho was also the film-makers' favourite district of London.

Wormold paced ahead, occasionally glancing back. But he seemed confident he wasn't followed. We kept well back. The narrow pavements were crowded so there were always plenty of people between us and him.

At the top of Wardour Street, Wormold turned left into Great Marlborough Street. I ran across the road to re-join Shirley. I felt hot and hoped Wormold would reach his destination soon.

Shirley nudged my arm and pointed: "There's a sign for Carnaby Street. I might peel off and check out some cool gear."

"Don't you dare," I said.

Up ahead, Wormold stooped to tie a shoe-lace. I grabbed Shirley's arm and turned round. Walk back slowly to make it look as though we're heading away from him. He's using an old ploy to pick out a follower in a crowded street. The inexperienced ones usually just stop as well. It's a sure giveaway."

We glanced back thirty seconds later. Wormold had finished pretending to tie his lace and was on the move again. We doubled our pace and headed after him.

He disappeared around the corner into Regent Street. We ran forward, but when we turned the corner we couldn't see him among the crowds of shoppers.

"We've lost him," I said.

"No we haven't," Shirley said. "Look." She pointed across the road.

Wormold was opening the door and entering a shop. We watched as he went inside, then turned and looked at each other's astonished faces.

The sign over the shopfront read: Aeroflot.

"That's the Russian state airline," I said.

"What's he doing in there?" Shirley asked.

"I don't think he's buying a ticket to Moscow," I said.

Chapter 7

For a couple of minutes we stood in the street staring at the Aeroflot offices.

Rush-hour crowds jostled around us. Buses ground along in low gear spewing diesel fumes. Taxis cruised by touting for fares. A busker placed his cap on the pavement, lifted a trumpet to his lips, and started on *London Pride*.

My mind was fizzing like a newly poured gin and tonic. And I could've done with one. A large one.

I'd read plenty of spy novels. I was looking forward to *The Spy Who Came in from the Cold*, which had just come out. I knew what a "dead letter drop" was. Could the Mercury Message Agency be used by the Russians as one? I'd heard that some of the staff of Aeroflot doubled up as spies. There'd be no reason why legitimate mail shouldn't be sent to its own offices. But if it suspected its mail was being monitored by MI5, perhaps it used the message agency for the sensitive stuff.

Which raised a question about the agency itself. Did it know it was being used for espionage? Its plaque outside was old. It had obviously been there for years, which would suggest the place was an ordinary business. Besides, Rudolph Strongbow was using it, too. He passed himself off as a representative of some phoney zip fastener outfit.

But Strongbow, I believed, was CIA. A true Yankee spook. Loyal to Uncle Sam. Did Strongbow know the Russians also used the place? Or was he using it because he did - and perhaps hoped to gain some information from that knowledge?

Gently, I took Shirley's arm. She was still staring in disbelief at the Aeroflot office.

"We've got to get back to Peter Street," I said. "I have to find a way to get into that message agency."

Shirley didn't say anything. She just turned her eyes upwards and shook her head as though I were stark raving mad.

We were back in the café opposite the Naughty Knickers Club.

We were nursing our second mug of weak tea of the afternoon. It wasn't any better than the first.

Shirley said: "How long are we going to sit here?"

I said: "I'm waiting for the message agency office to close. Then I may be able to find a way in. That's a four-storey building not including the basement. The club is on the ground floor and in the basement. The plaque says the agency is on the first floor. That means there must be something else on the two top floors. I may be able to persuade the doorman that I've got business upstairs. If I can, then perhaps I can get into the agency office and take a quick look round."

"What if you're caught?"

"I'll take my chances." Even as I said it, I realised I'd be taking a huge risk. But I'd talked my way out of tight corners before.

Shirley reached across the table and grabbed my hand. "I don't like it."

"I can't think of anything else to do."

Before I'd finished speaking, a middle-aged woman came down the stairs. She wore a grey two-piece suit - a jacket with wide lapels and pencil skirt. She was fixing a fawn cloche hat to her head with a hatpin.

I whispered to Shirley: "I think that must be Thelma Hughes, the woman I spoke to on the telephone."

Thelma entered the foyer and walked over to the doorman. She handed him a key, gave a peremptory wave, and stepped into the street.

The doorman ambled over to the desk, opened the top drawer and dropped the key in.

We watched Thelma walk down the street and turn the corner.

"Are you sure she was from the agency?" Shirley asked.

"I reckon so. But I wasn't banking on her leaving the key

with the doorman. I wonder whether she's left the key because someone else is expected this evening. Or perhaps the office cleaners need it."

"You won't be able to get into the office now."

"I will if I can borrow that key from the drawer."

"How are you going to do that?"

I smiled. "With your help."

Shirley turned a death-ray glare on me and said: "If this plan goes wrong, I'll peel your goolies and pickle them like onions."

"Actually, I prefer gherkins," I said. "But the plan can't fail."

"As Napoleon said as he advanced on Moscow."

I smiled. "We won't have snow on our boots."

I was being all confident with Shirley about my plan. But it felt like a troupe of Morris men were clog dancing inside my stomach.

The plan went like this. Shirley would flounce into the foyer of the Naughty Knickers Club like a stripper in search of a job. She'd persuade the doorman to show her to the manager's office. We guessed that would be downstairs where most of the action took place. While the doorman was away from his post, I'd scoot into the foyer, liberate the key from the desk drawer, and shoot up the stairs. Shirley would only need to lure the doorman away from the foyer for around thirty seconds for me to complete my part of the plan. Then she'd pretend she'd left something in her car parked nearby - I suggested her audition tape, to add an authentic touch. She'd explain she was going to fetch it but, really, scram.

Meanwhile, I'd use the key to enter the agency office. I'd take a quick look around and then leave, locking the door behind me. If the doorman challenged me, I'd say I'd had business with one of the other occupants upstairs. Later, I'd drop the key down a drain. Thelma from the agency would assume the doorman - or the cleaner, if there was one - had lost it. She wouldn't know I'd searched her office.

We left the caff and loitered in a shop doorway, just across from the club. A couple of well-liquored hooray Henry types staggered up the road and headed for the club. They tripped into the foyer and greeted the doorman in the kind of loud braying voice you acquire at the more expensive public schools.

"Evening Digby," one of them crowed. "How naughty are the knickers tonight?"

Digby the doorman managed a little bow without ripping the seat of his tight trousers and muttered some reply. The hooray Henrys ignored him and disappeared into the club.

The place fell quiet. Digby sat at his desk and counted his fingers.

"No time like the present," I said to Shirley.

"Save me the clichés. And don't dare tell me that fortune favours the brave. Because I'm not feeling like it."

"We'll meet around the corner in Berwick Street afterwards."

Shirley nodded reluctantly. She sashayed across the road like a stripper practising her bumps and grinds.

I checked the street to make sure no-one was taking an unhealthy interest in me. But everyone was too busy racing for buses and trains. They scurried along the narrow pavement swinging briefcases and shopping bags.

Shirley walked into the club like she'd just stepped into a spotlight on the stage of the London Palladium.

A little voice in my heart cheered her on: Go get him, girl!

I watched as she sidled towards Digby. She pointed her breasts at him like they were bazookas. The guy stood up and shuffled from foot to foot. I could swear that, even from the other side of the road, I saw his face colour.

Shirley said something to him. Digby shook his head. She moved closer. She made a little moue with her lips like she was going to kiss him. Instead, she whispered something in his ear.

Digby took a step back. Decided he quite liked being close

to Shirley and moved forward again. The poor bloke may have been a hero in the boxing ring but he was a patsy in Shirley's hands.

She took hold of his arm and caressed it while she said something else. Digby looked uncertainly towards the stairs leading to the basement, back at Shirley. She gave his arm an encouraging squeeze. He surrendered. Stepped away from his desk and headed for the stairs. Shirley followed close behind and the pair disappeared.

I charged across the road into the foyer. I raced around to the desk and yanked open the drawer. The key was lying on top of a dirty magazine. I grabbed it - the key, obviously! - slammed the drawer shut, and legged it up the stairs. I arrived on the first floor panting like a mountaineer who'd just scaled the north face of the Eiger.

The landing was lit by a single bulb that left the corners of the place in shadow. The floor was covered with cracked lino. The walls had that embossed wallpaper you see a lot of in doctors' waiting rooms. It had been painted brown a long time ago. There was a flight of stairs to the upper floors and one door. The place smelt of randy cats.

I silently inserted the key in the lock and turned it. I tried the door handle not expecting miracles.

Open sesame!

The door swung back on its hinges.

I stepped into the room and closed the door behind me. The evening sun streamed through a single window which looked out over Berwick Market. The room smelt of furniture polish. The rhythmic beat of music from the strip club throbbed up through the floor. Above the music, a posh voice - perhaps one of the hooray Henrys - shouted: "Get 'em orf!" There was a volley of coarse laughter.

There was a sturdy desk in the centre of the room. It had a large blotter and one of those old-fashioned ink stands with two bottles. One black ink, one red. To the right of the blotter there were two telephones - one for incoming, one for outgoing calls, I guessed. To the left, two stacks of wire baskets overflowed with papers. There were several pads of paper and a chipped mug featuring a donkey wearing a straw hat - "A present from Southend" - holding a selection of pens and pencils.

Beside the desk was a small bookcase. It held the telephone books and a few old copies of Kelly's - the directory which lists companies. The oldest volume was dated 1937. I picked it up and flipped to the Ms. The Mercury Message Agency was listed at the same address. That settled it for me. This was old enough to be a legitimate business. I would bet a pound to a paperclip Thelma didn't know that it was being used as a dead letter drop by spies.

One wall of the office was covered with floor-to-ceiling shelves loaded with box files. More than two hundred of them. The files had each been labelled with names in black indelible ink. I moved over to the shelves and peered at the names. They meant nothing to me. But most sounded like real businesses. The boxes had been shoved on the shelves at random. I couldn't see one for the Acme Zip Fastener Company. Or for Strongbow. Or Bellwether.

I moved back to the desk. There were four wire baskets in one of the stacks, three in the other. They were both stuffed with papers in no particular order that I could see. I looked at the document on the top of one of the stacks. It was a rate demand from the Borough of Westminster. Pay up or else.

There was no way I could riffle through the papers. They were too disorganised. Thelma would immediately know they'd been searched. That's the trouble with muddle. You can never put it back in exactly the same muddle. And people who live with muddle always know.

A faint round of applause filtered up through the floor. It reminded me that Shirley was downstairs. Hopefully, she'd fed them the line about the forgotten audition tape and scarpered. But I couldn't be sure. I had to find what I was looking for within the next few minutes or quit.

But that seemed impossible. There was just too much to sift through.

I moved around the other side of the desk and sat down in Thelma's seat. Her blotter was covered in jottings. Buy chicken for weekend. Pick up theatre tickets this eve. Lunch with Charlie Tuesday. Reynolds rings Bell.

Reynolds rings Bell.

That didn't sound like the other messages. Who was Reynolds? And why was he ringing a bell?

In fact, he wasn't ringing a bell. He was ringing Bell with a capital B. Could that be short for Bellwether?

I shot out of the chair and hastened over to the shelves with the box files. I started in the top left-hand corner and worked my way across shelf by shelf. I was sweating now and my heart was beating faster. The music from downstairs had raised its tempo as well.

Dah-dah-dum-dum. Dah-dah-dum-dum.

I found the Reynolds box file on the second set of shelves along. I pulled if off the shelf and flipped open the lid. There were about twenty or thirty message slips inside. Unlike the wire baskets, the slips were all filed neatly in date order. I took them out and flipped swiftly through them. I took out my notebook and copied down the messages on those that seemed most important.

Reynolds to Bellwether. More questions on plan. Call tonight.

Bellwether to Reynolds. Easy to fix signal. Sending details.

(The Bridego robbers had ingeniously found a way to make a green train signal turn red so that the Night Mail would stop where they wanted it to. Now I knew who'd helped them do it.)

Reynolds to Bellwether. Job tonight.

Bellwether to Reynolds. Hand special cargo to accredited

representative. No mistakes.

There'd been earlier messages but I didn't have time to copy them all. I replaced the message slips in the file in the order I'd found them and shoved the box back on the shelf.

I crossed to the door and felt in my pocket for the key.

The music downstairs ended with a ripple of applause. For a moment, there was silence. Somewhere in the building water gurgled through a pipe.

And then I heard steps on the stairs. Coming up from the ground floor.

They were the heavy steps of a big man moving slowly.

The steps of a man who expects trouble.

Chapter 8

Too late, I realised I'd forgotten to lock the door after me.

Perhaps the steps on the stairs were Digby from the foyer doing his night watchman act.

Clump, clump.

The footsteps reached the top stair and moved onto the landing.

If he tried the door he'd realise it wasn't locked. I could hide under the desk. Probably enough unless he searched the room. When he found the door unfastened, his first thought would be that Thelma had forgotten to lock up after her.

So he'd go back down stairs to get the key. And find it wasn't there.

Clump, clump.

The footsteps approached along the landing.

I looked under the desk. There was a wastepaper basket and a kind of fancy footstool arrangement. I didn't have time to move them and crawl under the desk.

Instead, I flattened myself against the wall so I'd be hidden by the door when it opened.

Clump, clump.

The footsteps stopped outside the door. I pressed myself against the wall and held my breath.

The door knob rattled but the door didn't open. I turned to the right and watched the door knob. It rattled again and then rotated ever so slowly. The door opened an inch and stopped. Eased a couple more inches, like it was being pushed by a small kid sneaking into a room.

Whuuuuumph.

The door flew open. And Digby charged into the room. I held up both hands to stop the door smashing into my face. Felt the force judder through my body as the solid wooden frame bounced off my hands.

Digby had his back to me. His head twisted from side-to-side as he searched the room.

I stepped forward. I lifted a leg, planted my foot in the small of his back and shoved with a force that would've shifted an elephant.

Digby stumbled forward and collapsed over the desk. The inkstand went flying and one of the stacks of wire baskets tumbled onto the floor. Thelma wasn't going to be pleased.

But I didn't pause to make an inventory of the damage or write a note of apology. Instead, I scrambled out of the door and slammed it behind me. I rummaged the key out of my pocket, shoved it into the lock and turned it.

I raced for the stairs. As I reached the first step the door shook and an angry voice yelled: "You're dead, you bastard."

But I was very much alive. And intended to stay that way. I clattered down the stairs praying that Shirley had already left the club.

I shot into the foyer and skidded to a halt. Two plug-uglies had appeared from nowhere. I guessed Digby had called them up from the basement before he'd started on his night-time round.

The plug-ugly on the left was about six foot six, had a shaved head, a spider's web tattoo on his right cheek and clenched fists the size of basketballs. The one on the right had dark hair in a crew cut, a black patch over his left eye and a barrel chest the size of an industrial boiler.

They blocked the way into the street.

They stood and studied me with their three eyes. They were trying to work out what had happened. The cogs in their brains were turning about as fast as a cartwheel stuck in a rutted road.

A suspicious guy (me) had just raced down the stairs and their boss was beating on a door and shouting four-letter words from the first floor.

They exchanged glances. Half a glance in the case of the pirate with the patch. They moved towards me. Slowly, like a pair of weary mastodons on their way to bed.

I stepped back towards the stairs to the basement.

And at that moment, I heard Shirley yell: "If you pinch my bum again, whacker, I'll pull your pecker so hard it'll ring the bells in Westminster Abbey."

I ignored the plug-uglies and raced down the stairs. I was in a bar area furnished with small tables and lit with red lamps. A fat bloke with a bald head and three chins had backed Shirley into a corner at the foot of the stairs. He had short legs and about eight arms each of which was trying to grab a bit of Shirley. She wrestled with two of the arms while one of the others foraged around her breasts and a couple more headed south towards her bum.

Shirley saw me hurtle down the stairs. She realised at once we had to get out of the place.

In a smooth single movement, she stepped back and lifted her left knee into the bloke's crotch. Shirl's knee hit him right in the wedding tackle with the force of a steam hammer. The bloke's eyes popped like a pair of fused searchlights. His tongue slipped out of the side of his mouth. His jaw hung slack and his legs crumpled underneath him.

I vaulted over him and joined Shirley. Her hair was mussed but her eyes were on fire.

I said: "The front way is blocked."

She said: "We can get out of the stage door. Follow me."

Behind me, the plug-uglies charged to the bottom of the stairs. The fat bloke was on the floor right in front of them. He was curled up like a giant slug. He was gripping his crotch and dribbling from his mouth.

The plug-uglies stopped in their tracks. They swapped one and half glances. They didn't know whether to chase us or help the manager look for his balls.

We didn't hang around to see what they decided. Shirley raced ahead of me down a long corridor. It had a row of dressing rooms off to one side. A blonde wearing nothing more than nipple tassels and false eyelashes popped her head out of a door as I dashed by.

She glanced at Shirley, now at the far end of the corridor. "You should chase me, darling. I don't run so fast," she shouted at my retreating back.

Shirley and I reached the stage door and pushed through it into a small yard. It was surrounded by a brick wall black with age. A battalion of flies buzzed around three grimy dustbins. A couple of bicycles had been chained to a drainpipe. On the far side of the yard, a wooden door set into the wall led out to an alley.

We yanked it open and ran down the alley into the street. We kept running for three streets until we turned a corner and fell into each other's arms panting for air.

"That was fun," Shirley said.

"How do they stop them falling off?" Frank Figgis asked.

"Stop what falling off?" I said.

"Nipple tassels."

It was the following morning. I was in Figgis's office and I'd been recounting my adventures of the previous evening.

I said: "Suction pads. Like the rubber ones you get on the ends of the arrows in a children's bow and arrow set."

Figgis's eyebrows hovered incredulously. "And that's enough to hold them on?"

"If you lick them."

"The nipples?"

"No, the pads."

Figgis scratched the back of his head. "Surely they'd fall off when the girl does that bit where she makes them rotate?"

"Not if she has a steely willpower," I said.

"And you say the stripper you saw had nothing else on apart from the tassels?"

"No, she was wearing false eyelashes. And a cheeky smile. But I didn't have time to stop and introduce myself."

Figgis reached for his Woodbines, realised the packet was empty, and tossed it into his waste bin all in a single practised movement.

"So you say. Are you sure you left nothing behind that'll enable the club owners or that Thelma Hughes you mentioned to identify you?"

"They won't be able to tell me from Adam. Or, in Shirley's case, from Eve. But that's not the point."

"Which is?"

"That Thelma now knows someone is taking an unhealthy interest in the affairs of the Mercury Message Agency."

"Do you think Thelma will call the police?" Figgis asked.

"I can't be sure, but I don't think so. For a start, I didn't take anything, so it's hard to say what crime if any was committed. I don't think the other tenants, especially the strip club downstairs, would be keen to see the cops in the building. And, finally, Thelma won't want news that she'd had a break-in getting back to her clients. I'm convinced she's running a legitimate business - and so are most of her clients. But they could worry that confidential information isn't safe if they heard there'd been a mystery break-in."

"So no problem," Figgis said. He took another packet of fags from his drawer and wrestled the cellophane paper off.

"Not exactly," I said. "Although I think Thelma doesn't realise it, both the Russians and Strongbow are using her agency for dead letter drops. If they heard about the break-in, they definitely would become suspicious. I saw messages between a person called Reynolds - there was no given name - and Elliott Bellwether. So they've been using Thelma's services as well."

Figgis lit up a fresh fag and took a long drag while he thought.

"I've given you your head on this one, because I sense there will be a big story at the end of it," he said. "But you need to wrap it up quickly. I can sense when His Holiness is getting twitchy and although I haven't told him precisely what you're up to, I can't keep it from him indefinitely. Besides, I've got to watch my own back with Pope."

I nodded. "I understand that. I think I've learnt a lot. I think the Bridego robbery was about more than the money."

"You'd have thought a cool two-and-half million would be enough for anyone," Figgis said.

"I think that was the bait to tempt the team who carried out the raid, but there were other brains behind it. And they had something else in mind."

"Such as?"

"I don't know, but I think we do know who the brains are - the Russians."

That had Figgis sitting up straighter. "You mean this was an espionage operation of some sort?"

"I think so." I told Figgis how Shirley and I had followed a man from the message agency to Aeroflot's Regent Street office. "I think the Russians use the agency as a message drop. And when I was in Brighton Beach, I visited the apartments where Bellwether lives. One of the residents told me he once heard Bellwether speaking a foreign language to someone. He didn't know what the language was, but it could be Russian."

"If this agency is a front for the Russkies, why did your CIA mate Strongbow give it as a contact number?"

"Because I think Strongbow is using it to try and penetrate the Russian spy ring. He knows they use the place - perhaps he's trying to work out how he can find out what information passes through Thelma's hands. It will all be in code, of course. The messages will be worded to sound like ordinary business transactions - like the ones I saw. One from Reynolds to Bellwether spoke of a 'special cargo' - presumably something they planned to snatch from the Night Mail train apart from the money."

"What do you think it was?" Figgis asked.

"I don't know. But it had to be something that was being sent from Glasgow to London. And something the Russians wanted a lot."

"Perhaps the Russkies already have it."

"Maybe, but I don't think so. Otherwise, why is Strongbow so eager to trace Bellwether? Perhaps Bellwether still has it. If we knew what it was, we'd be a lot closer to solving the mystery."

Figgis reached for his contacts book. "I've got an old mate on the Glasgow Herald. Jock McElroy. He's a good reporter. Knows things other people don't. Give him a call and mention my name."

Figgis handed me a slip of paper with a phone number. "But get a result - and get it soon."

Chapter 9

I sat at my desk in the newsroom, lifted the receiver on my telephone, and dialled a Glasgow number.

The phone was answered by a whisky voice: "Jock McElroy."

"Colin Crampton, Brighton *Evening Chronicle*. Frank Figgis gave me your name - and he sends his regards."

"Och! How is the old bastard? Has he smoked himself to death yet?"

"No, but he's still trying."

"Frankie Figgis would never give up. On smoking or landing a story."

"It's a story I'm calling about," I said.

"Oh, aye?" McElroy sounded wary. "I could do with a story in the silly season. If I don't find something soon I'll have to reheat a piece I did last year about sighting the Loch Ness Monster."

"I think the piece I'm working on may have something for both of us."

"Tell me more."

"It's about that Night Mail train that was hit in Buckinghamshire twelve days ago."

"Please say it was a Scottish team who pulled off the heist."

"Afraid not. That is to say, I don't know yet. And neither do the cops. But I was wondering whether you had any inside track on what the train was carrying."

"More bawbees than I'll see in a lifetime."

"Apart from that."

"Did they need more than two and half million smackers?"

"What about background?"

"Well, as I expect you know, the train was officially called a Travelling Post Office."

"But Night Mail fits better in headlines," I said.

McElroy grunted. "You may not know that it had twelve

carriages and carried seventy-two post office staff who sorted letters on the journey. But the laddies who robbed it were only interested in what was in the high value packages coach, which was the second carriage behind the engine."

McElroy wasn't telling me anything I didn't already know. I had to get to the point. I'd told him there could be a story in this for both of us. But I didn't want to give away too much too soon.

So I said: "I wondered whether the train ever carried any other items of value. Gold bullion, famous paintings, priceless jewellery. That sort of thing."

"I've heard nothing specific about that. Of course, I did a piece looking at the local angle at the time of the robbery. The usual procedure was for the high value stuff to be brought to the train and loaded under police escort. At the Glasgow end they've never had any trouble."

McElroy fell silent. He knew something else but he wasn't sure whether to tell me. I had to encourage him to keep talking.

So I said: "Did this happen each evening the train was due to leave?"

"You could rely on it. It was as certain as finding a drunk in Sauchiehall Street. After the story broke, I went down to the station and had a nose around. Bought a few whiskies for one of the porters after work. He let slip one rumour. He said after the Post Office vans left the night of the robbery, the train delayed its departure for around ten minutes. He'd never known that before. A flash car - possibly a Pontiac - drove into the station and an important looking guy carried a metal case aboard the train, then left. After that, the train pulled out."

"And he saw this himself?"

"With his own eyes, he claimed. And he said he was sober at the time. Which might just be true."

"Did he know who the person with the metal case was?"

"No idea. Naturally, I asked around, but I came up against a wall of denial. There was no extra delivery and the train wasn't delayed. It left on time, the stationmaster told me."

"So he was lying?"

"Like a flat fish."

We talked some more, but it was clear McElroy didn't have any more to tell.

I said: "Thanks for your help, Jock. If I find out anything about the mystery case from this end, I'll let you know."

I hung up.

Frank Figgis appeared on the other side of the newsroom. He pranced over to me in that high-stepping gait which meant he'd adjusted his braces too tightly again.

I said: "Jock thinks something apart from the money was loaded on to the Night Mail."

"Something worth more than the money?" Figgis asked incredulously.

I nodded.

"You better find out what it was, then," he said. "But don't forget I also want a piece about the latest developments in the Eileen Dudgeon murder."

I walked into Brighton police station still thinking about the mystery item put aboard the Night Mail.

It was hard to imagine anything more valuable to robbers than two and half million quid. Unless it was three and half million quid. It had to be something that someone wanted very badly.

But I put these thoughts aside as I stepped into the briefing room. The place was full with journalists from Fleet Street keen to bag themselves a decent murder story in the silly season.

I took a seat near the back next to a bloke I'd once met on a wounding-with-intent. We were both covering it in court - not doing it. Not that I wouldn't have done when a leathery hand landed on my shoulder. I looked up. Jim Houghton's face, pock-marked like the craters of the moon, was glaring down at me.

I said: "Kind of you, Jim, to give me a pat on the back for my scoop about the Dudgeon murder."

Houghton removed his hand so fast you'd have thought he'd just touched a live wire. (In a way, I like to think he had.)

He said: "That was my story."

I waved my hand to indicate the crowded room. "Not any more. Everyone wants a piece of it."

Jim grumbled something indistinct and limped off to his seat at the front. I was about to say something to my old wounding-with-intent mate when Ted Wilson walked in. He had a thick sheaf of papers under his arm. He took a place at the top table, rummaged through the papers and surveyed the room.

He picked up one of the papers and read a short statement which confirmed what everyone in the room already knew. The cops hadn't arrested anyone for Eileen Dudgeon's murder.

Ted called for questions and a few journos stuck their hands up. Mistake. Just ask the question. While your rivals look stupid waving their arms in the air, you're out front. If the cops haven't arrested anyone, there are only two questions worth asking - about motive and suspects.

So I asked them. Without bothering to stick my hand up first.

Ted shuffled through his papers and waffled a bit about continuing enquiries, analysis of evidence, and consideration of different options. In other words: he hadn't a clue.

Which was what I suspected. And on that inconclusive note, the press briefing broke up. I shot out of the room, nipped smartly down the corridor, and pushed my way into the men's lavvy. I hid in one of the cubicles while a couple of coppers spent a penny. Had a wry smile to myself. Wondered whether I could ever work the witticism into one of my articles. Coppers spending a penny. Get it?

The lavvy door banged twice in quick succession which I hoped meant both the plods had left. I nipped swiftly out, not forgetting to wash my hands on the way. When I got back to the briefing room the last straggler among the journos - a stringer from some obscure weekly - was just leaving. Perfect.

I didn't want any of them to know I had private business with Ted. He was still at the top table trying to pat his unruly sheaf of papers into some order.

I moseyed up and said: "There was a question I didn't want to ask in front of the children."

Ted gave a grim little smile. "Which probably means it's one I won't want to answer."

I said: "It's not about the Dudgeon killing. It's the Bridego robbery."

"You mean the Buckinghamshire job? I've had nothing to do with that."

"But you must have been hearing things on the bush telegraph. Cops are bound to boast about their part in a case this big."

"One or two bits of tittle-tattle - that's all."

"My question is about the search of Leatherslade Farm."

"Where the gang holed up afterwards. The investigation team have been searching it for a week. Yielding some useful clues, I've heard."

"Have you heard about anything specific that's been found?"

Ted looked up from his papers with suspicious eyes. "What sort of specific?"

"I'd heard rumours about a metal case. Wondered whether anything like it was found at Leatherslade?"

"I've not heard anything…"

"But you'll ask around?"

Ted raised his eyebrows. "Doing your job for you?"

I grinned. "Aren't we forgetting a few things?" There'd been several cases where the information I'd turned up had helped Ted make an arrest.

Ted finally got his papers into a neat pile. He shrugged. "I'll ask around," he said.

"So you are the good cop, after all," I said.

Back in the *Chronicle* newsroom ten minutes later, it didn't take me long to write up the press briefing.

There was hardly anything new to say. I rolled a couple of quick-fire folios out of the old Remington. I handed them to Cedric to take to the subs.

I'd been thinking about what Ted had said at the press briefing. When I'd asked him the question about motive, I was surprised he hadn't mentioned the search of Chaz's room. It wasn't a secret. I'd mentioned the fact in the piece I'd written for the previous night's *Chronicle*.

Of course, the search could have been coincidental. Perhaps the intruder who'd killed Eileen had been making a random hunt for valuables. But I didn't think so. Any searcher would start downstairs, not in a room which even a cursory glance would reveal contained nothing of value.

The more I thought about it, the more Chaz became the heart of the mystery. Chaz - the warehouseman who lodged with the wife of a former spy chief and hung out with rockers. Who was prepared to commit a robbery on a crowded holiday train. And who may have got away with it, if he hadn't been hit by a furniture van.

I was thinking about this when my telephone rang.

I lifted the receiver and Shirley's voice said: "It's lunchtime and the sun is shining."

"Is that an application for the job of restaurant critic or weather forecaster?"

"It's an invitation to join me for a walk along the front for lunch at that open air café by the Peace Statue."

"After the morning I've had I could do with some peace. I'll meet you outside the Palace Pier in ten minutes."

The seafront was crowded as Shirley and I strolled west towards Hove.

The sea sparkled with little points of light like diamonds. The beach was dotted with deckchairs. Children larked around in the water. A couple of old blokes with bald heads and pot bellies rolled up their trouser legs and dipped tentative toes in the water. Two teenagers hustled by scoffing chips wrapped in newspaper. A young mother with a polka-dot scarf and film-star sized sunshades pushed a pram with a bawling toddler.

How we all love to be beside the seaside.

Shirley linked her arm through mine. "Why can't the British weather always be like this?" she asked.

"Because if it was we wouldn't have anything to moan about."

We walked on in silence for a few moments.

"What are you thinking about?" Shirley asked.

"It's the story I'm working on. I can't make sense of it."

"Is it about that Chaz guy who got run down?"

"Partly about him. But there are so many threads in this story it's like a cat's cradle of a mystery. I can't work out why Chaz robbed Bellwether. I don't know what Rudolph Strongbow is up to. And I can't figure out what the Russian connection is with the Bridego robbery. They didn't want the money - but something else. Something sent from Scotland."

"Whisky?" Shirley said

"Russians drink vodka. And, anyway, a contact on the *Glasgow Herald* picked up a tip that it was something in a metal box."

We walked past the West Pier. A gaggle of children raced past us towards the dodgems. The rich aroma of chips cut through the sea air.

Shirley pointed ahead. "There's a crowd up by the Peace Statue. Some of them are waving banners. I can't read them from here."

"Don't need to. That circular sign is the Campaign for Nuclear Disarmament's symbol."

"Sure, I know that. I've never understood how CND chose it."

"It was designed by a bloke called Gerald Holtom. He used images from flag semaphore. He superimposed the N for nuclear over the D for disarmament in a circle. I guess the Peace Statue is a natural place to hold their demo."

The protesters were standing around the Peace Statue chanting as we walked up. Most of them were young and wore jeans or shorts and tee-shirts. They'd been marshalled into a line around the statue by a tall man with shoulder-length hair and a string of beads around his neck. He was wearing a kaftan and sandals. He carried a hand-written sign which read: *No US nuclear subs in Britain*.

He was followed by a woman with bare feet and a long swirly skirt. She held a hand-written placard which read: *Close Holy Loch base*.

I stopped so suddenly Shirley had walked three yards further on before she realised I wasn't by her side.

She turned and said: "You've got a look on your face like you've just discovered the lost chord."

She was right. I felt like "stout Cortez when, with eagle eyes, he stared upon the Pacific". And I didn't need any men to stare with wild surmise. I had enough of it myself.

I now knew what Bellwether wanted from the Bridego robbery.

Chapter 10

I sat in the café close to the Peace Statue and stirred my coffee.

Shirley said: "If you stir that any more you'll wear a hole in the bottom of the mug."

"I'm thinking."

"Does it hurt?"

"Not yet."

I put down my spoon and looked at the CND protesters. They were still marching around the Peace Statue. They were singing *We Shall Overcome*.

I said: "If I'm right, this story could go global. The *New York Times, Le Monde, South China Morning Post, Corriere della Sera*. Everywhere. Even *Pravda*. Did you know *Pravda* in Russian means 'truth'? There's another newspaper in Moscow called *Isvestia* - which means 'news' in English. Muscovites have a saying: 'There's no *Pravda* in *Isvestia* and no *Isvestia* in *Pravda*'."

"Keep your feet on the ground, cobber," Shirley said. She picked up her bacon sandwich and took a bite. Some of the brown sauce oozed out of the side. "First up, what's the story?"

"It's about what was in the secret metal case loaded onto the Night Mail in Glasgow. As we discovered in Soho, the Russians were taking a close interest in the heist. But they didn't want the money. They wanted what was in the case. But what could have come from around Glasgow that the Russians would want?"

"Not haggis, that's for sure."

"No, nuclear secrets."

Shirley nearly choked on her sandwich.

"I don't get it. What secrets?"

"Those protesters reminded me. A couple of years ago the government allowed the Americans to open a base for their nuclear submarines - the ones that can fire missiles at Moscow - at a place called Holy Loch in Scotland."

"Cute name."

"But not a cute place, as far as the protesters are concerned. They argue that having American nuclear subs there makes the loch a target for the Russkies. That's why they're protesting about it all around the country. But suppose the Americans sometimes have to transfer secret information from the base to London. The high value packages coach on the Night Mail would be the safest way of doing it. Much safer than by road or air. After all, until a few days ago, the Night Mail had never been robbed. Never even been stopped. It had a hundred per cent security record. I think the Russians must've been behind the robbery."

"But that Bellwether bozo was a Yank," Shirley said.

"He was certainly living in America. But that doesn't mean he was born American. Remember that the United States is a land of immigrants. Give me 'your huddled masses, yearning to breathe free' and all that. And don't forget there have been Americans who've spied for Russia before - like Rudolf Abel."

"You think Bellwether is a Russian? That means his name wouldn't be Bellwether."

"He originally called himself Arthur Crouch - and we know that was false. There's no rule which says that a crook has to limit himself to one phoney moniker. I need to find out more about Bellwether."

"How are you going to do that?"

"I'm going to call Jess Sheldon, the cop I met in Brighton Beach. She seems to have a line into the FBI. Perhaps she can access immigrant records or sources like that."

"And she's going to drop everything for your enquiry just because she loves your big blue eyes?"

I grinned. "I may have a card to play apart from that," I said.

"From up your sleeve, no doubt, you crafty bastard."

"Where else?" I said.

I lifted my mug and took a sip of the coffee. Pulled a

disappointed face.

"I hope my lead won't be as cold as this coffee," I said.

Back at the *Chronicle*, it took the international telephone operator twenty minutes to book me a line to the United States.

While I waited for the call, I wondered whether Jess would be able to find any more information about Elliott Bellwether. And, even if she did, whether she'd be willing to share it with me.

When she came on the line, she sounded as perky as she'd done when we first met.

"Hey, Colin, when you quit Brighton Beach, I thought we'd heard the last of you."

"Hoped, don't you mean?"

She laughed, not entirely out of politeness, I thought.

I filled Jess in on what I'd discovered since I'd returned to the UK. I heard her gasp, even above the crackling of the transatlantic line, when I told her about the rumble at the Naughty Knickers nightclub.

"Jeez, Colin, you sure like to live dangerously. Glad you're not running your scams on my beat."

I said: "I need to know more about Elliott Bellwether - about his background, where he came from. There must be something on file somewhere in the States. I hoped you might be able to help me."

"I'm not running an enquiry bureau here. There's real police work to do."

"I know that - and I wouldn't ask if there was some other way of getting the information."

"Well, there's nothing more on Bellwether in New York Police Department files. I've looked."

"But other departments hold different information. You could ask them."

"Call in favours, you mean? That always raises questions. Sometimes awkward questions."

Jess was going to turn me down. It was time to play the card I had up my sleeve.

"The questions are less awkward when your enquiries are linked to a live case," I said.

"Bellwether is not a live case for me - at the moment," Jess said.

"But Leone De Luca is."

A pause on the line. "Go on," Jess said.

"You know that he was the moving spirit behind Hank Shultz's murder?"

"Yeah, the guy who was croaked at Ma Koch's boarding house while you were in residence."

"You also know that you've not be able to link him directly to the killing," I said.

"With solid police work, we'll nail him in the end."

"That could take years. Meanwhile, De Luca is king of the rackets in Brighton Beach and beyond. And a thorn in the side of the cops."

"So what are you saying?"

"If I knew more about Bellwether, I might be able to find him. Perhaps there'd be enough to persuade him to rat on what he knows about De Luca. Perhaps that would be enough to nail De Luca."

"There's a mighty pile of perhapses there, Colin."

"Even a long shot is better than no shot."

Another pause. "You may have a point," Jess said.

"So you'll try to get more on Bellwether?"

"I'll give it a day. If there's nothing by this evening, you're on your own. I won't be picking up the phone to you again."

"I'll settle for that, Jess. And thanks."

I replaced the receiver and sat back in my chair. The newsroom buzzed with action as the deadline for the Night Final edition crept closer. Phil Bailey scooted into the room with a heap of cuttings from the morgue and headed for his desk. Sally Martin hit the keys on her typewriter like she wanted to punish it. Susan Wheatcroft ran a tape from the ticker machine through her fingers checking the latest stock market prices.

And I wondered whether Jess could help me land the biggest story of my career.

But the worry at the back of my mind was whether the story was too big for me. I couldn't afford to get it wrong. In newspapers there are mistakes and mistakes. Misspell a local dignitary's name and you get a slap over the wrist and write an apology for next day's paper. Wrongly accuse a gang of stealing nuclear secrets and you have everyone from the newspaper's proprietor to the darker departments of the government on your back. You find yourself out on the streets - and no-one willing to give you a job in newspapers ever again.

I sat at my desk and looked at my telephone, wondering whether Jess would find anything and call back.

The phone didn't ring.

It didn't ring for the rest of the afternoon.

So at half-past five I left my desk and walked round to Prinny's Pleasure. I'd arranged to meet Ted Wilson there. He was going to tell me whether anything unusual had been found at Leatherslade Farm, where the Bridego robbers had hung out after they'd pulled off their heist.

But the pub was empty when I walked in. The flock wallpaper - originally green, according to legend, but now grey - looked darker than ever. The sticky carpet seemed to cling more tenaciously to my feet as I walked up to the bar. And there was a scent in the air that was different. A sharper fragrance speared the heavy musk of stale beer - like a rose hiding behind a compost heap.

Jeff Purkiss was standing behind the bar, studying the label on a bottle of wine. He'd changed the shirt he'd been wearing for the last three weeks and combed his hair. I'd seen him do both in the past, but never at the same time.

I said: "Give me my usual."

He waved the wine bottle at me and asked: "Would you like a drop of this?"

"What is it?"

"Wine."

"I can see that. Does it have an *appellation contrôlée*?"

"It had a cork."

"Don't ever apply for a job as a sommelier."

"Why should I do that when I've got a thriving business?"

I looked around at the empty tables.

I said: "The only thing that thrives in here is bacteria."

"That's where you're wrong."

Jeff reached for a glass, turned to the optics, and poured me a large gin. He added two slices of lemon and an ice cube. He handed me the glass, reached under the counter for a bottle of tonic, and levered off the lid.

I freshened the gin with some tonic and took a pull at the fizzing drink.

I said: "What are you doing with that wine anyway?"

Jeff said: "Customer wanted a glass during the lunchtime session."

"No doubt a tourist who'd stumbled into the place by mistake."

"As it happens, he said he'd been told he could get fine wine and tasty victuals here."

"Victuals - that's not a word you often hear used."

It felt like an ice-cold blade had just been drawn down my spine. For I had heard that word not so long ago.

What had mystery man Reggie Derwent said to me on the flight to New York? *"I hear they serve some tasty victuals on this plane."*

"What was this tasty victual man like?" I asked.

"Superior kind of customer. Smart suit, striped tie, shiny

shoes. Well spoken. Public school, I shouldn't wonder. Might be Eton. He was curious to know whether I had any reporters among my regulars, the pub being so near to newspaper offices and that."

"And you told him?"

"That they're regulars. I mentioned your name, of course. He asked whether I knew what stories you were working on at the moment."

"And you told him nothing?"

"I asked him whether he'd like another drink. But he said one was more than enough. I like that - moderation in everything is my motto."

"Including personal hygiene."

"No need to get snarky. Just because I've got a new customer who takes an interest in the place."

It wasn't worth explaining to Jeff why he'd never see Reggie Derwent again. After I'd chased Reggie down that alleyway in Brighton Beach I didn't think I would. But he was still dogging my footsteps.

I was thinking about this when the pub door opened. Ted Wilson blocked out most of the light as he stepped inside. His trousers were creased, his jacket was done up on the wrong button, and his beard badly needed a trim. But from the way he bustled across the bar, I knew he had something to tell me.

Ted and I took our drinks to the corner table at the back of the bar.

He took a quick swig of his scotch and wiped his hand briefly across his lips.

"I've had a bit of luck," he said. "You remember Trevor Sparks who was my first oppo when I got promoted to detective inspector?"

It had been before my time on the *Chronicle*, but I'd heard tales of "Bright" Sparks who was a copper going places. Brighton was too small a town for his ambitions and he soon wormed his way into Scotland Yard.

I said: "Trevor is working on the Bridego robbery."

"You knew?" Ted sounded a bit disappointed. I'd spoiled his big surprise.

I felt a bit of a heel about it. So I said: "Someone who'd trained under you was always going to go far."

That seemed to satisfy him. He said: "I had a chin-wag with him on the dog-and-bone this afternoon. It turns out he was in on the Leatherslade Farm search. There's no doubt that was the place the gang hung out. They'd left all the mail sacks behind and the banknote wrappers. There were sleeping bags, food, empty beer bottles - looked like they'd had a party. There was even a Monopoly set."

"They could have played with real cash," I said.

"Trevor thinks they did. But, anyway, I asked him about the metal case. And they'd found one."

"Empty, presumably?"

"Not as you'd imagine," Ted said. "The case had obviously held microfilm. But here's the weird thing - it had all been burnt. It was just a heap of ash and goo in the case."

"Where was the case?"

"In the main living room of the farmhouse. It hadn't been hidden."

"Was anything else burnt?"

"They found matches and some cans of paraffin in one of the barns, but nothing else had been torched."

"Did Trevor have any theory why the microfilm had been burnt and nothing else?"

"He reckons it was a drunken prank. They'd grabbed something that was worth nothing and they decided to have a bit of fun."

Trevor couldn't have known that the metal case had been stolen to order. Had he, his theory would have made no sense.

Why burn something someone had taken a great deal of trouble to get?

I couldn't figure out why. It needed a bit of thinking about.

I said: "Thanks for your help, Ted. Appreciate it."

"Good to get a peek inside a big investigation." He drained his whisky. "I might treat myself to another."

"If you fancy something different, Jeff's opened a bottle of wine," I said. "*Chateau Insalubre,* I believe."

"If that's what I think it means, I'll stick to the scotch."

Chapter 11

"Have you ever read any Sherlock Holmes stories?" I asked Frank Figgis.

"A few. Never ceases to amaze me how he manages to come up with the right answer in less than eight thousand words."

We were sitting in Figgis' office. It was half an hour after my meeting with Ted Wilson.

I said: "My favourite story is 'Silver Blaze'. It's the one where Holmes talks about the mystery of the dog that didn't bark in the night time."

Figgis yawned. "What's all this got to do with the train robbery?"

"Because I think the solution to the mystery lies in the farmhouse that didn't burn down in the night time."

"You've lost me already."

I pulled my chair closer to Figgis's desk to make sure I had his full attention. It tended to wander, especially when he didn't have a Woodbine stuck between his lips.

"My theory goes like this," I said. "The Americans want to transport some secret documents held on microfilm from their base at Holy Loch to London. The safest way, they think, is in the high value packages coach of the Night Mail from Glasgow. The train is robbed - ostensibly to loot it for the cash."

"Why ostensibly?"

"I'll come back to that point in a minute. In fact, the robbery has been set up by Russian agents in order to capture the microfilm held in a metal case. The deal is that the gang who carry out the heist get to keep the cash as long as they hand the case with the microfilm of American nuclear submarine secrets to the Russians. But there's a twist in the Russkies' plans."

"Why doesn't that surprise me?"

"If the Yanks know the Russians have the microfilm, they'll

be able to limit the damage. We don't know what information the film contains but if it's something like codes and military plans, the Americans could simply alter them. The Russians would end up with old and useless information. But that would all change if the Americans thought the Russians hadn't gleaned any information from the microfilm - and didn't change their plans."

"But if the Russkies had the film, the Yanks would know they'd taken a look at it."

"Not if the Yanks thought the microfilm was accidentally destroyed before the Russians had a chance to retrieve it from the train robbers. And that's where the Russians tried to be clever. If my theory is right, they obtained a metal container which matched the Yankee one and filled it with a similar quantity of microfilm. The plan was for the robbers to burn down Leatherslade Farm, where they'd hidden out to divvy up the cash, so that the container and the microfilm would be totally destroyed. The cops would find the wreck of the case with the ruined microfilm and report back to the Americans. Big sighs of relief all round."

"But the robbers fouled up?"

"As only a bunch of smash-and-grab hooligans can. They didn't burn down the farm. The Russians should never have trusted them. My theory is that the robbers reckoned they had a few days before Leatherslade Farm would be discovered. But the police dragnet closed on the farm faster than they'd expected. They cleared out in a hurry, but not before burning the microfilm in the metal case. But they didn't have time to fire the farmhouse. Or perhaps they couldn't be bothered. After all, they'd got what they wanted - the money."

"But the crucial part of the plan was to burn the farm?" Figgis said.

I was pleased to see he was keeping up

"Yes. Instead of making it look like the film was accidentally burnt, they made it look as though it was deliberately destroyed. No self-respecting spy would do that. It must've set alarm bells ringing with the Yanks. They will know the real film is still out there."

Figgis reached for his fags, shook one out of the packet and lit up. He took a long drag and let out the smoke in a meditative sigh.

"But the Yanks will have worked out what you've just told me," Figgis said. "Probably without dragging Sherlock Holmes into it," he added, I thought unnecessarily.

"Yes. So will MI5, where I think my old mate Reggie Derwent comes from."

"And both will know that the real metal case with the genuine microfilm is still out there somewhere."

"But they don't know where."

"I think the answer must lie somewhere in what's happened so far," I said.

"So what are you going to do?" Figgis asked.

"I'm not sure," I said.

There was a light tap on the door. It opened and Cedric put his head round.

"Message for Mr Crampton," he said, holding out the paper. "Just come in."

I took the sheet and looked at it. "It's from Jess Sheldon, my contact at Brighton Beach police in New York. She's gleaned some more information about Elliott Bellwether, the man we first knew as Arthur Crouch. It seems his birth name was Vitaly Mikhailov."

"Sounds Russian," Figgis said.

I scanned my eyes down the page. "Jess has unearthed information from American immigration. Seems Mikhailov came from the Ukraine. He was in the Red Army, but deserted in the chaos after the Nazis invaded Russia in 1941. He finally made his way to the United States after the war, changed his name to Elliott Bellwether, and enrolled in a college to study law."

I read on some more.

"Jess says that he's now known to the cops as a shady attorney who helps sharks and conmen keep their scams one inch the right side of legal. No hard evidence of criminal activity. If there had been, he'd have been struck off as a lawyer."

I smiled at the postscript Jess had added to her message: Don't call us - we'll call you.

"Perhaps Mikhailov already has the microfilm," Figgis said.

"Perhaps," I said.

But I didn't think so.

"You really know how to show a girl a good time," Shirley said.

"I do my best," I said.

We were in my MGB racing along the coast road towards Peacehaven. I wanted to pay a return visit to the Ace of Spades café. The last time we'd called in, we'd left in a hurry with a gang of motorcycle rockers on our tail. But, since then, their leader Boss had been arrested and charged with attempted murder.

Of yours truly.

"Do you know what I hated about our last visit?" Shirley said.

"The fact we had to run for our lives?"

"No, the fact we had to drink coffee which tasted like the kind of stuff that gets left at the bottom of a dried-out billabong."

"We'll get the tea this time."

"As if that will make for a great night out."

I pressed my foot harder on the accelerator and the engine responded with a throaty roar. To our right, the sun looked like a blood orange sinking below the horizon. The sea heaved in a gentle swell as though a giant was turning over in his sleep under a vast blue blanket.

On the drive out of Brighton, I'd been telling Shirley about what I'd discovered during the day.

"So I think the stolen microfilm is still hidden somewhere. If I can find it first, I'll have a story that will make headlines around the world."

"And you'll have a bunch of angry Russkies after you," Shirley said. "Or should that be Yanks? Perhaps both. You're in way over your head this time."

"You're right. It was wrong to involve you. I'll turn the car round and drive you back to Brighton."

"Don't you dare. You'll need someone to pull your nuts out of the grinder."

I took my left hand off the steering wheel and patted her on the shoulder. "Thanks."

"What I can't figure is why we're going back to the Ace of Spades café. It was trouble last time. This time, we'll be about as welcome as a dingo at a dinner table."

We breasted the brow of a hill and sped down towards Peacehaven.

"The rockers' leader Boss had some kind of arrangement with Jerry Clark. He was mixed up in this business, but I can't work out how. Now that Boss won't see the outside of a prison cell for at least ten years, perhaps we can get one of the others to talk."

But when we drew up outside the Ace of Spades café, it looked as though we'd wasted our time. There'd been half a dozen gleaming motorcycles parked last time we called. Now there were none.

We climbed out of the MGB, walked into the café and looked around. A fresh layer of dust seemed to have settled over the place since we'd last visited. The old boy in a stained apron was still moping around in the kitchen. Dark smoke bubbled from a pan on the hob. The air smelt heavy with the fumes of long-fried bacon.

There was only one customer in the place. Marlene. Boss's girlfriend. Perhaps his former girlfriend. Unless she planned to stick by him while he did his porridge.

She was sitting at the back of the café, next to the table which held the little collection of James Dean memorabilia. She held a mug in both hands. Perhaps coffee. Perhaps tea. Perhaps she couldn't tell and didn't care. She cradled the mug like it was a baby. Like it responded to her affection. As the door slammed behind us, she looked up.

She recognised us immediately. Her back straightened. She pushed back a wisp of hair that had fallen across her face. Straightened her shoulders in the way people do when they expect trouble.

I ignored the bloke behind the counter who was wiping his hands on a tea-towel that looked like a leper's bandage. Shirley and I sashayed around the tables and chairs towards Marlene. She put down the mug and pushed back her chair.

I said: "We've only come to talk, Marlene. There'll be no trouble."

Shirley flashed a beaming smile. Marlene looked at Shirley and a shadow of a smile flitted over her lips.

We sat down at the table.

I pointed at Marlene's mug and said: "I'd buy you another but I don't want to poison you."

"Yeah, it's piss. I don't know how the old git gets away with it."

Shirley said: "I saw a pub down the road. We could go and talk there."

Marlene said: "I'm barred."

"Why?" I asked.

"Obvious, ain't it? I'm guilty, too. Just because I sleep with a bloke don't make me a killer. But folks around here think it does."

"That doesn't include us," I said.

"Too true, kiddo," Shirley said.

"I want to ask you some questions about Boss," I said.

"Why should I want to help you?"

"Because you can help Boss at the same time."

"Oh, yeah?"

I leaned forward. Showed Marlene my earnest face. "When Boss comes to trial, I'll have to give evidence as the victim in the case. I'll have to tell the truth, but the tone in which I give my evidence could have a big effect on what happens to Boss. He'll certainly go to jail, but if I give my evidence in a sympathetic way, he'll go to prison for fewer years than if I storm into the court like an avenging fury."

"Why should I believe you?"

"Why not? You've nothing to lose by taking the chance," I said.

"I believe him," Shirley said. "Except when he says he's not interested in my body."

For the first time, Marlene grinned. "Yeah, that sounds like a bloke."

I asked: "How long had Boss known Jerry Clark?"

"Since Boss worked down in Dorset."

"In Portland?"

"Yeah, in some Royal Navy place down there. Boss weren't in the navy or anything. He were civilian staff, humping stuff around, sweeping up their mess - that sort of crap. I think he met Clark then. Anyway, when I met Boss he already knew Clark. I was working as a hairdresser's assistant for a miserable old cow in a salon in Weymouth. Hated it. Boss had a bit of style. Usually had enough cash to show me some fun."

"But you moved to this area?" I said.

"Yeah, don't know why. It happened sudden like. Boss didn't tell me why, but I think it had something to do with that Clark."

"In what way?"

"Clark left the navy before his time. Bought himself out, I think they call it. Shipped up to Brighton and opened his business selling all that tourist crap. Don't know where he got the money. Perhaps an old aunt died and left him her loot."

"And that was the reason for Boss moving this way, too?"

"Seemed like it. The pair were always as thick as thieves. Not that they did much thieving. Just a way of saying."

"A figure of speech," I said.

Marlene nodded.

"Did Boss work for Clark?" I asked.

"Not like proper work," Marlene said. "But Clark gave Boss errands to run - paid him well for them. Boss would always be flush in the pub after he'd been on one of Clark's trips."

"Did Boss ever tell you where he went on these errands?"

"Naw. Asked him once and he told me to keep it out." She flicked her nose. "Meant it, too. Never asked him again."

I switched tack and asked: "How well did you know Chaz?"

"As well as I could without putting Boss's nose out of joint."

Shirley grinned. "Fancy him, did you?"

"Might have done. But Boss made it clear I should keep my legs together or else."

"But I thought Boss liked Chaz," I said.

"Don't know about liked. I think he might have been a bit afraid of him. Chaz was clever, see? He'd solve a problem with his brains, not charge in with his fists, like Boss. I cried when Chaz died, I don't mind admitting."

"What's happened to the rest of the gang? Do they ever come here now?"

"Not since the rozzers rounded us up and questioned us. Besides, I don't care. They're nothing to me."

She looked morosely into her mug. I thought she'd told us all she knew.

I said: "Thanks for your help. I'll keep my promise when Boss's trial comes."

Marlene looked up. Her eyes were wet with unshed tears. "Yeah, I believe you."

The old bloke behind the counter glared at Shirley and me as we walked out.

"Some people buy food and drink when they come in," he said pointedly.

"Perhaps that's why they don't come back," I said.

The door slammed behind us as we stepped into the car park.

Chapter 12

It was past ten o'clock when I arrived back at my lodgings in Regency Square.

I'd been doing some hard thinking while driving Shirley back to her flat. We'd talked over what we'd learnt from Marlene. Whatever Clark had been up to, Boss was in on it, too. Perhaps Boss was the heavy watching Clark's back for trouble. Or, perhaps, he played a courier role, as Marlene had suggested. Except that Clark hadn't trusted him to deliver the notorious attaché case to the man we now knew as Vitaly Mikhailov at the Black Rock café.

When I put the key in the lock at my lodgings, I still had more questions than answers.

I stepped silently into the hallway, taking care not to brush against the table with the glass ornaments which always tinkled when you knocked them. But it was no use. The Widow shot out of her parlour and blocked the way to the stairs.

She was wearing a floral apron over a grey blouse and tweedy skirt. She'd put her hair in curlers and a slash of lipstick, like a smear of blood, across her lips. Her eyes looked damp and I could tell she'd been crying. She smelt faintly of lavender water.

She said: "Will you answer one question for me, Mr Crampton?"

I said: "If that's the question, yes. I've answered it. Now I'd like to go to bed."

"Actually, that wasn't the question."

"What is it?"

"Are you happy here?"

"Deliriously," I said. I headed for the stairs, but the Widow shifted to one side to prevent me reaching them.

"I might have known you wouldn't give me an honest answer," the Widow said. She sniffled a bit.

I said: "What's the problem?"

"It's the new tenant. Mr Coniston. He's left."

"I didn't realise he'd arrived."

"He came at half past nine this morning and moved into the room that nice Valerie Hanley used to have. Naturally, I welcomed him with a cup of coffee and one of my rock cakes. He went into his room to settle in and I went out to do some shopping. When I came back two hours later, he'd gone."

"Permanently?"

"He left a note on the hall table saying the room wasn't really what he was looking for. And..." The Widow sniffled again. "He'd put the rock cake on top of the note as a paperweight."

I thought about that for a moment. Many of the Widow's tenants didn't last long. But two hours set a new record.

I said: "What was this Mr Coniston like?"

"I thought he was a very distinguished gentleman. The kind I try to attract. He wore a smart suit and a striped tie and when he'd first viewed the room he'd said it was 'pukka'."

That had my attention. Not many people went around describing things as pukka these days. But Reggie Derwent, the man who'd dogged my footsteps, used the word like a calling card. It was part of his pompous vocabulary which included calling grub victuals.

I cursed myself because alarm bells should've rung when the Widow originally told me a Mr Coniston was interested in the room. Derwent... Coniston... They're both lakes in the Lake District. I expect Reggie thought it was a ripping wheeze, as he'd no doubt call it, to disguise his identity by changing his name from one to the other.

The Widow took out a lace-fringed hankie and blew her nose.

I said: "I wouldn't upset yourself. If you've still got the rock cake why don't you have it with a cup of Ovaltine before you go to bed?"

The Widow brightened up a little at the prospect and moped

back into her room.

I headed for the stairs.

Normally, I'd have a lot of sympathy for a new tenant finding himself welcomed to the Widow's lodgings with one of her inedible pastries - caught between a rock cake and a hard place. But Reggie had booked in when he knew I'd be off the premises. And I knew why.

When the Widow conveniently went shopping, Reggie would've searched my rooms.

Since I'd moved in, I'd set little traps to monitor the Widow's visits to my place on the top floor. It's not difficult, but easy to get wrong. The idea of putting a paper tab between the door and the jamb so that it falls to the floor when the door's opened is a non-starter. It's so transparent, I'm amazed directors still include the idea in films. Anyone who is clever enough to enter a room will spot a trap like that instantly.

The best way is to set the traps so they're invisible. Most of my stuff I keep in a chest of drawers. There are three drawers and if I suspect the Widow may be making one of her periodic raids, I take out the bottom of the three drawers and insert an old train ticket between the back of the drawer above and the ledge on which it rests. If the drawer is opened, the ticket falls into the drawer below. I leave a few more old train tickets at the back of the bottom drawer so that just one ticket doesn't look suspicious. Undetectable and works every time.

And it had worked this time. The ticket had fallen into the bottom drawer. But there was something else with it. A calling card. Reggie Derwent's. There was a phone number and he'd written a message on the back of the card. "We need to speak."

When I arrived in the newsroom the following morning, I was still considering whether to give Reggie a call.

But when I thought about it more, I decided not to. He wouldn't have anything useful to tell me unless I had something to offer him.

Reggie was no doubt just one of a horde of spies and spooks hunting the missing microfilm. So far, it seemed, no-one had figured out where it was.

I glanced around the newsroom. Phil Bailey and Susan Wheatcroft were pounding their typewriters like they had some hot news. But there wasn't a lot of action from the rest.

A slow news day.

What every journalist dreads.

Before long, Figgis would be on my back looking for copy. I wondered whether I could whip up a front-page lead out of the missing microfilm. Trouble was, as far as official sources were concerned, the microfilm wasn't missing. Because it didn't even exist. I wouldn't be able to get anyone to corroborate my story. It would be as insubstantial as a soufflé which collapses as soon as it's taken out of the oven.

I was musing on this, when Freddie Barkworth, the *Chronicle*'s chief photographer, shoved through the swing doors and made his way across the newsroom.

He came up to my desk holding a couple of photographic prints in his right hand.

I said: "If that's another mugshot of me to use in a photo-byline, I don't want to see it."

Freddie grinned. "What a shy modest type you are - I don't think. In fact, you'll definitely want to see these."

"What are they?"

"You remember when you borrowed the camera to take some pictures of Arthur Crouch's passport after his attaché case was stolen on Volk's Railway?"

"Sure - and, by the way, Arthur Crouch is now called Vitaly Mikhailov. The camera was owned by a couple called Nat and Nettie. Earlier, they'd asked me to take a picture of them for their holiday album. We did that with Madeira Drive and Palace Pier in the background."

"I know. I developed the roll. You'll also remember that when you were taking their pictures, you accidentally fired off a couple of random shots."

"Just getting used to the camera," I said.

"That's what they all say. But, anyway, when I developed the film, I didn't take much notice of the accidental shots because they just seemed to be of crowds in Madeira Drive. But this morning, I was about to throw out the contact sheet, when I noticed something. Couldn't see it very well at first. When you look at a group of people on an inch by three-quarters contact, it's too small to see detail. But I used the magnifying glass and then decided to enlarge the two pictures. Glad I did because I'd not printed them full size before. Here they are."

Freddie laid them on my desk side by side. "Recognise anyone you know?" he asked. "Anyway, I'll leave them with you."

He loped off back to his darkroom.

I leant forward and looked closely at both twelve by nine inch prints. The first, taken at an awkward sideways angle, showed a crowd of tourists milling around, some heading for the beach, some for Black Rock station. The second, a bit straighter, showed the same group about twenty seconds later.

I looked at the first photo again. Then the second. I felt a hot flush around my neck and a new tenseness in my muscles.

In the first shot, the head and shoulders of Jerry Clark were visible. He was walking behind a blousy woman wearing a straw hat and a short man with a beer belly and knotted handkerchief on his head. In the second shot, Clark had moved forward and turned forty-five degrees to the camera angle so the whole of his right side was in the picture.

He was carrying an attaché case.

My brain felt like one of those new-fangled computers. Ideas were racing round it faster than I could control them. I had to focus and think calmly.

The attaché case Clark was carrying looked like the one Chaz had wrested from Mikhailov. But it couldn't be. At the time I'd accidentally taken that shot, Mikhailov's case was resting on his table at the Black Rock café. And later, he'd carried it on to a Volk's train.

So Clark wasn't just delivering a case with money and documents to Mikhailov. He must also have collected a case from Mikhailov. I knew what was in the case Clark had delivered. But what was in the case he'd taken? The case he was holding in Madeira Drive.

I picked up the pictures and headed for Frank Figgis's office.

Figgis looked at the pictures through a smokescreen from his ciggie.

"So what was in the second attaché case?" he asked.

"It couldn't have been the microfilm that was stolen in the Bridego robbery because the heist didn't take place until the early hours of the following morning," I said.

"And not his sandwiches," Figgis chipped in unhelpfully.

"I already know from information I found at the Mercury Message Agency that there were arrangements for someone to collect the metal case with the microfilm from the robbers. I think it was Clark. Perhaps the case Clark is carrying in the photo contained the instructions about the hand-over arrangements."

"That's just speculation," Figgis said.

"True, but what else could be in the case? Certainly not cheese and tomato sarnies. If whoever was behind this robbery trusted Clark to be the bagman who delivered Mikhailov's money, he could also be trusted to collect the microfilm. And if that were true, it would mean that Clark was an altogether more important figure in the conspiracy than I'd previously realised."

"But Clark just ran a company selling that tourist rubbish."

"True. But he'd been a chief petty officer in the Royal Navy based at Portland in Dorset. Think back, just two years."

I saw the idea form in Figgis's mind. "The Portland spy ring," he said.

"That's right."

A group of spies had been caught passing secrets about Britain's first nuclear submarine HMS Dreadnought to the Russians. They'd been arrested, tried and imprisoned. At the time, there'd been speculation that the police hadn't rounded up the whole ring.

"I think Clark was one of the members who evaded arrest," I said. "Somehow, he'd found the money to buy himself out of the navy and set up his business at about the time the spy ring was uncovered. I reckon that money must've come from his spymaster. And when I tackled Clark, he'd been so anxious not to be arrested, he killed himself. That was the mark of someone fanatically devoted to a cause."

Figgis drummed his fingertips on his desk. He was thinking hard.

Me, too. I cast my mind back to that final meeting with Clark. It had been quiet when I'd crept into his warehouse. I could just hear the sound of Clark moving boxes around on the metal shelves. But there was an astringent smell in the air - the stink of hot cellophane that the shrink-wrap machine made. Clark had been using it.

I remembered another detail from the Portland Ring spy trial. The spies smuggled photographs of documents to Russia on microfilm hidden inside antique books.

There were also books in Clark's warehouse. Guidebooks. Local histories. Joke books. I'd seen them as I'd crept towards him that evening.

And now I was certain I knew where the microfilm stolen in the train robbery was hidden.

Figgis's fingers stopped drumming. He'd made up his mind about something. "You must hand these pictures to the police and tell them what you know," he said.

"But this is a great story."

"And it will still be one."

"But if the cops know, every other paper will get to hear about it. We'll lose our exclusive."

"I don't want an argument about this. My decision is final."

He turned his attention to a pile of galley proofs to show the meeting was over.

I collected up the pictures and stormed out of the room. The time for arguing with Figgis was over. I had more important things to do.

Chapter 13

I stomped out of the *Chronicle*, but I didn't drive to Brighton police station.

I was angry. More furious than I'd been since I'd first stepped inside the *Chronicle*'s doors. And it was all down to Frank Figgis.

Back in his office, I'd wanted to clock him on the schnozzle.

Kerpow!

Give up the biggest story I'd ever had and hand my evidence to the cops? Not likely. In your dreams, Figgis. I couldn't understand him. He knew this story would make headlines around the world. And the *Chronicle* would have a scoop no-one would forget.

Hell, I'd risked death on a roof and been hunted by a pair of killers in a ghost train to get this story. And now Figgis wanted me to hand it over to the so-called forces of law and order. Well, no thank you.

I would hand my evidence to the police when I'd recovered the microfilm and written my scoop. And not before. I might even hand the film to the cops neatly wrapped in a package tied up with a bow. It would make a great picture for the front page.

I stepped around a young woman pushing a pram and headed down the street to the place I'd parked my car. I'd left it, as usual, in Jubilee Mews, a quiet street away from the crowds. I turned the corner into the mews, fished the keys out of my pocket, and unlocked the car.

I slid into the driver's seat and sat there with my hands gripping the wheel. I was still angry. And anger drives out rational thought. Figgis had just made the last stages of landing this story doubly difficult. I was out on my own without the backing of the *Chronicle* behind me. But, if necessary, I'd complete the story and sell it as a freelance. Any national paper in the country would pay good money for a scoop this big.

I'd calmed down and I'd thought it through. I knew what I had to do.

And no-one was going to stop me.

I put the key in the ignition and turned it.

The passenger door of the MGB opened and Rudolph Strongbow slid into the seat next to me.

He was holding a gun and had it pointed at my head.

I said: "I hope this doesn't mean you want the gold watch back."

Strongbow grinned, revealing a row of teeth that could have featured in a toothpaste ad.

I said: "It's so easy to regret impetuous generosity. Shirley didn't want a wristwatch, so I'm planning to sell it and buy a new cricket bat."

He said: "This isn't about the watch. It's about you sticking your nose into matters that don't concern you."

"You've just given a perfect description of investigative journalism. I couldn't have put it better myself."

"I'm not here for a seminar on journalism." He flicked the safety catch off the gun.

I said: "I wouldn't shoot me here. We're parked on double yellow lines. The wardens ticket cars with dead bodies in them."

"I'm not going to shoot you. Yet."

"From my point of view, it would be more convenient if you'd make an appointment. I expect there are others who'd like to get in before you."

"They'll have to wait. Now drive."

"Where?"

"Take the London Road out of town."

Strongbow settled back in his seat. But he held the gun firmly in his hand.

I pressed the starter button and put the MGB into gear. I eased the car out of its parking space gently, like I was lifting a baby from a cradle. I didn't want any sudden movement to jerk

Strongbow. He still had his finger on the trigger.

I turned out of the side street and headed for the London Road.

I said: "Where are we going?"

"You'll find out soon enough."

"I take it from this that our previous arrangement of payment for information provided has ended."

"It ended when you blundered into the Mercury Message Agency."

"I wondered why you'd given me a telephone number at an address being used as a message drop by Russian spies."

"I admit I underestimated you, Mr Crampton. It's not a mistake I usually make. I didn't expect you to link the telephone number to a physical street address. Still less, to put the address under observation, enter it and discover information that wasn't for your eyes."

"Until then, I thought you were CIA."

"That is what you were supposed to believe."

"But you're not CIA. You take your orders from an office in Moscow."

"You think too much. It's a dangerous habit when you're dealing with people like me. I believe there is an English saying: ignorance is bliss. It is very true in my world. It is safer not to know things which don't concern you."

"Safety first - is that it? The trouble with putting safety first is that you never know what's coming second."

"You will find what's coming second soon enough, Mr Crampton."

We were passing Preston Park on our way out of town. I glanced at the speedo. I was driving at thirty, just within the limit. I didn't want a traffic cop pulling me over and taking a bullet from Strongbow for his trouble.

I said: "I'd like to pull into the next petrol station."

Strongbow glanced at the gauge in the dashboard. "Your tank

is three-quarters full."

"I want to buy some wine gums to eat on the journey."

"You will not have an opportunity to alert the police from the petrol station. Besides, I will provide what little refreshment you require when we reach our destination."

"So this is not just an idle drive in the country."

"Nothing I do is idle, Mr Crampton. As you will shortly discover."

"I'm not such a slouch, either. As you have already discovered. In fact, I'd stick my neck out and say you're the mastermind behind the Bridego robbery."

"Normally, that would be the kind of statement which would force me to take severe action. But as you will not be in a position to repeat what I say, I see no harm in telling you. I'm not a modest man - it is one of my few faults. And, I must admit, I do take pride in having organised the job."

"So Mikhailov works for you?"

"Vitaly was an essential part of the plan. He contacted Willis Newton in the United States and discovered how to carry out the perfect train robbery. Then he took the information to England and briefed the team of common criminals and desperados we'd assembled."

"Because Newton couldn't take it himself?"

"Naturally. A crook with his record would have been watched from the moment he landed in Britain - even if he'd been admitted."

As we'd left the built-up area of town, I pressed the accelerator and picked up speed. We passed the twin stone pylons which mark the outer limits of Brighton and headed deep into the countryside.

I said: "This plan hasn't gone well for you, Strongbow. Mikhailov let you down when he allowed himself to be robbed by Chaz."

"That was, I admit, something I didn't anticipate but I've

satisfied myself that Chaz was a common robber."

"You were the one who broke into Eileen Dudgeon's house and searched his room. You killed Eileen."

"Not intentionally. I respect old people, as a good communist should. But then the lady returned from her church meeting sooner than I'd anticipated. I hoped merely to lock her in a room. But she slipped and fell down the stairs."

"At every step, you blunder along. Even your robber pals failed to burn the farmhouse to pretend the microfilm had been destroyed."

Strongbow swivelled his head sideways and gave me a thousand watt hate glare. "They were idiots - hopeless bunglers. They thought their lives were made as soon as they had the money. They failed to realise that getting away with a crime is the most difficult part."

"So why use them?"

"Because the crime had to be committed by British crooks to complete the illusion that this was just a normal robbery."

"So home-grown incompetence has ruined your plan and kept the world safe for democracy. Makes you proud to be British."

"You will not be so proud before this is finished. We may not have achieved everything but we will find the microfilm and we will take such value from it as we may."

"You have to find it first."

"I believe you know where it is. You will tell us."

"Why should I know where it is? I'm as much in the dark as you are."

"Before we have finished with you, Mr Crampton, you will wish you knew where it is."

There didn't seem to be much to say after that. Strongbow directed me to take the road past Ditchling. I drove on in sullen silence. We finally took a track between fields towards a farmhouse and barn. Both stood on a slight rise in the land.

We trundled up the uneven track at twenty miles an hour.

The car bounced over ruts and jounced on its springs.

Strongbow gripped the gun harder.

Ahead a weather-beaten sign with peeling paint was nailed to a rotting post.

I gaped like I'd just the seen the dark side of the moon - and it *was* made out of green cheese.

"This is a farm," I said. "A chicken farm."

"Hand me the car key," Strongbow said.

"I don't suppose there's any chance of you reconsidering your position on this?" I said.

"I am normally patient, but at the moment pressed for time. If you do not hand me the key, I shall put a bullet into your knee-cap. I am a reasonable man, so I shall let you choose which one."

"I've always thought my knees are my best feature. Not knobbly at all." I handed over the key.

"Thank you. Your knees will remain unharmed. For the time being. Now get out of the car."

I clambered out and stood beside the MGB wondering whether I could make a run for it before Strongbow joined me. I took a good look round.

We were in a farmyard with a small house on the north side. It had been built out of red brick and Sussex flint and, in its better days, would have looked like the kind of roses-round-the-door idyll that town folk dream of owning in the country. But it had run down over the years. One of the window panes was cracked. A couple of slates were missing from the roof. And the green paint had blistered in several places on the front door.

There was a stout barn to the west of the farmyard. It was built out of sturdy wooden planks and looked in better condition than the house. Perhaps that was because it was used for the farm's main business - keeping chickens. I could hear them clucking away inside. The air was thick with the kind of heavy stench which in the countryside means only one thing.

I swivelled around and saw the culprit. On the west side of the farmyard a rusty old tractor was hitched up to a slurry wagon. If stink was a colour, it would've been a kind of reddish brown - heavy dark undertones cut through with sharp slashes of scarlet. It invaded my nostrils like a swarm of wriggling insects.

To the south of the farmyard, fields rolled away for half a mile to a road. It was the road we'd approached on and I'd remembered there was a lay-by just before we'd turned off. As I watched, a grey car pulled into it.

Strongbow circled round the MGB and faced me. He still had the gun pointed at me.

He said: "I need to put you somewhere while I make some phone calls in the house."

I said: "Don't mind me. I'll just soak up the bucolic atmosphere."

"You can soak up the atmosphere in the barn. Is that bucolic enough for you?"

He gestured at me with the gun. I trudged towards the barn, trying not to look too enthusiastic about the situation.

The entrance was through a sturdy wooden door. It was held shut by two iron hook-and-eye catches - one at the top, one at the bottom. Strongbow deftly lifted the hooks out and opened the door outwards. The air that blasted through smelt putrid. A foul stench made up of sweating chickens and their festering waste.

Imagine you'd gone on holiday not realising that your lavvy had blocked up. You've left some milk and some herrings on the windowsill in the sun. And while you're away, next door's tomcat climbs through the window with a dead weasel, vomits over the hall carpet, and promptly dies. Oh, and the temperature stays above eighty Fahrenheit for the whole two weeks you're away. Then you come home and open the front door.

The smell from the barn was ten times worse than that.

Strongbow waved the gun at me again and I stepped inside. The door slammed shut behind me.

The place was lined with cages stacked eight high around the walls and down the centre of the barn. One chicken to a cage - each with its own water container and feeding bowl. The barn was lit by fluorescent tubes which did their best to resemble daylight. The tubes hung from cross-beams beneath the barn's vaulted roof.

I took a minute to become accustomed to the stench and wondered whether I'd ever get it out of my nose. It depended on how long I lived, I thought. In my present circumstances, I couldn't see any insurance company wanting to offer me life cover.

But I'd got myself into this mess and it was up to me to get out of it. What did prisoners who escaped do, I wondered? The first thing they did in those prisoner-of-war movies I enjoyed watching was to do a reconnaissance.

I walked around the place trying not to breathe too hard and looking for anything that could help. The cages, I noted, had slightly sloping floors so that when a hen laid an egg it rolled into a trough that ran along the front of the cages. There were dozens of eggs in the troughs. Collecting them hadn't been Strongbow's priority. Perhaps he ate Weetabix for breakfast.

At one end of the barn there was a pile of shallow wooden baskets - Sussex people call them trugs. I guessed the trugs were used to collect the eggs. There were some coils of rope. They were used in places for lashing piles of cages together. And there was a step-ladder - the kind that opens out like a capital A. It wasn't a very promising armoury, but it was all I had.

When Strongbow returned, he'd get down to the serious business of torturing me. I didn't know whether he'd do it in front of the chickens. Or whether he'd reason the sound of me yelling for mercy would put them off their laying. And I didn't know how soon he'd return. So whatever I did, I had to move fast.

And I'd had an idea.

Chapter 14

I had to find a way to distract Strongbow for long enough when he came back so I could grab his gun.

I trotted back across the barn towards the door. I looked up at the cross beams under the roof. They were about nine feet off the ground. One of them ran the width of the barn just three feet inside the door. I inspected the inside of the door. A couple of six-inch nails had been driven into the top of the frame - perhaps for use as makeshift coat pegs.

I hurried back to the pile of trugs and rope. I grabbed a couple of the trugs and a coil of rope I thought would be long enough for what I had in mind. I carried the stuff and dumped it just inside the door. Then I went back and collected the A-ladder. I set it up under the beam nearest the door. I took the length of rope and tied it to the handle of one of the trugs. Then I climbed up the step-ladder and balanced the trug on the beam. The rope hung down towards the floor.

I scurried down the step ladder, took hold of the other end of the rope and tied it securely around one of the nails on the door. I made sure to tighten up the rope so there was no slack between the door and the trug balanced on the beam. Then I grabbed the other trug and made my away along the cages collecting as many eggs as I could.

When the trug was full, I carried it back to the step-ladder, climbed up and carefully placed the eggs in the trug I'd balanced on the beam. When I'd finished I counted one hundred and forty three eggs in the trug - enough to make an omelette the size of a dustbin lid.

I climbed down the step-ladder, folded it up and carried it with the spare trug back to the pile of stuff at the far end of the barn. Then I went back to the door.

My plan was to position myself inside and to the right of

the door. If I listened carefully, I'd hear Strongbow remove the hook-and-eye catches. As soon as the door started to open, I'd shout: "I'm over here, Strongbow." He'd step through the door and look towards me. I hoped he'd not notice the rope as it moved outward with the door and yanked the trug with the eggs off the beam.

If I'd judged the distances right, the lot would hit him as he came in. In the confusion, I'd dive for him and wrestle the gun free.

With a bit of luck, the trug would knock Strongbow out.

If it didn't, I could end up dead.

I stepped behind the door and waited.

The chickens clucked and scratched and pecked. The noise was like background interference on an old vinyl record - only a hundred times louder.

Even so, I could still hear my own heart pounding. My mouth was dry. And I think I'd begun to smell like a chicken. I was sweating so much, I could've sworn I'd started to grow feathers.

I stood as still as a sentry and wondered what would happen if the plan failed. I tried to think about something else. But the only subject that came to mind was chickens.

It seemed hours - but was only minutes - before I heard the hook-and-eye catch rattle.

I tensed ready to shout and then dive at Strongbow when the trug and the eggs hit him.

The door opened an inch. Strongbow's shadow filtered through the gap between the door and the jamb. I heard his shoes scuff some gravel.

I tried to shout: "I'm over here, Strongbow." But the words came out as a croak. I sounded like a frog with laryngitis.

In one sweeping movement, Strongbow heaved the door open and stepped inside. He swivelled left in a well-practised movement and covered me with his gun.

I waited for the eggs to hit Strongbow.

But nothing happened.

Then I saw one end of the rope swing loose behind him. It had become detached from the nail on the door.

I glanced up. The trug wobbled precariously on the beam but didn't fall.

Strongbow followed my gaze. He saw the trug and the eggs. And grinned wolfishly.

"Ingenious," he said. "I commend you. I shall dine out on this story for years. People will buy me vodka just to hear me tell the story again."

"Seems a shame to spoil a good anecdote with any more unpleasantness," I said.

"I regret it's necessary. Amusing as your failed ploy is, you must learn a lesson. I must demonstrate my seriousness before we begin the interrogation. One bullet, I think. Not fatal, but somewhere painful. I think I mentioned the knee-cap."

I stepped back. Well, what was I expected to do? Strongbow was six feet away. He'd plug me with a bullet before I'd moved two feet.

I'd heard it was best to let the body go limp if you were expecting a bullet. Loose muscles sustain less damage than tense ones. That was alright for some prof pontificating in a laboratory. In the chicken barn, it didn't seem such a useful piece of advice.

Strongbow raised the gun and aimed at my left leg. "It's best not to move," he said. "I don't want to use a second bullet on you. Just yet."

I closed my eyes.

Waited for the agony to begin.

The blast of a gun filled the barn. My ears popped like they'd shot through the sound barrier. My body shook like a willow in a hurricane. But I was still standing.

There was no hole in my knee.

No blood.

I opened my eyes.

Strongbow was standing in front of me. The arm with the gun had fallen by his side. His fist became limp and the gun fell to the floor.

His lips moved but I couldn't hear what he said.

One thousand chickens had panicked. It was like they wanted to leave home. They screeched and threw themselves at their cages. The noise filled the place. The barn's old wooden planking pulsed with their fury.

But Strongbow appeared oblivious to it all.

His eyes had frozen in a glassy stare like a figure's in a bad painting. His face had turned white. And then a froth of blood bubbled through his lips. His mouth dropped open and he vomited a foul cocktail of blood and mucus onto the ground. Then he tumbled - in slow motion, like a marionette which has its strings cut one by one. He collapsed onto his knees. He looked at me with unseeing eyes and slumped forward onto his face. His limbs convulsed like they'd been plugged into a power circuit. And he lay still.

I dragged my gaze from his body to the figure who'd stepped into the barn behind Strongbow.

I hadn't seen Vitaly Mikhailov since, in the guise of Arthur Crouch, he'd had his dust-up with Chaz on the Volk's Railway.

I said: "Am I glad to see you."

He said: "Not too glad, I hope. You may have noticed that I also have a gun. And I have not hesitated to fire mine. As you can see, I have had my differences with Rudolph, but we both regard you as an obstacle to our plans."

I stood open-eyed and stared at the barrel pointing right at me.

So this was how it was going to end.

Death among the chickens.

Mikhailov smiled and tightened his finger on the trigger.

And then the trug with the eggs hit him.

"Run some more hot in for me, will you?" Mikhailov said.

He was sitting in a bath topped with soap bubbles in the deserted farmhouse. I was sitting on a bathroom stool covering him with his own gun. I'd locked Strongbow's weapon in the boot of the MGB. After all, he wouldn't be needing it any more.

I held the gun in my right hand and turned the hot tap with my left.

"I can't figure out how you rigged up that egg trick," Mikhailov said.

"It was supposed to hit Strongbow, but it didn't fall. I think your shot - the one that killed Strongbow - must have created a vibration which dislodged it."

"Damn wooden basket knocked me clean out. And these eggs are all over me." He sniffed. "I think some of them have turned."

I said: "What I can't understand is how you knew Strongbow had taken me to the farm?"

Mikhailov reached for the soap and worked up some lather.

"Strongbow has been riding me hard since this caper started. When that rocker guy snatched the attaché case off me, I decided I'd had enough. I wasn't going to play Strongbow's games anymore."

"That game being to deliver secret information to the KGB."

"Sure. I never wanted any part of it in the first place. But Strongbow had me nailed on a couple of deals I'd pulled as a lawyer in New York. Knew he could put me away unless I played ball with him."

"You could've gone to the cops."

"With my background? Get real. Besides, there was more. Strongbow knew I had relatives back in Russia. My kid sister has a good flat in Leningrad. Strongbow hinted that she could be swapping it for one room in a camp in Siberia if I didn't play ball. I may play both ends against the middle, but I'm a guy with a conscience. I couldn't do that to Valeriya."

"What did Strongbow want you to do?"

"I had to front the operation with the British team. Make sure it was all set up right and arrange for the special goods to be handed over to Strongbow's man. Then I could skedaddle back to the States and live happily ever after. There'd be some bonus bucks in it for me. Or so he said."

"But that wasn't going to happen."

"Types like Strongbow always want more. Besides, after the Volk's Railway thing, I'd screwed up. I decided I had to get Strongbow off my case."

"By killing him?" I said.

"Is there any other way? I wish I could think of one. I knew the guys who'd hit the Night Mail. I told them there was a new plan. I'd resigned from Strongbow's team and I wanted my share of the cash. Well, what could they do? They knew I had every detail of their plan and could squeal on them to the pigs. And, anyway, there was plenty of dough to go round - so what the hell? I walked away with the same share - a hundred and fifty thou'. Hey, I don't suppose you'd scrub my back?"

"You suppose right - and you still haven't told me how you knew Strongbow had brought me here."

"I'd asked the boys - great bunch of guys, incidentally - to keep their ears open for me while I fixed up a new fake passport. The boys had been sending me messages through that agency above that strip club in London. They told me there'd been a humdinger of a night at that club. Some guy and his broad running amok through the place."

"How did you know it was me?"

"I'd have figured it was you from the write-ups on the story you've had in that newspaper of yours. I guess Strongbow also figured it had to be you. I spotted Strongbow watching the *Chronicle* offices this morning. I'd been keeping tabs on him, waiting for an opportunity to croak him. I saw him pick you off in that cute sports car. I followed in a little grey saloon the Leatherslade guys had lent me."

"The grey saloon I saw parked in the layby down by the road?"

"Made my way across the fields. Looks like I arrived just in time for you. Not too bad for me either. Hey, we ought to celebrate with a drink. They got any beer in this dump?"

I reached over and pulled the plug out of the bath.

"What you doing?"

"It's time for a talk. I've got a proposition to put to you."

"Sounds great. But you gonna watch me towel off?"

"No, I'm going to cover you with the gun from the other side of the bathroom door."

We sat in wooden rockers on opposite sides of the empty fireplace in the farmhouse kitchen.

There was no beer in the place, but we found a bottle of vodka. I poured a generous measure for Mikhailov. He downed it in a shot and held out his glass for a refill.

I said: "Before we get drunk and start singing the *Volga Boatmen* song, let's deal with our outstanding business."

"We have outstanding business?"

"Yes, I have to decide whether to hand you over to the police, shoot you, or go with the third option."

"What is the third option?"

"To let you go."

"And if we go for that third option, what's in it for you?"

"We're going too fast. First I need some more information about you."

We talked for twenty minutes. Mikhailov told me how he'd had a job in a two-person law firm in Brooklyn. But a year later his partner was arrested for tax fraud and sent up the river to the state penitentiary. After that, honest clients weren't so thick on the ground. But those who wanted a lawyer to provide a veneer of legal respectability for their scams were willing to pay top dollar. One of them was Leone De Luca, then building his empire as *capo di capo* of the rackets in Coney Island and Brighton Beach. De Luca soon became Mikhailov's biggest client. Then his only client.

Mikhailov looked at his empty glass. I kept my right hand on the gun and poured him another shot with my left.

"But now the cops are closing in on De Luca," Mikhailov said. "He wants me to close down their investigation, but I've told him we've already bought all the crooked cops we can. Besides, the feds are taking an interest - and that just means big trouble."

"So what are you planning to do?" I asked.

"Before this, I'd planned to get my cash together and head to South America - Brazil maybe. Big country with a lot of future, they say. Besides, I've heard there are some great girls down there."

"And now you've got one hundred and fifty thousand, you'll be able to live like a king in Brazil."

"That's what I plan to do. And with that boodle, it won't be hard to find a honey to be my queen."

"But there's a price to pay," I said.

Mikhailov put down his glass. "What kind of price?"

"You know Lieutenant Jess Sheldon of the Brighton Beach police department?"

Mikhailov nodded. "You can't buy her. She's not for sale at any price."

"That's why I want you to hand over all the paperwork you've got on De Luca to her - or at least tell her where she can find it."

"But that will screw De Luca. He'll come after me."

"As you've said, Brazil is a big country - big enough to hide in. Besides, De Luca will be serving forty years minimum in maximum security. His goons will be caged, too."

Mikhailov stared into the empty fireplace. Perhaps he was thinking of what his life might have been if he'd been an honest lawyer. Or whether he'd have made more of his life if he hadn't deserted the Red Army. Or perhaps he was just thinking about whether he'd like the fire lit.

He looked back at me. "It's tough," he said. "But we have a deal. Get me pen and paper and I'll write a statement now. You can witness it."

I found some paper in a drawer. Mikhailov sat at the table and started to write.

It was more than an hour before he handed me a thick sheaf of papers. I took them and tucked them in my inside jacket pocket. I'd mail them by special delivery to Jess Sheldon.

I said: "You mentioned a sister in Leningrad. If you disappear, how will this affect her?"

"With Strongbow out of the picture, the KGB won't know what's happened. Rudolph won't even have told them about me - he'd have wanted all the credit for himself. The KGB will think he screwed up. Valeriya will be fine."

"So that concludes our business," I said.

"Before we leave, there's just one outstanding point," Mikhailov said. "What do we do with the body in the barn?"

"I think I know someone who will deal with that," I said.

Chapter 15

I draw the line at two people trying to shoot me on the same day.

Well, any reasonable person would.

I was tired of being the hunted rather than the hunter. I had to move into the end-game. Besides, I needed to write a story. When Figgis discovered that I'd disobeyed his direct order to deliver the pictures of Jerry Clark to the cops, he'd surely fire me.

Mr Plod wouldn't be too pleased to learn that I'd been running around the countryside in the company of gunmen.

And from the way the chickens were squawking when I finally drove away from the farmhouse, they weren't too happy to be left with the dead body.

I stopped in the village of Ditchling and found a phone box close to the pub. I took out the card with Reggie's phone number. The card he'd left down the back of my chest of drawers.

I dialled the number not expecting to reach him, but he picked up the phone after one ring.

I said: "You know who this, but you don't know where I am."

He said: "I have someone tracing the call as we speak."

"They can save their effort because I won't be here in one minute's time. I know what you want and I know where I can get it."

"Go on."

"But there's a deal."

"I don't make deals."

"In that case, I'll put the phone down and you can go back to your bosses with your tail between your legs."

"What deal?" There was a sharp angry edge to his voice.

"I tell you everything I know and hand over what you want. You fill in the background I don't know and let me write the story."

"How do I know you can deliver what I want?"

"You don't - but I can. We'll meet at half past nine tonight. Make it somewhere public where I can see what's going on around me."

There was a pause at Reggie's end of the line. He chuckled. "I have the perfect place. Somewhere you can see plenty going on around you. The Hall of Mirrors on Palace Pier. Nine-thirty it is."

The line went dead.

Bravado is great for convincing someone you can deliver on your promise.

But bravado isn't the same as confidence. Because bravado is for show and confidence is for real. And as I trudged back to my car from the phone box, I couldn't find as large a reservoir of confidence in me as I'd hoped.

I'd been fired up by my anger at Reggie's duplicity since the time he'd met me on the flight to America. But if I couldn't deliver on my promise, I was going to end up in the hands of the cops. And I'd be sacked from the *Chronicle*.

I unlocked the MGB, climbed into the driver's seat and sat staring through the windscreen. I was sure it was Clark who'd taken delivery of the microfilm. He'd obviously not had time to pass it on. Otherwise, why had everyone been running around trying to capture it? So it had to be hidden - and I was convinced he'd hidden it at his warehouse.

The night I'd visited him - my second visit - I knew he'd just used the shrink-wrap machine. What better place to hide the microfilm than in some piece of shrink-wrapped tourist tat? All I had to do was find it.

But that "all" took on a more worrying dimension as I fired up the MGB, put the car into gear, and pulled into the traffic. Somehow I had to get into Nobby's Novelties' warehouse. Then

I had to sort through thousands of items to find the one with the microfilm.

Nobby's Novelties still had police tape over the front door, but there were no cops around.

It was just after seven when I drew the MGB into the side of the road a hundred yards from the place. I climbed out of the car and ambled slowly towards the warehouse. The street was quiet. It was lined with offices and small workshops. The working day was long over and the folk who'd bustled about earlier had left for their homes.

As I approached the warehouse, a dark cloud moved over the sun and the street darkened. I hoped it wasn't an omen. But the wind was getting up. An old chip wrapper rustled along the gutters. Somewhere the loose lid on a dustbin rattled. An unfastened window was banging further down the street. I buttoned my jacket, put my head into the wind and headed towards the warehouse.

The police tape - Crime Scene: Do Not Enter - made sharp little cracking sounds as it flapped about. The warehouse door was firmly locked. The police would have left the building secure after they'd completed their enquiries. No unlocked doors, no insecure windows. Crime prevention by the experts.

But I thought there might be a way in that they'd overlooked. When Clark had thrown himself off the roof, he landed in a yard at the back of the warehouse. I'd noticed some steps leading down to a basement door. The cops would have made sure that was as tightly locked as the rest. But I'd also noticed there was an old-fashioned coalhole in the yard. Years ago, when the warehouse was built, it would have been heated by a boiler in the basement. The boiler would have burnt coal by the ton. The factory owners certainly didn't want dust-stained coalmen tramping through their building to deliver the stuff.

So they'd built a coalhole which - if I was right - had a chute to a bunker in the basement. If I could get into the basement, I reckoned the internal doors would be unlocked - and I could roam freely through the building.

An alleyway overgrown with ivy and infested with stinging nettles led up the side of the warehouse. I took a quick look up and down the street. Nobody was taking an interest in me, so I slipped silently up the alley. A gate led into the yard at the back of the warehouse. The gate was locked. Full marks to Mr Plod. But unlike the wall which ran around the yard, the gate wasn't topped with barbed wire.

The gate was one of those wooden jobs with a cross slat from top right-hand to bottom left-hand corner. It was about six feet high. I grabbed the top of the gate with both hands and planted my right foot in the middle of the cross-slat. Then I heaved myself up. I slipped off the cross-slat twice and grazed my hand the second time. But at the third attempt I got enough of a purchase to swing my left leg up on to the top of the gate. I heaved myself up and scrambled over.

I dabbed the grazed hand with my handkerchief and decided a minor injury was a small price to pay for a big story.

I took a quick look around the yard. Over the years, it had been used to dump stuff they no longer needed in the warehouse. There was a pile of old metal shelves, a couple of rusting filing cabinets, and some rotting wood which could have been anything. There was a heap of novelty ashtrays with the slogan: "Bugger Bognor" - George V. The quotation had supposedly been the late king's final words before he'd pegged it.

The coalhole was three feet to the side of the backdoor. (I tried the door: firmly locked. Score another to the cops.) The coalhole was topped with a cast-iron hatch that had been painted black. There was a heavy iron ring attached to the centre of the hatch. I bent my knees, grabbed the ring and heaved. The damned thing wouldn't budge. Not necessarily bad news. If the cops had been truly thorough, they'd have tried it themselves. If they couldn't move it, they'd assume nobody could. Thus it wasn't a threat to the security of the crime scene.

I crouched down and took a closer look at the hatch. It looked like the thing hadn't been opened since the days they sent canaries down coalmines. A hard crust of mud had settled into the crack between the edge of the hatch and the circular ring which secured it in the ground. I stood up and walked over to the pile of old shelving stacked on the other side of the yard. I selected a long thin metal strut from the pile and returned to the coalhole. I spent the next two minutes scraping years of old mud out of the crack. By the time I'd finished I'd opened up a clear gap between the holding ring and the hatch.

I cast the metal strut aside, seized the ring and heaved again. This time I felt a slight shift but the damned thing stayed resolutely closed. I stood up and stamped on it a couple of times. I figured some rust may have gathered in the gap underneath where the hatch and the ring met. Then I grabbed the ring again, took a deep breath, and heaved.

The hatch rose a couple of inches and slipped sideways. I realised why coalholes were usually round. A circle can never fall through a circle its own size - unlike a square or rectangle. I bent over panting like a navvy and tried hard not to let the hatch slip back. I gave another mighty heave. The whole thing came free from the hole. I rested it on the ground, stood up and sucked in some fresh air.

Then I bent down again and looked through the hole. There wasn't a chute - perhaps there'd never been one or perhaps it'd been removed years ago - but the floor of the basement was barely eight feet below the hole. If I lowered myself through the hole I should be able to drop to the floor safely.

A minute later I was standing on the floor of the basement praying that the cops hadn't locked the internal doors. The open coalhole gave a little light - enough to see a door on the far side of the room. I grabbed the handle and it opened.

With a smile on my face and a song in my heart, I skipped up the stairs to the warehouse.

The cops had left plenty of evidence of their search of the place. Boxes had been opened and contents turned out. But the search stopped at that. Of those items I could see that had been shrink-wrapped, none had been opened. I pondered for a moment the limits of human reason - how it was possible to conceive that something might be hidden in a cardboard box but not inside something contained in the box if it was wrapped. Decided that was one for the philosophers. Anyway, the police hadn't been searching for hidden microfilm. They'd been looking for anything that would explain Clark's suicide or Boss's attack on me.

But the cops' search had left me with a bigger problem than I'd imagined. Clark had had all his boxes neatly stacked and labelled on shelves. Now the stuff was all over the place. And I didn't know exactly what I was looking for.

I walked over to where the shrink-wrap machine stood. Cold now. And silent. I closed my eyes and tried hard to recall what Clark had been shifting around in the boxes when I'd caught him. I'd remembered seeing some Ditchling Beacon tea-towels in a box. But Clark must have already hidden the microfilm before I'd arrived. Otherwise, even Mr Plod would've stumbled across it.

Apart from the tea-towels, there'd been a book lying next to the shrink-wrap machine. Just the one. Which seemed strange at the time, because Clark was a wholesaler and dealt in bulk. There was usually a few dozen of any item.

But perhaps the book was left over from a batch Clark had been shrink-wrapping. It had a bright cover in reds and yellows. And a picture of a cartoon man laughing. I moved around the warehouse, dodging boxes left on the floor. There was still plenty of stuff on the shelves. I passed the Bexhill toilet-roll holders I'd seen on the first visit.

Towards the back of the warehouse, there were a couple of shelves devoted to books. They were mostly guide books and they were all shrink-wrapped. I guessed the aim was to stop browsers reading them in a bookshop. Or perhaps it was because the contents were so feeble no-one would buy them if they knew.

I hefted some of the boxes off the shelves and looked inside them. A guidebook to Worthing had a picture of the pier on the front cover. Chichester's featured the cathedral. Lewes's the ruined castle. None of them had red and yellow covers. None of them had a cartoon laughing man.

Perhaps I was on the wrong track anyway.

I decided to head back through the warehouse and search for boxes which might not have been properly sealed. But before I did, I reached up to the top shelf and hefted down the last cardboard box. The box had been sealed with duct tape. I took out my car key and cut the tape down the centre of the join in the cardboard. I opened the box.

Ho, ho, ho.

There was the laughing man. On the red and yellow cover of a paperback book. It was tastefully entitled: *Saucy Seaside Jokes.* "Shock the vicar with this unexpurgated selection of rude rib-ticklers," the back cover promised.

There were about twenty books in the box. They'd all been shrink-wrapped. I ripped off the wrapping from one of them and flipped through the pages. Nothing. Nor with the second book or the third. Before ripping off more wrapping I decided to examine the books more closely. Perhaps the shrink-wrap would indicate one that had been processed differently from the rest. I had most of the books out of the box before I held one in my right hand and stopped.

It felt lighter than the rest. I picked up one of the others in my left hand and compared weights. The right one was definitely lighter.

I ripped off the wrapping and opened the book.

I felt like it must be when you score a winning goal in the cup final at Wembley or a century in a test match at Lords.

The pages had been hollowed out in the centre to make a rectangular shaped hole. And a small packet in some blue waterproof material nestled in the centre of the hole.

I felt my heart do a little hop, skip and a jump. But there would be plenty of time to feel pleased with myself later. Right now, I had an appointment to keep.

I took the book and the blue packet and headed back to the coalhole.

Chapter 16

The wind had stiffened and there were a few spots of rain in the air by the time I reached Palace Pier.

I'd sat in the MGB and had a long think about what I should do after I'd climbed out of the coalhole. The blue packet was safe in my jacket pocket. I'd thought about opening it and studying the contents, but decided against. I'd promised Reggie I'd hand him the microfilm - and that's just what I planned to do.

If he kept his side of the bargain.

But Reggie had more tricks than a travelling circus. And I doubted whether I could trust him. He could rat on his promise. Then I'd be left without a big story - the only hope I had of holding onto my job at the *Chronicle*.

Despite the weather, the pier was thronged with people. An elderly couple huddled in their windcheaters and ate cockles in the lee of a pile of deckchairs. A group of children sucked on ice-creams as they chased each other in circles. A pair of young lovers smooched in the shadows behind the popcorn stand. The summer lights strung between the lampposts swayed in the wind. They cast a kaleidoscope of coloured reflections on the sea. The pier was alive with the chatter of happy holidaymakers. But the roar of the backwash from an incoming tide provided a sinister undernote to the scene.

Reggie had asked me to meet him in the Hall of Mirrors. It was towards the end of the pier, just around the corner from the hoop-la booth.

The crowds thinned out as I moved away from the landward end of the pier. By the time I'd passed the amusement arcade, there were only a handful of hardy souls huddling against the stiff south-westerly.

Many of the stallholders were shutting up for the night, but the hoop-la stall was still open. The place was run by a young woman with dark shoulder-length hair and an eager smile. She was wearing a red jacket like a holiday camp host. A name badge - Jenny - was pinned to her lapel.

"Three hoops for sixpence," she said as I passed.

I grinned. "I don't feel lucky at the moment," I said.

"You never know until you try," she said.

How true. I handed over sixpence and tossed them at the cuddly toys that were on offer as prizes. The first missed an elephant, the second a teddy bear, and the third a dog.

"I told you I was out of luck," I said.

Jenny smiled the kind of smile that would've persuaded many punters to have a second go. "I'll give you a consolation prize," she said.

She pointed to the back of the stall. Three minutes later I left without the consolation prize - but feeling a lot happier about my coming encounter with Reggie.

I had to fork out another tanner for admission to the Hall of Mirrors. The place wasn't exactly the Palace of Versailles. It was like a glass maze with distorting mirrors every few yards. In the day, the place would be filled with people giggling at themselves in the mirrors. But now it was deserted. The rising wind whistled through gaps in the walls. It created a low-pitched wail which rose and fell like an animal in pain.

I stepped cautiously into the maze. I passed a mirror which made me look like a seven-foot stick insect. I couldn't decide whether it was an improvement or not. The lights shifted in the wind and a misshapen shadow passed across the mirror. I looked away.

And then another shadow darkened on the other side of me. Like it was attacking in a pincer movement. There was a shuffling sound and a laugh. And Reggie stepped around a corner.

He stood in front of a mirror that made him look three feet tall and as round as a dumpling.

I said: "Good evening, Humpty Dumpty."

He chuckled. "It's an illusion, of course. A distortion of the truth."

"Distorted truth? That's why you feel so at home here, no doubt."

Reggie's lips twitched in a moue of annoyance. "Touché," he said. "But when you think of it, the mirrors merely show different versions of the truth. After all, we don't change - only what the mirror shows us."

"Is that what this charade is all about?"

"Let's move through the maze and discuss our differences. Perhaps we'll find a way out of both. And don't worry about privacy. I've arranged with the proprietor that we shall be alone here for as long as we wish."

Reggie moved around a corner of the maze and I followed him. A new mirror turned my head into a melon and my body into a pea.

Reggie said: "Have you brought the microfilm with you?"

"Information first, microfilm after," I said.

"Very well."

"Who was Charles Rickman?" I asked. "The man who called himself Chaz."

Reggie shuffled uncomfortably. Looked at himself in the mirror. Decided he didn't like the view and studied his feet instead.

"He was an MI5 agent. He specialised in undercover operations. His job was to pose as a motorcycle rocker and penetrate the chapter which hung out at the Ace of Spades café in Peacehaven. The group that venerated James Dean. Rickman threw himself into the job and studied the life of Dean intensely so that he'd be convincing."

"So that's why all the Dean paraphernalia in his room looked new. But why should MI5 want to spy on a bunch of harmless rockers?"

"Because we believed they were not as harmless as they

looked. In particular, it had come to our attention that one of them, Trevor Kerby - you knew him as Boss - was acting as a courier for someone we had a closer interest in."

"Jerry Clark of Nobby's Novelties."

"Precisely. You'll know about the Portland spy ring - Harry Houghton, Ethel Gee, Gordon Lonsdale and the Krogers - which we managed to crack two years ago."

"Not before they'd sold secrets about the Admiralty Underwater Weapons Establishment and *HMS Dreadnought* to the Russians."

Reggie twitched irritably. "They were given substantial prison sentences, but we always suspected there were others who'd slipped through the net. About a year ago, it came to our notice that Clark may have been one of them. A decision was taken at a high level to keep Clark under surveillance, in case he could lead us to any other traitors we ought to know about. We wanted to infiltrate an agent into Clark's company but that was difficult to do directly. Clark was a suspicious man - it was why he'd evaded our original round-up - and so we decided to try it through the rocker gang. Clark had regular contact with them via Boss."

"So that's why Chaz lodged with Eileen Dudgeon, the widow of your former chief?"

"We felt he needed a safe base from where he could make his reports."

"And that act of kind hospitality on Eileen's part cost her life. The CIA traitor Rudolph Strongbow admitted he killed Eileen when she caught him searching Chaz's room."

"That was an unfortunate consequence."

"Unfortunate you call it. I call it fatal."

Reggie twitched his neck. "Anyway, let's get back to Rickman. He played his part well, worked his way into Boss's and then Clark's confidence, and landed a job at the warehouse."

"From where he no doubt first got wind of Clark's involvement in the Bridego robbery?"

Reggie nodded. "We knew there was going to be some attempt to steal information but we didn't know when or where."

He strolled further into the mirror maze. I followed.

"But you knew about Arthur Crouch, also known as Elliott Bellwether and Vitaly Mikhailov?" I said.

"Yes. Rickman reported that Clark had visited the man a couple of times after he'd arrived in Britain. He discovered at the last minute that Clark was going to hand a large sum of money, together with a false passport and ticket out of the country, to Mikhailov in return for information. We suspected that was a payment for plans about the robbery. It was a last minute decision, but I authorised Rickman to intercept the plans."

"But Chaz snatched the case with the money, not the one with the plans."

Reggie studied himself in a mirror. It made his legs ten feet tall and the rest of his body insignificant.

He shrugged. "We got it wrong. Improvised plans. Always room for error. Rickman only saw Mikhailov after he'd swapped cases with Clark."

"So Mikhailov already had the case with the money and had passed the plans to Clark," I said.

Reggie nodded. "Rickman thought the hand-over was due to take place at the other end of the Volk's Railway. He thought Mikhailov still had the case with the plans. That's why he attacked him on the train."

"And I chased Chaz because I thought he was a common thief."

"There was nothing common about Charles Rickman. He was a brave man."

"But you're telling me he died under the wheels of a furniture van because of a mistake?"

"The service paid for him to have a handsome funeral - we even chose music he'd like."

"I'd bet he can't wait to thank you in the afterlife."

Reggie's head drooped. I pushed past him further into the mirror maze. I couldn't stand how sanctimonious the man was.

"Don't blame yourself for what happened to Rickman," he said. "Any good citizen seeing what he thought was a robbery would have had a go."

"I don't blame myself. I blame the man with the twisted mind who ordered him to do it."

"One has to make difficult decisions," Reggie said stiffly.

"Does one?" I said.

I took a look at myself in the next mirror. My head and legs were normal but I seemed to have grown an enormous beer belly.

"What do you see when you look at yourself in the mirror, Reggie?"

He glanced over my shoulder and smirked. "Certainly not that."

I said: "After the robbery on the Volk's train, you lost track of Mikhailov. How was that?"

"We had a man down. Rickman's death had to be covered. We couldn't let even the police know what we'd been doing. Our surveillance of Clark dropped at the same time. A regrettable lapse."

"And you've also missed the fact that the CIA traitor who'd masterminded the robbery had entered the country and was trying to retrieve the microfilm. That, as it turned out, placed my life at risk."

I told Reggie how I'd been kidnapped by Strongbow and how he'd been shot in the chicken barn by Mikhailov.

For the first time since our meeting, Reggie seemed subdued. He'd lost his bounce and bubble. "We'll take care of that. We can't have dead Russian spies lying around the countryside."

"To spoil our green and pleasant land," I said. "Incidentally, you won't have the opportunity to thank Mikhailov for potting

Strongbow. He's leaving the country. Besides, as he explained to me, he was a reluctant participant in this farrago. He's no model citizen but he was blackmailed into this. Unlike some people I could mention."

I turned the final corner of the maze and headed for the exit.

"Thanks for the meeting, Reggie, Great location. It's helped me to see things in a completely new perspective."

Reggie hurried after me. "Aren't you forgetting something?"

"The microfilm?"

"Yes."

"I don't have it with me."

"But you assured me you..."

"Follow me."

We stepped out of the House of Mirrors. The wind plucked at our jackets and I felt a flurry of rain on my face. The pier had emptied. The stalls had closed but the hoop-la stand was still open. It shone like a rectangle of light against the blackness of the sea behind.

"Indulge me, Reggie. Have a go at the hoop-la before you leave the pier."

Reggie looked at me as though I'd asked him to jump into the sea wearing concrete water-wings.

He said: "I came here to claim the microfilm, not win a teddy bear."

I said: "Why not do both?"

He cricked his neck in that irritable gesture again. I walked up to the stall and said: "Three rings for Mr Derwent please."

Jenny handed them to him. He looked at them like he didn't know what they were for. He shrugged his shoulders and threw them with an angry force. They scythed across the stall and crashed into the backing cloth.

"Bad luck," I said. "You didn't win a cuddly toy."

"But you do get a consolation prize," Jenny said. She held up a miniature plastic fish bowl by a string handle. A solitary goldfish circled the bowl.

"A goldfish?" Reggie said incredulously.

"A shark would be more appropriate for you," I said. "You're a complete bastard, you know."

"Yes, I rather take pride in that."

"Good night," I said. "We mustn't do this again some time."

I headed off down the pier.

I left Reggie gawping at the goldfish - and the little blue waterproof package at the bottom of the bowl.

Chapter 17

I arrived back in the newsroom close to midnight bizarrely wondering what Reggie would do with the goldfish.

The place was empty apart from Charlie Timson, who was duty reporter for the graveyard shift.

He looked up from his typewriter when I strolled in and said: "Don't know why you've showed up. Nothing much happening. The only story I've got is about the new Women's Institute chairwoman. Not exactly going to hit the front page."

"Caused a lot of trouble in the morgue, though. All three of the Clipping Cousins were vying for the job. They were driving Henrietta Houndstooth crazy."

"Not any longer," Charlie said. "All three Cousins lost out. Mrs Hogg-Tomlinson withdrew her resignation. She's carrying on for another year. And I'm supposed to make half a column out of it." He ran his hands through his hair in a kind of despairing gesture. "You got anything better?"

"I think my piece will make a few column inches," I said. I didn't want Charlie knowing I'd got a world scoop. He wouldn't leave me alone to write it.

Charlie went back to thumping the keys of his typewriter in a resentful way.

I sat at my desk and hammered out two stories on my old Remington. The first was a piece to lead the front page - on the truth behind two railway robberies - on the Volk's train and at Bridego bridge. Then I'd pounded out a four-thousand word backgrounder for inside the paper. It told the whole story from beginning to end, including my visit to Brighton Beach in America.

By the time I'd finished, the first light of dawn was filtering through the grime-encrusted newsroom windows and I had a fat stack of folios beside my typewriter. Soon after that, early shift reporters started to arrive.

I called Frank Figgis at his home number and suggested he got into the office straight away.

Figgis's smile was so broad I could see every one of the eleven yellow teeth he had left.

We were sitting in his office half an hour after I'd called him. He showed all the signs of having dressed hurriedly and gulped his breakfast. He wore a frayed shirt, had forgotten to put on his tie, and had left his fly-buttons undone. He had something that looked like a piece of bacon stuck between two of his front teeth.

He finished reading the last folio of my story and replaced the pile on his desk.

He said: "This is the hottest story we've ever had."

"Hotter than the Trunk Murders?"

"Hardly moved the thermometer compared with this. It's a story that will run for weeks. And go national."

"International, I'd say."

"You're right. And we've got it."

Ahem! I coughed politely. "Did I just hear you use the first person plural in connection with the provenance of the story?"

Figgis looked away embarrassed. But barely for a second. There was more brass in Figgis's neck than the bells in St Paul's Cathedral.

"Any story is a team effort," he said.

"I could have done with a few members of the team on hand when a couple of ruffians threatened to shoot me in the chicken barn."

"Yes, I loved that part of the story. I can see the trug with eggs being a comedy highlight when they come to make a film of this."

My tired old eyes opened wide at that. "You can see them making a movie?" I said.

"Bound to," Figgis said. "It'll pack 'em in."

"So I take it the fact I didn't hand those pictures Freddie Barkworth gave me to the police is forgiven?"

"Let's say forgotten."

"Let's say never mentioned again."

"Very well. As it happens this story will do me no end of good with His Holiness. There'll be no talk of easing me out now."

Figgis reached for his Woodbines. "I'm reserving the whole front page for your lead story and five pages inside the paper for this background piece."

He picked up my folios from his desk and flicked appreciatively through them.

There was a single rap on the door. It opened and Cedric came in. He was holding a large white envelope.

He said: "Sorry to interrupt, Mr Figgis, but this was just delivered at reception. Man said it was important."

Figgis grabbed the envelope and ripped it open. He took out a single sheet of paper.

He put on his reading glasses and held the paper inches from his nose while he read. I watched as his eyebrows drew together and a frown deepened on his forehead.

"Not bad news?" I asked.

"The worst," he said.

"About my story?"

"We've had a D-Notice."

"You mean a Defence Notice. The kind the government issues when it wants to stop a story being published," I said.

"Yes, when they think a story will damage the national interest," Figgis said. He tossed the D-Notice onto his desk. "It means we can't publish your articles."

I thumped Figgis's desk so hard with my hand a fine cloud of dust flew into the air.

"Reggie Derwent promised he'd tell me everything in return for handing him the microfilm," I said.

"But he didn't promise he'd let you publish it."

"That was implied."

"Nothing is implied when you're dealing with types like Derwent."

I said: "D-Notices are only advisory. They're a request from the government not to publish something they say damages the national interest. Too often, that means their interest."

"Maybe, but in this case, the wording of this letter means they're serious."

"Let's publish anyway. What was it the Duke of Wellington once said? 'Publish and be damned'."

"If we do in this case, we'll be damned," Figgis said. He stubbed out his ciggie and threw the butt into his waste bin. "Besides, I'll have to show this to His Holiness. When it comes to difficult stories, he's got the backbone of a jellyfish."

I felt defeated. I suppose I should have raged with anger. But I was just too tired to scream and shout. I'd been through too much. Heard too many lies. Seen too many killings. I'd discovered the truth that others had tried to hide with their duplicity. And now the government thought its D-Notice would tidy me and my story away, as if it had never happened. Out of sight, out of mind. Well, it wasn't going to be like that.

I stood up and headed for the door.

"Where are you going?" Figgis asked.

"Home to bed. I've had no sleep for thirty-six hours. But this isn't over. Not yet."

Figgis looked at me with sad eyes. "Remember that at least I know what you've achieved. This is a great story. And you'll always know that, too."

He looked at me with an intensity in his eyes I'd never noticed before. "Don't do anything stupid," he said.

"Anything stupid?" I said. "How do you think I got the story in the first place?"

Epilogue

Nine months later…

The letterbox rattled and something heavy landed on the doormat.

I turned over in bed, put my arm around Shirley and said: "The newspapers have been delivered."

We were in Shirley's flat. A thin April light filtered through the curtains.

Shirley said: "*Uuuuurgh.* I'm asleep."

But she rolled over and put her arms around my neck.

"Aren't you pleased we sold that Strongbow gold watch and bought a double bed," she said.

I kissed her. "I can see the benefits," I said.

"You wanted to buy a cricket bat."

"I've changed my mind on that. I score more this way."

"If you want to bowl this maiden over, you better get the papers."

I climbed out of bed, trotted barefoot into the hall, and collected them from the mat.

When I returned to the bedroom, Shirley was sitting up and rubbing sleep from her eyes.

I handed her *The Guardian* and the *Daily Mirror* and kept the *UK Press Gazette*, the journalists' weekly trade paper, for myself.

Shirley grabbed the *Mirror* and turned to the crossword.

I opened the *Press Gazette* at the news pages, saw the main headline - and whooped with delight.

Shirley dropped the *Mirror* and leaned towards me.

"That boring old rag doesn't usually get you going," she said.

"It's the best news I've had this week. Ben Stoker has won a Pulitzer Prize."

"What's that?"

"It's a prestigious prize for writers. There are prizes for novelists and playwrights, but mostly for journalists. Each year they hand a prize to a journalist who's written the best editorials, to one who's performed a great public service and so on. Ben's won the best reporter award."

"Ben was the old guy who edited the *Brighton Beach Banner*, wasn't he?" Shirley asked. "I thought you said he was down on his luck."

"Looks like it has changed," I said. "When I was in Brighton Beach, he told me it had always been his ambition to win a Pulitzer. He won the prize for his exposé of a CIA agent who'd become a Russian spy and organised a daring train robbery in Britain. He wrote the story for the *Banner* as an exclusive, but it was picked up and splashed by all the other American papers."

Shirley grabbed the *Press Gazette* from me and devoured the story about Ben's Pulitzer.

"It doesn't give any of those details about his story here."

"It can't. Ben's story was given a D-Notice in Britain. No-one in this country published it."

Shirley put down the paper. "Yeah, I remember you telling me. All your hard work down the drain. You didn't get any credit for it."

"School of hard knocks. You get used to it in journalism. But it's great to know the story has made a big splash - if only overseas."

"I wonder how Ben got to hear about it," Shirley said. "I thought only you'd got the whole tale."

"Yes," I said. "I wonder how Ben did hear about it."

I grinned in a way I knew would make me look a bit smug. But I didn't really care. Reading the news in the *Press Gazette* was enough of a prize for me.

Besides, we all claim our victories in different ways.

Read more Crampton of the Chronicle stories at:

www.colincrampton.com

About Peter Bartram

Peter Bartram brings years of experience as a journalist to his Crampton of the Chronicle crime mystery series. Peter began his career as a reporter on a local newspaper before working as journalist and editor in London and, finally, becoming freelance. He has done most things in journalism from door-stepping for quotes to writing serious editorials. He's pursued stories in locations as diverse as 700 feet down a coal mine and Buckingham Palace. Peter wrote 21 non-fiction books, including five ghost-written, before turning to crime with the Crampton of the Chronicle mysteries.

Follow Peter Bartram on Facebook at:
www.facebook.com/peterbartramauthor
Follow Peter Bartram on Twitter at:
@PeterFBartram

A message from Peter Bartram

Thank you for reading my Morning, Noon & Night trilogy. I hope you have enjoyed reading it as much as I enjoyed writing it. If you have a few moments to add a short review on Amazon or Goodreads, I would be very grateful. Reviews are important feedback for authors and I truly appreciate every one. If you would like news of further Crampton of the Chronicle stories, please visit my website - the address is at the top of this page.

More great books from Peter Bartram...

HEADLINE MURDER

When the owner of a miniature golf course goes missing, ace crime reporter Colin Crampton uncovers the dark secrets of a 22-year-old murder.

STOP PRESS MURDER

The murder of a night watchman and the theft of a saucy film of a nude woman bathing set Colin off on a madcap investigation with a stunning surprise ending.

FRONT PAGE MURDER

Archie Flowerdew is sentenced to hang for killing rival artist Percy Despart. Archie's niece Tammy believes he's innocent and convinces Colin to take up the case. Trouble is, the more Colin investigates, the more it looks like Archie is guilty...

MURDER FROM THE NEWSDESK

Seven short stories featuring Colin Crampton - download free from Amazon.

30858885R00220

Printed in Great
Britain
by Amazon